Also by Lucy Score

RILEY THORN NOVELS
The Corpse in the Closet
The Blast from the Past

KNOCKEMOUT SERIES
Things We Never Got Over
Things We Hide from
the Light
Things We Left Behind

BENEVOLENCE SERIES
Pretend You're Mine
Finally Mine
Protecting What's Mine

SINNER AND SAINT
SERIES
Crossing the Line
Breaking the Rules

WELCOME HOME
SERIES
Mr. Fixer Upper
The Christmas Fix

BLUE MOON SERIES
No More Secrets
Fall into Temptation
The Last Second Chance
Not Part of the Plan
Holding on to Chaos
The Fine Art of Faking It
Where It All Began
The Mistletoe Kisser

STANDALONES
By a Thread
Forever Never
Rock Bottom Girl
The Worst Best Man
The Price of Scandal
Undercover Love
Heart of Hope
Maggie Moves On

BOOTLEG SPRINGS
SERIES
Whiskey Chaser
Sidecar Crush
Moonshine Kiss
Bourbon Bliss
Gin Fling
Highball Rush

THE
DEAD GUY
NEXT DOOR

LUCY SCORE

Bloom *books*

Sourcebooks and the colophon are registered trademarks of
Sourcebooks. Bloom Books is a trademark of Sourcebooks.

Published by Bloom Books, an imprint of Sourcebooks
P.O. Box 4410, Naperville, Illinois 60567-4410
(630) 961-3900
sourcebooks.com

Originally published in 2020 by That's What She Said Publishing, Inc.

Cataloging-in-Publication data on file with the Library of Congress.

Printed and bound in the United States of America.
LSC 10 9 8 7 6 5 4 3 2

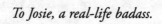

To Josie, a real-life badass.

1

The dead talked to Riley Thorn in her dreams. The living inconveniently telegraphed their secrets to her over grocery conveyor belts and in crowded restaurants.

She did her best to ignore them all.

In fact, right now, the only thing she was talking to was her breasts.

"Heading south on 83 toward the bridge. We've got company," she said through gritted teeth.

"Oh my God. She's lost it. She's talking to her tits," one of her back seat passengers whined.

"I talk to mine all the time. Don't you?" another announced.

"I do not know if I speak to any body part," the only man in the vehicle mused. "Perhaps I should try it."

"You people are *not* normal," complained the final back-seat tagalong.

Ha. Normal.

Normal had been Riley's rebellion against a patchouli-scented, homegrown-vegetable-selling, séance-attending child-hood. *Normal* was her middle name. Well, not technically. Her *legal* middle name was the worst possible middle name in the history of middle names. She'd change it if it didn't involve actually writing it down on paperwork and handing it to another human being.

Normal was what she longed for now as she jammed her foot down on the accelerator. The stolen pickup truck lumbered up to speed while Ram Jam howled "Black Betty" at full volume.

Her front seat passenger slapped fresh magazines into her guns.

"It looks like the cops," Riley reported, wondering if she should pull over or if it would be the last mistake she'd ever make. Red and blue lights flashed on in her rearview mirror. "You can't shoot at cops!"

There was a loud bang, and one of her back seat passengers shrieked. "They're shooting at us! Bad cops!"

Just then, the night sky lit up to the right.

"They're not shooting at us," Riley insisted over the music. Fireworks exploded to their right as City Island's pyrotechnics crew went balls to the Fourth of July wall. There was a baseball stadium full of families enjoying both the nation's favorite pastime and birthday, completely unaware that the bad guys were closing in on a group of what had been until last week relatively normal citizens.

She desperately wished she could have been one of them. Innocent. Happy. Her only concern the inflated prices at the beer stand. But no. She'd made one stupid mistake, one seemingly innocent decision, and now she was going to end up in the Susquehanna River in a stolen truck full of weirdos.

The unmarked sedan behind her veered into the left lane, and she knew exactly what the occupants were going to do. It blared into her mind in high definition.

"Everybody get down!" she shouted and slammed on the brakes.

All five of her passengers hit the deck just before a hail of bullets took out the windows on the driver's side.

"Pretty sure they're shooting at us now," one of the smart-asses pointed out.

"You think?" Riley yelled back.

Glass rained down, and the smell of burning rubber assailed her nostrils.

"We're taking fire," Riley yelled in the vicinity of her breasts. If anyone was talking back, she couldn't hear them. Not over the fireworks or the screaming or the rock song wailing at full blast on the radio with the broken volume knob.

She peeked over the wheel. Black tire tracks led up to the car sitting sideways across two of the bridge's three southbound lanes. Two men stood in front of the car, legs braced, guns drawn. She couldn't go back. There was only one way to get past gun-toting bad guys barricading the road to freedom. She could only hope the truck's massive engine block would protect them enough to make it work.

"Everybody hang on," she said grimly as she revved the engine. A shower of golden sparkles rained down from the sky above, drifting toward the inky black of the river.

"What's the plan?" her front seat passenger asked, calmly chambering rounds in both guns.

"I'm gonna ram them."

Step one. Accelerate to thirty miles per hour.

"I blame you, Nick Santiago," she yelled to her breasts again and mashed the gas pedal to the floor. She couldn't tell which pops and booms were fireworks and which were bullets peppering the front of the truck.

"Ohhhhhhmmmmmmm," hummed the large Black man wedged into the back seat in the midst of three shell-shocked waitresses.

"What the hell is Studly doing?"

"How should I know? Maybe we should hum with him?"

Riley blocked out the back seat *ohms*.

Step two. Aim for the center of the front wheel.

Her passengers abandoned their *om* and joined together in a chorus of screams and regrets. Bits and pieces from each of their lives flashed before Riley's eyes. She had half a second to appreciate the irony that it was other peoples' lives and not her own. Because that was what her quest for normal had earned her. A too-quiet, forgettable life.

"I should have stayed in school!"

"I never should have given that guy a BJ!"

"I should have had that second hot fudge sundae!"

Riley never should have answered the knock on her door two weeks ago.

Boom.

2

The soothing sounds of digital wind chimes and chanting monks yanked Riley from an unsettling dream about an elderly woman obsessed with lymph nodes.

She slapped at the buttons on the expensive gradual progression monstrosity she'd stolen from a very stupid man and pulled the blanket over her head. Here, in the space between sleep and work, she was alone. Blissfully, quietly alone.

No intrusive thoughts from strangers to acknowledge. No dead grandmothers to appease.

Here, under the covers, everything was normal.

Well, as normal as a broke, divorced, thirty-four-year-old proofreader who hailed from a long and distinguished line of female… Never mind. She didn't like to think about the special "talents" that ran in her family. Especially not first thing in the morning.

It was a summer Tuesday. Which meant her cubicle mate, Bud, would bring in sushi just past its expiration date and then spend most of the afternoon in the bathroom. Donna, the front desk gargoyle, would be wearing a withering glare and take out her Monday night church bingo losses on anyone who wandered past her desk.

It also meant that Riley would treat herself to the one and only fancy coffee drink she budgeted for the week.

With the siren's call of caffeine fresh in her mind, she dragged herself out of bed and shuffled for the bathroom in the hall.

"Riley!" a thin, reedy voice called from one of the lower floors. "Fred needs help with his Kindle again."

"Okay, Lily," she yelled back.

Riley's mother took a ceramics class with Lily Bogdanovich. So when Riley had found herself on the other side of a changed lock on the front porch formerly known as hers, Lily had happily opened her attic.

The crumbling stone mansion on Front Street belonged to the Bogdanovich twins. Lily and Fred were elderly siblings who had inherited the house, half a racehorse, and every issue of *Playboy* published between 1972 and 1984.

Never having families themselves, the Bogdanovich twins had set up an off-the-books flophouse in the mansion, opening their guest bedrooms to complete strangers.

Riley had space on the third floor that included room for a bed, a small living area, and a microscopic kitchenette that couldn't handle much more than microwave popcorn and toast. The plaster ceiling followed the odd, grandiose rooflines of the ancient architectural wreck in hard angles and weird slants. But the dormer windows offered a decent view of the Susquehanna River as it meandered its way south on the other side of Front Street.

The downside?

"Keep it down out there," the downside snarled from behind his closed door.

Riley shared a bathroom with the tenant across the hall. Dickie Frick was a grumpy, presumably perverted old man. His welcome mat said FUCK OFF, and he always left his dirty underwear on the floor in front of the sink. She didn't know much more about him except that he sometimes remembered to flush the toilet, had a job that involved working late, and, depending

6

on his mood, liked to watch *NCIS* reruns or porn.

Ignoring Dickie, she left the bushy rose wallpaper and hunter-green woodwork of the hall behind and stepped into the bathroom.

There they were. The tighty-not-so-whities. On a yawn, she reached under the sink and pulled out the pair of plastic salad tongs she'd stashed there. Trying not to look too closely—she'd made that mistake once—she made the short journey to Dickie's door and tossed the briefs over the knob before returning to the bathroom.

The room had a decades-past-its-heyday charm. The sink was bile yellow as was the claw-foot tub. The floor was covered in a dingy black-and-white-checkered tile. It creaked dangerously whenever she got into the tub, but it had yet to give up the good fight against gravity.

She shoved a toothbrush into her mouth and a hairbrush into her thick shoulder-length hair. Her mother's side's Ukrainian genes had won the genetic wrestling match. Her hair was dark brown. Her eyes were the same, just a little too big for her face. Heavy lids made her look bored even when she wasn't. The upside was, if she took the time to bother with eye shadow, she could really rock the hell out of a good come-hither stare.

Not that she was come-hithering anyone right now. The divorce still stung. And there was that whole being broke thing. She didn't want to meet someone new and have to explain to him why her roommates were all on Medicare. If anyone with a badge asked, she was supposed to call them all Aunt and Uncle So-and-So.

Morning bathroom business taken care of, Riley returned to her room, still yawning. She'd been short on sleep for most of her life. It was the dreams. They'd only gotten more annoying, more insistent, the older she got. Turning on the TV, she listened to the perky news team banter about the latest vigilante activity in the city while she dressed. A group of unidentified adults in masks had tracked down a repeat offender of the litterbug classification and filled his car—incidentally illegally parked in a handicapped spot—to the roof with trash.

"Harrisburg mayor Nolan Flemming had this to say about the vigilantes."

The screen cut to a shot of the mayor, whose main claim to fame since his election was his Kennedy-esque hotness, on the steps outside his office building downtown. "I have full confidence in our police department. No one in our fair city is above the law, and citizens must remember that though justice may move slowly, it will still be served. Taking the law into your own hands is not only dangerous; it's illegal."

Dressed for the day, Riley grabbed her leftovers out of the fridge and headed down the skinny back staircase. It was a tight corkscrew, dangerous for anyone who wore a shoe size above a woman's eight. Down two flights she went, catching signs of life on every floor.

She peeled off into the kitchen on the first floor, a sunny room with butcher-block counters and ancient mint-green cabinets that required a stepladder to access.

Fred, the oddly muscular senior citizen, was wearing his side-part toupee and a Hall and Oates T-shirt. He happily handed over his e-reader to her so she could work her youngish person magic, which consisted of connecting to the Wi-Fi and hitting Sync.

"You're the best, Riley," Fred chirped while his Yoga Poses for Sexy Seniors downloaded.

"Don't pull any muscles," she warned. "See you later, Mr. Willicott," she said to her other neighbor.

"Who the hell are you?" groused the elderly version of Denzel Washington as he poured coffee into a bowl. She wasn't sure if his memory was faulty or if Mr. Willicott just didn't give a shit about anything.

Ducking out the back door, she inhaled a breath of fresh almost summer. June in Pennsylvania was nice.

Maybe she'd take an hour or two of vacation time and leave early today, she mused as she unlocked her Jeep.

"Yeah, maybe do some fishing."

"I'm not going fishing, Uncle Jimmy," she muttered, turning the key and cranking the stereo. The Jeep had belonged to her now-deceased uncle. It became hers after she'd had to return the BMW her ex-husband had tried to surprise her with after forgetting her birthday. Again.

Jimmy, her father's brother, had died doing what he loved best: napping in his boat after drinking a six-pack of cheap beer. The coronary took him out before he could wake up and finish his triple-decker roast beef and fried onion sandwich. The man was dead but not exactly gone. His spirit lingered in the Jeep she'd inherited. Her sister refused to ride anywhere with Riley, claiming she could still smell the ghost of the Styrofoam cooler of fish the man had once forgotten about for a week in the dead of summer.

She pulled out onto Front Street with the river to her right and Harrisburg to her left. As the state capital, parts of the city were almost impressive. The capitol complex, with its green-glazed terra-cotta dome and postmodern fountain, drew crowds for tours year-round. Then there were the not-so-nice parts. The don't-walk-down-the-street-alone-at-night parts, the easily flooded parts, and the what's-that-weird-smell parts.

Of course, it wasn't just crime and weird smells that had given Harrisburg its notoriety. There was that brush with bankruptcy thanks to an incinerator debacle, and then there were the millions of city dollars tied up in a collection of Wild West artifacts for a museum that never happened.

Despite all this, revitalization was slowly oozing in from the city's borders. Festivals along the riverfront drew huge crowds. Family-friendly 5Ks snaked their way down city streets. Breweries and restaurants popped up in once-abandoned store-fronts. And long-empty buildings found new owners with renovation budgets.

Little Amps was a hip coffee shop that roasted its own beans and attracted the kinds of people who enjoyed the inconvenience of not going through a chain drive-thru. The coffee was excellent, but the parking was stupid. The building sat on a corner on the skinny one-way Green Street. Riley circled twice before getting desperate and slipping into a spot down the block tagged with a faded paper sign that read, No PARKING UNTIL FURTHER NOTICE, HARRISBURG PARKING ENFORCEMENT.

"*I wouldn't do that if I were you*," Uncle Jimmy's voice sang in her head.

She ignored it. The sign had been there for the last six weeks, and as far as she could tell, the parking office was just screwing with drivers at this point.

She waited for a rusted-out pickup and a shiny Tesla to cruise past before crossing the street. A guy with dreadlocks and a lot of facial piercings held the door for her as she jogged up the two concrete steps into the shop. There was a line, as there always was on weekday mornings. But no one else seemed to be in the hurry that Riley always was. They all probably had make-their-own schedules or work-from-home jobs.

Lucky bastards.

The higher-ups at the marketing firm where she worked had freaked out over the suggestion. Employees were required to be in the building for exactly eight hours a day, five days a week, in order to get paid. Her boss, Leon Tuffley Jr., a crotch-scratching "charmer," told them all that there was no way he was paying employees to "pretend" to work when he knew damn well they'd all be "drinking beer naked and farting around."

In an unspoken rebellion, the offended employees had since dedicated wildly inappropriate amounts of time to social media and computer games during work hours. It had been the only thing to unite them.

Riley shifted her weight from foot to foot, tantalized by the smell of Honduran dark roast. Unless everyone in front of her was ordering a black coffee, she was going to be late. Again. And Donna, the front desk sentinel of indeterminate age and humanity, was going to be a pain in the ass about it. Again.

After nearly a year at Sullivan, Hartfield, Aster, Reynolds, and Tuffley, Riley had yet to see the woman smile, say, "Excuse me," when she elbowed someone out of her way in the snack room, or wash her hands before leaving the restroom.

"Should I shave the ol' bikini line in case we have sex tonight? Or should I not shave it and hold out for one more date?"

Instinctively, Riley glanced over her shoulder. The woman behind her was studying the menu board, but apparently her mind was on more important things. Things that a stranger such as herself should *not* be eavesdropping on.

Opening a news app, Riley drowned out the private thoughts of strangers and focused on more local happenings.

"Welcome to Little Amps," the barista said cheerfully when Riley arrived at the front of the line. "What can I get you?" The barista's hair was chopped short and shaved on one side. Her cat-eye glasses were a bright shade of raspberry that matched the tips of her hair. The tattoo at the base of her thumb was a penguin with heart eyes. She also had swollen lymph nodes on one side of her neck.

Not that Riley could actually *tell*. But she knew.

Oh shit. Not again. Not here.

Her nose twitched.

"Uh, I'll have the cold jar, please," she croaked, looking everywhere but the girl's neck.

"Tell her," the grandmotherly figure from her dreams insisted. *"Tell her. Tell her. Tell her."*

Riley pressed her lips together. She wasn't doing this again. She'd already had to stop going to her favorite sandwich shop for lunch. And then there was the dive bar over on Fifth Street that she'd never set foot in again.

"Say it!"

She rubbed a palm over her nose. It was still twitching.

These stupid messages were ruining her life. She needed a damn mute button. It wasn't like they were true. They *felt* true, but they were probably just deranged compulsions.

On cue, her phone rang.

"Hi, Mom," Riley said. The barista was pouring milk over ice and cold brew into a to-go jar. If customers brought their jar back, they got ten percent off their next order. She *really* wanted that discount.

"What's wrong?" Blossom Basil-Thorn demanded. The nasally Wisconsin accent was always more pronounced when she was worried about her daughters.

"Nothing," Riley lied.

"Lying. Skip to the part where you tell me the truth. Was it another dream?"

She heard a bang and a clunk on her mom's end of the call. "What are you doing?" she asked.

"Making homemade laundry detergent while your father makes the leak in the sink worse," her mother said. "Now, tell me about the dream."

"Can't right now," Riley hedged.

The barista screwed on the lid, whistling a jazzy little tune, completely unaware of the battle that was waging inside her customer.

It wasn't even real, she told herself. It was just a stupid dream, and the girl in front of her had perfectly normal lymph nodes. She probably didn't even have a dead grandmother.

"Ah," her mother said, understanding. "You need to tell whoever it is whatever it is, Riley. It's a gift. You're wasting your talents by ignoring them."

"It's not a gift," Riley argued. She handed the girl cash, and when their fingers brushed, she saw the barista as a five-year-old standing on a stool in Great-Grandma Ida's kitchen as a very alive Ida taught her how to mix pancake batter.

Crap.

"I gotta go, Mom," Riley said and disconnected. She stood rooted to the spot for a second, debating whether she should wait for her change or just run.

She'd forked over a twenty. She needed that change.

"Tell her this instant!"

Riley wondered if death had made this Ida lady more authoritative or if she'd always been that way.

"Here's your change," the barista sang, handing over the bills.

Visions of lymph nodes danced in Riley's head. She stuffed a dollar in the tip jar and cleared her throat. "Ida wants you to get your lymph nodes checked," she whispered.

There. Happy, Ida? Another public place officially ruined. She was definitely going to have to start going to coffee shops and restaurants in disguise so she could at least keep coming back after these stupid revelations.

"Wait. What? Who?" The barista's mouth fell open in an *O*, and she stared.

See? She didn't even have a great-grandma Ida.

"Do you mean my great-grandma?" the girl asked.

Well, shit.

Riley started to back away. "Just get them checked. Right away."

"Wait!" the girl called after her. The rest of the customers who weren't jamming out to indie folk rock in their earbuds watched Riley hurry toward the door.

Skidding to a halt, she swore, then dashed back to the register. "I'm just going to take this," she said, her cheeks flaming as she grabbed the coffee.

She could kiss that ten percent discount goodbye. Because this jar was never coming back.

3

S he was four minutes late, and *of course* the side door was already locked.

Frazzled and annoyed, Riley walked around the building to the front entrance. Sullivan, Hartfield, Aster, Reynolds, and Tuffley was housed in what had once been two row houses. The floors were uneven, the ceilings low, and the walls were painted a morale-crushing gray that Tuffley got at a discount when a local jail accidentally ordered too many five-gallon buckets of industrial paint.

The reception area was one of the only presentable spaces in the office, with its dull green carpet, fake plants in brass pots, and four matching vinyl chairs that faced a watercooler. The watercooler—and the rest of reception—was guarded by the aforementioned short round angry receptionist.

"Morning," Riley said.

"Looks like *someone* couldn't be bothered to show up on time again," Donna hissed, her beady little eyes doling out judgment behind floral-rimmed glasses. Donna took things like lateness or long lunches or making too many photocopies at one time as a personal insult. She'd once reported a graphic designer for "walking weird."

Riley ignored the snide little woman and hurried down the hall toward the cubicle farm, but not before she heard Donna say into her phone, "That Thorn girl was late again. I must be the only one in this building who takes their responsibilities seriously."

The shabby hallway connected the two buildings. It opened into a room with more gray walls, fluorescent lights, and ten cubicles crammed together at the center, well away from any actual natural light. Riley slipped into hers. She shared it with Bud, the graphic designer who never removed his earbuds, didn't shower often, and did obsessive amounts of research on ultimate Frisbee fails. In the year that she'd been with the company, they had had only one conversation. That was the day the fire alarm went off, and she had to tap him on the shoulder to tell him to evacuate.

The bright side? Bud didn't have many internal thoughts for her to accidentally overhear.

The cubicles on either side of them were empty, thanks to a spring round of layoffs. But when Riley had asked if she could move to a different desk, the answer had been a firm no.

It was the answer for every question ever dared to be asked within these walls.

No, she could *not* leave early for a dentist appointment. No, she could *not* move her lunchtime to 1:00 instead of 12:45. And no, she could most definitely not hang up the flyer for her sister's yoga studio on the community bulletin board.

It was a shitty job with a shitty company. But divorced TV-news-writer pariahs couldn't be choosers. She needed to stick it out for one more year and twenty-one days—yeah, she had a countdown on the calendar in her apartment—before this position went from red flag to a sign of stability on her résumé.

Her desk was littered with job jackets containing printouts of incredibly exciting things like pellet stove schematics and magazine ads for bathroom stall dividers. Another exciting day for a proofreader.

Riley turned on her monitor, gave it a whack in the top

right corner to make the green lines disappear, and began her morning ritual: cyberstalking her ex-husband and his girlfriend on social media.

Griffin Gentry was Channel 50's most popular morning news anchor. He spent more money on spray tans and voice coaches than most people spent on mortgages. He'd claimed that the news was in his blood. But in reality, his blood was in the media group that owned the station. His father—who most definitely tried to slip Riley the tongue on her wedding day—was an executive vice president with the company and had some good ol' nepotistic pull.

By the time she'd come on board at a bright, shiny twenty-eight, full of high hopes and big dreams, Griffin's reputation had been edited and sanitized. He hadn't noticed her for two full years. It wasn't until the office Christmas party, when a drunken Griffin had accidentally knocked her to the floor when she exited the restroom, that he'd bothered learning her name.

He'd noticed her after that, and she'd let herself be dazzled, flattered, even grateful for the attention. They'd survived two years of dating and a year of marriage before Riley couldn't ignore the red flags anymore.

The bustiest of which was weather girl Bella Goodshine.

Scrolling through the twenty-four-year-old's Instagram feed was Riley's favorite self-flagellating hobby. Bella had *Baywatch*-style long blond hair and wide blue eyes that made her look constantly startled or starstruck. That was probably what had first drawn Griffin to the bubbly meteorologist. Or her very large breasts.

Riley was no slouch in the boob department, but she didn't advertise like Bella.

The perky blond dressed like a naughty sorority sister and had the disposition of a children's TV show star. When Riley had burst into her own bedroom to find her husband standing pantsless in front of the mirror, Bella had politely spit out his cock and given her a chipper, "Oh, hi!"

Riley's response had been less friendly and much, much more costly.

Bella's Instagram account was a perfectly curated highlight reel of a woman adored by both the public and her "dreamy" boyfriend. *Barf.*

Riley got to experience the heart-shaped pancakes Bella's "sweetie" made her for Valentine's Day along with the rest of the woman's sixty-five thousand followers. A number that grew exponentially every time she posted another bikini shot.

But it wasn't a bikini day. No. Today was much, much worse.

"You have got to be kidding me," Riley murmured under her breath.

The short video clip showed a slim hand with Pepto Bismol pink nails angling this way and that to capture as much light as possible on a blindingly huge diamond ring.

"…thrilled viewers with an on-air proposal…" said the announcer.

Congratulations, Biffin!
Hottest couple ever.
#relationshipgoals

Riley's cell phone rang. She didn't need to look at the caller ID to know who it was.

"Hey, Jas."

"That tangerine weasel gave her *your* ring." Jasmine Patel was Riley's best friend, partner in crime, and wing lady. Frankly, Riley wasn't sure how she'd earned the honor. They'd met in junior high when Jasmine's mother had moved her dermatology practice to Camp Hill.

Jasmine had been the instant cool girl in school, arriving secure in the confidence of winning the genetic lottery. She got her natural grace and freakish cardiovascular stamina from her uncle, who played soccer professionally in the UK. The straight-As-without-trying brains were guaranteed for the third daughter of a doctor and a PhD-wielding historian. And then there was her appearance.

Her long glossy black hair was always elegantly sleek, even when she woke up with a hangover. Her cheekbones were the stuff of legends, as was skin that had never once permitted a blemish to bloom. Jasmine had been the first girl in seventh grade to get boobs. Also the first girl to tell ninth-grade football hottie Bryson to keep his hands to himself.

While Riley had spent her adolescence obsessed with being normal, Jasmine had railed against it. If there was an expectation, she ignored it. If there was a rule, she broke it.

And if some asshole ever dared hurt one of the people she loved, Jasmine Patel was the Don Corleone of payback.

When the judge had ordered Riley to pay damages to her lying, cheating ex-husband, Jasmine had calmly strolled out of the courthouse, got in her SUV, and rammed it into the driver's side door of Griffin's Audi convertible.

She'd pleaded "bee in the car." Coupled with her good looks and the fact that Griffin had taken up two handicapped spaces, the cops had let her off with a warning.

"I almost feel sorry for her," Riley confessed to her best friend.

Champion grudge holder Jasmine snorted. "Please. She's old enough to know that marrying a dickless moron who cheated on his first wife is a shit idea."

"I'm sure they'll be very happy together," Riley said. At couples' plastic surgery appointments and across conference room tables while their attorneys hashed out a prenup.

"How do you feel?" Jasmine asked.

Riley found it comforting that there was more rage than pity in her friend's tone. "Like I want a gallon of tequila," she admitted.

"I can make that happen," Jasmine promised.

Riley gave a humorless laugh.

"Look, I'm worried about you, and not just because your ex is a self-absorbed toadstool," her friend said.

"I'm fine," Riley insisted. "Everything is fine."

"No, you're not. You're living in a sketchy retirement home.

Working a dead-end job. You're not dating. And I bet you a bottle of that tequila that not only did you *not* put on mascara this morning; you're wearing gray or black."

Riley was wearing gray *and* black.

"Not everyone needs a colorful closet, Jas."

"Listen, girl. You need to accept the fact that your attempt at boring and normal failed. Stop clinging to the hope that one day you'll wake up and be someone else. You need to embrace who you are and get back out there. You are *stagnant*. Stir things up. Slap on some concealer, bust out something that shows cleavage, and *do* something."

"Doing something involves money," Riley pointed out.

Jasmine snorted. "Honey, if you walked into a bar with a pouty face, you wouldn't pay for a drink or dinner or possibly even your rent. It depends on what bar we go to."

Jasmine had never paid for a drink in her life.

"I think you're overestimating my appeal," Riley said wryly.

"Are you depressed?" her friend pushed.

"No. Of course not." Maybe. Probably.

Riley's computer made a *whoosh* noise, and a new email popped into her inbox.

Subject: On-Time Arrivals to Work

She heard the squeak of Donna's orthopedic shoes on the industrial tile in the hall.

Riley heaved a sigh. "I have to go."

"Okay. But do yourself a favor and stay off social media today. Do *not* watch the proposal video. I'll call you later."

Of course there was a proposal video. "Thanks," Riley breathed.

She disconnected and then did what she always did when she received a passive-aggressive memo from the supervisory staff. She abbreviated Sullivan, Hartfield, Aster, Reynolds, and Tuffley to SHART in the signature line of her outgoing email messages.

Then she brought up Channel 50's Facebook page and cued up the "surprise engagement" video.

4

After watching Griffin theatrically get down on one knee in the middle of Bella's explanation of a high-pressure system a dozen or so times, Riley buried herself in work. This included spending the entire afternoon double-checking that all three hundred links on a township's horrifically outdated website no longer took users to the porn site that had hijacked them.

She slogged home through the afternoon commuter traffic, windows down and music up to drown out Uncle Jimmy's fishing suggestions. Her phone rang when she got to the mansion's parking lot. It was her sister, Wander.

"Hey," Riley said, shifting the Jeep into park and cutting the engine.

"Hi." Wander's breathy Zen tone made a simple greeting sound like the ringing of a meditation gong. If a meditation gong were ringing over a backdrop of three screaming kids. "I just heard about Griffin. How are you?" she asked.

"I'm fine. Really," Riley said, repeating her refrain. "It's not like I want to still be married to him." She grabbed her purse, lunch bag, and unreturnable coffee jar and headed for the back door.

"Of course not," Wander agreed. "But it's still normal to have feelings about the situation. *I* have feelings about it."

Riley let herself into the house. The smell of something very strong and very not great wafting from the kitchen hit her in the nose. She made a beeline for the back staircase to avoid her neighbors. "Oh really? What are *your* feelings?" she asked her sister.

"I find myself wishing karma worked more swiftly," Wander said.

It was her sister's equivalent of Jasmine smashing her car into Griffin's. Riley laughed. "I appreciate your frustration on my behalf."

"I mean, the man sued you after you caught him cheating on you in your own home," Wander continued. "I realize that his journey is his own, but I don't care for the fact that he dragged you along for the ride before leaving you in the gutter."

Her sister could really commit to a metaphor.

"I'm fine," Riley said again.

"It's not fair that you're still paying for his mistakes and he gets to just go on with his life." Wander's voice wasn't as soothing now. It was vibrating with a deeply suppressed rage.

"Maybe you should take a breath? Do some meditating?" Riley suggested as she climbed the stairs.

The screaming reached a crescendo on Wander's end of the call. "Girls, if you can't lower your volume and find a way to behave as a community, I'll make you churn homemade butter again."

There was a chorus of "noooooo" and then the relative quiet that can be achieved with three girls under the age of eight in one room.

Riley heard her sister take a deep breath, followed by a second one.

"I'm going to consult my spirit guides," Wander decided.

"About your ex-brother-in-law getting engaged or your kids fighting?" Riley asked, tackling the last flight to the third floor.

"Both. But also you. I'm concerned that there's an obstacle standing in your way of finding happiness."

"I'm happy," Riley lied.

Wander snorted elegantly. "I can smell that lie from here."

"You're so weird." Riley laughed.

"You could be too if you just gave yourself the permission."

Between the second and third floor, Wander had to go save a child's hair from the Velcro strap of a sneaker. With the chaos of her sister's life still ringing in her ear, Riley let herself into her quiet, peaceful apartment.

But today, her space didn't feel so quiet or peaceful. It felt... sad. Lifeless. Also suspiciously neater than when she'd left it this morning. The throw on the back of her ratty couch was folded and draped on the wrong side. The clean laundry she'd brought home from her parents' house Sunday was neatly folded on her coffee table. The stack of mail she'd had the energy to open had clearly been pawed through.

Mrs. Penny, she thought. Her second-floor neighbor had made breaking and entering—and tidying—into a hobby.

Riley's nose twitched. And she immediately suppressed whatever "message" or hallucination was trying to come through. When it was too quiet, her brain did stupid things like trying to predict the future or attempting to read minds. Since she didn't have three daughters to yell at or the desire to strike up a conversation with any of her neighbors, she would find her own distraction. She changed into gym shorts and a tank and jogged back downstairs with feigned enthusiasm.

"Joining us for dinner, Riley?" Fred called out from the kitchen door. He wielded a spoon coated in something so dark it was almost black.

"We're recreating that spinach thing from the Indian place," Lily announced behind him. "Fourth time's the charm!"

The Bogdanovich twins' hobbies in restaurant recipe re-creation rarely ended well on Indian night. They could manage an Italian dish, and even their beef and broccoli was passable. But they had yet to make a palatable Indian meal.

"Wish I could," Riley fibbed, stuffing earbuds in her ears. "Gotta run!" She waved and headed out the front door before they could try tempting her with burnt, homemade naan.

Once outside in the not-spinach-scented air, she cranked

her music to drown out any stray thoughts from passing strangers that might accidentally lodge in her own brain.

The mossy, muddy Susquehanna flowed lazily to her right. Late afternoon sun flickered on its surface. It wasn't so bad. A little humid, a little mosquito-y. But the grass and trees were a healthy green, and the river didn't smell too much like fish.

See? She could do things. She wasn't stagnant.

A shirtless runner with a six-pack of abs and a shoulder-pec-bicep tattoo gave her the what's-up nod. She smiled back, but he was too busy calculating how many scoops of protein powder he had left and didn't notice her boobs or her smile.

She walked until she got hungry—about half a mile—then returned home and snuck up the front staircase to avoid any more supper invitations.

Her dinner choices were limited to a single-serving frozen pizza or the last container of homemade vegan lentil soup from lunch with her parents Sunday.

The pizza won.

She preheated the thirty-year-old oven and gave in to the siren song of her couch. Face-planting on it, Riley reached for the remote. Mrs. Penny had definitely been here. Her Netflix history included four episodes of her neighbor's favorite guilty pleasure, *Beyond the Picket Fence: Gruesome Unsolved Crimes.*

Riley queued up the next episode of *her* guilty pleasure, *Made It Out Alive.* The survival show helped to keep things in perspective. Sure, she was divorced and broke, and her stupid ex-husband was probably buying a new custom-tailored tux, but at least she hadn't been mauled by a grizzly bear in the Canadian wilderness.

Yep. It was all about perspective.

———

She was contemplating a fourth slice when she heard the creak in the hallway through the paper-thin walls. Worn from decades of feet, the floorboards groaned in protest when anyone approached either apartment.

It was probably Dickie.

She had no idea what the man did for a living, but he kept odd hours. She usually only saw him Saturday mornings as she was reluctantly leaving for early morning "family yoga" and he was coming home from wherever dirty old men spent their Friday nights.

She heard the knock across the hall and wondered if it was one of the second-floor neighbors complaining about Dickie "stomping around like a maniac" again. The knock sounded again. More insistent this time.

That wasn't a neighbor. They all had a tendency to announce themselves like, "Yoo-hoo! It's Lily from downstairs," or "Dickie, turn that porno shit off! My grandkids are visiting."

Riley heard the footsteps and lolled her head against the back of the couch to eye her own door. The knock sounded a second later.

She heaved herself off the couch, debating whether she really wanted to meet anyone who would voluntarily knock on Dickie's door. The debate was settled when she snuck a peek through the peephole.

He was tall, at least according to the fish-eye view, and dressed in jeans and a T-shirt. He was looking down at something in his hands, but the top of his head held the promise of full-face hotness.

She opened the door and confirmed full-face hotness.

Yep. Tall. Broad shoulders, muscled chest. Bronze skin. Short dark hair that curled just a little on top. Assessing eyes under thick brows, full lips bookended by matching deep dimples barely disguised under rebel razor stubble.

And those eyes. Blue-green like the ocean on a sunny day. They sucked her in.

The vision hit her fast enough that she didn't have time to fight it. Her nose twitched so hard she felt her lip curl Elvis-style.

For a second, the sexy stranger vanished in a cotton candy fog of pink and blue. Then she saw a hideous bedspread in yellows, oranges, and greens. A lava lamp cast an orange glow from the other side of the bed. Those ocean eyes boring into hers as his body covered hers. Tattoos. One on his chest. One on his bicep. None on his neck—thank God. His mouth was on hers as he dragged her underwear down her thighs.

"Riley," the vision stranger breathed as he lined up his very, very nice cock with her center.

"Nick," Vision Riley gasped as he drove into her.

The TV remote slid out of her hand and hit the floor. The vision—or more likely the exercise-induced hallucination—retreated.

Sexy Stranger cleared his throat. "I'm looking for Jorge Alvarez," he said.

"That's me," she croaked, hypnotized by his dimples.

He glanced down at the clipboard he was holding and back up at her. "You're Jorge Alvarez?" One of those dark eyebrows quirked.

Since when were eyebrows sexy?

Either the guy was too handsome to be smart, or he had an excellent poker face.

"Kidding. I don't know any Jorge Alvarezes," she said. "Alvari?"

He was still staring at her, and Riley gave passing thought to how disheveled she must look. Her hair was in its sloppy postwalk knot. She had pizza sauce on her tank top and probably an entire serving of oregano in her teeth.

Don't smile, she ordered herself.

He nodded and made a note on the clipboard. "Do you know most of your neighbors?" he asked. He gave off a cop vibe. A really, really good-looking cop vibe.

"Of course," she said, crossing her arms. "We're all related."

This guy hadn't shown a badge, but there was something "official" about him.

"Hmm," he said, clearly not believing her. "I have a Jorge Alvarez at this address down for three boxes of Nature Girl Chunkie Munkie Choco Nut Bars. He hasn't paid yet."

"*You're* selling Nature Girl candy?" she asked. No self-respecting cop would pretend to participate in an adolescent girl organization fundraiser.

"My niece did the selling. I'm collecting from the deadbeats trying to stiff her out of her candy money."

There was no way in hell she'd missed a Nature Girl canvasing the house selling candy. She loved the Goosey Gooey Caramel Nuggets. This hot guy with his eyebrows was definitely lying. "Uh-huh. Sure," she said.

"You're sure Mr. Alvarez doesn't live across the hall?" he pressed.

"Positive."

He gave her a flash of dimple and a swoop of eyebrow. "Do you know who *does* live across the hall?"

"Yes." She swooned internally.

He waited a beat and then turned on what she assumed was his best weapon: his smile. Those dimples deepened and beamed out hotness.

"You don't give much up, do you?" he asked, all charm.

"Not to strangers who knock on my door looking for fake neighbors when there's a nice, neat nameplate next to the door with the current resident's last name."

He cleared his throat again and glanced over his shoulder at the nameplate. "So Mr. Frick lives there?"

Riley just smiled.

He turned back to his clipboard and made a note. She shifted to peek at the paper.

"That looks pretty official for a Nature Girls order sheet."

He flipped the folio closed and dropped it to his side.

"Thanks for your help, Ms…" He trailed off.

She pointed to her nameplate.

"Thorn. Fitting," he said with a wink. Those dimples got impossibly deeper. She bet they'd hold pencils.

"I didn't catch your name," she said, extending her hand.

He paused for a second before taking her hand. "I'm Nick."

Well, hell. Score one for the vision.

Her nose gave a twitch. *Bedspread. Lava lamp. Sex.*

She shook her head, dislodging the scene from her brain. His grip was strong and warm and felt way too much like it had in her…dream. He squeezed her hand tighter, and her thighs quivered in response.

"You're not really collecting candy money, are you, Nick?"

He met her gaze levelly. His grip stayed firm. "Now what would give you that idea, Thorn?"

What was she doing sharing an extra-long handshake with a hot stranger who was obviously lying to her face? Riley released him and wiped her palm on her shorts. "There is no Chunkie Munkie Choco Nut Bar."

"What are you? Some kind of—"

"Nature Girl candy connoisseur," she finished for him. "What's your niece's name?"

"Esmeralda." It rolled off the tongue almost as easily as the truth.

She narrowed her eyes. "No one is named Esmeralda."

"Thanks again for your help, Thorn." His grin was a flash of temptation and danger. "See you around." With a wave of his paperwork, he headed toward the stairs.

"Anytime, Nick." If that was his real name. "Would you like me to tell Dickie that you stopped by?"

He paused and turned back to face her. "Maybe it would be better if you didn't mention this to your…"

"Uncle," she filled in for him.

"Yeah. Maybe don't mention this to your uncle."

She had a feeling he was going to say that.

5

To Nick Santiago, the best thing about working for himself was that he got to set his own hours.

When everyone else in the city got up early and was on the road fighting morning commuter traffic, he slept until eight, hit the gym, chugged a protein shake, and took his sweet-ass time wandering downstairs to the office. He'd gotten a deal on the first-floor storefront and upstairs apartment from his aunt Nancy, who was a Harrisburg property maven.

The timing had been right when the last tenant, a sketchy vape shop, moved out. So Nick had signed a three-year lease and set up shop. That had been—well, hell—two and a half years ago. Time still managed to fly without the demarcations of a traditional work schedule or wedding anniversaries or first days of school, he realized. But it was the way he preferred it. He liked his life. Liked working for himself.

Except for all the fucking paperwork. And walking in on his cousin getting a lap dance in his wheelchair from his wife

"Seriously?" Nick said, dumping his sunglasses on the empty desk and picking up the stack of mail.

"Mmph, sorry, man." His cousin Brian wrestled his tongue back from his wife's mouth. Nick's cousin was a blond-haired, glasses-wearing reformed ladies' man with a brain that constantly sifted through data. Jose was tiny, lean, and maybe just a little mean. Most of the time, her expression was completely unreadable. To anyone too stupid to notice details—like the knife tattoo on her shoulder—Josie looked like a pretty girl with a goth wardrobe. But she was as fragile as barbed wire and as flowery as poison ivy.

In high school, while Brian had been elected homecoming king and Josie had been voted most likely to go to jail for homicide, Nick had the distinction of collecting the most detentions in school history. A record that still stood.

The three of them had been best friends since elementary school when Dax Dipshit tried to dump third-grade Brian out of his wheelchair on the playground. Nick had been in the middle of getting his ass kicked by Dipshit—actual name Dipler—and his two cronies when new girl Josie wandered into the melee and punched Dax right in the nuts.

Josie was the problem solver of the team, if the problem could be solved with force. She enjoyed sidling into dangerous situations and being underestimated. She was almost as good a shot as Nick was and better at hand-to-hand combat.

Brian was a one-man gossiping geek team. If there was information to be dug up, he would find it. Technically, he only worked for Nick part-time. The rest of the time he ran his own cybersecurity company.

Nick's contribution was, well, doing everything else it took to run the business…except paperwork. He was observant, street-smart, and good at getting information out of people, women especially. He also had no problems doing the heavy lifting of armed security and surveillance jobs.

Together, the three of them made Santiago Investigations into a reasonably successful investigations business.

Bill. Junk. Bill. Nick threw them back on the desk, deciding to ignore them until absolutely necessary.

Thanks to a good run of pharmaceutical rep layoffs and armed security gigs in the spring, Santiago Investigations had enjoyed some positive cash flow. However, with summer just getting started, things were slowing down a bit. More people were vacationing rather than serving divorce papers and hiring security. That just meant his schedule could be even more flexible until business picked up again.

"Any messages?" Nick asked.

Brian wheeled closer to his monitor setup while Josie perched on the edge of the desk like a deadly bird of prey.

"Stoltzfus called. He wants eyes on his wife," Brian reported.

Nick rolled his eyes. "Again?"

"Again," Brian confirmed.

"Why doesn't he just get a divorce already?" Josie pulled out a three-inch blade from her boot and went to work cleaning the dirt from her fingernails.

"Anything else?" Nick asked.

"Chad called in sick. Kids gave him the stomach bug they were circulating. Just in time for half a dozen serves to come in."

Process serving was Nick's second-least favorite part of the job. Which was why he hired Chad, a middle-aged, stay-at-home dad, to dole out divorce papers and summonses on nights and weekends.

"Another one for Mustangs," Josie reported.

Mustangs was a gay club half a block down from the capitol complex. An ex-partner was being a pain in the ass and suing. Nick had served the club so often that he joined the owner's drag poker game every few weeks. At least when he could afford to lose to Lady Ophelia Everhard.

Nick could confirm that luck was definitely a lady.

"Did you track down that Frick guy?" Josie asked him, closing the blade and slipping it back into place.

"No luck," he said. "Place is one of those big monstrosities on Front Street. Looks like a flophouse." He thought of the pretty neighbor with the pizza sauce on her tank. He'd always been a sucker for big brown eyes. And pizza.

"What's that look for?" Brian demanded.

"What look?"

Josie's eyes narrowed. "You got all dreamy-faced for a second."

"I'm not dreamy-faced," Nick argued.

His employees shared an annoying look.

"Don't start that marital telepathy bullshit," he complained.

"You met someone," Brian sang.

"Oooooh," Josie crooned.

"I hate working with family," Nick complained before stomping into his office and shutting the door.

His office was…functional. It was the least offensive way to describe the windowless room with its threadbare, shit-brown carpet that clashed mightily with the pea-green file cabinets. His desk was a dented gray metal with drawers that stuck unless punched in exactly the right spot.

But the rent was cheap, the internet was fast, and there was a great deli right around the corner.

Maybe someday he'd upgrade. Give the place a face-lift. Put down roots or whatever. But for now, it worked as is. Just like the rest of his life. Low maintenance. Low responsibility. Easy.

He unloaded his files, his Glock, and his badge from the backpack before logging into the system and officially starting his day.

He spent a tedious hour updating files for clients. Then he answered the handful of emails that had come in that morning. There was a request for a "proof of life" from an insurance company and a potential armed security job that sounded a little too sketchy for his liking. He accepted the proof of life, declined the security gig, and mapped out a route for evening serves.

The client wanted another attempt on Dickie Frick.

Normally, if he didn't have any luck on a serve, he'd turn it over to Chad or Josie for another attempt. But then he wouldn't get to see the pizza sauce neighbor again. An attractive hot mess with a smart mouth living with a bunch of senior citizens and lying about family ties? The mysterious Ms. Thorn interested him.

He drummed his fingers on the metal desktop, debating.

Ethics weren't exactly Nick's favorite thing. Other people's moral codes always felt a little too restrictive for him. Like wearing a necktie. He generally did the right thing. He just didn't like having someone else dictate what the right thing was.

In this case, he was just curious, not up to something nefarious. And that was good enough for him. He called up Facebook's search engine and keyed in "Thorn" and "Harrisburg."

It took some scrolling, but he found her. Riley Thorn. The profile picture was definitely her. She had her arms around two other women. They were all wearing sunglasses and laughing. Private profile. Smart.

Profile Picture Thorn was wearing one hell of a diamond engagement ring and a diamond-encrusted wedding band. Rings that had most definitely not been on her finger last night. He'd checked.

"Nice to meet you, Riley Thorn," he said to himself. Annoyed that his curiosity wasn't magically appeased, he decided it was time for a break.

The deli was a short walk away, and it was a good, almost-summer day. He got the usual—cheesesteak in the garden, raspberry iced tea, and extra napkins. He dropped a few bucks in the tip jar and left, heading in the direction opposite the office.

"Nice day," he called out a block later to the bearded guy sitting on a folding chair in the doorway of a barbershop.

Perry was a Third Street fixture. As close to homeless as a person could get without making it official, the sixty-something-year-old slept in a dilapidated shack near the railroad tracks that the bank and township tax collector had given up on long ago. Perry acted as a one-man neighborhood watch and unofficial crossing guard for a handful of blocks on Third Street.

Nick and his fellow business-owning neighbors kept an eye out for the guy, supplying him with whatever essentials he needed. At least when Perry allowed it.

"It certainly is," the man agreed, lifting his face to the sunshine and closing his eyes. His bushy white beard was neatly coiffed, which meant the barber had talked him into a chair this morning.

Nick took the empty seat next to him and unwrapped the cheesesteak. He handed over the tea and half of the sub.

"Much obliged, Nicholas," Perry said.

"How's life?" Nick asked, divvying up the napkins.

"Blissfully uncomplicated. Yours?"

Uncomplicated was what Nick strived for. Every time he'd brushed up against complicated, it had ended in disaster. Better to travel through life unencumbered. "Living the dream, my friend," he said.

They ate in silence for a few minutes, people watching and soaking up the sun.

"Heard there was more vigilante action last night," Perry said, breaking the companionable silence.

"Heard that too," Nick said. If anything happened within city limits, Perry usually knew about it. "Any idea who's organizing it?"

Perry gave the shrug of a man without worries. "You know how it goes. We tend to get fed up when the powerful stop paying attention to the people who put them there," he philosophized.

"Think it'll become a real problem?" Nick asked.

"Doubtful. They're probably just good, frustrated people having a little fun in the name of justice. It'll burn itself out," Perry predicted.

"Any good neighborhood gossip?" Some people had entertainment news shows or gossip blogs or soap operas. Nick had Perry.

"Oh, plenty. You know that pretty gal lives over on Forster next to the church?"

Harrisburg's population might have made it a city, but the tight-knit neighborhoods made it feel more like overlapping small towns most days.

"Short skirts, fancy sunglasses?" Nick asked, drawing her out of his memory banks.

"That's the one. Seems she came home early from a business trip and found her husband making a candlelight dinner for two."

"I take it that second place setting wasn't for her?" he guessed.

"No, indeed. The second plate belonged to a gentleman known for his conservative politics when it comes to gay marriage."

"You don't say."

"Just goes to show you can say anything you want, but that don't make you a different person than what you are down deep."

Nick nodded in agreement, his mouth too full to comment.

"Seems the good-looking gal gave him the boot and threw all his stuff out on the front porch for him to collect. I might have helped myself to a fancy tie or two," Perry said.

"You'd look good in a tie," Nick said.

"I think I would too. How goes the investigations business?" Perry asked, changing the subject. "Got any hot ones?"

"Pretty lukewarm right now. But it'll pick up again soon," Nick predicted.

Perry nodded sagely. "Gives you more time for the ladies. Maybe you should pay the pretty gal on Forster a visit? Commiserate with her."

Nick shook his head, thinking about the expensive suits, the perfectly coiffed hair. "I don't think so. I think even a palate cleanser with her would be complicated."

"Complications make the world go round," Perry mused.

Nick laughed. "That is the exact opposite of what you preach, my friend."

Perry gestured at him with the sub. "The way I choose to live my life is not providing a commentary on how you should live yours. You're a young, healthy man, Nicholas. Complications are the best part of life. I'm starting to get concerned about you."

This coming from the guy who went without running water for most of 2017. "*You're* concerned about *me*?"

"I am."

"You're the one who doesn't have a bank account," Nick pointed out.

"And you're the one who hasn't been out with a girl in what? Two? Three months?"

"It hasn't been that long," Nick scoffed. *Holy shit. It really had.*

"You've either hit a dry spell or..." Perry paused to take

a long, contemplative sip of his tea—"your appetites are changing."

"I assure you, my appetites where women are concerned are just fine," Nick insisted.

"Then maybe you're getting tired of the buffet and you're thinking about finding that one right entrée."

Nick eyed his friend. "Have you been making bathtub jungle juice again?"

6

Riley's parents lived in a two-story brick home on the outskirts of Camp Hill, a town just across the river from Harrisburg. Things were quieter there. Yards were more uniformly groomed. Cars were more expensive. Kids walked home from school for lunch, and moms went to Pilates classes. It was nice. Normal.

But normal wasn't exactly a word that got thrown around when it came to the residents of 69 Dogwood Street.

Riley's dad, Roger, had retired a few months ago from his warehouse manager job of thirty-plus years. After a week spent lounging around in his underwear, he'd started a second career as a trivia night host for local bars. He'd swapped his uniform of steel-toed boots and button-downs for flashy tracksuits and orthopedic sneakers. Business was booming. Three nights a week, he was paid under the table in cash and free beer to lead West Shore bar patrons through categories like sports heroes, famous criminals, and gangster cinema.

Riley's mother, on the other hand, had never bothered with the pretense of normal. While friends' moms had been packing lunches after work or driving their kids to 137 activities, Blossom Basil-Thorn had been making her own yogurt, turning the backyard into a jungle of vegetables and flowers, and raising free-range children. Riley had been walking herself to school since she was six. At seven, she was making her own breakfast, and by twelve, she'd built a network of friends' parents who didn't mind another kid in the car on the way to volleyball games.

There was also the matter of the neon sign found in the sunroom window facing the street. When Blossom plugged it in on Mondays, Wednesdays, and Saturday mornings, the words PSYCHIC READINGS glowed proud and purple.

Riley climbed the steps. Noting that half of her mother's army of plants had been moved to the front porch, a sure sign that summer was here, she let herself in through the front door.

The smell of something—was that burnt cabbage?— assaulted her nose. *Just another typical family dinner.*

"Adult child entering the premises," she called out. She and her sister knew better than to walk in unannounced. Their parents enjoyed an annoyingly healthy sex life in their empty-nest years.

"Back here," her dad yelled.

"Are your pants on?" She waited for verification.

"For now," Blossom sang.

Sighing, Riley followed the short hallway back to the kitchen.

She found them leaning over a casserole dish on the stove, the source of the stench. "Smells like liquid garbage that a raccoon ate and shit back out," her dad observed.

"I don't care what it smells like. You're eating it," her mom said, whacking him in the butt with a wooden spoon. The Wisconsin twang issuing orders was the unique soundtrack to Riley's childhood. "The doctor said you need to get your cholesterol under control, and that's what we're doing."

"She didn't mean by starving me," he complained. "Rye Bread, you're with me on this, aren't you?"

There had always been two teams in the family: Riley and her dad versus her sister and mother.

Roger had called dibs on first-name naming rights on the first kid, which was why Riley was Riley and not Amethyst-Lavender. Blossom got to choose Riley's never-to-be-mentioned middle name. They swapped for their second child, which explained why her sister was Wander Nancy.

"Smells...interesting," she said.

Her parents paused their bickering for the traditional Thorn greeting. A hearty hug from her father and uncomfortably intense eye contact from her mother while Blossom squished her daughter's cheeks between her hands.

"You're upset," Blossom decided after invading Riley's personal space.

"Why would I be upset?" Riley asked, sidestepping the observation and extricating herself from her mom's grasp. She made the mistake of sticking her face directly over the casserole dish and seared her nasal passageways. "Gah! What is this? Ammonia?"

"I told you," Roger said triumphantly. "I'm not eating that garbage." He picked up the mail stacked up on a turquoise side table clustered with purifying crystals, succulent plants, and a pile of scratched-off lottery tickets.

"It's not garbage. It's cabbage casserole," sniffed Blossom. She turned to her daughter. "It's called forced fasting," she whispered to Riley. "I made it up. If he gets hungry enough, he'll dig into the veggie salad I put in the fridge."

Her mother was a diabolical manipulator, but she only used her powers for good as a rule.

"Now, is this smudgy aura of yours related to that dumbass getting engaged to the woman he cheated on you with?" Blossom asked.

Riley picked a peeled carrot stick off the cutting board and bit into it. "I'm fine," she insisted. She needed to get that tattooed on her face.

"Of course you're fine. But *are* you though?"

"It's not like I'm going to buy them something off their registry or anything. But it doesn't really have anything to do with me. Maybe this is just proof that life isn't fair." Her ex-husband was planning a honeymoon to Fiji while she was living with Dickie Frick the underwear dropper.

"Sometimes karma takes her sweet time to work things out," Blossom said, shoving the casserole back into the oven. "All you need to do is ask yourself if you're mad at Griffin the human fungus or yourself?"

"Pretty sure I'm mad at him," Riley said, this time sneaking a slice of cucumber. *She* hadn't cheated or lied or gotten her significant other fired when the marriage ended. She'd been the dutiful wife. The hardworking employee.

"Hmm," her mother said, turning back to the stove to stir whatever was simmering on the burner.

Hmm was never good.

"Don't 'hmm' me, Mom," Riley complained.

"Hmm," Blossom repeated.

Riley started to count backward from ten. Her mother only made it to six.

"If you *really* want to know what I think—" she began.

"I really don't," Riley interjected.

"I think you're upset with yourself for rejecting your gifts, which you know would have prevented this entire situation. If you hadn't been so concerned with repressing—"

Roger stormed back into the kitchen waving a letter like a battle flag. "That helmet-headed garden gnome next door reported us to the township for hanging laundry in the backyard," he yelled.

Her father's other retirement hobby involved ramping up the long-standing feud he had with their goody-two-shoes neighbor, Chelsea Strump. Proving that it was a small world and that apples didn't fall far from their trees, Chelsea just happened to be Front Desk Donna's niece. She was as committed to her hair spray and blue eyeliner as she was to labeling herself a stay-at-home mom, though both her kids were in college…on the opposite side of the country. Which was probably not a coincidence given Chelsea's aggressive parental helicoptering. She still drove a minivan and still sat on the PTA. Her husband traveled for work—which Riley guessed was another noncoincidence—leaving his wife far too much time to keep track of infractions committed by neighbors.

"First the garden, then the fence height, now this!" Roger stomped around the kitchen table.

Blossom's backyard vegetable patch and herb containers spiraled out of control every summer. She didn't pull weeds because "they were living things too," which meant that every summer, the quarter acre turned into a snarl of greenery. Chelsea claimed the pollen from the weeds was affecting her health.

Roger had erected a fence between the properties right around the time Chelsea's second son went off to college. She'd filed a complaint with the township claiming the fence height was one inch too tall according to code. In retaliation, Riley's father had spread exactly one inch of mulch on his side of the fence.

"Now, Roger. She's just a sad, empty woman who's lost her sense of identity," Blossom reminded him.

"She called your bras a 'pornographic eyesore,'" Riley's dad read.

"That greasy, close-minded slug trail had better learn to mind her business," Blossom said, eyes narrowing.

"Incoming little souls," came a musical voice from the front of the house.

"We're all fully clothed," Riley yelled back.

There was a stampede of tiny feet, and Riley's three nieces exploded into the kitchen. Roger Thorn was drowning in estrogen, but he didn't seem to mind, high-fiving each granddaughter as they stampeded in.

Their mother, Wander, floated into the room on a cloud of Zen. She was the kind of beautiful that made members of both genders pause to take notice. Her rich dark hair was confined in long box braids. She had their mother's heavily lidded eyes, her biological father's cupid's bow lips, and a leanly muscled physique. If she hadn't been just as beautiful inside, Riley could have worked up an intense dislike for her sister.

"Is that lunch I smell, or am I channeling someone?" Wander asked serenely, placing a serving dish of sliced apples and homemade yogurt on the table.

"See? Your sister doesn't have a problem using her gifts," Blossom announced, giving Riley a pointed look as she boosted a granddaughter up on her hip.

Riley rolled her eyes. She remained unconvinced that a psychic snoot was a gift.

"Hesty, dat stinks," six-year-old Rain announced.

When Wander announced her first pregnancy, mother and daughter spent a weekend divining appropriate grandmother names before settling on Hestia, the goddess of hearth and family. As it turned out, "Hestia" was quite the mouthful for little kids.

"Pop-Pop!" River, the oldest at eight, launched herself at Roger.

Four-year-old Janet ignored all of them and quietly tucked herself into the cabinet under the sink.

"How are you?" Wander asked, wrapping her yoga-toned arms around Riley and giving her a tight squeeze. She was dressed in a flowing skirt and a cropped tank that showed off abs no mother of three had the right to.

"I'm fine," Riley insisted, returning the hug.

"Your sister is upset about you-know-who giving you-know-what to you-know-who-else on the morning news," Blossom said. She gave Rain a smacking kiss on the cheek before putting her down.

"Of course you are," Wander said, catching a shoe Janet hurled from her cabinet hideaway. The chaos of family never seemed to faze Wander. Riley wondered if it was a by-product of her conception. "Who wouldn't be? Speaking of ex-husbands, Raphy's coming to dinner. He's bringing organic strawberries for dessert."

"Wonderful!" Blossom said.

Unlike Riley, Wander had managed to maintain a friendly relationship with her ex. Actually, both of them. One was

41

legally an ex-husband. She showed her commitment to the other through a handfasting ceremony, which turned out to be able to be untied rather than divorced.

Raphael fancied himself to be an up-and-coming artist. Apparently "up-and-coming" meant paralyzed by self-doubt. The man hadn't produced a single sketch or painting in all the years the family had known him. He had, however, managed to produce two of Wander's three girls and a small mountain of credit card debt when he decided that buying his own pottery kiln would unlock his creativity.

Spoiler alert: It hadn't.

"Come into the studio. We'll do a cleansing," Wander offered to Riley.

"And a tarot reading," Blossom piped up.

"I don't need a cleansing or a reading," Riley insisted.

"Yes, you do," her sister and mother responded in unison.

———

"You're squandering your gifts," Blossom said, pointing her spoon in Riley's direction.

They were crowded around the battered green table that once had been a respectable natural oak until her mother got into her furniture-painting phase. Roger was chowing down on the salad. The kids were eating tuna salad sandwiches, leaving the rest of them to stir the bitter sludge of cabbage casserole around their bowls.

"Mom, give it a rest," Riley said wearily.

"I'm just saying, if you had been tuned in, you would have realized what a huge mistake Griffin was in the first place," Blossom insisted.

"Thanks, Mom. That's exactly what I need to hear right now."

"Sometimes the words that hurt the most are the ones you need to hear the most," Wander said with an uncomfortable amount of eye contact.

"Listen to your sister," Blossom insisted.

"Don't listen to either of them," Roger said. "You're fine

just the way you are. Now, show me how to turn on the security camera again. I wanna see if Strump noticed all the bras I threw in the tree." He pushed his phone in her direction.

"Whose bras did you throw in what tree?" Blossom demanded.

"When is the last time you even had a vision?" Wander asked Riley. "Repressing these things can be dangerous. You might think you're protecting yourself, but you could just be bottling up all that power until one day it implodes."

Riley opened the app on the phone and thought of the barista. Then she thought about Nick the candy guy…and that hideous bedspread…and the feel of him between her legs.

She cleared her throat. "Can we please talk about something else?"

"I started making my own sketch paper," Raphael announced cheerfully in his rumbling baritone. His textured Afro gave him an extra four inches in height on an already tall, gangly frame.

"Good for you, sweetie," Wander said placidly.

Riley met her sister's gaze across the table and raised an eyebrow. Wander gave a little eye roll. Under all those essential oils and box braids was a judgmental human being who Riley loved dearly. Maybe they didn't see eye to eye when it came to psychic abilities, but they were family. And surviving a free-range childhood together had made them friends too.

"Have you done any interesting readings lately, Blossom?" Raphael asked.

"Well, you know I can't ethically divulge details. *But* I did have a reading that revealed a breach of trust. A week later, my client caught her husband with another man. Good for him for living his truth, but a cheater's still a cheater. She threw him out on his keister and then chucked all his stuff out on the porch."

"That must have felt very empowering," Wander said.

Riley felt a greasy, lingering shame in the pit of her

stomach and thought of the envelope back at her place. The one that arrived like clockwork every month. Could she have predicted this ending to her story? And if so, would she have even believed it?

7

Riley trudged up the stairs of the ancient stone mansion. After dinner with her family, she had printed out the municipal laws for her father so he could figure out a new legal way to piss off the neighbor. Then she'd spent an hour playing with her nieces while her mother did a tarot reading for Raphael, encouraging him to channel his creativity.

She had just gotten to the third floor when the bathroom door opened.

"Oh, come on, Dickie," she groaned. "Can't you at least wear a bathrobe?"

"Nope," the man said, shuffling his skinny, naked ass toward his room. "Gotta air out the boys."

Riley gagged and clamped a hand over her mouth. Her neighbor's wrinkly white left butt cheek sported a middle finger tattoo. *Classy.* "Yeah? Well, air them out behind closed doors," she called after him.

He slapped the tattoo and walked through his open door. In an instant, Dickie's naked ass was replaced by something else. The hallway shifted on its axis, and Riley slapped a palm against the wainscoting to keep from pitching over.

Her nose twitched violently, and she felt herself falling through fluffy cotton-candy clouds.

"What the—"

But the falling sensation lurched to a stop. The pastel clouds thinned just enough, and she found herself peering at Dickie's open door.

But it was dark now. And he was wearing a robe—thank God—and calling someone a cocksucker. He stepped back to slam the door, but there was a black-gloved hand shoving it open and pushing him into his room. A second hand came up within her line of sight. This one was holding a gun.

"Oh God," she croaked.

The gun fired twice, making her ears ring dully. Dickie crumpled to the floor. She heard footsteps running over the buzzing in her ears. The clouds obscured her vision, but she could smell gunpowder residue and blood. Her vision tunneled in on Dickie's lifeless eyes. He looked pissed off and surprised as a dark puddle slowly spread beneath him on the wood floor toward the Fuck Off welcome mat.

"What the—"

The vision vanished as quickly as it had come on, leaving her weak and dizzy. And super close to barfing.

Dickie's door was closed. There was no gloved gunman standing next to her. She slid to the floor, sweating and shivering. Her heart pounded out a staccato SOS in her chest. The taco she'd snarfed down on the way home after her mother's cabbage casserole threatened to revisit the world via the wrong end.

She could hear Dickie's TV. Hear him moving around in his room. He was alive. Not dead on the floor.

"Not real," she whispered. It wasn't real. It was food poisoning. It was a cabbage-induced hallucination. She crawled to her door and let herself in.

The tidal wave of nausea took her by surprise. She stumbled for the kitchen trash can and threw up mightily. So much for the taco.

The floor seemed like a nice place to curl up and die. She lay down on the rug in the kitchenette and stared up at the plaster ceiling.

Someone shot Dickie.

Dickie was dead.

But it wasn't real. He was clearly alive. Her rational brain scrambled for an explanation while the malfunctioning part replayed the vision over and over again.

Her phone was ringing from wherever she'd dropped her purse. It was her mom. But Riley was too tired and dizzy to answer it. Blossom had most likely been awakened mid-snore by the sense that something was very wrong with one of her daughters.

Her mom's abilities fell mostly in the divination realm. Palm reading, tarot cards, sometimes tea leaves. But Blossom also had heightened motherly instincts that reported whenever one of her daughters was in trouble.

Riley was too nauseous to have the ignoring-her-gifts conversation for the nine millionth time. Her mother wouldn't see food poisoning hallucinations—she'd see evidence of clairvoyance.

"I didn't just see the future," Riley told herself between slow deep breaths. "I had a hallucination. It was the cabbage. Food poisoning."

She waited until she was relatively sure she wouldn't hurl again before pulling herself up to standing. Her legs were shaky, and she was sweating like a hairy guy in a sauna.

Opening her door, she stood and stared at Dickie's door. She could hear *NCIS* coming from within. Dead men didn't watch reruns. She closed the door and flopped down on the couch. Maybe she'd watch a few minutes of TV to tune out and pull herself back together before she cleaned out the trash can.

The urge to vomit returned when she scrolled through channels and accidentally paused on Channel 50, which was showing a clip from Griffin's morning proposal.

She stabbed the power button, erasing the happy couple's expertly contoured faces.

The sudden silence caught her attention, and she went on full alert.

Dickie never turned the TV off this early. Maybe something was wrong?

She sat, debating for another moment before she couldn't take it anymore. "Dammit," she muttered, unlocking her door and peeking out into the hall. The rest of the house was still quiet. There were no strange footsteps on the stairs. No gun-toting bad guys tiptoeing up to the door.

What if Hot Nick the fake candy guy was involved? What were the odds that a total stranger would just happen to come looking for the man whose death she'd just envisioned... witnessed...imagined...hallucinated...under false pretenses?

Was Hot Nick a deadly assassin?

And if so, what had Dickie done to piss him off?

Also, what did being physically attracted to a murderer say about her?

"This is ridiculous," she muttered to herself. Creeping over to Dickie's door, she pressed her ear against the wood. She held her breath and listened.

There was a creak on the other side. A quiet shuffle and another creak. Was it her neighbor still airing out his genitalia? Or a dimpled cold-blooded killer disposing of evidence?

The door was thrown open, and she yelped, stumbling back.

"What the hell are you doing?" Dickie demanded. He was wearing a bathrobe now, but—in true creepy old man fashion—he hadn't bothered to tie it.

She had never been so reassured to see wrinkly man parts in her entire life.

"Nothing. Nothing. I was just—"

"Spying on me with your big ear pressed up against my door?"

Riley had always considered both her ears to be of normal proportions.

"I, uh, heard your TV go off, and I was concerned."

"Concerned?" He cackled. "If you want a piece of the ol' Dickie, you don't gotta make excuses." He pointed suggestively toward his crotch region.

"Look, I already threw up once tonight. I was just worried you…fell…" *Into a pool of his own blood. After being murdered by a good-looking stranger who lied about candy.* "Just keep Little Dickie covered up, and forget I was ever here," she told him, heading back to her room.

"They all want a piece of the Dickster," she heard him say as he closed his door.

"Gross." But at least "the Dickster" was alive.

Back in her own room, she cleaned out her vomit can, reset the locks, and dug out her lucky signed Hershey Bears hockey stick. It was the closest thing to a weapon that she had.

Just in case.

Her phone rang again.

"Hey, Mom," she answered wearily. "Nothing's wrong. I'm fine."

8

Pennsylvania provided very few months when it was comfortable to sit locked in a car for long hours at a stretch. June could go either way. It could be breezy and seventy degrees or eight thousand degrees and humid.

Camped out at the far end of the gravel lot behind Dickie Frick's place, Nick was grateful for the breezy evening. The mansion had probably been impressive a few decades ago. Now, it just looked like an oversize funeral home that had fallen on hard times.

A Jeep pulled into the parking lot, radio blaring. Nick admired the view as Riley Thorn hopped out in cute gym shorts and a T-shirt. She opened the back and leaned in to grab some bags.

Very nice legs.

And now he felt like a lecherous stalker. If people realized how easy it was to watch them without their knowledge, no one would leave their home again.

She froze, mid-lean, before dropping her grocery bags on the ground and looking right at him.

"Shit," Nick muttered.

He did his best to duck, pulling his ball cap lower over his eyes. But he was a tall guy, and Riley Thorn was apparently a suspicious woman. She crossed the lot toward his vehicle.

He pretended to be enthralled with the GPS on his phone when she knocked on his window.

"Selling more candy?" she asked, crossing her arms when he rolled the glass down.

"You shouldn't be confronting a stranger alone in a parking lot," Nick said. Bad things happened to good people all the time.

"What? I'm supposed to let one of my eighty-year-old neighbors do it for me?" she asked, crossing her arms.

Something obviously had made her even less trusting than the last time their paths had crossed.

"Stop staring and get in," he ordered.

"Yeah. Okay." She snorted. "Get in the car with a stranger so what? You can take me to a secondary location and murder me?"

He sighed. "I didn't want to have to do this but..." Nick flashed his badge at her. "Get in."

She blinked, then complied.

"Nice to see you again, Thorn," he said when she climbed into the passenger seat.

She pulled out her phone and snapped a picture of him.

"What are you doing?"

"Sending your picture and a description of your car to my sister in case I go missing," she told him. "Let me see your badge again."

He handed it over and waited.

"You sneaky son of a bitch! You're not a cop. This says 'private investigator.'"

When she reached for the door handle, Nick hit the automatic locks.

"I swear to God, I will scream bloody murder while punching you in the junk and calling 911," she threatened.

"Relax, Rambo," he said dryly. "I'm not kidnapping you. I'm keeping you from blowing my cover." He pointed at the minivan that came squealing into the lot. It stopped, taking up two spaces and a good portion of the thruway. A woman in at

51

least her early one hundreds with purple streaked hair spryly jumped out from behind the wheel.

"Listen, Nick, if that is your real name," Riley began.

But he held up a hand. "I'm Nick Santiago. I'm a devilishly handsome private investigator, and I'm looking for Dickie. Now hang on for a second."

Bad Park Job Lady was eyeing Riley's groceries where she'd left them behind the Jeep. The woman squinted through the thickest prescription eyeglasses Nick had ever seen. He felt reasonably confident that she couldn't see four feet in front of her, let alone to the back of the lot. But he'd been wrong before.

"Well, shit," he muttered when she zeroed in on his car and headed their way. He'd been made by two out of two residents. Sitting in the lot had been a stupid idea.

"Santiago," Riley said, enunciating the syllables while she typed on her phone. He heard the whoosh of a text message. "If you murder me, my sister is going to be very displeased," she warned him.

"Listen, Thorn. I will give you whatever you want if you don't blow my cover right now. If I have to talk myself out of another trespassing arrest—"

"Another?" she hissed.

"Anything. Thorn. Anything you want."

There was a knock on his window. He considered himself to be a good reader of people. But the woman next to him wasn't giving a hint of what she was thinking. He had no idea if he was about to be sold out.

Nick rolled down the window and pasted on his most charming, dimple-flashing smile. He'd discovered that weapon in preschool and had wielded it with deft precision ever since.

"Is everything all right, Riley?" the woman asked, giving Nick the magnified evil eye. She was so short she could barely see over the door into the vehicle. *What was with the mausoleum residents being so suspicious?*

He held his breath and his smile.

"Everything's fine, Mrs. Penny," his passenger seat prisoner said grudgingly.

"In that case, who's the stud?" Mrs. Penny demanded, still eyeing him with suspicion.

Riley waited just a beat too long, and Nick took matters into his own hands.

"I'm Nick, Mrs. Penny. Riley's new boyfriend."

His "girlfriend" choked on what he could only assume was her own saliva. Nick reached over and slapped her on the back while still grinning at the elderly woman.

"About time you moved on from that smug shit sandwich," Mrs. Penny said.

He wondered if Smug Shit Sandwich was the guy who'd put the rings on her finger. He gave Riley's shoulder an affectionate squeeze. "You okay there, babe?"

She looked like she was one second away from reverting to her junk-punching plan.

"Great," she rasped to his relief. "Just great."

"Well, Nick. I'm Mrs. Penny, and after a background check, you're welcome here anytime for dinner…or breakfast." She gave them a slow, disturbing wink.

"Uh. Thanks, Mrs. Penny. It was nice to meet you," he said, releasing Riley and offering his hand out the window. The woman's grip was surprisingly strong.

"Mrs. Penny, did you get your driver's license back?" Riley asked.

The woman turned a shade of pink. "You know, I think I might have left my iron on. I'd better go check! Toodle-oo!"

Nick watched as she trucked toward the back door of the building.

"First of all, how old is Mrs. Penny? She looks like she's a hundred and five, but she moves like she's in her forties," he observed.

"She's eighty. Now, please leave without murdering any of my neighbors."

Baffled, he grinned. "You seriously think I'm here to murder someone?"

"You knocked on my door under false pretenses looking for Dickie Frick, *not* collecting candy money. Then I find you lurking in the parking lot two days later. You're obviously up to no good," she pointed out.

"So you'd get in a car with someone you thought was a murderer? That's irresponsible. Didn't your parents teach you about stranger danger?"

"First of all, no. My parents didn't teach me about stranger danger. Second, I can junk punch a whole lot harder than any of my neighbors, so I'd rather you have to go through me to get to them. And third, excuse me, *stalker*. You don't get to pass judgment on me."

"You shouldn't take unnecessary chances, Riley."

"Don't tell me what to do, *Nick*."

They sat in a short, tense silence.

"Thanks for not blowing my cover," he said finally.

"I didn't do it for you. I did it to get Mrs. Penny away from your car."

"I'm not here to hurt anyone," he promised, flashing her a grin.

She appeared to be immune to his dimples. This was uncharted territory for Nick Santiago.

"You said if I played along, you'd give me anything I wanted. I want answers. Why are you stalking me and my neighbors?" she demanded.

"I'm not *stalking*. I'm *surveilling*. There's a very important legal distinction."

"Semantics," she said. "Why are you 'surveilling'?"

"Well, before you stood on my hood and gawked at me like a Bieber fan, I was trying to catch your neighbor Dickie—"

"My uncle," she corrected. "And I was not gawking."

"Yeah, right. And Mrs. Penny is your second cousin once removed, and I'm actually selling candy," he scoffed.

"You were creeping, and I spotted you creeping. You're a conspicuous creeper."

"*Surveilling.* I'm a conspicuous *surveiller*, and no, I'm not." Nick sighed. "You're the first neighbor to spot me."

"Most of my neighbors are nearsighted and half-deaf. What do you want with Dickie?" she demanded.

"All I want to do is hand him a couple of papers."

"And then what? Shoot him in the head?"

Pretty Riley Thorn has quite the imagination.

"I'm a private investigator, Thorn, not a hit man. I don't generally shoot people," Nick said with an exasperated laugh.

She gave him a long, searching look that felt like she was prying into his soul. He was most definitely imagining the tingle he felt in his chest.

They sat there locked in a staring contest, and when Riley finally blew out a breath and relaxed against the seat, the tingle in his chest went away.

"Okay. How much trouble is he in?" she asked.

"Some," he said evasively.

She spied the papers on the dash and grabbed them.

"Hey, Nancy Drew, hands off the paperwork."

"Trademark infringement?" she read and collapsed against the seat with a relieved laugh. "Wait a minute. Dickie is only fifty-seven? He looks like he's a hundred."

Nick snatched the papers back. "Apparently he's perverting the Nature Girl brand without the organization's permission."

"Ew. Dickie owns that gross bar?" Her nose wrinkled, and she got even cuter.

Nature Girls was a bar on the seedier end of Harrisburg that dressed its servers up in pornographic knockoffs of actual Nature Girl uniforms. They wore short pleated kilts, cropped button-downs, and suspenders covered in naughtier versions of Nature Girl pins.

"You don't know what your uncle who lives across the hall from you does for a living?" he teased.

"We're not a close family."

"You live together," he pointed out.

"People don't get killed over trademark infringement, right?" she asked, ignoring his question and looking very, very serious.

"Not usually. But they do get sued for a lot of money. Like your fake uncle here if he doesn't respond to these papers," Nick explained.

That seemed to appease her, and Riley visibly relaxed. "So you chase people around with papers for a living?" she asked, stretching her legs out.

He couldn't help but send her thighs an admiring glance. "Sometimes."

"Your job might be more boring than mine," she said, looking around the interior of his vehicle. It was littered with protein bar wrappers and empty bottles of water.

"You don't find all this glitz and glamour impressive?" he asked. "By the way, don't drink out of that Mountain Dew bottle."

"How long have you been sitting here?" she asked, eyeing the bottle with a mix of fascination and horror.

"Two hours so far today. Client said they'd pay for it."

"Hate to break it to you, but he doesn't usually come home until ten on Thursday nights."

"Christ," he said, glancing down at his watch. "I'm not sitting here for another three hours. Are you sure about ten?"

She nodded. "Thursday nights, he comes home, showers, and watches *NCIS* reruns."

"How thin are your walls?" he asked.

"You can practically see through them."

It was time to turn up the charm.

"Okay, let's go," Nick said, hitting the unlock button and opening his door.

"Where?" she asked, scrambling out.

He crossed to her Jeep, stuffed the serve papers into one of the grocery bags, then looped the handles over his wrists. "Your place," he said.

She wrinkled her nose. It was a cute nose. "Have you lost your mind?" she asked.

"What kind of boyfriend would I be if I watched my girl carry all this stuff up all those stairs?"

"A fake one?" she shot back.

But he was already heading in the direction of the back door.

9

Nick's ass going up stairs turned out to be the distraction Riley had been looking for. Staring at worn denim moving over taut muscle had an anesthetizing effect on the panic she'd spent all day squashing.

Griffin's ass had always been a little too flat for her liking. He didn't have any tattoos either. Or dimples. He'd also never voluntarily carried anything anywhere. Not groceries, not laundry, not even Riley across the threshold on their wedding night.

He claimed it was because his hands were an important part of his job. He'd taken his class in on-camera gesticulations very seriously.

Nick, however, carried groceries like a champ, *and* his ass was much, much nicer. She also caught a glimpse of ink on his upper arm when it peeked out from the sleeve of his T-shirt.

Her brain coughed up another glimpse of that hideous bedspread and glorious naked flesh, causing her to stumble on the stairs. She wondered if there was any way to will one vision to actually happen—naked hot Nick—while preventing another—dead Dickie.

"You okay back there?" he asked with the sexy arch of an eyebrow.

"Yep," she lied. "Falling down the stairs is a hobby of mine."

He gave her an I-know-you-were-checking-out-my-ass grin before continuing up.

They made it all the way to the third floor without spotting any other neighbors.

Riley stepped past him and unlocked the door. "Come on in," she said, glancing nervously at Dickie's closed door.

Her underwear-dropping neighbor would be royally pissed if he knew she'd helped a PI track him down. But if her vision actually came true, Dickie had bigger problems than trademark infringement.

Nick wasn't here to hurt Dickie. She was reasonably certain. Maybe she didn't exactly know how to wield her whackadoo "gifts," but she wasn't getting any homicidal maniac vibes from him.

Besides, it would have taken her two trips to haul all the groceries herself.

"Nice view," Nick said, nodding toward the river through the dormer windows. He put the bags down on her sliver of countertop and started unpacking them.

Riley blinked and then stepped in to start putting the food away. "Thanks."

"Might be the ugliest couch I've ever seen," he said, eyeing the offending brown-and-green-checkered love seat.

He wasn't wrong. The previous tenant must have had a cat, because stuffing was actively trying to escape one of the arms. "It came with the room," she said.

He held up a bag of cheese curls in one hand and seaweed crunch treats in the other, the look on his face questioning.

She took both bags from him and opened the cabinet above the sink. The cheese curls went in first, followed by the seaweed bag propped in front as camouflage.

"What?" she asked, noting his appraising look.

"You're a good girl, aren't you?" he said.

She was immediately offended because he sure as hell didn't mean it as a compliment. "Excuse me?"

"You live alone, but you make your bed every morning," he pointed out.

"A lot of people make their beds every day," she said haughtily.

"You didn't blow my cover in the parking lot when you had the chance just because I asked you nicely."

"I didn't want to cause a scene and endanger my eighty-year-old neighbor," she insisted.

"You didn't do it because I asked you not to. It's as simple as that. *And* you like my dimples *and* my ass, but you haven't flirted with me at all." He said it with a suggestive eyebrow wiggle.

"Oh please. Maybe I'm just not attracted to you," she shot back.

"Yeah. I don't think so." He said it with the confidence of a man who was every woman's type, which only served to annoy her further. "Face it, Thorn. You're a good girl. A nice girl. A rule follower."

"Spoken like the high school bad boy who never grew up," she huffed.

"You wound me, Thorn."

"I doubt that."

His grin was lethal. "You know what I like about a good girl?"

"Please. Enlighten me," she said with an eye roll.

He reached into the cabinet above the sink, plucked out the seaweed snacks, and tossed them to her. "Behind every good girl facade is the urge to do something bad." He pulled out the bag of cheese curls, opened it, and helped himself to one.

He was standing in her kitchen, flirtatiously offending her, *and* eating her snacks. She was both outraged and outrageously turned on. "Okay, buddy. My turn," she said.

"Have at me," he said, opening his arms in invitation.

"Fine. You're one of those rebels with no cause. The rule-breaking, I-can't-be-tied-down-to-a-job-or-a-woman type. I bet you've tossed your fair share of leather jackets over your shoulder in your bad-boy career. You *claim* you don't want normal because normal is boring. But that's all a facade."

"What is it I really want, Thorn?" he asked. Those blue-green eyes were warm, entertained.

She wasn't sure which one of them was enjoying the naughty, naked vision that started playing in her head. "Maybe you get off on the whole black sheep routine not because you hate normal but because you don't think you can hack it. Maybe you *want* to be the guy who shows up on time with no-reason roses or doing day care drop-offs, but you don't think you can. Because you don't think you're reliable or responsible enough."

Nick studied her for a long beat, and then the smug, gorgeous son of a bitch popped another cheese curl into his mouth. "I like you, Thorn."

"Gee, I'm *so* happy to hear that," she said dryly. She snatched the bag out of his hand and pretended not to watch him lick the cheese dust off his fingers.

"You know, I was thinking..." he began.

She knew exactly what he was thinking. "Nope."

"Since we're dating and all," he continued.

"Not dating," she corrected.

"And since I need to wait for your fake uncle..."

"*N-O.*"

"How about I order us a pizza, and we hang out here in your conveniently located apartment? Have ourselves a date night?"

Nick Santiago was dangerous. Maybe not in the here-to-murder-her-neighbor way, but he definitely was not safe. "Thanks, but I'll pass," she said.

"See. There's that good girl again," he teased, taking a step toward her. "Saying 'I'll pass' instead of 'Get the hell out of my apartment, Nick.'"

The testosterone exploding forth from his pores was acting like a drug on her body. Her heart was tapping out "hot guy alert" in Morse code, and her nipples had at some point turned to stone.

"Thanks for the help. Now, get the hell out of my apartment, Nick," she said.

He flashed her that killer smile again, and she knew she'd only managed to entertain him.

Zing! Hormones instantly flooded into her system. But Riley Thorn was smarter than hormones.

She took him by the arm and escorted him to the door.

Nick paused in the doorway, his eyes locking on hers. She could smell his dryer sheets and deodorant, feel the delicious heat his body pumped off. She wondered if he was about to kiss her. Or maybe *she* was about to kiss *him*.

"See you around, Thorn," he said, chucking her on the chin.

"Bye, Nick."

She watched him leave. Worn denim over muscled ass. White T-shirt flexing over broad shoulders.

"Yoo-hoo, young stranger!" Riley heard Lily call. "Can you help me move some furniture in my bedroom?"

Riley crossed to the top of the stairs. "Nick's leaving, Lily. He doesn't have time to come to your bedroom," she yelled.

Nick glanced up and sent her another sexy grin, accompanied by a casual salute.

"Look at the patootie on that one."

Riley couldn't argue with Lily's inner observation as Nick Santiago walked out of both their lives.

10

Nick juggled his haul and jabbed the doorbell with a finger. The gong-like sound of it echoed inside the monstrous house.

"Come in!" bellowed someone from inside.

Nick shook his head. Security obviously wasn't a priority here. He should have a chat with Riley about that. He let himself in and found the foyer empty.

"Gimme a hand, will you, sonny?" a voice wheezed from the room to his left. Nick spotted an elderly gentleman perched on a cushion in the middle of the floor of what looked like a fancy living room stuffed with furniture. The man's feet and legs were at weird angles, as was the toupee slipping down over his forehead.

Nick dumped everything he was carrying on the hall table and crossed to the man.

"Are you stuck?" he asked, offering a hand.

"The ol' hip joints lock up sometimes in lotus pose," he said, gripping Nick's hand and rocking from side to side.

It took both hands, most of his upper body strength, and a good two minutes to untie the elderly yogi. There was a sickening chorus of joint pops and a crack that sounded like bone snapping in half before the man finally unwound his limbs and made his way back to his feet.

"Whew! Thanks for the hand, whippersnapper," he said, wiping the sweat from his brow. "I'm Fred, by the way."

Nick gave him a once-over to make sure no bones were poking through the skin.

"I'm Nick," he said, letting go of Fred and feeling relief when the guy didn't crumple back to the floor.

"Nice to meet ya," Fred said, shuffling out of the room without asking Nick who he was or why he was there.

Nick gathered his stuff, locked the front door, and headed up the stairs. On the second floor, he heard Mrs. Penny cursing through her closed door. "Think you can use dragon fire on me, you goddamn amateur? Eat my icy acid, you son of a bitch!" He hoped she was gaming.

The third floor was much quieter. At least until the bathroom door flew open. A Carrie Underwood song about cheating exploded into the hall. And so did Riley Thorn, wearing nothing but a blue bath towel. She smelled like something bright and citrusy.

She shrieked when she spotted him. The wireless speaker she carried hit the floor with a thump. So did the bucket of shower supplies when she hunched over to assume a panicked defensive stance.

The towel slipped very nicely from breasts to belly button.

Reluctant gentleman that he was, Nick turned around to face the stairs.

"What are you doing here?" Riley gasped.

He held up the pizza box in one hand. "Date night?" he offered.

"No!" He heard her scrambling behind him to fix the towel. "You just want to use me for my apartment."

"Definitely not *just*," he said. He'd only gotten a glimpse, but it had been one hell of a glimpse.

"Despite what this looks like, I have some self-respect. I'm not going to let you just show up, look at my boobs, and then camp out in my apartment until Dickie comes home."

"They're great boobs. And the pizza has bacon on it." He

opened the box over his shoulder so she could see it. "Come on, Thorn. Just an hour or two, some free pizza, and then I'll be out of your hair."

Her groan was frustrated and conflicted. He smelled victory.

"How about now?" he asked, hefting the bag in his other hand. "Chocolate marshmallow ice cream."

She sighed, and he knew he'd won.

"Ugh. Fine. Give me two minutes to get dressed."

"No need to on my account," he joked.

"Hilarious. Two minutes," she reminded him, snatching the pizza out of his hand. He was still grinning when she slammed her door, leaving him and the ice cream in the hall.

Exactly two minutes later, Nick was just raising his knuckles to knock when the door opened. She'd combed her wet hair back from her face and—unfortunately—put on a pair of shorts and a Shippensburg University T-shirt. There was a slice of pizza in her hand. She looked cute, fresh, annoyed.

He brushed past her, enjoying another hit of citrus, before heading to the doll-size kitchen where he produced two plates from the cabinet.

"Come on in. Make yourself at home," she said dryly.

"You're not going to be annoyed the whole time, are you?" he teased.

"I can almost guarantee I'll be annoyed as long as you're in my apartment," she shot back.

"Here." He handed her a plate with another slice on it before plating two of his own. He ripped off two paper towels and gave her one.

"You could have just waited in your car," Riley complained as he headed for the couch.

He sat and toed his shoes off. "Why do that when I can have date night with my new girlfriend?"

"You're so weird," she said. "Water, beer, or a soda?"

"Water." He wanted the beer. But technically, he was on duty.

She put two glasses of water on the coffee table and sat down next to him.

The ugly couch was as comfortable as it was attractive. It was small enough that their elbows were touching. Her skin was still a little damp from her shower, and that was wreaking some havoc on his gentlemanly efforts.

"You seem tense, Thorn," he observed.

"Gee, I wonder why?"

"If it makes you feel any better, seeing you half-naked was the highlight of my week," he offered. Hell, probably his month. "I'd be willing to even the score, you know. To make you feel better."

Her laugh was a little warmer. "Keep your pants on," she told him.

Her phone buzzed on the coffee table. The screen lit up with the name "Mom."

They both watched it.

"Aren't you going to get that?" he asked.

"Definitely not."

"You're an interesting girl, Thorn."

"I'm not," she insisted.

"Sure, you are. You're an enigma. A mystery."

"I know what an enigma is," she said, shooting him the side-eye.

"What's a girl like you doing in a dump like this?"

She peered at him over her second slice of pizza. "I don't actually know how to take or answer that."

"Is there more than one way to take that question?"

"You could mean any number of things. For instance, you could be wondering what a girl as obviously insane as I am is doing living on her own and not in some kind of asylum. *Or* you could be wondering how badly someone had to screw up to land here with half of Harrisburg's AARP members for roommates and the couch from hell."

He grinned. "Your brain must be an exhausting place to be," he predicted.

"You have no idea," she said.

"Seriously, how did you end up here? You're what? Thirty? You went to college," he said, gesturing at her shirt. "Then what?"

She sighed, and her shoulders started to inch away from her ears. "Thirty-four. Nicely done, by the way. It's a long, boring story, and you don't seem like the type of guy who likes to be bored."

Nick had a hunch there was absolutely nothing boring about Riley Thorn.

"Come on, Thorn. I'll tell you all my secrets if you tell me yours."

"Oh, I doubt that," she said lightly.

"More pizza, or are you ready for ice cream?" he asked, holding up his empty plate.

"Ice cream," she decided.

"You talk. I'll scoop," he said, returning to the kitchen and digging out a pair of bowls from her minimalist kitchen supplies. "What's a smart-doesn't-appear-to-have-any-serious-drug-problems-or-mental-issues woman like you doing in a dilapidated mansion with thirdhand furniture and no cable?"

"It can all be summed up by saying I make poor life choices," she said, dropping her head to the back of the couch and watching him.

"Lost your life savings in a Ponzi scheme?" he pressed. He was a curious guy by nature. He liked knowing people's stories, their motivations, the whys and hows that brought them to their present. That innate nosiness was part of what had set him on his previous and current career paths.

"If you consider marriage a Ponzi scheme, then yes," she said.

"Ah. The shit sandwich Mrs. Penny mentioned," he guessed, digging into the ice cream.

"You've got a good memory," Riley said. It sounded more suspicious than complimentary.

"I do when I'm interested in something."

Bowls and spoons in hand, he returned to the couch.

"Mrs. Penny is *very* interesting," she quipped.

"You're no snooze fest yourself, Thorn. So you got married."

"I got married to the wrong guy who I desperately wanted to be the right guy. Fun fact: wanting something desperately doesn't magically make it happen. He cheated. We got divorced. His family lawyer was a shark, and I dragged myself out hemorrhaging profusely. Metaphorically speaking. He got the house, the car, and my job, and here I am a year later, living out my days as a proofreader and live-in tech support for senior citizens."

She was matter-of-fact, not woe-is-me, and he liked that. "He cheats and still gets everything? *Shit sandwich* sounds accurate," Nick mused. He watched her stir her ice cream clockwise.

"He got engaged again yesterday. With the ring he made me give back," she said. "She's twenty-four."

"Ouch."

"I kind of feel sorry for her. She doesn't know what she's getting herself into." She shook herself and scooped up some ice cream. "Enough about me. You ever been Ponzi-schemed?"

He winced. "I'm not the settling-down type."

"No. *Really?*" She went heavy on the sarcasm.

"Enlighten me, Thorn. What tipped you off?"

"That whole bad-boy confidence thing. You're too sure of yourself. I can tell you've never had a woman damage your self-esteem over the long term," she teased.

He laughed, and she smiled at him, those brown eyes warm and bright.

"Funny," he said.

"Seriously though. Have you ever done a long-term relationship?" she asked.

He was distracted by the way she slid her spoon out of her mouth, the way her hair fell over her face when she looked down at the bowl. He brushed it back for her, and she looked up at him in surprise.

"I'm more of a buffet guy than a one-entrée type," he told her, remembering what Perry had said.

She surprised him with a laugh. "Maybe that's where I went wrong. I picked an entrée and got food poisoning. Next time, I'll head for the buffet."

He shook his head. "No, you won't. You're the monogamous kind. You *like* settling down."

She laughed again. "You say that like it's the equivalent of getting chased by homicidal clowns."

"Well." He gave a shrug. "Yeah. It is."

"Is that why you're a PI and not something more—"

"Boring? Soul sucking? Oppressed?" he offered.

"I was going to say *structured*."

He shuddered. "I'm not a fan of structure or security. I like calling the shots, even if that means I have no one else to blame for my mistakes."

"Hmm." She was studying him with interest. "Where do you see yourself in five years, Mr. Santiago?" she asked him.

"What is this? A job interview?"

"A social experiment."

He leaned back against the worn cushion. "I don't know. I guess I see myself where I am now doing what I'm doing now," he said. "Maybe just with nicer stuff. What about you?"

"In five years? I want a job I love. A non–shit sandwich significant other. At least one dog and a kid or two. And a bank balance that I don't have to check every single day to make sure I can afford a cup of coffee. Quiet. Peaceful. Happy. Normal."

"Adventure. Novelty. Excitement," Nick responded, pointing a thumb at his chest.

"Clearly this pretend relationship will never work out," she said smugly.

"But if you ever want to sample this buffet, let me know," he offered, waving his hand down his body.

She snorted. "I fell for the spray-tanned 'good' guy. I'm not going to rebound with the tattooed bad boy. We have *disaster* written all over us."

"Disasters can be a lot of fun," he pointed out.

She rolled her eyes. "That is such a Nick Santiago thing to say."

———

By 11:00 p.m., Dickie Frick was a no-show, and Riley had gotten increasingly anxious.

"This is weird," she said, coming back to the couch from her ninth trip to her peephole. The later it got, the more nervous she seemed.

"Probably got hung up at the bar," Nick guessed.

"You don't think he's in trouble, do you?" she asked, chewing on her lower lip. She looked legitimately concerned.

He cocked his head. "What makes you say that?"

She shrugged three times in a row and looked over his shoulder rather than in his eyes. "I don't know. Maybe just a feeling."

His fake girlfriend was lying to him.

Nick waited.

"I mean, do you ever just have a gut feeling that something's not right?" she asked. Her back was ramrod straight. Those brown eyes looked pleadingly into his, and he found himself nodding.

"Sure. Instincts. More people should listen to their gut," he said.

"What if your gut is telling you something insane?" she asked, leaning in just a little closer. The cushion dipped under her weight.

Right now, his gut was screaming, "Kiss her," and he had every intention of not taking his own advice. "I guess you have to weigh the consequences of not listening to your gut," he said.

If he kissed her, he'd be giving her the wrong idea. He wasn't looking for "something," and Riley Thorn was a "something" kind of girl. She was the kind of girl who deserved dinner dates who showed up on time and someone who remembered birthdays and anniversaries. Someone who'd be home by 5:30 every night and volunteer to coach T-ball.

He was not that kind of someone.

"I was afraid you'd say that," she sighed. The sigh turned into a yawn.

He glanced at his watch. "I should go," he said.

"Do you want me to text you or something if Dickie comes home?"

If. Nick's spidey sense tingled at that particular word choice.

"Do you have a reason to believe he's in trouble?" he pressed.

She was still—too still—for a long beat before she finally said, "Not a good one."

Her face was close. Those big brown eyes and the worry in them were playing his protective instincts like a damn fiddle. She jumped, and he glanced down, wondering what had startled her. Apparently it was the hand he'd unconsciously put on her bare knee.

They both stared down at the point where their bodies touched.

Not only was she not threatening to punch him in the junk, Riley was leaning ever so slightly into his side. Like an invitation. His gut started a go-for-it chant that was echoed in his groin. If a cute pair of shorts and sad brown eyes were all it took to work him into a sexually frustrated lather, the farther he stayed away from her, the better.

He didn't do complications. He didn't want to feel responsible for someone again.

"So maybe don't worry about it then," he advised, giving her leg a platonic pat before pulling his hand back. "Besides, you're not responsible for his welfare, Thorn. You can't protect other people from themselves. It never works out the way you think it should."

"Hmm."

He got to his feet, suddenly anxious to get some distance between himself and Riley's shapely legs. "Thanks for the couch time," he said, slipping back to the slick, careless charm.

She rose too and escorted him to the door for the second time that day. Only this time, he knew it would be the last.

"Thanks for the pizza," she said. She still looked worried, and he hated that he wanted to fix whatever it was for her. Old habits died hard.

"Don't worry about letting me know when he gets home," Nick said. "I'll catch him at the bar tomorrow." He'd been avoiding Nature Girls since it was more of a gun-behind-the-bar, what-are-you-looking-at kind of place and played the odds that he could catch Frick at home.

"Sure. Bye, Nick." The way she said it told him she got the message.

"See ya around, Thorn," he said, tapping the papers against his palm and taking one last look at the pretty girl with the sad eyes.

11

The coffee coated her computer monitor in a fine brown mist.

Coughing, Riley made a grab for the box of tissues she kept on her desk and mopped up the mess. Her morning Bella Goodshine stalking had just taken an unexpected turn. Bud, headphones on, shot her a suspicious look and then went back to ignoring her.

She restarted the video from the beginning.

"Gretchen Gallagher reporting for Channel 50 from Little Amps Coffee Roasters, where I'm told an employee recently had a life-changing encounter."

The camera panned over to the pink-haired barista, and Riley adjusted the volume on her headphones.

"Tell our viewers what happened, Maris," the reporter prompted.

"Well, it was Monday morning, and a woman ordered a cold jar to go, and as I was cashing her out, she said, 'Ida wants you to get your lymph nodes checked.' I was like, 'What?' but she basically ran out the door. I was pretty freaked out because Ida is my great-granny. She died four years ago."

"Oh crap," Riley murmured to herself, a feeling of dread beginning to percolate in her intestines.

"So what did you do?" the reporter asked, hanging on the barista's every word.

"I went straight to the doctor," Maris answered.

"Please don't be sick. Please don't be sick," Riley chanted.

"It turns out I have thyroid cancer," Maris said, her eyes going wide. "But we caught it early, and it's very treatable."

"Is there anything you'd like to say to the psychic Good Samaritan?"

Maris turned to the camera, her eyes watery, her smile wavering. "I'd just like to say, ma'am, you and Great-Grandma Ida saved my—"

Riley closed the interview and yanked off her headphones. In all her adult years of vision having, there had never once been any concrete evidence that what she was "seeing" was true. She'd never followed up to see if any of the other against-her-will warnings were even necessary or if any of the "lost" items she'd been compelled to locate for strangers were ever found.

This was bad. Very bad.

If Great-Grandma Ida really had reached out from beyond the grave and barista Maris really did have thyroid cancer, that meant Dickie Frick could actually end up with a face full of lead.

Well, crap.

She spared the back of Bud's head a glance. He appeared to be in the middle of a very long Reddit rant and probably wouldn't pay her any attention. She picked up the phone and dialed her mom.

"Riley! Sweetie, how are you?"

"Mom, I have a hypothetical question, and you can't get all worked up about it, okay?"

"Hang on. Let me put my dye aside. My new alpaca wool came today." Riley heard a thump and a muttered curse. "There. Okay. You have my full attention," Blossom announced.

Riley took a breath. "If someone sees something that hasn't happened yet—"

"If a clairvoyant sees the future," her mother corrected.

"Whatever. Does that mean they can stop it or change what happens, or is it going to happen no matter what?"

"Sweetie, it's all so nuanced. You can't—"

"Not *me*. *Someone*," she insisted.

"Fine. *Someone* could have a vision of something that might happen, or it might represent something else. Like the tarot cards."

"So sometimes a gun isn't a gun?" Riley asked hopefully.

"There are no guns in tarot, silly. But say you or *someone* dreamed of, oh, I don't know…a big pile of snakes slithering around."

"Uh. Gross?"

"Snakes can represent several different things," Blossom said, ignoring her.

"So visions or dreams aren't always literal?"

"They're rarely literal. Honestly, only the most powerful clairvoyants have that kind of direct link to the future or past. Most deal with messages that need to be decoded."

Powerful? That adjective had never applied to anything in Riley's entire life besides her ex-husband's legal team.

"What if a clairvoyant had a nightmare while they were wide awake that their neighbor was shot and killed?" she asked.

"Oh, well then, I'd suggest to the neighbor that they get their affairs settled," Blossom joked.

"Mom!"

"Kidding! We're talking about serious gifts here. Most of us get our messages filtered through symbolism and nuance. A vision like that would be so powerful the receiver would be completely unable to deny it."

"What about changing the future?" Riley pinched the bridge of her nose. "Like if someone sees the future, are they obligated to change it? Should they change it? Are they even capable of changing it?"

"I don't have a definitive answer for you, sweetie. Even if someone were capable of changing the future, that someone would have to question whether it would be ethical to do so.

You know your grandmother is on the ethics committee of the North American Psychics Guild. She'd be able to provide more guidance in that area," Blossom said. "You should give her a call."

Elanora Basil was a dour, terrifying matriarch. She was also one of the most well-known mediums on the East Coast. She'd been offered her own reality show and had dismissed the offer as "poppycock." Also filed under *poppycock* was her granddaughter's rejection of the family gifts.

"Thanks, Mom. I was just…wondering," Riley said, having no intention of calling up her grandmother for a chat about psychic ethics.

"Any time, kiddo! I hope this helped."

It hadn't. Not one little bit.

———

It took Riley four tries to actually get out of the Jeep in front of the police station on Walnut Street. She immediately got back behind the wheel and slammed the door.

"Nope. This is so stupid. What am I supposed to do? Go in there and say, 'Hey, I had a psychic vision that my neighbor is going to get shot'?"

"Beats doing nothing and then feeling like crapola when he gets murdered."

"Not now, Uncle Jimmy."

"Just sayin', even if he is a prick, you'd feel bad if he was a dead prick, and you could have done something about it."

Her dead uncle had a point.

Riley swore under her breath and closed her eyes. "This sucks," she muttered to herself.

She took a deep breath and did what she never did: tried to be psychic.

She called up the vision from memory and walked through it step-by-step.

It was steadier this time. Or she was. Either way, the third-floor hallway wasn't tilt-a-whirling around, and she wasn't barfing up tacos. It was dark. The house was quiet. And through those weird puffy clouds, she could just make out a shadow moving toward Dickie's door. She did her best to mentally pan down.

Sweat broke out on the back of her neck, but she clung to the scene for dear life. Black sneakers wavered between clouds. Black sneakers with red flames. A leather-gloved hand knocked lightly.

The TV noise on the other side of the door cut off. Then footsteps.

"Don't answer the freaking door, Dickie," Riley said, hoping that if she could change the vision, she'd also change the future.

But the dumbass answered the door. He was dressed in that tattered robe and, once again, hadn't bothered to secure it.

"I told you," he grumbled. "You got a problem, you bring it up with your boss, you cocksucker." They were Dickie's last words. He started to slam the door, but that gloved hand stopped him. The gun came up. Fired.

Riley shook herself out of it. Sweat ran like Niagara freaking Falls down her back. Her heart was pounding, and her breath came in short, sharp bursts like she'd just run half a mile after the ice cream truck. A wave of nausea hit her.

Was it any wonder she blocked this crap? Who the hell wanted to feel like this all the time? It was like opening herself up to a case of the flu.

Still shaking, she slid back out into the June sunshine and shut the car door.

"You can do this," she told herself. "Go on in there and tell them Dickie Frick is going to get murdered. And then run before they break out the straitjacket." Straightening her shoulders, she took one last shaky breath and marched across the street.

A lifetime of TV shows had promised her a busy bullpen of uniformed officers and detectives drinking bad coffee and talking shit. Instead, she found a stark waiting room with sturdy wooden chairs lining three of the walls. Flickering fluorescent bulbs lit the space. Signs forbade visitors from bringing weapons, tobacco products, and pets inside. They also required visitors to wear pants and shoes.

Two of the chairs were taken, one by a very pissed-off-looking mom who was asking Siri to find the closest military school, the other by a bearded man wearing a jacket much heavier than the weather called for and stained, baggy sweatpants. He was snoring.

There was a plexiglass window in the wall next to a locked door. Riley approached.

"Can I help you?" The officer on the other side of the glass was in uniform, but—given the grilled chicken salad and worn paperback at his elbow—it looked like getting dressed was as close to the action as he got.

She stepped closer. "I think something bad is going to happen to my…uh, friend," she said. No need to tell him more information than necessary in case he decided to call for some nice burly orderlies.

The officer blinked very slowly. "Um-hmm." His name tag read Sergeant Cornelius.

"I think someone is going to try to hurt him," she said.

"What makes you think that?" he asked with a stifled yawn. Apparently, she was boring him.

She gave up on subtle and went for it. "Look, someone might show up at his apartment and maybe shoot him."

"Are you telling me you're planning on shooting your friend?" the sergeant asked, still not nearly interested enough.

"Uh, no." This guy's listening skills fell well below adequate.

"Good," he grunted. "Because that's a hell of a lot of paperwork."

"Look. I just think he's in trouble, and maybe if you talked to him or staked out his place—"

"Are you on any medications or have you recently gone off a medication?" he asked, tapping out a beat with the pen in his hand.

"No."

"Any illegal drugs?"

"No."

"Do you have any evidence that your friend is in danger?"

She wondered how many unhinged people this sergeant saw on any given day.

"Well, no," she conceded.

Riley saw him write down *5150?* on the notepad next to his salad. Everyone who'd lived through the bad Britney years knew that a 5150 was an involuntary psychiatric hold. He was focusing on the wrong problem.

She hitched her purse higher on her shoulder and got ready to bolt. "Look. His name is Dickie Frick. He lives on Front Street, and something bad is going to happen to him. It's going to be someone he knows. *Not* me. I've done my civic duty. Now it's up to you to make sure he doesn't get murdered."

"Uh-huh. Okay. Ma'am, why don't you have a seat out there, and I'll see if I can find someone to take your statement?" He crossed out the question mark.

Definitely not happening. Work probably wouldn't let her use PTO for being thrown in jail. "I gotta go," she said and hustled out the door. "Shit. Shit. Shit." She dashed across the street and jumped into the Jeep. Her hands were shaking so hard she dropped the keys twice before she got them in the ignition. *Worst getaway driver ever.* Fortunately, the bored sergeant hadn't meandered out of the building yet, gun drawn.

Still, she wasn't taking any chances. Jamming her foot on the accelerator, she peeled out of the parking space.

"How did it go?"

"Not now, Uncle Jimmy."

"You still have half an hour in your lunch break. We could do some fishing."

12

Dickie lived through the night. Riley knew this because she stayed up until dawn, leaning against her door with her hockey stick at the ready. There was no manual on timelines for visions coming true. She knew *this* because she spent two hours of her all-night vigil scouring the internet for such a manual.

She was so exhausted that she fell asleep in corpse pose during Wander's afternoon yoga class and snored until her father nudged her with his hairy bare foot.

"You look terrible," Lily announced when Riley slumped through the back door. Her neighbor peered at her through steamed glasses over a simmering pot of almost-like-Olive-Garden marinara. "Don't you think that new boyfriend of yours deserves the teensiest bit of effort?"

"Boyfriend?" Riley yawned.

"Hot guy, tight buns. Carried your groceries," Mrs. Penny said, peering over the screen of her laptop.

"Oh. Right. Nick." One meal with her, and Nick had gone from fake boyfriend to "See you around." At least her bad luck with men was still intact.

"The hottie with the heine," Lily said and giggled, wiping her glasses on the front of her frilly kitty-cat apron. The woman was eighty years old and more boy crazy than a thirteen-year-old at a Jonas Brothers concert.

"What does this Nick guy do for a living? What's his last name? Did you run him to see if he has any priors?" Mrs. Penny was less *boy* crazy and more just plain crazy.

"Nick's…in sales," Riley hedged. She wasn't going to see him again, but she also didn't have the energy to share that information with her neighbors. If she did, she'd have to decline Mrs. Penny's offer to set her up with some distant relative and spend an hour scouring her eyeballs after Lily gave her more worksheets detailing Kama Sutra positions.

"What kind of sales?" Mrs. Penny pressed.

"Uh, insurance?" Riley said. "Have either of you seen Dickie today?" she asked, changing the subject.

Mrs. Penny snorted. "Saw that walking skid mark leave for work about an hour ago."

If he was at work, he wasn't getting murdered across the hall. The terrifying ticking clock in Riley's head got a little quieter.

"The cops didn't stop by, did they?" she asked innocently.

"Police? No! Are you okay, Riley?" Lily asked, waving the marinara spoon in her direction. "Whoopsies!" A splatter of sauce hit the floor, reminding Riley a little too much of the blood in her vision. She gagged.

Mrs. Penny eyed her suspiciously through thick glasses. "Is this about that shitweasel getting engaged? You didn't have him whacked, did you?"

"Griffin?" Riley said. "No. Nope. Happy for him. Everything is great. Oh, hey. Unrelated. Can everyone remember to keep the doors and windows locked at all times?"

"Gosh, Riley. I don't know if we can," Lily said, pouring a little red wine into the sauce and then taking a tipple straight from the bottle. "Mr. Willicott lost his keys in 2009."

Riley closed her eyes and took an exasperated breath. "If I make new keys for Mr. Willicott, can we start locking up around here?"

"Probably, dear," Lily said brightly.

Riley escaped to the quiet of the third floor. At the top of the stairs, she stared at Dickie's door, debating.

She'd gone to the police over a hallucination. Wasn't her civic duty fulfilled?

"If I were an underwear-shedding, perv-bar-owning guy," she mused out loud, "would I want to know if someone thought I was going to be murdered?"

Looking at Dickie's door, she recalled the marinara splatter and sighed. "Crap."

Inside her apartment, she grabbed a notepad and pen.

Dickie,

Don't answer your door late at night. Someone might shoot you in the head.

Sincerely,
Riley

Nope.

Dickie,

I hallucinated your brutal murder. Can you maybe be extra careful for the next week or so? Also, keep your underwear off the bathroom floor.

Best wishes,
Your Neighbor

Hmm. No.

Dickie,

Someone might be coming to murder you, and I think you

know them. If you know what I'm talking about, please go to the police and don't answer your door.

A concerned citizen

Just the right balance of warning and "you're now responsible for your own life," she decided.

Satisfied, Riley slipped the note under his door and returned to her apartment. There. She'd gone to the cops—who had ignored her—*and* she'd personally warned the victim. Her hands were officially clean. Short of hurling her body in front of Dickie's if bullets started flying, there was nothing else she could do.

Well, except...

She glanced at her phone. Maybe there was one other thing.

————

After a communal spaghetti dinner, Riley returned to her apartment, changed into her summer pajamas—yoga shorts and a tank top—and settled on the couch to watch how to ram a car on *Made It Out Alive*.

It was after midnight when the telltale creak in the hallway jolted her out of other people's survival. Anxiety rising, she tiptoed to her door and peered through the peephole.

It was Dickie. Alive and...well, normal. He was standing in his doorway, holding her note.

Relief was swift. Life saved. She'd done her duty. Now, she could get back to normal.

The son of a bitch crumpled up the paper and tossed it over his shoulder into the hall.

"Seriously?" she hissed.

He slammed his door.

"You're welcome," she called through the door. "Jerk."

She was definitely not going to be the guy's human shield now. Maybe just one quick sweep to check the doors and windows downstairs, and she'd officially forget the whole thing. She padded down the stairs to the first floor.

Both the front and back doors were unlocked, and a window in the front parlor was wide open.

"It's like living with a bunch of toddlers," she grumbled, locking everything up tight. They were all going to have to have a long conversation about safety this weekend.

Under a cloud of annoyance, she returned to her apartment, locked her door, and decided to watch one more episode before bed.

———

When she jolted awake on the couch, the TV screen was asking her if she was still watching. There was no noise other than the usual creaks and groans of an old house full of old people, but something had woken her.

Something like a knock.

Was that Dickie's voice? Was he talking to someone in the hall?

Tripping over the blanket tangled around her legs, she was only halfway to the door when she heard two quick bangs followed by a definitive thump.

"No, no, no, no," she chanted and grabbed the hockey stick.

Holding her breath, she looked through the peephole and caught a glimpse of movement in the dark hall. Dickie's door was open.

"Shit." Her heart was hammering so hard she could feel it in the roots of her hair. She couldn't believe this was actually happening.

There was something round and shiny hovering in the dark, like an orb. The orb disappeared, and she realized that she was squinting at Dickie's closed door.

What if I'm imagining everything? What if I'm still asleep on the couch? She glanced behind her, half expecting to see herself drooling on a pillow. Nope. She was definitely awake.

She heard another sound. The haunted house creak of Mrs. Penny's door on the second floor. She lived directly under

Dickie. If the woman heard the shots and came to investigate, it would be a third-floor bloodbath.

There was a noise somewhere on the stairs. Loud, fast footsteps. She had no choice. Gripping the hockey stick, she flung her door open.

"Stay in your rooms and call 911," Riley shouted and charged for the stairs.

She was halfway down to the second floor when she ran full speed into a solid figure dressed in black.

Caught!

She would have screamed, would have bludgeoned the stranger, but gravity and forward momentum had other ideas.

Together, they plunged down the stairs.

Riley's shoulder and hip took the brunt of the impact. Then every other body part took a turn as the much larger, heavier body used hers as a cushion. Repeatedly.

She hit the landing with an "oomph" turned war cry when the attacker landed on her chest. Blindly, she struck out kicking and flailing as hands clutched her shoulders.

She was not going to get murdered. Her mother would never forgive her.

Lights burned to life.

"Jesus, Thorn! Knock it off!"

She paused mid-flail and opened an eye. Nick was sitting on top of her.

"Did you kill him?" she groaned. "I can't believe I let you buy me pizza."

"Thorn," he said, pushing her hair out of her face. "Are you okay?"

"What in the holy hell is all this racket?" Mr. Willicott bellowed.

"Everyone stay in your rooms," Nick yelled back.

"Who are you?" Fred wanted to know.

"That's Riley's boyfriend," Mrs. Penny shouted.

Great. Now her neighbors were going to think she was dating a murderer.

"I heard cannon fire!" Mr. Willicott shouted. "Goddamn river pirates!"

"I think someone drove a truck into the building," Lily offered.

"Did you kill him?" Riley asked Nick.

His gaze darted up to the third floor. "I was in the parking lot and heard the shots," he said grimly. "I was running up the stairs when you threw yourself at me."

"You're sure?" She winced. The shock was fading, and pain began to bloom everywhere. She couldn't tell what hurt the most. It all hurt. A lot.

"Sure I didn't sneak in here, fire two shots, and then wait for you to hurl yourself into me on the stairs? Yeah. Positive." Nick was running his hands down her arms and legs. "Is anything broken? Can you sit up?"

"Ungh. I think I'm okay."

"Riley, I called 911, and they want to know what happened," Fred yelled from downstairs. "Should I tell them about the river pirates?"

"Tell them you heard gunshots in your house," she called weakly.

Nick helped her into a seated position, and the stairwell swayed. A symphony of nauseating pains sparked to life.

A curtain of red blurred the vision in her left eye. "Oh my God, is that blood?" She slapped a hand to her forehead and yelped. "Am I decapitated?"

He yanked her hand down and probed at what she could only assume was a gaping wound that would horribly disfigure her for life.

"It's barely a scratch," he promised. "You're only going to need a couple of stitches."

"Scratches don't need stitches."

"Maybe just some superglue then. Let's see if you can stand," he said.

"Ask the police to send their most handsome officers," Lily yelled to her brother.

"Just leave me," Riley begged. "Go check on Dickie."

"Let's get you on your feet first," Nick said.

Despite the raging inferno of pain, Riley realized there wasn't going to be a rush to get into Dickie's apartment.

"Okay," she sighed. The spinning slowed to the speed of a drunken, lopsided merry-go-round.

Nick held her against him when she swayed. "Put your arm around me."

She tried to lift her arm and felt the nausea rise. "It's not working."

"Shit, honey. I think your shoulder's dislocated. We need to get you to a hospital."

"No hospital." She winced as her arm flopped uselessly. "At least not till after…"

They both looked up the stairs again.

"I'm coming up," Mrs. Penny shouted unnecessarily from ten feet away.

"What did she say?" Lily hollered. "Should I come upstairs?"

"Stay in your rooms," Riley insisted.

Nick slid one arm around her waist and the other under her knees, scooping her up like a bride. "Try to keep your arm still, okay?" he said, starting up the stairs.

Her shoulder felt like it had been trampled by a runaway elephant. The rest of her felt like a small pickup truck had backed over her a few times. "What are you doing here?" she asked him, gritting her teeth.

"I heard gunshots," he said again.

Riley could feel his heart thumping steadily against her. She wondered if it was adrenaline or the fact that he was lugging an adult woman up a flight of stairs.

"He had a visitor," she said. "I thought the guy went down the stairs, but if you didn't pass him—"

"Must have gone out the fire escape," he said, holding her against his very nice, warm, safe chest. "What the hell were you doing throwing yourself down the stairs with a hockey stick after a shooter?"

"Ah, crap! My Bears stick!" She peered over Nick's shoulder. Her hockey stick was splintered in pieces on the landing. "Wait. Why were you even here to hear gunshots?"

"Frick gave me the slip at Nature Girls. Thought I'd swing by and see if his car was here."

"It's a million o'clock in the morning," she pointed out, wincing.

"Yeah, well, he pissed me off. Had his bartender give me the runaround while he ducked out the back. Figured I could ruin his night here."

"Pretty sure someone else beat you to it," she said.

They got to the top of the stairs, and Nick hauled her into her room. Propping her against the wall, he flipped on the lights and did a quick, sexy sweep of the room with his gun drawn and his back pressing her into the plaster.

Even with pain and adrenaline having a finger-snap *West Side Story* battle in her nervous system, Riley still managed to feel the hormonal "zing" with his weight against her.

"Lock your door," he ordered gruffly, stepping back into the hall.

"Why? What are you going to do?" she whispered, limping after him.

"I'm going to check on Frick."

They both stared at the closed door across the hall for a beat. It was deathly quiet on the other side.

"What if someone's still in there?" she hissed, clutching at his arm with her working hand.

He looked down and cupped her face. "It's going to be fine. I'm just going to open the door and look around inside. Ten seconds tops."

"I really like your dimples," she confessed, then frowned. Apparently pain made her loopy.

His grin was quick but strained. "Stay focused, Thorn. I want you to close and lock the door. Don't let anyone in but me."

She shook her head. It seemed cowardly to retreat now. But she was also pretty sure that Dickie Frick was dead behind that door, and she didn't want to be haunted by his real-life death. The vision had been bad enough.

"I'll stay in the hall while you go take a look," she decided. A decent compromise. "If you find a dead Dickie, I'll call 911 and tell them it definitely wasn't river pirates."

He gave her a long look, then nodded.

He crossed the hall and pressed his ear to the door just like she had only a few days earlier.

Nick glanced over his shoulder at her and winked. She rolled her eyes.

The doorknob turned silently in his hand, and he was inside in a second. From her sagging position against the opposite wall, she watched him sweep the room with a level of competence that screamed *cop*.

"Make the call, Thorn." His voice was calm and firm.

Riley's hands shook, so she wedged the phone in her relatively useless right hand and used her left to dial 911. "What do I say?" she hissed.

"Tell the operator you heard gunshots in your building."

"Is he dead?"

"How upset are you going to be?"

13

In the fourteen minutes it took to have lights and sirens surrounding the mansion, Nick got Riley onto her couch, pressed a wad of paper towels to the cut on her forehead, and secured her bad arm to her side with the tie of a bathrobe.

He wasn't going to think about the fear that had gripped him when he'd heard the shots fired. He had just pulled into the lot and confirmed Frick's shitmobile was there when he'd heard the shots. All he'd been able to think about was getting to her.

There was something about Riley Thorn that made him feel a lot of really stupid feelings he didn't want to feel.

Prior to the two slugs to Dickie Frick's head, he would have said those feelings fit neatly in the lust box. After? Well, now he wasn't so sure. The woman had hurled herself down the stairs after someone she thought was a murderer.

Stupidly brave was apparently quite the turn-on for him.

Even now, with him standing between her and anyone that came up those stairs, his hands still weren't completely steady. Her face was pale, which made the blood on her forehead stand out even more. Head wounds bled. A lot. Rationally, he knew this, but it did nothing to squash the blooming rage in his gut.

She was in pain and needed a doctor. But there was fucking protocol.

He glared and paced as the EMT checked her pupils.

"How's our girl doing?" Mrs. Penny, the purple-haired tenant from the parking lot, tottered into the room wearing a set of men's pajamas and holding a glass of bourbon. She had gamer headphones around her neck.

"Mrs. Penny, you should stay downstairs," Riley called out wearily. Her voice sounded strained, and Nick cursed the investigating officers for taking their sweet fucking time arriving on scene.

"I had to come up and see what all the fuss was," Mrs. Penny harrumphed. "Willicott says some pirate firebombed Dickie's apartment."

"There was no firebombing and no pirates," Riley told her. "You should go downstairs and tell Mr. Willicott that."

Instead, Mrs. Penny made herself comfortable on the couch next to Riley. "Well, since I'm here and you have that Netflix thingy on this TV, I'll just keep an eye on you. Young man, mind scooching over?" she asked the EMT.

"Well, if it isn't Nick 'the Forehead' Santiago," came a familiar voice from the doorway.

"Sergeant Jones. Always a pleasure," he said with a genuine smile. Mabel Jones was a short, curvy uniformed cop with a foghorn laugh and a pretty cute snore. They'd been on a few dates back in the day. Their parting had been amicable. Thankfully. Last time he'd checked, she was the best marksman in the department.

"How the hell did you land yourself in the middle of this mess, Nicky?" she asked.

Despite the friendly tone, it was a professional question, and he knew better than to give too much information. He was standing ten feet from a homicide. Like it or not, he was a suspect. A situation that wasn't going to surprise half the Harrisburg PD.

"How about we go out in the hall?" he suggested, jerking his chin in the direction of the open door.

Jones gave him an all-knowing look that traveled to the bleeding, battered Riley, who was watching them while the EMT sealed a second butterfly bandage to her forehead.

"Sure," Jones agreed, leading the way.

She waited for Nick's feet to cross the threshold before going all cop on him. "You wanna tell me how you just happened on a DB in a house you don't live in in the middle of the night?"

"Nick was just visiting his girlfriend, Riley," a voice called out over the whir of the lift chair. "We were worried she'd given up on men after being married to that camera-ready robot, you know," the woman shouted. Her white hair stood up in tufts. Her fuzzy bathrobe was open over an almost sheer pink housedress.

"Girlfriend?" That cracked Jones's implacable good-cop facade. She grinned. "About damn time."

Nick skated a hand over the back of his neck. "Yeah." He drew the word out. He was walking a fine line here. Lying to the cops was usually not a great idea. It was even worse when he was about to become a suspect.

"It's a new relationship," the woman said, climbing off the lift chair. "But we're hoping it sticks. We've all got our fingers crossed for a happily ever after."

"Lily, don't say anything to them without your lawyer present!" Mrs. Penny tottered out of Riley's apartment and into the hall. She waved her cane at the sergeant. "Anything you say will incriminate you, and they'll throw your ass in jail."

"Are you up yet?" a male voice shouted from somewhere below.

"I'm sending it back, Mr. Willicott," Lily yelled back and stabbed at the buttons on the chair.

Mrs. Penny peeked into Dickie Frick's open door, where a tech from forensics was photographing the body.

"Why don't you two wait somewhere else?" Jones suggested, trying to usher the women away from their dead neighbor.

"Why don't you make me, five-oh?" Mrs. Penny shot back.

The third-floor hall was getting downright crowded, Nick thought.

"What have we got, Sergeant?"

Nick closed his eyes. "You've got to be fucking kidding me."

"Santiago. I should have known." Detective Kellen Weber looked just as douchey as the last time Nick had seen him. Even at two in the morning, the guy was wearing a fucking tie and that smug-ass smirk.

"How's the nose, Weber?" Nick asked.

The detective's eyes narrowed above an almost imperceptible twist to the otherwise straight blade of his nose.

"DB with two GSWs to the head discovered in his own apartment," Jones reported crisply.

"What are you lookin' at, copper?" Mrs. Penny demanded, giving the detective the evil eye.

"That's *Detective* Copper," Weber said evenly.

"Why don't we go check on Riley?" Lily suggested at full volume, linking her arm through Mrs. Penny's.

Mrs. Penny glowered at Weber and Jones. She pointed two fingers at her giant lenses and then at the cops. "I'm watchin' you two. So don't even bother trying to plant evidence!"

"No, ma'am," Jones agreed.

The two women tottered into Riley's apartment. "You poor thing! Look at all that blood!" Lily howled.

"You didn't shoot Dickie over the underwear thing, did you?" Mrs. Penny asked Riley.

Nick shut the door before Riley's neighbors managed to fertilize any more seeds of suspicion.

"What are you doing here, Santiago?" Weber demanded.

Nick shrugged and gave him a tight-lipped smile. "Not much."

"Please, don't elaborate," Weber said. "I'd love nothing more than to slap cuffs on you and drag you downtown."

"You remember what happened last time you put cuffs on me," Nick said darkly.

"He's dating the across-the-hall neighbor," Jones filled in, shooting Nick a warning look.

"Great-niece," Mrs. Penny shouted as she wrenched open Riley's door. "She's our great-niece."

"All of you?" Weber looked skeptical.

"You got a problem with family, po-po?" Mrs. Penny demanded.

Nick felt the heat of her glare as it was magnified through her glasses.

The hum of the lift chair was approaching the top of the stairs again. The grumpy, Denzel-esque Mr. Willicott was wearing a bathrobe over suit pants and a FEED ME TACOS AND TELL ME I'M PRETTY T-shirt. He was followed by toupeed Fred, the elderly yogi Nick had met on his last visit.

"Gentlemen, we need you to wait in your own rooms," Jones said, ignoring the futility of corralling elders.

"Too late, cutie pie!" Fred said cheerfully. "Willicott already took the chair up. It'll take him half an hour just to get back down there. I'm Fred, by the way. Single. Spry. Ready to mingle."

"Who is Riley Thorn to you?" Detective Fun Sucker asked Mr. Willicott, who was very obviously the only Black man in the "family."

"Who?" Willicott asked.

Fred elbowed him.

"Oh, right," Willicott grumbled. "He's my great-nephew."

"Ha! This one's a comedian," Fred said, twirling a finger around his ear as he shoved Willicott toward Riley's apartment. "Willicott's my ex-brother-in-law, but we love 'im like family."

"What's that smell?" Willicott demanded.

"Decomposing flesh," Mrs. Penny announced.

"Is that my T-shirt?" Nick heard Riley ask inside.

"Back to why you're calling in dead bodies," Weber said, drawing Nick's attention.

Nick shoved his hands in his pockets. "I felt like it was something you'd want to know about."

Weber stepped in on him. "Drop the rebel-without-a-clue act, Santiago."

"As soon as you drop the asshole routine."

"Loose fucking cannon," Weber shot back.

"Smug shit," Nick growled.

"Gentlemen, can we get back to our murder vic?" Jones suggested.

"Detective, looks like the back door was kicked in," another uniform, this one out of breath from the three-floor climb, announced.

"Uh, yeah. That wasn't the shooter. That was me," Nick said.

Jones rolled her eyes and he thought he heard her mutter, "Oh, for fuck's sake."

"You carrying?" Weber asked, all business.

"Yes," Nick snapped.

"Turn over your weapon, smart-ass," Weber said triumphantly.

"Seriously?"

"We've got a DB with a double tap. You're on scene with a gun, and you just confessed to breaking in," Weber pointed out.

"He was in a hurry to get to his girlfriend on account of the sex they were gonna have. Right, Nick?" Lily called from the doorway, sending him an exaggerated wink none of the law enforcement officers missed.

"Gimme the gun, Santiago."

Nick stared hard at the detective's ever so slightly crooked nose. Jones helpfully held out an open evidence bag.

"Fine," he said. "But I want a receipt and a formal fucking apology when I also turn over my dashcam footage that proves I was still in my truck when the shots were fired."

"Cry me a river, pretty boy," Weber said snidely.

"Kiss my ass, shithead."

"I hate to break up the bromance or whatever this is, but I think I'd like to go to the hospital," Riley announced from the doorway. She was leaning against it like it was the only thing keeping her upright.

"Maybe you don't have a problem withholding treatment, *Detective*, but I do," Nick said, moving to Riley's side and slipping his arm around her waist.

"You can go as soon as you answer some questions," Weber said, his tone marginally warmer when it was directed at Riley.

"Save the charm, Detective Dick. She's taken," Nick announced, pulling her in closer and not minding at all the way she melted into him.

"I'm sure you'll do what you always do, Santiago. Get bored and move on to something more exciting," Weber snapped.

Nick bared his teeth and fantasized about shoving Weber ass over face down the stairs.

"Why don't we go inside?" Riley suggested, her grip on Nick's waist tightening as if she knew exactly what he'd been considering.

"Coroner's on her way up, Detective," one of the uniforms reported.

"Sit tight, Ms. Thorn, and I'll be with you in a minute. Then we can get you to a doctor," Weber said solicitously just to piss Nick off.

14

Riley leaned heavily on Nick as he helped her limp back to the couch. She wheezed out a sigh when he gently lowered her back onto the cushion.

Everything hurt. Her shoulder. Her hip. Both knees. Her forehead. A wrist. A bicep. Her entire ass. The EMT reported that she didn't appear to have broken anything but that she still needed a head-to-toe going-over. Riley felt like she'd caught the flu, got hit by a city bus, and then was tossed in an industrial dryer with a load of bowling balls.

Nick crammed himself onto the couch next to her and slung a protective arm around her. Giving in to the exhaustion, she sagged into his side and rested her head against him. Here she could focus on the low hum of relief that came from touching him. He was solid and warm and a very nice place to rest her weary, bloody head.

"So someone finally offed the old sleazebag," Mrs. Penny mused behind them. She'd picked up a stack of Riley's unopened mail and was thumbing through it. Riley was too tired to protest.

"Can't say I'm surprised," Fred said from the floor where he sat pretzel legged.

"I remember six years ago when I was bringing in the groceries, and that noodle-nosed bran muffin didn't even hold the door for me," Lily huffed. "Nope. He just let it shut right in my face. And me with an armful of bags."

Lily was one of the sweetest human beings on the face of the earth. But she also had a reputation for holding grudges. Fail to hold a door for her when she was having a bad day, and she wouldn't cry at your funeral.

"You got anything to eat around here?" Mr. Willicott barked at Sergeant Jones as if it were her place.

"There's eggs in the fridge," Riley called out weakly.

Mrs. Penny held up an envelope with a law firm logo on it to the ceiling light and squinted.

"I'll take that, Mrs. Penny," Riley said, holding out her good hand.

Disappointed, her neighbor handed it over, and Riley stuffed it between the couch cushions.

Nick quirked a sexy eyebrow, but she pretended not to notice. She was physically injured and emotionally scarred, gosh darn it. All these nosy busybodies could suck it.

"I need more plates," Mr. Willicott yelled from the kitchenette where something was sizzling away on the stovetop.

"Go across the hall," Lily suggested.

"There's probably brains and blood all over the place," Mrs. Penny reminded them.

Riley squeezed her eyes shut and tried not to think about blood and brains. Another vision had come true, and despite everything she'd done, Dickie had still ended up dead. It was a lose-lose as far as she was concerned.

"I don't know if Dickie owned dishes anyway. We can improvise," Fred said, untying his legs and rising from the floor.

His shorts were entirely too short, Riley noted in a detached, slipping-into-a-pain-coma kind of way.

"Ms. Thorn, I need to ask you a few questions." The handsome detective was back. So was the very insistent muscle twitching just beneath Nick's left eye. A person didn't have to be actually psychic to pick up on the fact that Nick hated Detective Weber. Or that the feeling was mutual.

"Riley already gave her statement to a uniform," Nick snarled.

"Here you go, sweetie!" Lily pushed a coffee mug of scrambled eggs into Riley's good hand. Surprised to find that she was in fact hungry, Riley wedged the mug between her knees so she could eat with her left hand.

The detective sat down on the coffee table facing her and flipped his notebook to a blank page. "Be that as it may, she left out the fact that she went to the station on Walnut Street two days ago and reported that one Dickie Frick was in danger."

Well, hell.

"How did you—" Riley's question was cut off.

"Surveillance footage and your license plate," the detective said.

"Real nice, copper," Mrs. Penny sniffed. "Good enough to search a license plate but can't be bothered to save a man's life with advance notice. Another five-star day for the Harrisburg PD."

Detective Weber ignored the jibe.

"Is this your handwriting, Ms. Thorn?" Detective Weber held up a piece of paper that had been smoothed out and stuffed in an evidence bag.

Shiiiiiiit. Riley dropped her fork.

Nick leaned forward, his eyes skimming the note.

"We found it crumpled up in the hallway," the detective announced.

This entire situation was getting stupider by the second. An idiot was dead because he ignored the warning that should have saved his life. She was being questioned by the cops she went to for help.

Her nose twitched. *Uh-oh.* And now it was getting harder to focus on what the detective was saying because there was a very insistent dead father figure who kept nudging at her consciousness.

"Tie clip. Tie clip. Tie clip. Tell him."

What was it about dead people that made them so pushy?

Riley shook her head, trying to dislodge the ghost. "I'm sorry. What were you saying, Detective?" she asked.

"I was asking you how exactly you knew Frick was in trouble. Were you in a relationship with him?"

The other occupants of her apartment started laughing, then wheezing.

"Our Riley dates men like Hot Nick here," Lily announced with an appreciative gleam in her eyes.

"Or that ex-husband of hers. I mean, the guy's a tool but a hot one," Mrs. Penny said, fanning herself with an old credit card statement she'd liberated from Riley's plastic bill bin.

"TIE CLIP."

"Give me a minute, will you?" she muttered under her breath in exasperation. The last time she listened to her psychic "urges," it hadn't gone exactly to plan.

"Ms. Thorn, I'm going to need you to tell me exactly how you knew your neighbor was in danger *now*. Not in a minute. Do you know who did this?" Detective Weber was very, very serious now.

"Tie clip."

This was what she got for trying to do the right thing. A dead guy poking at her and a live detective ready to slap cuffs on her.

"I had a feeling," she said, choking out the words.

"A feeling," Detective Weber repeated. "A *feeling* made you call the tip line eight hours ago and disguise your voice like Cookie Monster."

So much for the *anonymous* part of the anonymous tip line. "That was not Cookie Monster," Riley argued. It had been her best impression of Mr. Willicott.

"Thorn," Nick said quietly, shaking his head. Her fake boyfriend was telling her to *for real* shut up.

"Are you interfering with my investigation?" Weber asked Nick.

"Listen, genius," Nick snapped. "Why in the hell would she warn you about a murder if she was going to commit it?"

"People do all kinds of crazy things," Weber said. "I'd think you'd remember that."

Ugh. She was exhausted, pissed off, sore from head to toe, and the last thing she needed was a pissing contest in her apartment.

"I didn't kill Dickie. I don't know who did," Riley cut in. "Sometimes I just…know things." Heat flushed her cheeks.

There was no reaction from either man.

She rolled her eyes, which made her headache worse. "Like before they happen. Or I know things that I shouldn't know." God, this was humiliating.

"She's a psychic, dear," Lily said helpfully, popping up over the back of the couch. She was eating eggs out of a soup bowl.

"A psychic?" the detective repeated.

"I don't identify as a psychic," Riley said quickly.

"Her whole family is psychic," Lily insisted.

"I'm not psychic. Officially," Riley said lamely. "I just sometimes know things. Like about Dickie. And that the tie clip your dad gave you fell between your washer and dryer."

The detective's face went stone still.

"Okay. That's enough," Nick decided, standing. He gently pulled her to her feet. "I'm taking her to the hospital. If you have any more questions, ask them with a lawyer present."

The detective stood too. "Make sure you get me that dashcam footage if you don't want to be spending the night in jail, Santiago."

Nick responded with a middle finger over his shoulder.

They left her neighbors in her apartment. It was a slow, painful two flights of stairs. Riley refused to wuss out and use the lift chair. But they managed to eventually make it to the parking lot. Nick helped her into his SUV.

They were both quiet as he pulled out of the lot, leaving the flash of red and blue lights in the rearview mirror.

"You wanna talk about the whole psychic thing?" he asked finally.

She didn't bother opening her eyes when she shook her head. "Nope. You want to tell me why you and the detective hate each other's guts?"

"Nope."

15

Nick pulled up to the hospital's emergency department entrance and threw on his hazard lights. "Let's go get that shoulder looked at, Thorn," he said. Hitting up the city hospital's emergency department in the middle of the night was always a crapshoot.

He half carried her into the waiting room and manhandled her into a chair near the front desk. It didn't appear to be a full moon.

There was a snoring homeless woman sprawled across three chairs with a pushcart of belongings next to her. On the other side of the room, a kid vomited profusely into a bucket on his exhausted mother's lap. A pair of EMTs wheeled a convulsing woman on a gurney in through the doors. The guy in the bloody T-shirt at the admitting desk looked like someone had poked a few holes in him.

"Stay here. I'll park and get you checked in," Nick said to Riley.

She had her eyes squeezed shut.

"You okay?" he asked, leaning in and laying a hand on her good shoulder.

"I'm an empathetic vomiter," she hissed from between clenched teeth. "Trying not to barf."

He grinned and ruffled her hair. "You're pretty cute, Thorn."

She groaned but gave him a ghost of a smile.

After finding a space in the parking garage, he headed straight to the nurse at the desk. He leaned against the counter and smiled dashingly. No one was immune to his charm. Or his dimples.

The woman leaned forward and peered over the reading glasses on the end of her nose. Her knowing grin caught him by surprise. "Well, well, well. Nicky Santiago."

"Holy shit. Roberta? How's Teddy doing?" he asked.

"Since you arrested him? Great. Married. Two kids. Works in administration for the Senators baseball team."

"Good for him," Nick said.

"He's on the straight and narrow now," she promised. "What did you bring me tonight?" Roberta asked, shooting Riley a glance.

He cleared his throat. "My girlf—*fiancée* hurled herself down a flight of stairs chasing a murderer."

"Fiancée, huh?" She slid a clipboard and cheap plastic pen toward him.

He'd thought the rest of his explanation deserved more attention.

"Yeah. Finally settling down," he said, flashing her the grin. "I think she's got a dislocated shoulder. Maybe needs some stitches. Should be in and out real quick."

"I'll see what I can do," Roberta said.

He tapped the desk. "Appreciate it. Tell Teddy I said hi."

He returned to Riley and took the chair next to her.

"Did they say how long of a wait it'll be?" she asked, leaning into him.

"I've got an in at the desk," he said, angling himself toward her. "They'll take you back in a minute."

"An 'in,' you say?" She looked at the nurse. "Dated her daughter?"

"Arrested her son. By the way, we're now engaged."

That got her attention. "You and the nurse? Congrats."

"You and me, Thorn," he corrected.

She frowned. "We are? When did that happen?"

"Around the same time you threw yourself at me on the stairs."

"That wasn't a proposal," she said dryly.

"Come on, Thorn. I don't want Detective Dickface sneaking back there to harass you. If we're engaged, they'll let me go back with you. I'll play security."

"I'm not convinced that you're not just trying to find an excuse to see my boobs again," she said.

"You don't want me waiting out here all by my lonesome, do you?"

As if on cue, the homeless woman woke up with an explosive fit of coughing.

"Fine. I accept your proposal. Where's my ring?"

"You left it at home in the lockbox because it's not safe to wear at night. I almost lost an eye last week when I rolled over to spoon you."

"You've put a lot of thought into this fake engagement." Her smile was sleepy, pained.

"I just think fast on my feet. Now, let's do some paperwork." He picked up the clipboard. "Name: Riley Thorn." He drew out the syllables as he wrote. "Riley short for anything?"

"No."

"Middle name?"

She shifted uncomfortably in her seat. "Uh, nope."

"Nope, you don't have one, or nope, you won't tell me?"

"Won't tell you. It's horrific. There's something very wrong with my parents." Up close, her eyes were the color of bourbon.

"This isn't making me not want to know it."

"Moving on," she said and slapped the clipboard with her good hand. It fell out of his hands.

"Oops. Sorry. Depth perception," she said.

Just then, the little boy tossed his cookies for the third time.

"Oh God," Riley groaned, closing her eyes.

Nick abandoned the paperwork and put an arm around her.

"No puking," he insisted. He pressed her face into the crook of his neck and covered her ear with his palm. He was definitely *not* cuddling her. He was just keeping her from barfing all over the floor. Really, he was doing them all a favor. He was heroic like that.

Minutes later, a big guy in scrubs called Riley's name.

"Only family," he said to Nick.

"He's my fiancé," Riley lied.

Roberta shot Nick a double thumbs-up.

The nurse grunted, clearly not caring that *the* Nick Santiago was engaged, and led them through the doors and down a hall to a row of hospital beds separated by curtains. It was busier back here. More patients. More staff. The noises and smells of the human body in distress created a special kind of sensory experience.

"Wait here," the nurse said, gesturing at a bed before drawing the curtain closed.

They both sat on the bed, and Riley sagged down onto the mattress in the fetal position. He stretched out next to her. "You know, this relationship is progressing a little fast even for me," he said conversationally. "We're engaged and in bed together, and you haven't even bought me dinner yet."

"I guess that makes you easy," she said dryly.

"I prefer the term 'cheap date.'"

She winced. "We're in the emergency department. There's nothing cheap about that."

"Then it's only fair that I put out," he offered.

She gave a pained laugh and then was quiet for a long minute.

"I can't believe I'm being spooned in the hospital by a private investigator after my neighbor got murdered across the hall."

"I can't believe I'm spooning a hot psychic in a hospital bed."

"You're so weird." She yawned. "And I'm not a psychic."

They must have fallen asleep, because the next thing he knew, the curtain was being briskly drawn back by a woman with black-rimmed glasses that matched her inky curly hair.

Nick swiped at the drool on the corner of his mouth and in Riley's hair.

"Let's get you upright," the woman said in a no-nonsense tone.

"Come on, Thorn. Up we go." He climbed out of the bed and helped ease Riley into a seated position.

"Okay…Riley," the woman said, consulting her form. "I'm Lisa, your on-duty PA. What brings you to the ED tonight?"

"I fell down the stairs," Riley said.

The PA turned a shrewd eye on Nick.

He put his hands up. "Whoa, hang on. I carried her back up the stairs."

Lisa didn't look convinced.

"It was my fault," Riley said. "I didn't look where I was going—"

"Sir, maybe you should wait outside." Lisa opened the curtain for him and gestured toward an empty chair on the other side of the hall.

Riley laughed. "It's fine. He can stay."

"Your choice. Now, I just need you to put on this gown," Lisa said.

"Get out, Nick."

———

Dawn was breaking as Nick wheeled Riley with her relocated shoulder, three stitches, and bruised flesh out the automatic doors of the emergency department. Her arm was in a sling, and there were circles as dark as bruises under her eyes.

The smell of coffee wafted temptingly from the gift shop café behind them. Early commuter traffic was already beginning to snarl on Second Street just beyond the parking garage.

"Ready to go, champ?" he asked, parking the chair on the sidewalk.

She rose and immediately wobbled.

He slid an arm around her waist to steady her. "How about you wait here? And I'll get the car," he offered.

"That sounds—"

"Riley!"

Her face, already stark white against the bandage on her forehead, went even paler.

"Oh shit. Oh no. This is not happening," she whispered.

"Is that…?" Nick trailed off as he stared at the man in the suit jogging toward them, clutching a microphone. A cameraman hauled ass behind him.

"Griffin Gentry," Riley filled in for him. "My ex-husband."

"I thought he'd be taller," Nick mused as the petite primped putz came to a halt in front of them.

"He does most of his interviews standing on a box," she said.

"Riley Thorn, Griffin Gentry from Channel 50 News," he said into the microphone.

"I know who you are," she said, rolling her eyes.

"What can you tell us about the brutal murder of your next-door neighbor in the early hours of today?" he asked.

Gentry's blond hair was perfectly coiffed and sprayed with industrial shellac. His suit was somewhere between gray and a light purple. He wore a lavender shirt, a purple paisley tie, and loafers with tassels. The man's teeth were a shade of white not known to exist in nature.

Speaking of *not found in nature*, his skin was a dusky orange, and he was wearing a thick layer of foundation. A tangerine weasel.

"No comment," she said, dodging the microphone he shoved in her face.

"Back off, buddy," Nick said, escorting her toward the garage and away from the moron. But Gentry jumped in front of them again.

"Is it true that you're a suspect in the homicide?" Gentry asked, shoving the microphone in her face. "Channel 50 is aware of your history of anger management issues and violence. Would you like to make a statement about your involvement in the death of Mr. Frick?"

"Seriously, Griffin?" Riley said, exasperated.

Nick had had enough.

"Listen, shorty, you think *she's* got anger issues, you ain't seen nothing yet," he threatened, putting himself between them. "Now, get out of our way, or I'll pick you up and find a dumpster."

"I'm a journalist," Gentry whined, his voice a full octave higher.

"Why don't you go shower off that cologne? It's making my eyes burn. Then you can explain to your viewers how exactly you know Ms. Thorn. And that she divorced you after you failed to keep your tiny dick in your—"

"Okay! I think we got enough here," Gentry squealed, covering the camera lens with a hand.

"Come on, Nick," Riley said, tugging on his arm. They left Gentry at the entrance to the parking garage and headed for Nick's vehicle.

They almost made it.

"Riley! Wait up!" Gentry called, jogging after them, this time without a microphone or a camera.

They didn't stop, but with her pained gait, it didn't take long for Gentry's stumpy legs to catch them.

"Who is this guy? Your bodyguard?" He snorted at his own joke.

"I'm her fiancé, genius. And if you don't get out of her face right now, I'm going to knock you down and mess up that snazzy suit," Nick told him.

The guy took a self-preserving step back. "Fiancé?" Gentry looked him up and down. "What? Did you decide to get engaged just because I did?"

"Go away, Griffin," Riley said through gritted teeth.

"You owe me, Riley," he wheedled.

She wheeled on him, then winced. But when she opened her pretty brown eyes, there was bloody murder in them. "Exactly what do I owe you? *You* cheated on me. *You* sued me. And *you* cash my check every month," she snapped.

Now Nick *really* didn't like this guy.

"Come on, Ry. I'm trying to make the move to the evening

desk. Help a guy out." Gentry cocked his head to the side and flashed her those white teeth.

"Does he think he's being charming right now?" Nick asked Riley.

"He thinks he's charming all the time," she told him.

Gentry pouted. "Look. Just give me an exclusive on this. I get you on camera. You can tell your side of why you shot that guy. I've got a one-on-one with the mayor for the six o'clock news tonight. Between the two, I'm basically guaranteed a spot on the desk."

"I didn't shoot anyone," she argued wearily. "Why don't you just have your dad fire someone again?"

"Riley, Riley, Riley." Gentry reached out like he was going to do the old push-the-hair-behind-the-girl's-ear move. She recoiled like a turtle going back in its shell.

Nick moved between them again and grabbed the guy's wrist. "Gentry, man, I swear to God. If you don't remove your finger from her vicinity right now, I'm going to break it. And then I'm going to sue you for assaulting my nose with that god-awful cologne."

Gentry sniffed at his shoulder and frowned. "You don't like it? It's pheromone-based."

"It smells like cat piss. Now, get the fuck out of my way, and don't come near my woman again."

Nick gave the guy a helpful shove so he could put Riley in the passenger seat. When she was situated, he shut her door and took a menacing step toward Gentry that had the guy scurrying back toward the news van.

"You'll be sorry," Gentry squealed over his shoulder as he jogged back up the ramp.

Nick got behind the wheel and looked at Riley. She had her eyes squeezed shut.

"*That* guy?" he said finally.

She opened one eye. "I don't know what I was thinking."

16

I say we install cameras and motion sensors around the perimeter." Mrs. Penny gave the living room floor a *thunk* with her cane as she paced.

Nick had delivered Riley to her front door after the hospital with a "take care" and what felt like a smoldering look. But there had been no offers to call or visit her later.

She couldn't blame him. The whole psychic thing and run-in with her ex-husband would have scared anyone off. She'd pout about it after the "neighborhood watch" meeting called to address the "dead neighbor thing."

"I still think this could be a paranormal phenomenon," Lily insisted as she swiveled around and around on the stool in front of the organ someone had stuffed into a corner a few decades ago. "I think we need to have the place exorcised."

Mrs. Penny snorted. "A spirit doesn't shoot deadbeats in the head with a Smith and Wesson. It was a human, and now we need a security system with laser beams."

"We don't have that kind of budget," Fred said from the pink meditation cushion in the window seat. "We could take turns patrolling."

"And do *what* if you catch someone breaking in?" Riley

asked. She was wedged onto a green velvet divan between a stack of pillows Lily had thoughtfully arranged for her and Mr. Willicott, who seemed to think she was one of the pillows.

Realistically, she was the only one in this house who had a chance at being able to outrun a wannabe murderer or at least surviving the heart attack if she found one hiding in the basement.

"We could hire a self-defense expert!" Lily suggested. "There's this handsome martial arts man at my gym."

"When did you start going to the gym?" Fred asked his sister.

"Let's all get guns," Mr. Willicott said, perking up. This was the first time Riley could remember him contributing something conversation-related since they'd met.

"You'd find a way to shoot yourself in the ass," Mrs. Penny argued.

The doorbell rang, and they all froze.

"Is it another murderer?" Mr. Willicott shouted.

"I bet it's the ghost," Lily said, sounding a little too enthusiastic about that possibility.

"Only one way to find out." Mrs. Penny yanked open the door, and in walked Riley's mother.

"Oh no," Riley groaned, girding herself for the guilt trip.

Blossom dumped her hemp shopping totes in the foyer and hurried to her daughter's side. "You poor thing," she crooned, fussing over Riley's bandage and sling.

"I was going to call you, Mom," she fibbed.

"Don't be silly," Blossom said, pulling a dusty afghan off the back of the divan and tucking it around Riley's legs. "You've been through so much. Why would you even think to call me? Besides, Lily called me and told me your *fiancé* took you to the hospital."

Uh-oh. Danger zone.

Riley recognized that diabolical sparkle in her mother's otherwise guileless eyes. This was forced fasting–level Blossom Basil-Thorn.

"Now, you just cozy up in here. I'll warm up my boneless

bone broth. While that simmers, I'll do a top-to-bottom smudging," Blossom said cheerfully.

"Thank you, Blossom," Lily called after Riley's mother.

Blossom waved a clump of sage and disappeared into the back of the house.

"Back to the meeting," Mrs. Penny announced.

"We need a code word," Fred said with a lot of confidence for a man who had put his toupee on backward that day.

"A code word?" Riley, more concerned that her mother was about to exact her revenge through soup, couldn't follow the conversation.

"In case one of us is being held hostage or abducted. If the bad guy has one of us, we'll use the code word to alert the others." Mrs. Penny obviously had no trouble following the unraveling thread.

Riley wasn't sure how a code word would prevent a gun-toting bad guy from breaking into the house and shooting someone else. "Maybe we should just start locking the house?" she suggested.

"Then how will we lure the bad guys in?" Lily wanted to know.

"Wait. Why are we luring them in?" Riley asked. She really needed to go to sleep. For two days.

"So we can use the *code word*. Keep up, girlie," Mr. Willicott bellowed.

"Harbinger." That was Mrs. Penny's suggestion. Or she was calling someone in the room a harbinger.

Riley's body was one low throb of pain. It made paying attention more difficult.

"Swiss cheese," Fred tried.

"But what happens if I need you to pick up some Swiss cheese at the market?" Lily pointed out. "You'd think I've been abducted."

"Good point. What's a food none of us like?" Mrs. Penny wondered.

"Pizza," Mr. Willicott said.

"Pizza?" everyone echoed in horror.

"What kind of monster are you?" Mrs. Penny hissed.

"I don't like the hard shell," Mr. Willicott grumbled.

"Shell? You mean crust," Fred said.

"No! The yellow crispy shell that holds all the meat and lettuce."

"I think you're thinking about a taco," Riley said.

"That's what I said. Tacos," Mr. Willicott said grumpily.

"Have you seen the neurologist lately?" Lily asked sweetly.

"Let's focus, people," Mrs. Penny said, clapping her hands. "We need a code word that we'll all remember."

"Ciabatta," Fred suggested.

"Cha-what now?" his sister asked.

"French toast?" Mrs. Penny tried.

Blossom wandered past the doorway barefoot and waving a bouquet of smoking sage.

"How about cabbage casserole?" Riley suggested.

"Code word: cabbage casserole," Mrs. Penny mused. "I like it."

"Great. Can I go to bed now?" Riley asked.

There was a knock at the front door. Everyone over the age of seventy scrambled out of their seats.

"What do we do?"

"Is it the killer?"

"We should have got those guns!"

"Anyone have something we could hit him over the head with?"

"I got a lamp!"

"Put that down, Fred. I paid ten dollars for that at a garage sale!"

"Harrisburg Police," a weary voice called from the other side of the door.

"You got a warrant, copper?" Mrs. Penny demanded through the door.

Even from the divan, Riley could hear the man sigh. "I'd like to talk to Riley Thorn."

Mr. Willicott opened the door, and Detective Weber walked in. He'd lost the tie and jacket and rolled up the sleeves of his button-down. He looked almost as tired as Riley felt.

"Have a few minutes?" he asked her.

Great. Now she had to give up her nap for an interrogation. Well, she'd have plenty of time to sleep in prison.

"Yeah. Sure." She didn't think she could make it up the stairs on her own, so she limped back to the kitchen and closed the pocket door behind them. "Do you want some water or something?" she asked, dropping onto one of the vinyl chairs around the table.

"No, thanks." The detective took the chair across from her and sat. Wordlessly he reached into his pocket and dropped something on the table between them.

It was a tie clip.

She sighed.

"I have a lot of questions," he said.

"Join the club," she said.

"Why don't you start by telling me how it works?" he suggested.

"If I knew that, I'd be able to control it. And if I could control it, I'd block out these ridiculous visions and stop having conversations with dead people." She scrubbed a hand over her face to hide the fact that her nose was twitching. "Your dad wants you to know he doesn't blame you."

The detective sat there stone-faced for so long, Riley wondered if he'd fallen asleep with his eyes open.

"Tell me about how you knew Frick was going to be murdered," he said finally.

She gave him points for not shifting gears and demanding to know all about the message his dead father just sent.

"I didn't know it was going to happen. I'm not exactly a practicing psychic. I didn't even know until recently that these things were visions and not cabbage-induced hallucinations."

He wisely let the cabbage thing go.

"You had a feeling something was going to happen to Dickie. How did that come about?" he tried again.

Riley yawned mightily. When Weber didn't turn into a human and suggest she go to bed and talk to him later, she

114

told him about the vision in the hallway, the visit to the police department, the note.

"Why didn't you go to him personally?"

She leaned in. "Detective Weber, I have something to tell you. There's someone out there who wants you dead, and they're going to knock on your door and shoot you in the head. I don't know who or when, but it's probably going to happen. So how about that rain in the forecast for Tuesday?"

"Point taken."

"Am I still a suspect?"

"Right now, you're the only person of interest we've got since your boyfriend exonerated himself with dashcam footage."

"Haven't you heard? He's my fiancé now," she joked.

"You could do better," he said.

A low moan came from the hall.

The door slid open, and her mother stood there with a phony smile pasted on her face, smoking sage clutched in her hand.

Riley sighed. "This is my mother, Blossom Basil-Thorn," she said, making the introductions. "Mom, this is Detective Weber."

"I'm so happy to meet you on such an auspicious day, Detective," Blossom said. "After all, how often does your own daughter get engaged *and* accused of murder on the same day without telling you anything?"

"Oh boy," Riley whispered.

Detective Weber looked a little nervous.

"Mom, we'll talk about that later," Riley said, nodding toward the door.

"Don't mind me. I'll just stir this boneless bone broth with the knife in my back," Blossom insisted, stomping to the stove.

"You can't make those jokes around a homicide detective," Riley pointed out.

"I've heard worse," Weber admitted.

Since her mother wasn't leaving the room anytime soon, Riley slumped back in her chair. "So what now? Am I under arrest?"

"Should you be?"

"Do you really think I killed Dickie?"

"I'm more concerned with the facts. You had prior knowledge of the situation. You were here when the crime was committed."

"Lots of people were here," Blossom announced to the broth she was whipping into a vortex. That was the thing about her mom: even if Blossom was mad, she still had her family's back.

"What's my motive?" Riley asked, too tired, too sore to care at this point.

"Sometimes people don't need much of a motive," he said. "Did I mention your fingerprints were found on his door?"

She rolled her eyes. "I bet you found everyone's fingerprints. We're a nosy, close-knit group."

"Not close enough to introduce your mother to your fiancé," Blossom grumbled.

"Mom!"

"There you are!" Jasmine Patel, in all her beautiful glory, stormed into the kitchen. Her dark hair flowed out behind her like the cape of a tough yet benevolent superhero. The detective looked the way all men did when Riley's best friend entered a room: dumbstruck.

"Hey, Jas," Riley said weakly.

"What the hell happened to you? Why didn't you call me?"

"Join the club," Blossom said, whirling around, clutching a ladle.

"Hey, Blossom." Jasmine waved.

"Who did call you?" Riley asked.

"Lily. She said something about an evil spirit committing a murder, and you falling down the stairs and getting engaged."

"Jasmine, this is Detective Weber, who is considering whether to arrest me. Detective Weber, this is Jasmine."

Jasmine went on the beautiful angry woman attack. "If you think that Riley has anything to do with whatever the hell happened, you're an idiot. What *did* happen by the way?" she asked, turning back to Riley.

"Your friend's great-uncle was shot and killed in his room last night," the detective answered.

"Regular uncle," Riley corrected him. "He was only fifty-seven."

"Really?" Blossom asked in surprise. "I thought he had to be at least ninety."

Jasmine leaned in to examine the diameter of Riley's pupils. "Did you hit your head?"

"Repeatedly."

"Jimmy's been dead for two years," Jasmine said, shooting a look at Blossom, who was violently drying a bowl with a dish towel.

"Not Jimmy. Dickie."

"Wave-the-cannoli, leave-the-underwear Dickie?" Jasmine asked, confused.

"Yes. That *Uncle* Dickie," Riley said.

"Oh. Right. Oh. Ohhh!" Jasmine recovered nicely. "Listen, Detective… What was your name again?"

"Weber," he answered.

"Detective Weber, if you want to question my client, you'll need to go through me first."

"You're a lawyer?" he asked.

Jasmine was an estate and elder law attorney. Her client meetings took place in dated living rooms crammed with knickknacks, not interrogation rooms.

"You're damn right I am," she said, poking him in the chest with a very red fingernail.

Riley felt like that probably wasn't allowed. Poking a cop was probably like touching the Liberty Bell or hugging one of the guards at Buckingham Palace. It just wasn't done.

"Hey, Jas, do you mind getting me a glass of water?" Riley asked, adding a dry croak for effect. There was no reason for them both to go to jail.

"Of course, babe. Anything you want. You better watch yourself, mister," she threatened Weber with that same pointed finger.

"Detective," he reminded her.

"Mister Detective," Riley said, then started to laugh. Not the normal laughter of a regular person who found something entertaining. No. This was the unhinged, deranged, hiccupping gasp of a lunatic who desperately needed sleep. This was the delayed hysterical reaction of a woman who had been pushed too far. A woman who had tried to save a dumbass's life. A woman who had cushioned the fall of the very fine, very dense body of Nick Santiago, who was never, ever going to see her again. A woman who was hanging on by her fingernails while her cheating ex-husband booked first-class tickets for his second honeymoon.

"Oh boy," Jasmine said.

"I think she might need that water," Weber observed as Riley cackled on.

"That's not a water laugh. That's a tequila laugh," Jasmine observed.

"Did you know that Riley's engaged?" Blossom said from the sink.

17

H i." There was a deep baritone coming from the end of Riley's bed when she woke from a much needed six-hour nap. After Detective Weber had decided not to arrest her. Yet.

A very tall, very muscled Black man with a perfectly proportioned shaved head was attached to the voice.

He smiled.

Riley fell out of bed. "Oof!" Her body was indignant at the added abuse.

"Yoo-hoo, Gabe!" Lily tottered into the room wearing a shiny pink jogging suit. "I brought you some tea."

"You are too kind. Thank you." His voice boomed around the room.

"What the hell is going on here?" Riley demanded, climbing back to her feet and yanking the sling off her bad arm and preparing to fight. She looked around before remembering that her hockey stick/personal weapon was no longer in one piece.

"I am Gabe," he said, flashing her that smile again, this time over the rim of a posy-ringed teacup.

He was built like a Mack truck, making the dainty teacup and saucer look doll-size in his hands. She wasn't picking up on dangerous murderer vibes, but that didn't mean they weren't lurking beneath the surface.

"Is this a dream or a vision?" Riley whispered, scrambling over the bed to get between the stranger and Lily.

"I very much like your very short pants," Gabe said, politely admiring her peace-sign underwear.

"Lily, you have *got* to stop letting people into the house," Riley insisted, grabbing a pair of discarded shorts off the floor and dragging them on.

"I remember when my breasts were that perky," Lily sighed as she puttered around the room straightening up. "Don't waste these years, Riley! You take those perky breasts, and you put them in that Hot Nick's face every chance you get."

Riley crossed her arms over her tank top. "You both need to go," she insisted.

Lily looked disappointed and glanced longingly back at Gabe. *"I'd like to run into him naked and greased up."*

Upset and now considerably grossed out, Riley blocked out Lily's dirty thoughts and guided her neighbor toward the door. "You can't let strangers in the house anymore. We all need to be more careful."

Lily left, muttering about young girls not appreciating the fine men crawling all over them.

Turning to face the intruder, Riley crossed her arms again. "I'm not interested in anything you're selling."

"I am not selling anything," he said, beaming at her. "I have been sent to guide you."

"That explains nothing," she said. "Did you just wander in off the street? Are you here to rob me? Because as you can see, I've got nothing worth stealing."

"A minimalist lifestyle is something to aspire to." He took another dainty sip of tea.

He looked way too happy, way too fit, and way too calm to be human.

If psychics were real, did that mean vampires and werewolves were real too?

"Are you a vampire?" she asked.

He chuckled magnanimously. "I am not. I am a guide. Your guide."

"Gabe, don't take this the wrong way, but you're not making any sense."

He put the cup and saucer down on the bed and rose to his full height. Riley wasn't great at estimating, but he looked to be about eight feet tall.

"Your spiritual guide," he announced, pressing his palms together at his chest.

Her eyes narrowed. "Are you some kind of new age Jehovah's Witness?"

She waited for his next round of magnanimous chuckles to subside. Apparently, this guy thought she was hilarious. "I am not," he said finally.

"Yeah. Thanks. But I'm not buying. I'm not missing any religious figure that you'd love to tell me about, and I do not want to donate to fund a mission trip to a town that will have to rebuild whatever your well-meaning volunteers erected to feel good about themselves."

Riley grabbed him by the arm. Her fingers didn't even reach a third of the way around his biceps. But he still allowed her to lead him to the door.

"You have many bruises," Gabe observed. "Are you aware of them?"

She was painfully aware of them.

"I am," she said, giving him a push across the threshold.

"Are we going out?" he asked.

"You're going out. I'm staying in."

He stood there smiling, and she slammed the door in his face.

"I'll just wait then," he called cheerfully through the door.

Riley limped back to her bed. She debated going back to sleep, then realized that beneath all the aches and pains was a ravenous hunger that didn't feel like being ignored. Also, she *really* needed to have that talk with her neighbors about letting strangers in the house.

She put on a bra and a clean T-shirt, thought about running a brush through her hair, then decided there was no point to it. She looked like she'd gone a round with a Rock 'Em Sock 'Em Robot and lost. And it wasn't like she had a fake fiancé to impress. Nick Santiago would never show his sexy face around here again. Not after the whole psychic revelation. Not that she blamed him. In her experience, guys didn't deal well with that kind of information. Griffin had never known. He'd only thought her family was "eccentric."

Cautiously, she opened her door and peered into the hall. The yellow crime scene tape starkly crisscrossed Dickie's door. But spiritual guide Gabe was nowhere to be found. Relieved, she hobbled to the stairs.

Three flights of stairs in her condition? Nope. She pushed the call button for the lift chair and, while she was waiting, brushed her teeth.

What felt like forty minutes later, she made it to the first floor. Someone was cooking something that smelled edible, which ruled out her mother. Even after a lengthy explanation and lengthier apology, Blossom was not happy with her oldest daughter. Riley now had a long list of things she should have done differently, starting with accepting herself and her gifts and then moving right on down the line to telling her mother everything the moment it happened.

She followed her nose back to the kitchen and stopped in the doorway.

Lily and Fred were parked at the table watching Mrs. Penny pepper Gabe with questions while acting as his sous-chef. There was a pot of something sinful-smelling simmering away. Next to it, Gabe was flipping grilled cheese sandwiches on a griddle.

Riley's stomach growled audibly.

"What is it you do for a living, big fella?" Mrs. Penny asked. Her wrinkled hands arranged neatly sliced vegetables around a bowl of dip on a serving tray.

"I am a spiritual advisor," he said, moving his attention to the pot.

"Like a priest?" Lily wanted to know. "Or do you still get to have sexual relations?"

"More like a teacher," Gabe explained.

"What does a spiritual advisor teach?" Fred asked.

"Whatever it is the student needs to learn."

Riley rolled her eyes and limped into the room.

"Your friend here is quite the cook," Mrs. Penny said, gesturing wildly with a knife.

"He's not my friend," Riley argued, taking a step back in case the woman got too animated with her weapon hand.

Gabe looked hurt, and Riley felt as if she'd just kicked a puppy in the face. "I hope you will grow to think of me as such," he said sadly.

"Riley Thorn, you hurt this handsome beefcake's feelings," Lily said. "Apologize to our new neighbor right now!"

"I'm sorry, Gabe—whoa. Hang on. What?" Riley asked, slumping into a chair at the table.

"Gabe is staying with us now. I made up the second first-floor parlor for you," Lily said to him. "You can share the hall bathroom with Mr. Willicott."

"Wait a minute. You're letting him stay?" Riley sputtered. "He's a stranger—no offense, Gabe—who shows up on the doorstep less than twenty-four hours after Dickie was murdered, and you move him in? How do we know he's not the murderer?"

It was like age had taken their ability to practice self-preservation. Next, they'd be celebrating Hug an Axe Murderer Day.

"You're all banged up and grumpy. No judgment," Fred said, holding up his palms. "I'm an excellent judge of people. Gabe here is obviously no threat."

Fred had once changed Ted Bundy's tire in a grocery store parking lot.

"I must agree with this kind man," Gabe said seriously. "I am very nonthreatening."

Riley gave up. Her battered body didn't have the energy to argue with senseless goofballs.

"You will feel better once you have eaten," he insisted.

He put a bowl of tomato soup and a grilled cheese sandwich in front of her. She was so hungry she decided to ignore the possibility of the food being poisoned.

Fred, Lily, and Mrs. Penny dug into their food. Gabe sat down next to her with a glass of water. His chair let out a whimper as he settled his very large muscles on it.

"Aren't you eating?" she asked around a big mouthful of melty goodness.

He gave her a benevolent smile. "I am in the midst of a fast."

This guy was definitely not human. Or the food was definitely poisoned.

But hey, everyone had to go sometime. Might as well go with a belly full of melted cheddar.

"A fast what?" Lily piped up.

Fred took a noisy slurp of soup.

"I am not eating food," Gabe explained. "I am ingesting water to cleanse my body of toxins so I can better serve in a physical and spiritual capacity."

Mrs. Penny eyed him, a blob of tomato soup smearing one of the lenses of her glasses. "What do you bench? Three twenty-five? Three fifty?"

"Four hundred," he said.

Fred's sandwich fell out of his hand and hit the table with a squishy thwack. "Maybe I should start fasting?" he said.

Now the muscled stranger was going to start starving her neighbors. Riley threw her napkin down. "Okay. This is ridiculous. Front porch. Now," she said to Gabe. She could lock him out of the house if need be, and there would be plenty of witnesses on Front Street.

"I would be delighted to speak in private," he said, rising from his chair.

She picked up her soup and sandwich. "Great," she said dryly. "Let's go."

Gabe followed her to the front of the house like a happy puppy.

She was out of breath by the time they reached the front door. She really needed to start working out. Limping out on the porch, Riley dropped down on one of the wicker chairs and stuffed the grilled cheese into her face. "Why are you here?" she demanded with a full mouth.

"I was sent to guide you." He took a sip of water and smacked his lips. "Ahh."

"Guide me where?"

"In your spiritual development."

"Listen, Gabe, I am not going to join your church or whatever. You can't convert me. I'm unconvertible." She tried the soup. Its deliciousness annoyed her.

"I am not here to convert you. I was sent to help you develop your connection with your gifts."

Her eyes narrowed, and she stopped chewing. "Sent by who? Whom? Whatever."

"Your grandmother."

Well, shit.

Her spoon clattered on the wooden planks beneath their feet.

"Allow me," he said, picking it up for her. He handed it back to her. When their fingers brushed, she caught a glimpse of Elanora Basil's stern, lined face, her silver hair scraped back in her usual disciplined bun. The strands of onyx and amethyst she always wore for protection glittered around her neck. Riley could feel the woman's disapproval radiating through the vision.

"Would you excuse me for a moment?" she whispered hoarsely.

Gabe dipped his head and pressed his palms together. "Of course."

"No, no. Don't do that. Don't do that bowing thing," she groaned.

She got up and limped to the far end of the porch. Stuffing the last of her sandwich into her mouth, she dialed her mother's number.

Blossom answered on the second ring.

"Riley, I love you and want you to know you're very important to me. But I'm in the middle of something right now."

"Mom, Grandmother sent me a man."

"Yeah, well, your father got a spite cow," her mother retorted. "I'll call you later."

"What's a spite cow?" But Blossom had already hung up.

She dialed her sister next.

"Riley. How are you feeling? Do you want to borrow my healing candles and crystals?" Wander offered.

"There's a large Black man here by the name of Gabe saying Grandmother sent him to be my spirit guide or teacher or whatever," Riley explained.

Wander was silent for a beat. "That does sound like something she'd do."

"What am I supposed to do?" Riley hissed.

"Whatever you do, don't send him back. You do not want to piss off that woman," Wander warned.

"I know." Grandmother's disapproval was scarier than ten haunted houses and a Halloween movie marathon. "But why now? She's always left me alone before."

With Wander, Grandmother had always demanded a full report on the efforts she was making to maintain and grow her gift, as if there was a lot you could do with a psychic schnoz. When it came to Riley, it was, "How is your volleyball season?" or "Happy birthday. Here are some socks with cats on them."

"Oh, I don't know. Maybe it's because you've spent the last thirty years trying not to have powers, and now you're predicting murders?" Wander mused.

Wander was such a loving, open, Zen-like spirit, her snark always managed to sneak up and surprise Riley.

"By the way, Fred was in class this morning, and he said you're dating a guy who pushed you down the stairs." Wander was Fred's favorite yoga instructor.

"We're actually engaged," Riley joked airily. Quickly, she filled her sister in on the fake boyfriend turned fake fiancé.

"Well, that explains Mom's mood in class today."

"Don't worry," Riley assured her. "After the whole I'm-a-psychic revelation and spending half the night in the emergency department with me, I think my fake engagement is over."

"Like Mom always says, if he can't handle who you are, he doesn't deserve you," Wander said matter-of-factly.

"Speaking of Mom," Riley said. "I called her, and she said something about a spite cow and hung up on me."

"You know Mom and Dad. If there's a way to make life weirder, they'll find it. Now, do you want me to come over and help you with your spiritual guide?"

Riley glanced over her shoulder at Gabe, who was beaming rainbows at a butterfly that had landed on his finger.

She sighed. "No. I'll figure it out."

18

I t had been a long-ass week, and it was only Wednesday morning.

Tired, grumpy, and annoyed with the world, Nick gave Brian and Josie a cursory grunt before shutting himself in his office. He wasn't in the mood for another round of "Did you call her?" and "Are you going to call her?"

Most of the hours since Sunday morning had been spent reminding himself of all the reasons why he should definitely not reach out to Riley Thorn.

He'd even gone so far as to write up a list of reasons why he should stay far, far away from her.

1. He liked her. A lot.
2. He felt protective of her. And that never went well.
3. He didn't want to get snared in the "monogamy and marriage" trap. And Riley looked like the kind of girl who could distract a man into forgetting his own endgame.

So instead of checking in on her like he wanted to, he was here. Pissed off with himself and everything else.

He turned on the local news for background noise and

dug into the stack of files on his desk. His office looked like a paper avalanche was about to occur. While most of the world had moved beyond paper copies, process serving still placed an obnoxious amount of importance on originals. And Nick, being Nick, didn't feel like his time was best spent alphabetizing shit. So it sat in great precarious piles where it would live until either something catastrophic happened or he had no other choice but to take a week organizing just to see the carpet again.

The news story on the TV caught his attention. That idiot Griffin Gentry was describing the latest "gang activity" in the city. Grainy video surveillance showed a group of individuals dressed mostly in black and wearing an amusing variety of masks leaving a guy hog-tied in the middle of the pedestrian bridge between downtown Harrisburg and City Island.

Nick stared at the screen and wondered if Gentry was sitting on a phone book to look as tall as his cohost.

In a voice a full octave below the one he normally spoke in, Gentry informed viewers that law enforcement had discovered that the victim was actually a pickpocket with a lengthy rap sheet. He had four outstanding warrants, not to mention three stolen wallets on him.

"Dumbass," Nick muttered at the screen. Just looking at Gentry pissed him off all over again. He'd done a little digging on the guy, the results of which hadn't improved his opinion of the man.

His desk phone buzzed, and it took him a moment to recognize the sound. Generally his door was open. If Brian or Josie needed something, they just yelled.

"Yeah? What?" he said after managing to stab the right button.

"You've got a potential client out here who wants to discuss a job," Brian reported.

A distraction from paperwork and Riley. Exactly what he needed. "Send them in," Nick said. He glanced around, realizing he should have at least taken a minute to clean up. But the office door was already opening.

"Nicholas." The emphasis was on the "ass."

He nearly fell out of his chair.

"Mrs. Zimmerman?" The woman of his teenage nightmares stood frowning in his doorway. Gone were the black-and-gray tracksuits that she'd donned for decades to run thousands of students through the Presidential Fitness Test. In their place, she wore somber black slacks and a dark gray tank top that showed off her still impressive biceps. Her steel-gray hair was cut short, emphasizing the sharp lines of her face. She'd been gray when he had her for phys ed in ninth and tenth grade. He'd, perhaps unfairly, assumed she'd been near ninety then. However, twenty years later, she looked exactly the same.

Definite vampire genes.

"I see you're still a mess," she noted, her disdainful gaze taking in the disarray.

"Just a little behind on the filing," he said, recovering. He stood and gestured toward the only chair not buried under files. "Please, have a seat."

She sat gingerly, as if she expected something sticky to ruin her clothes. He thought about the protein shake he'd spilled last week and hoped he'd remembered to clean it up.

"What can I do for you?" he asked, trying to rein in his long-dormant teenage panic.

She sat staring at him for much longer than necessary. He wished he had shaved and worn something besides the wrinkled T-shirt he'd pulled off the floor of his closet.

This was the effect Mrs. Zimmerman had on all students. Even dimpled teenage rebels.

After overhearing some admittedly embellished locker room talk during gym class, she'd pulled him aside and put the fear of God into him. Her lecture on why real men didn't need to prove their manhood by detailing their sexual exploits had stuck. So had the uncomfortably detailed list of the consequences of unprotected sex.

Nick had never kissed and told again. He'd also never forgotten a condom. Hell, his backups had backups.

"If you find yourself capable of professionalism, I'd like you to find the person who murdered my nephew."

He gave himself points for not spitting the now-cold coffee in her face. There were a lot of ways that sentence could have ended. Find my car keys. Find out what my neighbor is growing in their backyard. Find out where my ex-husband spent my alimony money.

He had not seen the murdered nephew thing coming.

"What happened to your nephew?" he asked, setting the mug down.

She gave him a steely-eyed glare of disappointment. "Why don't you tell me, since you're the one who discovered his body?"

"Dickie Frick is your *nephew*?"

"Was. Seeing as how he's dead now."

He tried to do the math. Either the entire family had vampire genes, or they aged prematurely.

"He was my sister's son," she continued. "My sister is a pathetic doormat of a human being who excelled at nothing but making terrible choices in life. Her son was a disgusting disappointment. However, despite their shortcomings, they are both family. And family—even disgusting disappointments—deserve justice."

"Uh, okay. So why hire me?" he asked. "Why not let the cops do their job?"

"Have you seen the news in the past five years?" she scoffed. "Not only does our fair city have the highest murder rate in its history, it has also attained the distinction of having most of those crimes go unsolved. Something is rotting in Harrisburg, Nicholas. And I don't trust the authorities to prioritize finding justice for my disgusting nephew."

"But you do trust me?" he said. He could feel the grin spreading across his face. "You like me. You've always liked me, haven't you?"

She rolled her eyes, but there was a distinct twinkle in them. "Don't be ridiculous. I've never liked a student. You're all hormonal disgraces to the human race," she sniffed.

"Of course we are. But to clarify, you want to hire *this* hormonal disgrace because you believe I'll get you justice."

She sighed as if the conversation pained her. "Stop fishing for compliments, Nicholas. I have no control over what you choose to believe. Are you taking the job or not?"

Taking the job meant definitely seeing Riley Thorn again and not avoiding her like he'd planned. "I'm in," he announced.

She gave him a stately nod. "Fine."

They discussed terms and negotiated his fee until both parties were satisfied.

"Would you like something to drink?" Nick offered. He could probably scrounge up a tea bag from cold season last year. Mrs. Zimmerman looked like a tea drinker.

"Whiskey. I presume you have some in your desk."

She presumed correctly. It felt like a trap. But sometimes it was more fun falling into a trap than avoiding it.

He punched his bottom drawer open and produced a bottle of Jack Daniel's along with the two reasonably clean glasses.

"I'm counting on you, Nicholas, to get my family the justice they're due," she said as he poured. "The police are being awfully tight-lipped about their investigation."

Make his high school gym teacher proud, solve a case his ex-partner was working, and spend more time with Riley Thorn?

Nick suddenly wasn't so pissed off at the world anymore.

Nothing like a challenge to get the blood moving.

19

T here's a man here to see you. With flowers."

Riley was dragged from the low hum of boredom that was seeping through her pores into her bloodstream by Donna's uncharacteristically cheerful voice on the phone.

A man with flowers to see her? If it was Griffin trying to charm his way into an exclusive interview about Dead Dickie, she was going to make him eat the flowers. She limped around the corner and got a shock when she spotted Nick Santiago looking fine and flirty with an armload of roses.

His dimples were locked and loaded.

Donna looked like she was going to vault over the desk and devour him alive.

"What are you doing here?" Riley asked, crossing her arms over her chest, something she could do now without the sling.

She was getting tired of men just popping up in her life. She'd had to sneak out of the house just to get past Gabe this morning. He'd been following her around since his arrival, asking her when she would be ready to start their training.

"Can't the luckiest guy in the world stop by and say hi to his beautiful fiancée?" he asked, all charm. He pushed the flowers into her arms and, before she could react, dropped a kiss on her forehead. It felt like it set her skin on fire.

Donna's jaw unhinged, and her mouth fell open. "*Fiancée? How does* she *rate a prime steak like* him? *She must be blackmailing him.*"

Riley closed her eyes and exhaled sharply. The last thing she needed right now was to be inside Donna's head. "How did you find me?" she hissed at Nick.

"PI, remember?"

The nosy receptionist wheeled her chair closer, straining to hear their conversation.

"Let's go in the conference room," Riley decided. She closed her fingers around his wrist and was once again jarred by the jolt of skin on skin. That ugly bedspread popped unbidden into her head again. Maybe she should have a sit-down with Gabe if it meant she could stop falling into sex fantasies at the drop of a hat.

She pulled Nick into the windowless room with its dark wood-paneled walls and cheap laminate table. This was the room most client meetings occurred in. Management thought it was impressive. Riley thought it looked like the interior of a coffin.

Closing the door behind them, she dropped his wrist and resumed the annoyed crossed-arm position.

"How are you feeling?" he asked, those blue-green eyes running over her body.

He'd been the only one in the building to ask her since she'd shown up to work on Monday with her arm in a sling and bruises covering eighty percent of her body. "Fine," she said. If *fine* meant so sore she had to give herself a pep talk before getting off the toilet. "What are you doing here?"

If he asked her to tell him what number he was thinking of, she was going to hit him in the head with the trash can. She'd use her good arm.

"I need your help," he said, leaning one very fine ass cheek on the glossy conference table.

She blinked. "With what?"

He gave her one of those slow once-overs, that eyebrow hook, and another shot of dimples. "I caught a new case today," he said, picking up a SHART pen and clicking it.

She counted the clicks. The marketing department had cheaped out. Sure, they looked okay on the outside, and they mostly did the job you'd expect. But each pen had between thirty-five and forty-two clicks in it before the spring mechanism exploded. One of their more nervous sales reps had nearly lost an eye in the middle of a big pitch.

"Mazel tov. What does that have to do with me?"

"You, my lovely fiancée, are my access." *Click. Click.*

This didn't sound good.

"Access to what exactly?"

"Dickie Frick's aunt hired me to find out who killed him," Nick said.

"Aren't the cops handling that? Isn't that their job?" The guy wanted to track down someone who willingly put two bullets in a human being's head. This was exactly the kind of man she did not need to get involved with.

Click. Click.

"The family isn't happy with how the investigation is proceeding. They want to make sure Dickie gets justice."

"That means you have to hunt down a murderer."

He spread his arms wide. "All part of the glamorous life of a PI. Who happens to be engaged to the deceased's next-door neighbor."

"You want me to get you into his apartment," she said, finally understanding.

Click. Click.

"And access to the rest of your roommates. Someone in that house has to know something. Also, please don't tell me you're claiming them in your family tree, by the way. We're engaged. You can give up the pretense."

She sniffed indignantly. "If we're fake engaged, then I can claim any fake relative I want."

He reached for her and drew her between those long legs. "Come on, Riley," he said, all charm. "Give a guy a break." He pushed up the sleeve of her cardigan and examined the bruise on her forearm. "Damn, Thorn. I bet the rest of you is purple."

She batted his hand away. "Oh, right. You care so much about my welfare," she said with no shortage of sarcasm. "I'm at work, Nick. Can we get to the point?"

"If you help me, I'll pay you."

Okay. Money talked. A few extra bucks a week would go a long way. "You'll pay me to be your fake fiancée so you can interrogate my neighbors and hunt down a person who killed a man? How does any of this sound normal to you?"

"Live a little, Thorn. It'll be fun."

He was so confident. So charming. So smooth. She wanted to smack him.

"I don't want to have fun," she said, sounding distinctly pouty.

His grin sharpened. "Sure you do," he countered.

There was a smolder there in those inky-lashed eyes. His thighs brushed hers, and he slid a hand up her jaw, around her neck, and into her hair. It was a gentle yet inevitable pull that brought her forehead to his. She put her hands on his chest. She wasn't exactly pushing him away, but she also wasn't grabbing him and yanking those unfairly full lips to hers.

Heat that was more than just the slow simmer of humidity bloomed between them. Her body forgot how to breathe.

They stayed like that for a long while. Hell, it might have been the rest of the day. Riley wasn't sure since all measurements of the passage of time abandoned her along with most biological functions.

"I need to think about it," she gasped, finally sucking oxygen into her burning lungs.

He released her, and she took a step back.

Nick stood, and for a second, she thought he might pin her against the door with those agile-looking hips and kiss her until she suffocated.

Instead, he pulled a business card out of his back pocket and held it out. "Come by my office after work," he said. "Meet the team."

"The team," she repeated.

"Yeah. Stop by. Get a feel for me as more than just your devastatingly handsome fake fiancé."

"Maybe," she hedged.

There were those damn dimples again. They had a hypnotizing effect. The man could probably convince a teetotaler gathering to go wine tasting.

"See you later, Thorn." He winked, all swagger and confidence, as he opened the door.

Alone in the coffin room, Riley sank down in the closest chair. She was dazzled by so many Nick Santiago pheromone fumes in such a confined space. She picked up the pen. Clicked it.

The spring shot out and whizzed past her face before banking off the wall.

With a sigh, she took the flowers and went back to her desk. She had just uncapped her red marker when her desk phone rang again.

"There's *another* one here to see you." Donna sounded incredulous.

"Another what?" Riley asked.

"Man."

With a frown, Riley hung up and made the trek back to the reception area.

There, perched on one of the chairs, was a placidly smiling Gabe. He was dressed in black gym shorts and a black tank that looked like it had been painted on. Donna was staring at him, her mouth agape.

"I'd spend an hour biting his hamstrings."

Riley sent up a prayer that she hadn't just overheard that from Donna's brain.

"What are you doing here?" Riley demanded.

Gabe rose, towering over her like a giant cuddly grizzly bear.

"I wish to take you to lunch so we can discuss your training."

"Training?" Donna was leaning so far over the reception desk that she was practically horizontal.

Ah, crap.

Riley looked hard at her uninvited visitor. "My *personal* trainer," she said slowly, willing the bear of a man to keep up with the lie. She wasn't sure how telegraphing mental messages went, but she did *not* need Gabe blabbing to Donna about her psychic inabilities. "For the wedding."

"Ah, yes," he said, catching on. "I am Riley's personal trainer. She would like much larger biceps for her wedding."

"You'd think she'd want a smaller ass," Donna sniped.

"You seem to carry an unusually large burden of hate and disappointment for such a small person," he observed. "Have you tried meditation?"

Donna's mouth fell open even farther, and Riley thought she heard the woman's jaw crack.

"I'm taking an early lunch," Riley decided, dragging Gabe out the front door.

"Yes. We will discuss caloric intake," he said, waving over his shoulder at the flabbergasted receptionist.

"Are you trying to ruin my life?" Riley demanded once they hit the sidewalk.

"This is a confusing question as I am clearly trying to improve your life," he said, easily catching up to her with his freakishly long, muscular legs.

"You can't antagonize a coworker who hates me and expect it to improve my life," she argued.

"And you cannot refuse to stand up for yourself and expect your life to improve."

The gigantic man had a point. "It's easier this way," she said, trying to ignore his point…and the way his dark skin seemed to shimmer in the sunlight like his entire body was dusted in some kind of angelic bronzer.

Was he the epitome of human perfection, or was he something otherworldly? Had her grandmother sent her some kind of guardian angel?

"Is it?" he mused in his deep baritone.

"You sound like my mother."

"Your mother must be a highly evolved person."

"Do you have money?" she asked, changing the subject. She'd left her wallet at her desk, and she really needed to eat her feelings.

"Of course."

"Good. You can buy me lunch."

Riley eyed the mixing bowl–sized tossed salad postfast Gabe was namaste-ing across the table and ignored the gaggle of other people's thoughts that were intruding on her own.

No dressing. No meat. No croutons.

He was definitely not human.

It struck her that Gabe and Nick were polar opposites. One structured and disciplined, invested in long-term results, the other a wild card looking for a good time. Where did she fall on that scale? She considered the healthy-ish turkey wrap that she was eating on the lunch break she'd taken early. Eh. Probably somewhere in the middle.

"Okay. So tell me about this training you're so excited about," she said reluctantly.

He lit up. "Your grandmother instructed me to provide any training or support necessary to help you navigate your powers," he said.

"I don't understand why she'd think I would want to 'navigate my powers,'" she complained. "I had a vision that my neighbor was going to get murdered. I went to the police. I warned the neighbor. He still got murdered. And now I'm a person of interest in the crime."

She noted that the burly bearded guy at the deli counter was either worried about someone named Candy or running out of candy.

"I can see how that would be frustrating for you," Gabe said, hanging on her every word. He was a freakishly good listener.

"What's the point of hearing other people's thoughts or seeing the future if I can't do anything about it? Why would I want that?"

He nodded. "Being who we are meant to be is not always easy."

"I don't *want* to be this. I want to be normal. Ordinary."

"No one is meant to be ordinary. We are all extraordinary," he said, his brown eyes beseeching her.

"Yeah? Well, I just want to be ordinary." That was all she'd ever wanted. To be normal. To fit in.

"It is here that our beliefs diverge, Riley," he said. "Life is an adventure to be lived, not a series of repetitive days to survive."

She frowned at him. "Would you please stop talking in fortune cookies?"

"I am unfamiliar with fortune cookies," he said, still smiling.

"Seriously? I wish I would have known that. We could have had Chinese food."

There were two women at the table next to them. The first, in the perky pink polo, was jabbering on and on about Malcolm from accounting. The second was methodically twisting the ends of her long black braids around her finger and suffering in silence.

"Please. Shut. The. Fuck. Up. My God. When is the last time this girl breathed? I'm never gonna get this time back. Hang on. Hello! Who is Mr. Hot Chocolate over there?"

Riley noticed the woman with the braids zero in on Gabe.

"I would very much like that," Gabe said.

"Huh? Sorry. What?" Riley asked.

"Have food from China with you." His puppy-dog sincerity was as sweet as it was annoying.

"Look. I just want you to understand that you were sent here under false pretenses. I don't want to learn to use my powers. I want them to go away."

He beamed at her. "The best way to quiet your powers is to learn how to control them."

The contents of her wrap flopped onto her plate. "You can teach me that?"

"How to control your powers? Yes."

She put down the wrap. "You can teach me how to block all this stuff out?"

"If that is what you wish. It would be my pleasure," he said, giving her a little bow.

20

Santiago Investigations was housed in a small brick duplex turned storefront on Third Street. The block was a mix of residential and commercial spaces where the parking was tight and the air smelled like early home-cooked dinners and laundry drying.

Riley had thought about Nick's offer all afternoon. And while the extra money would come in handy, she really didn't want to get involved. She'd rather forget the whole thing had ever happened and move on with her boring life and stick to her boring plan.

She tucked the Jeep into a space down the block. A movement in her rearview mirror caught her eye. A dark sedan stopped in the street three cars back. She felt the hairs on the back of her neck stand up. Cops.

"Looks like you've got company, girlie."

"I can see that, Uncle Jimmy."

"Think they're coming to arrest you?"

Her dead uncle was annoyingly chipper about the possibility. "I didn't do anything besides ask them to do their jobs," she complained. "And now I'm carrying on a conversation with an empty Jeep. *That* doesn't look crazy or suspicious."

Frustrated, she got out and slung her purse over her

shoulder. Deciding it was best to pretend she hadn't noticed that she was being followed, Riley dutifully crossed at the crosswalk. Once on the sidewalk, she paused between parked cars and pretended to tie her nonexistent shoelace.

Behind the wheel was the grumpy-looking Detective Weber in a tie and dark sunglasses.

"Crap," she whispered to herself. It felt like at any moment, he was going to jump out of the car and handcuff her. The fact that she *felt* guilty annoyed her even more. She hadn't done anything wrong. And if he was still convinced she had something to do with it, she was going to have to do his stupid job for him and prove her innocence.

"You do know you're wearing sandals, don't you, Ms. Thorn?"

Riley looked up and realized the detective had rolled down the window and was looking at her.

Well, shit.

She stood up. "Just, uh, doing some stretches," she said, making a show of raising her arms over her head. Totally normal. Completely nonchalant. "Can I help you with something?"

Please say no. Please say no.

"You're just stretching, and I'm just driving around," he said.

A lie for a lie.

"Okay then," she said, wondering if she should throw in a quad stretch for good measure.

"Tell Santiago I said hi," Detective Weber said and drove off.

Riley decided it would be best not to relay that message and hurried down the block to the office.

A large plate-glass window looked in on the reception area, which housed two desks and a wall of dented green filing cabinets. Riley opened the door, pretending like she'd visited her fake fiancé a hundred times before.

The guy behind the far desk gave off sexy nerd vibes. He was dividing his attention between three huge computer monitors and the woman perched on the desk swinging her combat boots. They both turned to look at her.

Cute nerd grinned. "You must be Riley," he said. He pushed away from the desk, and she spotted the wheelchair for the first time. "I'm Brian, Nick's cousin and doer of everything he doesn't want to."

"I'm Josie, Nick's bodyguard," the woman said. There was a fifty-fifty chance that wasn't a joke.

Josie was petite, but there was definitely a don't-fuck-with-me vibe. It probably had something to do with the knife tattoo on her shoulder.

"Hi," Riley said, exercising her stellar conversational skills. "I'm Nick's fake fiancée."

Four eyebrows raised. The cousin and the bodyguard exchanged a look. It was the kind of telepathy that existed between people who'd known each other for a very long time.

"It's nice to meet you, Riley," Brian said, grinning.

"Are you two…?" Riley pointed her finger back and forth between them.

"Married? Yes. Ovulating? Also yes," Josie announced, leaning back on her hands. She gave her husband a seductive look.

A door, the same army green as the cabinets, between the two desks opened, revealing Nick and his dimples.

"Hey. Glad you could come," he said.

No matter how many times she saw him, he was still delicious looking. Like a giant ice cream sundae that she knew would give her a stomachache if she ate the whole thing, but she still really, really wanted it.

"Riley was just explaining your engagement," Josie said, batting long lashes in Nick's direction.

"Fake engagement," Nick and Riley said in unison.

Brian and Josie shared another knowing look.

"Come on back, Thorn," Nick said, shooting his employees a glare.

When Riley glanced over her shoulder, she saw Brian and Josie making obscene kissy faces. Nick flipped them the bird.

"I hate when they get all telepathic," he grumbled, then seemed to think better. "Ah, sorry. No offense."

"None taken. Good luck with your ovulating," Riley called to the happy couple.

Nick shut the door.

Much like his SUV, Nick's office was a disaster. The trash can was overflowing with hoagie wrappers, and every flat surface in the room was buried under files and stacks of paperwork. There was a path that cut from the door to behind the battered metal desk. The carpet beneath was shit brown.

He ushered her to the only other chair that wasn't serving as a temporary filing cabinet.

It was a bit of a relief to know that Hot Nick didn't have his life together everywhere. It humanized him and those devilish dimples.

"Nice place," she quipped.

"I've been busy, and I hate paperwork," he said by way of an explanation.

"So because you hate it, you're just not going to do it?" she clarified.

"Life's short. Why waste it doing things you don't want to do?"

The life philosophy of Nick Santiago, ladies and gentlemen.

"Are you hoping that the paperwork fairies will magically appear overnight and start filing?" she asked.

"If you tell me the tooth fairy isn't real, this fake engagement is over."

He tossed her a bottle of water and got one for himself from the mini fridge she hadn't noticed since it too had sixty pounds of paperwork and a backpack on top of it.

"So," he said. Nick didn't take the chair behind the desk. No, he leaned against the front of it, stretching those long legs out in front of him until her feet were between them. Worn denim over muscled thighs. His T-shirt—Freddy Mercury, another point in his favor—was a faded classic that fit him as if it had been handmade for his chest and shoulders.

It was annoying how everything about him was unequivocally hot.

"So," she repeated.

"You're here."

"So it would seem."

Nick grinned. She noticed his left dimple seemed maybe a millimeter deeper than his right. "Are you willing to continue our temporary engagement?" he asked, drawing her attention away from his facial perfection. "For semi-generous financial compensation, of course."

His expression was downright lecherous. She liked it.

"I haven't made up my mind yet," she told him.

"Then I'll just have to convince you."

Yes, please.

"Here's how I see this going," he continued. "We hang out at your place. You provide the access for me to casually interview your neighbors."

She crossed her legs, bumped a bruise, and immediately uncrossed them. "Do you honestly think that one of them knows something?"

He shrugged and took a swig of water. "They all knew Frick a lot longer than you. It's possible one of them knows something that will be helpful."

"It's more probable that they all know a whole lot of nothing, and you'll drown in inappropriate, loud small talk."

"I think I can handle it. Little old ladies love me. I'm charming. Which brings me to the next ask."

Riley unscrewed the cap on her water. "What's that?"

"A sleepover."

She choked and bobbled the bottle. Gasping and coughing, she watched in horror as a geyser of spring water gracefully arced from the bottle through the air before splashing down on Nick's crotch.

"Shit. Sorry," she said, jumping up and looking for napkins or paper towels.

She found a box of tissues and grabbed a fistful.

"Relax, Thorn, it's just—"

He cut off abruptly when she pressed a handful of tissues to his groin and began to dab with enthusiasm.

"Boss, we're heading out—whoops. Sorry to interrupt," Josie said with a wicked grin.

"It's just water," Riley insisted, still blotting tissues to his crotch.

"Sure it is. Have fuuuuuun," she sang as she closed the door.

"For the love of God, Thorn," Nick said, sounding pained. He grabbed her wrists.

It appeared that spilled water was now only a secondary problem in his crotch region.

They stood that way—Riley trapped between his thighs, Nick's hands gripping her wrists, and a conspicuous hard-on between them—for a long moment.

She looked at the ceiling. It seemed safer. There was a hum vibrating through her body that started where his fingers touched her skin. It was redirecting her nerves to feel something other than the soreness that accompanied hurling oneself down a flight of stairs.

His laugh was low, husky. "You're cute when you're embarrassed and turned on."

She ignored the latter part of his statement. "Your employee thinks I was...you know." If her face got one degree hotter, her skin would start to melt.

"Who cares what people think?"

Ugh. It was such a typically hot, confident, badass, black-sheep thing to say.

She cleared her throat. "What were you saying before... that?" She pointed in the direction of his erection.

"A sleepover," he said with a dirty, dirty grin.

"A sleepover," she parroted. "You want to have a sleepover. With me."

"I want to search Dickie's apartment. And what better way to do that than while spending the night with my fiancée?"

"Oh." She didn't know if she was more relieved or disappointed.

There was something blooming, burning in the air between them, and Riley had concerns that she was the only one who

147

felt it. Had she just walked into a cloud of pheromones? Was she just that overdue for an orgasm that she couldn't handle even the most casual of touches? Were her wrists a previously undiscovered erogenous zone?

"Breathe," Nick said smugly.

"Huh?" she croaked.

"You haven't taken a breath in about a minute."

Desperately, she sucked in a breath. "Have too," she argued.

He ran his hands up her arms and back down, eyeing her. "You know, if we're going to sell this engagement thing, you can't jump out of your skin every time I touch you." His thumbs rubbed little circles over her pulse.

He was playing a game with her, and she didn't know the rules.

"So what do you say, Thorn? Be my fake fiancée? I promise it'll be a good time."

Riley didn't need to be psychic to know that Nick Santiago was not the get-down-on-one-knee type. Unless it was to spread a woman's thighs and use his tongue to take her to a new level of orgasmic bliss.

"Um. Okay."

His smile was triumphant. "Good. How about I take you to dinner to celebrate?"

21

"Why do you need thirty pounds of paperwork to go to dinner?" Riley asked with suspicion as Nick slid behind the wheel of his SUV.

He waited to answer until she was belted in and his GPS app was calculating the first stop. "Thought you could help me do some serves on the way."

The look she shot him was pure gold. Annoyance. Trepidation. Surprise.

"Come on, Thorn. It's the least you could do since you mauled my crotch in front of an employee."

"You're such as ass."

He gave her knee a squeeze and then consciously put his hand back on the wheel, heading south. He liked touching her. And that was a potential problem. In his office, all he'd thought about was how much he wanted to clear his desk, strip her naked, and show her how limber his tongue was.

It had seemed safer to get her in the car. But now he was running calculations on back seat dimensions. One thing was for sure—Riley Thorn made him think about sex.

"What better way to get to know each other than by being locked in a car together on a boring road trip that includes such central Pennsylvania highlights as the sketchy side of York and a mobile home park in Peach Bottom?" he asked cheerfully.

She groaned. "You sure know how to show a girl a good time."

"Have something better to do?" he asked.

Her sigh almost fogged up the inside of the windshield. "Nope."

"Think of it as an adventure," he advised. "And if you're a good girl, I'll buy you dinner *and* snacks."

"I *do* like snacks," she mused.

They agreed on music—'80s hair band—and interior temperature, signs that, had he been looking for them, would have indicated compatibility outside the bedroom. But compatibility that didn't involve nudity had never been a priority for Nick. So he didn't quite know what to do with it.

Riley skimmed serves while he piloted them south on Interstate 83. Farmland and mega warehouses flanked the rolling hills of the highway.

"Tell me about this psychic thing," he said.

She glanced up from a divorce and waited a beat. "There's not much to tell," she said finally.

"How does it work? Do you see in pictures, or do you hear stuff like voices?"

Once again, she was looking at him with suspicion like she was waiting for him to get to the punchline.

"What?" he asked.

"Aren't you going to ask me to give you the winning lottery numbers or ask me what number you're thinking of?"

He snorted. "Get that a lot?"

"No one's actually interested in what it's like, just what it can give them."

"I'm interested," he insisted.

"Okay. So then, I guess both," she said grudgingly. "Like sometimes it plays out in my head like I'm watching TV, and sometimes it's really insistent whispers, but they're coming from inside my head."

"What was it with Dickie?" he asked.

"Awful," she said. "I thought it was a food poisoning hallucination at first. I ran into him in the hall between our apartments, and it just hit me. Like a movie playing out. Dickie was answering his door and calling someone a cocksucker. There was a hand wearing a glove and holding a gun. *Bang bang.* Dickie goes down, looking surprised and pissed off."

"Cocksucker," Nick repeated. Odds were, Dickie knew the person on the other end of the gun and hadn't expected them to put some brass in his brain.

"Sometimes I dream about dead people telling me things," she confessed.

"How do you know when a dream is just a dream?"

"I don't really. That's part of the problem. I don't have any control over it, so I can't just tap into it and use it like a tool. I also apparently can't turn it off. Yet."

"That must be annoying," he guessed.

"It is," she said emphatically.

"Is there like a Hogwarts for psychics? Or some kind of training?" he asked, genuinely interested.

That got a smile out of her. "No Hogwarts unfortunately. But there's a guild, and apparently there are things I could learn to manage it," she said, her focus out the window.

"You kind of make it sound like a disease," he pointed out.

"It feels like it. These messages invade my head, and it makes me sweaty and nauseous and clammy and shaky. It's like getting a bad flu in five seconds. I threw up tacos after the Dickie vision."

"Does every clairvoyant feel that way?" he asked. Yeah, so maybe he'd done a little internet research on the whole psychic thing.

She shrugged. "I don't think so. But it's not something that I get into with others."

"I want points for not directly asking you why you don't want to embrace this whole thing."

"Points awarded," she said and then looked at him. "My turn for questions. What's with you and the detective?"

He drummed his fingers on the wheel. "We used to be partners."

"I'm guessing it didn't end well."

"That's a safe assumption," he said, signaling to take the South Queen Street exit.

She waited pointedly.

"We didn't exactly see eye to eye on anything," Nick said, giving in.

"It's hard to picture you as a cop. You don't seem like you like rules."

And Weber lived for them. "I prefer puzzles. I thought it would be different if I was the one enforcing the rules."

"Were you wrong?" she asked.

The sun slanted in through the glass, highlighting subtle threads of red in her hair.

"Turns out I don't like being told what to do and when to do it."

"Is that why you're not married either?" she asked smugly.

"That would be a factor," he said, navigating down a one-way street crowded with crumbling row houses.

He swung into a parking space between a tricked-out Suburban with custom wheels and a two-tone Honda with an aftermarket spoiler and two flat tires.

Riley handed over the first serve, a court summons in a stolen property trial.

"Stay here and keep the doors locked," he instructed.

Her brown eyes widened. "Is it safe here?"

"Reasonably," he said, stepping out of the car. "But there's a charming retired car thief down the block who might try to talk you out of the car so he can help himself to it. Happened to me twice before I wised up."

He got lucky on the serve. Mr. Reggie Johnson was home and not too pissed off about the papers.

By the third successful serve, Nick was starting to think Riley was a good luck charm.

"Why are you doing serves?" she asked him after a grandma

with a pack of Chihuahuas gave him two cookies for serving her foreclosure papers on a beach condo.

He magnanimously handed over one of the cookies. "It's all part of the exciting and glamorous life of a PI. Also, the guy who usually does serves is down with the plague. It's on me to pick up the slack."

"Do you like your job?" she asked.

He thought about it. "I like my life," he decided. "I get to call the shots. I get to sleep in if I want. Work late if I feel like it. I can take my mom out to lunch in the middle of the day or fly out to Vegas for a long weekend without checking in with anyone."

Riley groaned.

"What?" Most women usually had this response to his white-knuckled grip on his bachelorhood.

"I think I want to be a bachelor," she said wistfully.

"You can be a bachelor with different equipment. There's no genitalia requirement."

"My entire life is based on other people's rules and schedules. I can't even take a sick day without having four supervisors weigh in on it."

"Whose fault is that?" he asked.

"Mine. Everything always is."

"Poor little Riley Thorn," he teased. "What are you waiting for? Some white knight to sweep in and clean everything up for you?"

"Hey. Pot, kettle. You're the one waiting for a paperwork fairy to show up and wave her wand. I'm not waiting for a white knight. I'm still paying for the last one."

There was a story there that she wasn't sharing. He'd add it to the list of mysteries surrounding her, which already included items such as what the hell had she been thinking getting herself married to Griffin "Cheese Puff Dust" Gentry?

"Two more stops, and then I'll feed you," he promised, changing the subject.

———

They stopped at a little twenty-four-hour diner in the middle of nowhere Pennsylvania.

"Do people always tell you more than they should?" he asked as soon as the server wandered away, their orders stowed in her apron.

"What do you mean?"

"Josie and Brian, for instance. I didn't know they were trying to get pregnant," he said.

"I guess I've never noticed," she said, tracing a finger over the edge of the table.

He pointed at her. "I think that's the first lie you've told me."

She laughed and then leveled him with a smug look. "Actually it's the third."

He leaned in. "I can't tell if you're fucking with me."

"Good," she said.

Either she knew how to push his buttons, or his bullshit detector was on the fritz.

They ate their burgers and then hit the road, homeward bound.

It was dark now. The moon was coming up, and the traffic was light. His work was done, and he had managed not to talk Riley into the back seat. All in all, he was pleased with himself.

If he'd been the boyfriend type, he'd be holding her hand right now. Instead, he changed the station to oldies.

"So," she said, finally breaking the silence. "Did you ghost me because of the whole psychic thing?"

"Ghost you? What are you talking about? I didn't ghost you," he lied. He'd totally ghosted her.

"Now who's lying?" she teased. "Did you disappear on me because I had a vision my neighbor was going to get whacked?"

He turned onto Forster Street. "No. I disappeared on you because I'm attracted to you."

"That's even weirder," she decided with a frown.

He could feel her gaze on him in the dark as he caught the light for Third Street. "I'm attracted to you, but you're the settle-down-and-be-monogamous type."

"I am not!"

She sounded insulted, and he laughed. "Please, Thorn. You have white dress, family dog, and day care drop-off written all over you."

"Yeah, in the *future*," she said as he lined up to parallel park across the street from the office. "But right now, I'd settle for a few nights of sweaty, meaningless sex."

He'd been aiming for the parking space behind her Jeep and instead launched the rear wheel of the vehicle up onto the curb.

Her laugh rang out over the crooning of the Drifters.

"You did that on purpose," he accused.

She gave a sexy one-shouldered shrug. "Maybe. Thanks for dinner, Nick."

When she got out, he followed her to the Jeep. He stood in the open door while she settled herself behind the wheel.

"Hey, Thorn?" Their faces were inches apart in the dark.

"Yeah?"

"What number am I thinking of?"

Her smile was slow and dirty. His blood abandoned his brain, speeding south. "Sixty-nine, and I didn't need to be psychic to know that."

22

Nature Girls was a shithole bar located in a shithole building in a seedier section of the city. Nick remembered his time on this beat well. A rookie cop with shiny shoes and a stiff blue uniform.

Shootings. Muggings. Carjackings. Gang activity. Drug busts. Homeless altercations. It was much the same now. The current mayor had run on the promise that he'd clean up the city and make it safe again.

Here, there was still a good percentage of the population who had dug their roots into this neighborhood decades before and had no intentions of abandoning their brick row houses and their tiny storefronts to the criminal element.

There was a bright-yellow shop one block down that had the best empanadas in the city. They had to paint over graffiti at least once a month, but business was brisk. Cut down a side street, and there was a bakery that had been in business for forty years. On Sundays, the owners' family handed out free bread.

Nick felt what he'd always felt when he walked these streets: an odd mix of desolation, hope, and pride. Could the people win where law enforcement had failed? He hoped so.

Somewhere in the distance, he heard glass break followed by shouts.

He locked his vehicle and set the alarm for good measure before joining the scattering of pedestrians on the sidewalk. None of them paid any attention to whatever was happening down the street. It was safer that way. Smarter that way. No one witnessed anything here. That way, there wasn't any need for retaliation.

Nature Girls was open according to the half-burnt-out neon OPEN sign in the one and only window that hadn't been boarded up on the facade. It was afternoon. Business didn't pick up until nine or ten at night when, under the cover of darkness, hard drinkers slunk out of the shadows and through the front door to order cheap liquor and terrible food.

He tugged his ball cap a little lower and stepped inside. The metal door slammed ominously behind him. No one bothered to look up. It was the kind of place where dreams and secrets went to die.

The bar was small by anyone's account. And no one would have called it clean. The interior looked even grimier than the first time he'd set foot inside. The floor, an ancient green vinyl tile, was stained and peeling. Also sticky. The ceiling was low and held up by sporadically placed supports. At some point, an enterprising owner had thought to class the place up with fake tin ceiling tiles that matched nothing.

The bar was stickier than the floor, which was saying something. There were wear marks every foot or so from decades of sweaty elbows. Mismatched barstools lined the L shape. There was also a collection of tables and chairs—all empty given the time of day—scattered around the floor between the ceiling jacks. A jukebox sat in the corner with a thick cobweb above it. Opposite the front door was a pair of swinging saloon doors that led to a narrow hallway with restrooms.

The entire place felt like the basement bar in a fraternity house.

Nick took a seat on a stool and waited for the scowling

bartender to put down his vape pen. It was a different guy than the last time he was here, he noted with relief.

"Get you something?" the bartender asked. He was a grizzled white guy with a stringy beard that trailed down into a braid. He wore a bowling shirt open over a stained tank top. A thick gold chain peeked out of thick white chest hair.

"Yeah. Lager." Nick nodded toward the tap.

There were three other patrons at the bar. One looked as though he'd passed out. The other two kept their eyes glued to a horseshoe tournament on the greasy TV screen behind the bar.

A server shoved through the saloon doors, calling what might have been a good-natured "Fuck off" over her shoulder to someone behind the scenes.

The uniform was ridiculous. Her pleated plaid skirt stopped about an inch below her crotch. The shirt was a white button-down that ended in a knot just beneath her breasts. A blue sash was worn beauty-contestant style. But instead of Miss Pennsylvania, it was covered in sexually suggestive pins. She had what looked like platinum-blond hair worn shaved almost to the scalp everywhere but the top of her head. The faux-hawk was purple.

"'Sup," she said to the bartender, blowing a bubble with her gum and strolling over to the touch screen at the service bar.

The bartender grunted his greeting and put a plastic cup in front of Nick. *Classy. Probably too many injuries from broken glass*, he guessed. The mirror behind the bar was broken in two places.

The server abandoned the register and wandered over to the jukebox. She plugged in a code, and screaming death metal filled the bar.

The other patrons, at least the conscious ones, didn't flinch.

The front door opened, slammed shut again. Nick eyed the newcomer in the mirror. A short, stocky guy with a shaved head and bushy black brows. He ignored everyone and headed into the back through the saloon doors. The bartender and server shared a look.

Nick took his shot when the bartender paused in front of him to refill a bottle of Patrón…from a plastic bottle of Captain Dennis tequila.

"That the new owner?" Nick asked. "Didn't know if you'd stay open without Dickie."

The bartender grunted again but this time eyed him. "Do I know you?" His voice was a rattly rasp.

Nick had been trying to figure out the same thing. It was possible, probable even, that he'd arrested this guy a few years ago. "You don't look familiar," he lied.

The bartender leaned forward menacingly. "You smell like a cop."

Ah, shit.

This got the attention of the two conscious patrons at the end of the bar. They flicked dead-eyed glances his way before returning their focus to the TV.

"Not a cop," Nick said easily and picked up his beer.

The bald guy reappeared from the back with files tucked under his arm. This time, he gave the bartender a nod before heading out the front door. Nick would have liked to follow him, but the guy had been moving at a fast clip, and there was no way to catch up without making it too obvious.

"I'll tell you what I told the rest of your cop buddies when they tossed the place. Fuck. Off," the bartender snarled.

"Relax, man," Nick said. "There's no problem here." He forced himself to finish the rest of his beer leisurely. And when he was done, he left a ten-spot on the bar and walked out.

The server was leaning against the building in the alley, smoking a cigarette and texting.

"You a cop?" she asked, cigarette clamped between her lips.

"Nope. Just looking for some answers."

"Twenty bucks, and I'll give you answers," she said, blowing a cloud of blue smoke in his direction.

He smelled a setup. But sometimes even setups were educational.

He fished a bill out of his wallet, held it up between two

fingers. She waited a beat before stepping forward and snatching it out of his hand.

"We don't like questions around here," she said, tucking the money into her bra.

"I hope that's not your only answer," Nick said. "Who's in charge now that Dickie's dead?"

She shrugged and looked bored. "Dunno."

"Who's paying the bills? Who's signing your paychecks?"

She snorted. "Does this look like the kind of place with a payroll department?"

"Give me something," he insisted.

"Who wants to know? You think the cops care about figuring out who shot Frick's face off?"

"Maybe Dickie's family cares."

Her laugh was dry, humorless. "Dickie had a family? Ha. I always pictured him living alone in some shithole watching pornos and eating bad Chinese takeout."

"Can you think of anyone who would have wanted him dead?"

She shot him a you-dumbass look. "Only everyone who ever met him. Guy was a dick."

"How long have you worked here?" Nick asked.

"Listen, you've about used up that twenty bucks."

"You haven't given me anything worth twenty bucks."

"Six months. Now either cough up another bill or go."

He went. And when he got back in the car, he checked his dashcam footage, hoping to see a car or, better yet, a license plate for Baldy. But no such luck. The guy had walked out and headed down the block before disappearing around the corner. Nick watched and waited for a vehicle to cruise through the intersection, but none did for five full minutes.

23

I t had been yet another mind-numbing day at the office for Riley, made only more so in comparison to her road trip with Nick the night before. She'd learned that process serving wasn't exactly glamorous, high-flying fun. But there were no production meetings, no passive-aggressive office memos, and no annual reports to proofread.

She zipped into a parking space on the street and hauled her yoga mat out of the back seat. A dark sedan cruised by, and Riley thought she recognized Detective Weber's profile behind the wheel.

Dammit. If she was still at the top of the suspect list, she really was going to have to do his job for him and track down the killer.

But first, yoga.

Wander's studio occupied the second floor of a tidy brick building on Twenty-First Street in Camp Hill. The first floor belonged to an antique store that didn't mind the smell of incense or the sound of chiming gongs above.

"Wait up!" Jasmine, in head-to-toe Lululemon, jogged toward her. Her long hair flowed out behind her in a glossy curtain. She carried a mat that matched the deep purple of her pants. Riley guessed that most of the people on the street were watching her move in slow motion. "Girl, you better tell me everything there is to know about this Nick guy before we get upstairs," she demanded.

Riley laughed. Wander had a thing about everyone entering the studio in silence.

Jasmine opened the heavy glass door to the stairs.

"Not much to add," Riley said. "The deal is we continue to pretend to be engaged so he can hang out at the house and interview my neighbors. He thinks he can get more information out of them as my fiancé than as an investigator."

It was a long, steep flight of stairs. They tackled the first step together slowly in as much deference to Riley's soreness as their desire to gossip.

"So it's just business? That's it?" Jasmine looked disappointed.

"Well, there was *some* flirting." Riley smugly recalled Nick nearly driving the car into a streetlamp. "But he's under the assumption that I'm shopping for husband number two. And I'm of the opinion that my lady parts are so rusty I don't know if they could actually handle a night with Nick Santiago in my bed."

Jasmine was shaking her head. "Girl, we need to get you some WD-40 and a shot of confidence. You're amazing. He'd be lucky to take your lady parts for a spin."

"I love you, Jas, but you're delusional."

"You have an allegedly attractive man—according to your man-crazy neighbor Lily—who carried you upstairs, drove you to the hospital, yelled at your ex, and then concocted a scheme to pretend to be engaged to you. He's interested. And unless you're biologically dead, you're interested too."

Riley *was* interested. And terrified. Casual sex with Nick wouldn't be casual for her. It would be life changing, world rocking, potentially vagina ruining. It was like strapping on a pair of skis for the first time ever and plummeting down a black diamond trail. She felt like it would be smarter to start on a bunny trail until she could get the hang of things again.

"We'll see," she said noncommittally and stepped into the studio before Jasmine could bring up any of several good points on why she should get naked with Nick.

The space was crowded with bodies in various stretches on the wide plank floors. The incense was smoking. The crystals were aligned. The bolsters were stacked.

Gabe opened his eyes from the hero's pose he was perfecting and waved. He gestured toward the empty space around him. Apparently the rest of the class preferred to admire the man—celestial being? godlike spirit?—from afar.

"Who. Is. That?" Jasmine whispered.

"Tell you later," Riley said out of the side of her mouth.

Wander shot them a loving yet warning glance from the front of the room. They both zipped their lips and unrolled their mats. Between the incredibly athletic Black man on her left and the long-legged Indian attorney on her right, Riley felt like an inferiority sandwich.

Her parents bustled in, not speaking but still causing a ruckus with Velcro mat straps and excessive grunting to remove shoes. Her dad waved at her, then nodded in Gabe's direction with exaggerated eyebrow movement. His questions didn't need to be vocalized.

Is this the guy your crazy grandma sent you?

Riley nodded and turned back to the front of the room when her sister started the music.

"It's warm yoga tonight," Wander said, beaming at the crowded class. The windows were open to bring in the summer evening heat. "Tonight we'll be working on unfolding and opening, accepting where we are physically and mentally while working to go deeper, to find more joy, more sweat, more passion. Let us begin."

Oh boy. Just what Riley needed.

———

Her body hurt. Her muscles ached. Her joints felt like concrete. Sweat rolled and dripped and trickled its way down her body to the mat and floor. By the time Wander took the class into corpse pose, Riley felt like she'd been wrung out and left to dry. She also felt marginally better.

Her sister ended class with a serene "Namaste" echoed by the rest of the now enlightened students.

Riley stayed where she was, a limp, soggy corpse, while Gabe led a spontaneous round of applause.

"Thank you, Gabe," Wander said, coming to kneel next to Riley's mat. "You were a wonderful student."

"And you were a magnificent teacher," he said.

Riley opened one eye and rolled her head to the side to look at Jasmine. "Are they flirting?" Riley asked.

"Either that or complimenting each other's sublimeness," her friend answered.

"Great class, kiddo," Roger said. "I gotta get out of here. Trivia starts in half an hour at Arooga's. You feeling better, Rye Bread?" he asked.

Riley gave him a thumbs-up. "All good, Dad."

"Good. Come by and meet my cow this weekend." He gave Blossom a kiss on the forehead and an affectionate tweak on the nose before ambling toward the cubbies on the back wall.

"Cow?" Jasmine wondered.

"Don't ask," Riley said.

"Gabe, it's wonderful to meet you," Blossom said, joining them. "I'm so happy you're here to help our Riley finally discover her gifts."

"It is my honor to be here," Gabe said.

"Yeah. About that," Riley began with a yawn. "Maybe we should start this training some other time?"

"I've waited thirty-plus years for this moment," Blossom reminded her. "Now is good."

"May I join you?" Wander asked.

"By all means, of course," Gabe said.

Great. Now Riley was going to have an audience.

"I'm *not* missing this," Jasmine said, dropping back down onto her mat.

Gabe got to his very large feet and asked permission to collect a few items for the training. Wander scampered off to help him.

Blossom patted Riley's knee. "Now, don't be nervous. We're all here to help you."

Riley groaned. "Mom, I don't really want to do this. Especially not with an audience. I already feel like crap, and every time I get hit with a vision or something, I get all sweaty and sick. Do you really want me to barf in Wander's studio again?"

The first time had been during hot yoga with a hangover.

"Sweetie, it's easier if you open yourself to it and just go with it. Stop trying to fight it or control it." Blossom perked up. "It's actually just like vomiting!"

Gabe returned with a hulking bicep full of pillar candles in purples and whites and a collection of amethyst crystals.

Wander handed out meditation cushions.

"Me too?" Jasmine asked, delighted.

Where Riley had always envied Jasmine's genius brain and effortless good looks, her best friend had made a big deal out of the Thorn women's psychic abilities. Until right this second, Riley had assumed that it had been the teenage equivalent of a supportive "No, those pants don't make your ass look huge."

"Of course. We all have gifts. Intentional cultivation of those gifts can be the beginning of a great journey." Gabe said.

"He sounds like a—"

"Fortune cookie," Riley finished the thought for Jasmine.

They settled in a semicircle around Gabe on thick cushions. Riley dragged her feet into the appropriate cross-legged pose, noting that her twinges and pains were marginally better after an hour of yoga.

"Please choose a candle," Gabe instructed as he methodically lit each one with a match, the flame never seeming to get close to his fingers. "Watch the flame dance and flicker. Let it be only the light that you see."

She wondered what she could scrounge up for dinner

tonight. She should have asked Fred before he left class what they were having.

"Allow your mind to settle, your breath to deepen. It is in this state of peace and nonjudgment that your gifts can open."

All this talk of opening irked her. Bad things happened when people were open. People didn't want you to be real and vulnerable. They wanted you to shut up and do what you were supposed to do.

She shot a glance to her right and was disappointed to find Jasmine fixated on her candle. She sighed. Great. She was alone in her cynicism.

Something drilled into her leg. It was her mother's freak-ishly strong finger sending her a warning. Blossom had been gifted with steel rods for fingers and wielded them when necessary.

Fine. She would try.

Riley cracked her neck, rolled her shoulders, and picked a candle at random.

If she got this over with fast enough, she could be having dinner in—

She was floating on nothingness. No, that wasn't quite right. It was pink and blue ether. Or clouds. Or cotton candy. Whatever it was, it felt thicker than air. Thick enough for her to be suspended in it, to be connected to it.

There was a cacophony of voices like she was sitting in a theater surrounded by people. She couldn't see anyone, but she could feel them. And hear them.

"My son is missing out on the life he's meant for by marrying that dingbat with the boobs."

"I've sent them every sign I can to tell them I'm fine and the afterlife is great, but none of those yahoos have paid a lick of attention."

"She needs to know that the secret ingredient to my porridge recipe is vanilla bean extract."

Voices crowded in on all sides of her, and Ether Riley held up her hands. "Can everyone just shut up for five seconds?"

"Excellent work." Gabe's voice was pleased.

"I didn't do anything. And they all keep yelling at me," she complained. The nausea was already rising in her empty stomach.

"You have opened yourself. Now, it is time to control it."

"Control? How?" She was shouting just to hear herself over the demands of the dead.

"Why is she screaming?" she heard Jasmine ask.

"Because I can't hear myself think," Riley yelled.

"Ask them something," Gabe suggested.

"Like what?"

"Something you want to know."

Something she wanted to know. How to be normal? Yeah. Right. Like a bunch of ethereal blabbermouths were going to know that.

What was for supper?

"Uh. Okay. What's for supper tonight?" she asked.

The voices dropped down to a dull roar, and Riley saw, or thought she saw, meat loaves in tins in an oven.

She liked meat loaf. And she didn't feel so sick now.

"What are you seeing?" Gabe asked.

"Meat loaf."

"She loves meat loaf," Blossom stage-whispered from somewhere far away.

Riley ignored them. "Um, how about: Is Griffin going to live happily ever after? No! Wait!" She shook her head. She didn't really want the answer to that one. It wasn't like she wanted him to live a life of misery with weeping boils. But she also really didn't want to know that he'd avoid karma forever. "Okay, how about this. What do I need to know?"

The voices disappeared completely. There was nothingness, and then there was something. She was hurtling through space, heading toward a tiny prick of light.

"I don't think I'm doing this right," she yelled.

"Stay there. Be open," Gabe's distant voice instructed.

Did he sound concerned? Had she ripped down some

psychic veil? Was she hurtling toward hell? Could she still be sent to jail for a crime she didn't commit if she were in hell? Would she survive long enough to have meat loaf?

The light was getting brighter, bigger, until she was pushing through weird cotton candy clouds and stepping into it.

Uh-oh.

It was a small room lit by a ghastly orange glow emanating from a lava lamp tucked into the corner. The bedspread, that god-awful orange-and-green floral blanket, was rumpled and half on the floor.

It probably had something to do with the tangle of naked bodies writhing on top of the bed. She watched as Nick Santiago used that very talented tongue to tease his name from...big-time uh-oh.

Her lips. Vision Riley was buck naked, pulling his hair, and thoroughly embracing having an equally disrobed Nick move over her body.

Not Currently Engaged in Sexual Intercourse Riley covered her eyes. "Oh my God," she said, feeling all kinds of things in all kinds of places.

"What do you see?" Gabe's voice asked soothingly from a distance.

There was no way in hell she was sharing this particular vision. She was basically having sex in front of her mother right now, and that was not cool. Not cool at all. Could Gabe see this? Was this some kind of psychic sex tape?

"I see more meat loaf," she lied.

And then she was back. Like the snap of a rubber band. She'd been pulled and stretched and then released back to the present.

"I swear I could smell Uncle Jimmy's aftershave," Wander was whispering. "Like a warm, lovely cloud of it."

"I just saw like a lot of blue," Jasmine said, sounding disappointed. "Like when you squeeze your eyes shut too tight."

"Jasmine, let me do a tarot reading for you," Blossom insisted at Riley's elbow. "I feel like I'm bursting with spirit guides right now."

Riley sagged off her cushion and onto the floor. She was sweaty and spent. And very hungry. At least she didn't feel like she was going to projectile vomit. Improvement.

"Riley?"

She felt her mother's sausage fingers prodding her arm. Then big warm pancakes of hands were tapping her cheeks.

"Meat loaf," she whispered and opened her eyes.

"What the hell happened?" Jasmine asked. "Are you all right?"

Gabe was grinning down at her. "You are very powerful indeed."

Blossom jumped to her feet. "I knew it! *I knew it!* In your face, Carol Loomis! My daughter is a savant! And your creepy Ouija board–manipulating son is a loooooooooser!" She danced an inappropriate boogie around the studio.

"Mom!" Wander was both amused and horrified.

"What? Oh, sorry." Blossom seemed to remember where she was and hurried back over to where Gabe was helping Riley sit up. "What happened? Tell us everything so I can put it all in the guild newsletter!"

"Could you, uh, see what I saw?" Riley asked Gabe, trying to sound like a woman who hadn't just foretold really great sex. She avoided making eye contact with everyone.

"Riley accessed a realm in the Other," Gabe explained.

The Other meaning Cotton Candy World, she guessed.

Wander pressed a glass of water into Riley's hands.

"The Other?" Jasmine asked. *"Why can't I be cool and psychic like the Thorns?"*

Riley blinked. Had her beautiful genius of a best friend just wished she could be more like *her?*

"I like to think of it as the beyond," Gabe was saying. "The Other can be experienced through senses outside the traditional limited ones."

"I saw meat loaf in the oven," Riley said. She took a big gulp of water, let it soothe her tight throat. "Everything was behind these big fluffy clouds, and I had a hard time seeing through them."

They were all hanging on her every word. Her mother was taking notes in her phone.

"I texted Lily when you said meat loaf, and she sent this," Blossom said, crawling over to shove her phone in Riley's face. "Look at this." Little tins of mini meat loaves lined up in the oven.

If the meat loaves were real, then… Holy. Shit. She was going to have sex with Nick Santiago, no-strings bad boy extraordinaire.

"Oh, this is so exciting! I can't wait to tell everyone I know," Blossom crowed.

"Mom! No! No telling anyone. I don't need the world to confirm that I'm a freak," Riley groaned.

"You are most certainly not a freak," Gabe said. "You are a powerful, gifted clairvoyant."

"Yeah? Well, I don't need Mom taking out a billboard on the Camp Hill bypass to tell the world about it," she said and frowned.

He laid a massive hand on her shoulder. "Do not worry. This is the first step in learning to control your abilities," he promised.

Control. Stop. Whatever. As long as this meant she wasn't going to have to live with voices in her head anymore.

24

H e wasn't nervous. Pfft. Nick Santiago didn't get nervous. He'd gotten a haircut because he was due for one. The new pajama pants in his bag were because he didn't have time to do laundry. And the six breath mints he'd downed on the ten-minute drive to Riley's? Well, she didn't need to suffer because he'd ordered onions on his sub at lunch.

He was definitely *not* nervous about platonically spending the night with her. He eyed the overnight bag on the passenger seat. *Great.* Now he was lying to himself.

It had to be the platonic thing. If they'd been planning to have a few hours of strings-free naked fun, he'd be fine. He was confident when it came to sex. He had a track record of proven results backing him up. But this pretending to be a boyfriend—now fiancé—without any of the physical stuff, well, it was messing with his head.

"Get yourself together, man," he muttered. He climbed out of the SUV and crossed the parking lot, debating whether he should use the front door like a guest or keep it casual by using the back door.

Nick fired off a text to Riley, letting her know he'd arrived, and let himself in the unlocked back door. He heard a congenial ruckus coming from the front of the house. The kitchen was to his right through an open pocket door painted an unappetizing mint green. A large Black man with the most perfectly formed head Nick had ever seen was dropping one ice cube at a time into a shiny bucket.

"Hey, man," Nick said, edging into the kitchen. Riley hadn't mentioned any new roommates. Definitely not any built like Under Armour models.

"Hello. I am retrieving ice for happy hour," the man announced, hefting the bucket out of the sink. Each bicep was the size of Nick's head.

"Do you live here?" Nick asked.

"I do. I am Gabe, Riley's very close friend," the man said.

Nick didn't care for the sound of that. "I'm Nick. Riley hasn't mentioned a close friend named *Gabe*."

"I am training her for her wedding night."

"Her wedding night?" Nick repeated. "Hang on. *I'm* the guy she's marrying. If there's training to do, I'll be the one doing it."

"You are a very lucky man. She is an incredible woman," Gabe said with a wistful quality that Nick *really* didn't like.

"Gabe, do you need help with the ice?" Riley appeared in the door with an empty glass and a smile. She was wearing the kind of shorts that would have kept teenage Nick up at night and a cute scoop-neck tank that gave adult Nick more than a few dirty ideas. Her smile faltered for just a second. "Nick! Hey." She looked guiltily back and forth between the two men.

She damn well better feel guilty. Moving in a new "very close friend" right under her fiancé's nose? That shit wasn't cool.

Fake fiancé.

He'd just remembered that part. Big Guy Gabe was looking at Riley like he was a loyal golden retriever.

"Hey, beautiful," Nick said, deciding to prove a point. Dropping his bag on the floor, he pulled her into his arms, pinned her against the wall, and went for the gold. His lips didn't brush hers. No, they devoured. His tongue didn't slip into her mouth. It invaded.

He meant to mark his territory. Not produce a porno. But

he *really* liked how her mouth felt under his. Riley didn't seem to mind either. So maybe he went a *little* over the top with the performance. Maybe he could have stopped thirty seconds earlier. Maybe he could have kept his hands from slipping under the hem of that shirt to skim over the smooth skin of her waist. He could have definitely not growled when he caught that sexy little moan of hers.

Thank you, six breath mints.

Nick pulled back and felt a caveman-like pride when her knees buckled. Despite his little dry spell, he still had it. What he didn't have was his own balance. He tipped a little too far to the side and rammed a shoulder into the doorjamb. Now, she was the one looking smug.

"Do you have issues with vertigo?" Gabe asked. "I can help you rearrange the crystals in your ears to make you steadier on your feet."

Shut up, Gabe.

"My balance is just fine," Nick said, crossing his arms and making sure to flex his own biceps. Maybe they weren't gladiator-sized, but they were nothing to be ashamed of.

He should have done push-ups in the parking lot first.

"Gabe, this is Nick," Riley interjected. "Gabe knows we're not really engaged and that you're investigating Dickie's murder. Nick knows that I am…you know…"

"A superior clairvoyant with unparalleled gifts?" Gabe suggested.

If Riley Thorn had a fan club, this guy wanted to be president.

"Who *is* this guy?" Nick asked his pretty, fake fiancée whose lips were now pink and swollen. Bigger question: Why did she trust him?

She worked up a blush. "Well, he's my trainer."

"Your trainer?" He was not a fan of the idea of Gabe the Gargantuan getting Riley all sweaty and then helping her stretch.

She looked over her shoulder to make sure no one else was within earshot. "We're telling people he's my personal trainer, but he's kind of my…" She looked beseechingly at Gabe.

"I am Riley's not-fake spiritual guide," Gabe announced grandly.

If the guy was waiting for a standing ovation, he sure as hell wasn't getting one from this audience. "Hang on a second," Nick said. "Aren't spirit guides supposed to be spirits?"

Yeah, he'd done some more googling. Big deal.

"Spirit guides are not among the living," Gabe agreed.

"So what I hear you saying is you're either dead or not human," Nick said with a straight face.

Riley rolled her eyes, but he caught the lift at the corners of her lips.

"I am most definitely alive," Gabe said stiffly.

"Gabe is my spiritual guide, not spirit guide," Riley cut in. She pinched Nick's forearm hard. "We just started working together."

"So the better you get at this psychic thing, the less you'll need extra-large Dwayne Johnson here?" Nick pressed.

Gabe looked like someone had just punched a teddy bear in the face. "I can only hope that Riley's need for my services will outlast your need for hers," he retorted.

Nick stepped in on the mountain of a man and looked up. "Are you accusing me of using her?"

"Okay. Let's stop this conversation right here," Riley said, wedging herself between them. "I don't need more drama and weirdness in my life."

"I would not dream of complicating your life," Gabe promised.

Nick wasn't about to make any such promises. "Oh, come on, man. She's engaged. You can stop with the sucking up."

"Nick, shut up," she growled.

"I agree with Riley," Gabe said. His blinding smile was really starting to piss Nick off. "You should definitely cease talking."

"Listen, Andre the Giant, if you don't stop flirting with my fiancée, I'm going to find a step stool, climb it, and punch that smile off your face."

Riley slapped her hands to his chest. "Nick, get a grip. If you can't play nice, then the deal's off. Got it?"

Gabe peered over Riley's shoulder, his smile smug. But Nick was used to being the troublemaker. And it was usually the troublemaker who got the girl.

"Where's the ice? I got room-temperature martinis in here," Mrs. Penny bellowed from the parlor.

"Coming!" Riley called back. "Come on, *gentlemen*. Remember, Gabe. You're my personal trainer. Nick, you're my fiancé."

"I think we have our roles straight," Nick said.

"Do not underestimate these people." She wagged a finger in his direction. "They might look old and helpless, but I've seen them make Food Dude drivers cry."

"Honey, don't underestimate my charm," he said, flashing her a wink.

He followed her into the parlor where he'd helped untie Fred's legs. It was still crowded with mismatched furniture and now also the elderly. Mrs. Penny was behind a small mahogany bar, eyeballing her pours in a cocktail shaker. Her cane was propped against a bookcase stuffed with leather volumes of books that looked as if they hadn't been opened in a few decades and the kind of knickknack debris that accumulates over a lifetime.

Mr. Willicott, the Denzel Washington look-alike with the short-term memory of a stoner, had his face buried in a hardback romance novel. Fred the Freakishly Flexible was sitting cross-legged at the organ, noodling out what sounded like a funeral dirge. Lily, dressed in a plaid nightgown, was draped across the weird-looking green velvet couch thing like she was having her portrait painted.

"'Bout damn time," Mrs. Penny snapped when Gabe delivered the bucket of ice.

"My apologies, Mrs. Penny. I hand-selected each cube for you. I did not wish to disappoint you with inferior ice."

"Well, aren't you a charmer?" the elderly bartender purred.

"Oh, for fuck's sake," Nick muttered under his breath.

Riley elbowed him in the gut.

Which reminded him, maybe he should step up his gym workouts. He didn't need the sixteen-pack that was on display under the big guy's skin-tight T-shirt. But maybe a few more planks and crunches a week were warranted.

"Nick's here, everybody," Riley said with feigned cheer.

"Whatcha got in the bag?" Mrs. Penny asked as she added Gabe's hand-selected bullshit ice to a cocktail shaker. "Sex toys?"

"Uhhhh…" He wasn't sure how to handle that one.

"Nick is spending the night," Riley said dryly.

"So definitely sex toys," Mrs. Penny repeated.

"Don't embarrass the kids," Lily admonished.

Nick was knocking on thirty-eight and took mild offense to being called a kid.

"Sex with or without accessories is a normal, healthy function," Fred weighed in unnecessarily.

Mr. Willicott grumbled under his breath and turned the page in the novel.

"You know, in some ancient cultures, it was typical for tribes to wait outside the hut while relationships were consummated. They would chant and sing. Riley, we'd be happy to sing outside your door while you make love since it's been so long for you," Lily offered.

"Kill me now," Riley whispered to Nick.

He used the opportunity to slide an affectionate arm around her waist and give Gabe a come-at-me glare. "I don't think we'll need any chanting, but thanks," he told Lily, giving Riley a squeeze.

"Dirty gin martinis up," Mrs. Penny announced.

"Lily has been taking anthropology courses on the internet," Gabe explained, picking up four of the drinks in his massive hands. Spiritual Guide Gabe could bitch-slap someone into oblivion with one of those flesh-toned pizza trays.

He delivered the first to Riley and then reluctantly gave one to Nick.

"And Mrs. Penny is taking an online bartending course," Riley said, crossing her eyes at Nick over the rim of her glass.

He grinned. Damn, she was cute.

Fred cut off his funeral dirge to take the martini Gabe proffered.

"Happy happy hour, everyone," Lily sang from the couch.

Nick grabbed Riley's free hand and dragged her over to the love seat across from Lily. He crammed himself onto the cushion next to her. Gabe took the hint and sat by himself in a huge wingback chair near the organ. He took a careful sip of his martini, eyes widening then blinking rapidly.

"What is this?" Gabe asked.

"Alcohol, big guy. More specifically, gin," Mrs. Penny called.

"I have never had alcohol before," he said.

The dude was definitely not human.

"This is nice. Do you guys do this often?" Nick asked, priming the pump for his low-key, super strategic interrogation.

"Every Friday," Mrs. Penny said, stepping out from behind the bar with an extra-large martini glass filled to the brim.

"All of you?" he pressed.

"Smooth, Santiago. Real smooth," Riley whispered.

"Well, not *all* of us," Fred said conspiratorially.

"Like putty in my hands," Nick said over the rim of his glass only loud enough for Riley to hear him. "What about Dickie?" he asked.

"Who?" Willicott grumbled, putting his book down. "Man can't find a quiet place to read."

"The dead guy," Fred yelled in Willicott's direction.

"Who's dead?"

"Dickie Frick. The guy who lives on the third floor," Mrs. Penny shouted. "Someone shot him in the head."

"When did that happen? He owes me money," Willicott complained. He picked up his martini and sniffed it.

"How much did he owe you?" Nick asked.

"Who?" Willicott asked, taking a sip of gin.

"Mr. Willicott, how much money did the dead guy upstairs owe you?" Riley enunciated each word at full volume.

The man rose from his chair and wandered out of the room.

"That's probably the last we'll see of him," Lily said. "He gets lost in the hallway sometimes. Did I ever tell you about the time I was coming home with groceries?"

"I don't think so," Nick said.

"Here we go again," Riley muttered.

He toyed with the ends of her hair as Lily launched into a long-winded story involving bags of groceries and Dickie not holding the door for her. Nick didn't find it relevant to his investigation, but at least someone was talking about the deceased. Eventually one of them would say something important.

"Two thousand, one hundred, and fifty dollars."

Everyone turned toward the doorway. Mr. Willicott stood there, peering at the small leather notebook in his hand.

"Dickie owed you two grand?" Nick asked.

"Yeah. I had the Mother Chuckers in the championship last weekend. They eked one out over the Balls of Glory," Willicott said.

"Uh, are you saying you were betting on the summer rec dodgeball league?" Riley asked.

"And winning," Willicott said, waving his notebook. He sat back down in his chair and picked up his martini and novel.

"What is dodgeball?" Gabe asked.

"Hafta go down to the bar and see if I can get my cash," Willicott mused.

"Dickie was running a gambling ring out of Nature Girls?" Nick clarified.

"Well, don't that beat all," Mrs. Penny said. Her martini vat was half-empty already.

"Why the recreational league?" Riley asked.

Willicott shrugged. "Summer's slow for sports. Dickie ran books on everything. I lost four hundred bucks on toddler soccer last summer."

"Told you, Thorn," Nick said.

25

I don't get it," Riley hiccupped as she led the way upstairs. Most of their neighbors were still in the parlor working on their fourth round of martinis. Nick had slipped her his third one to stay sober for the planned breaking and entering. She'd managed his and dumped hers in a fake plant. She wasn't exactly drunk, but she sure wasn't sober.

"Don't get what?" he asked. His hands settled on her hips from behind, and she stifled a tipsy purr.

"Have fun having sex," Lily called up the stairs as she tottered past.

"Thanks, Lily," Nick said.

Riley heard the smile in his voice and tried not to picture the dimples. He was just putting on a show, playing the role of a guy in love with a girl, she reminded herself.

But his hands stayed where they were even after her neighbor disappeared.

"You know, being here with you makes me nervous," he said suddenly.

"Really?" She'd applied deodorant twice, dusted her apartment, and—because why not—even did a quick smudging with leftover sage incense her mother had stashed in the Bad Vibes Emergency Kit.

His grip on her hips stopped them both on the stairs. "Yeah. It was right about here that I caught you midflight."

Oh, that. "I promise not to tackle you down the stairs tonight," she said.

"Back to what you don't get," he prompted.

She started for the third floor. Nick's hands stayed firmly planted, and she tried not to think about why they were there or where else they'd been…er…would be. "Sports betting. It's legal now in Pennsylvania. Can't someone just walk into the casino and place a bet?"

"Even easier than that," he said cheerfully. "You can open an app or a website and gamble your life savings away."

They got to the top of the stairs, and she turned to look at him. He released his hold on her and gripped both railings, the picture of casual. Nick Santiago made a woman think he had all the time in the world to explore her.

"So why would Dickie be running some junior league bookie business when people can do it legally?"

Those dimples were putting on a show for her under a respectable layer of stubble. His eyes, that annoyingly enchanting mix of blue and green, were framed by sexy crinkles that she hadn't yet fully appreciated.

"What's the fun in doing something legal, Thorn?"

The bad boy in tight jeans and a rumpled T-shirt made an excellent point. Sometimes bad was fun.

Ugly orange and yellow flowers flashed into her mind. A lava lamp with fat lazy bubbles. Nick. Naked. *Holy guacamole.*

"Riley?"

Gabe's voice cut through her lust-fueled fantasy, startling her. She very nearly took another header down the stairs, but Nick caught her.

"Huh? Wha…? Yeah?" she sputtered.

Nick was standing very close to her. The tips of his scuffed boots touched her toes. A few of his fingertips had found their way under the hem of her tank again and were currently setting the skin of her abdomen on fire.

"Is everything all right?" Gabe asked, peering up at them from the first floor.

"Uhhhhh."

"She's fine, Optimus Prime," Nick said without breaking eye contact with her.

Could Gabe see her vision? Could Nick? Both were acting like weirdos. It was the last thing she needed. Two men in her head.

"I'm fine," she said lamely.

Gabe gave her a long, searching look, then nodded. "If you need me, I will be down here."

"She won't need you tonight," Nick promised.

———

Riley tried hard to ignore the barefoot Nick on her couch by making them a quick dinner of chicken and pasta.

They convened on the couch with plates and laptops. His long legs stretched out, bare feet resting on the coffee table. She sat cross-legged next to him, balancing computer and plate. Just another fake couple enjoying a fake Friday night in.

She scrolled through the yoga studio's Facebook page stats. Engagement and followers were up. Tonight, Wander was hosting a flow class with a live DJ followed by a walk to an organic wine bar and tarot readings.

In the Thorn family, her mother and sister were the stars, and Riley was the assistant sitting at home on a Friday night.

She sighed.

"What's that for?" Nick asked.

"If we were really dating, what do you think we'd be doing right now?" she asked.

His wolfish expression and the butter-melting, heavy-lidded gaze that traveled over her body said it all.

"*Besides* that. The sun isn't even down on a Friday, and I'm in for the night. My sister has a live DJ and strobe lights, and I'm on my couch scheduling posts on her social media."

"You know, we have a few hours to kill before everyone settles down," he mused.

"And how do you propose to kill time?" she asked.

He raised an eyebrow and opened his mouth.

"Besides sex," she interrupted.

"Besides sex? Huh. That'll take a little more time, but I can come up with some options."

"Options that don't cost anything, seeing as how my shoestring budget is double-knotted?"

He winked. "Honey, some of the best fun is free."

"Stop talking about sex."

He laughed and patted her thigh. "I'm not. Well, not *just* sex. Come on. Grab a pair of shoes and your keys."

"Where are we going?"

"To find some Friday night fun."

They snuck down the back staircase to the parking lot. Nick opened the driver's side door of Riley's Jeep and climbed up to release the soft top. "What are you doing?" she asked.

"It's illegal to have the top up on a night like this," he insisted.

She'd had the top down once, and after eating half her own hair and getting caught in a rainstorm, she'd decided it wasn't worth the effort. But heading south on Front Street with the warm air whipping through her ponytail and a grinning Nick behind the wheel, she wondered how many other kinds of fun she'd decided weren't worth the effort. The sun was dipping low, turning the sky and river orange and gold as he took the Market Street Bridge.

Riley was pleasantly surprised when he exited onto City Island, a low swath of land that squatted in the middle of the river, separating the East and West Shores. It was home to, among other things, the Harrisburg Senators baseball stadium, a red-and-white riverboat, and a crapload of parking for people who worked downtown.

It was a nice spot. Except for the flooding and the mayfly hatches.

"Maybe he's taking you fishing? I like this guy."

Shut it, Uncle Jimmy.

"No baseball game tonight," she observed as he pulled into an empty space in the parking lot.

"Nope." He flashed her a grin. "Let's go."

They got out of the Jeep, and Nick took her hand to lead her up the concrete steps. To the right was the pedestrian bridge that connected the island with the city. On the left was a carriage house for the Harrisburg Police Department's horses.

Nick pulled her down the asphalt path in front of the stables.

"Where are we going?" she asked. Everything worth seeing on the island was north, not west.

"Let me be spontaneous and romantic here, okay?" he complained.

"I think you're taking this fake relationship a little too seriously." She thought about the sex scene that had played out in her head. Maybe he wasn't the only one.

The western span of the Walnut Street Bridge rose before them. It had once spanned the entire river, but a flood in 1996 famously took out its center sections. The skeletal remains on both shores were all that was left behind.

"We're not supposed to be here."

"Live a little, Thorn," he teased, pulling her around the barrels and No Trespassing signs that were clearly intended to dissuade foot traffic.

She stepped carefully onto the metal grating, peering at the water below.

"Perfect timing," Nick said, squeezing her hand. She looked up.

"Oh, wow." The fat globe of the setting sun was just beginning to kiss the tree line on the West Shore. "Not bad, Santiago," she said as orange and pink blazed like fire in the sky, flickering on the surface of the river.

Music and laughter floated to them from the restaurant carved into the opposite shore.

He stood behind her, hands resting on the metal rail in front of her, boxing her in but not quite touching her. Her entire body buzzed with awareness as the sun disappeared, taking with it its warmth. But she had a new heat source. Nick Santiago.

"The way I see it, Thorn," he said, his voice low and rough in her ear, "is you try so hard to be normal, you forget about what's really important."

"What *is* really important?" she asked a little breathlessly.

"Picture this. You're on your deathbed."

She knew better than to actually visualize it lest she accidentally find out how and when she was going to die.

"What's your regret? That you didn't convince more people how normal you are or that you didn't take more moments like this?"

"They don't have to be independent of each other," Riley argued. "I can be normal and still have fun." Probably. Maybe.

"But are you?"

"How many girls have you brought out here?" she asked, changing the subject and turning to face him. She could picture teenage rebel Nick impressing the good girls out of their underwear with his sunset-on-the-bridge routine. She'd have fallen for it. And she'd have treasured that memory forever.

"Have you ever thought about focusing on what something means for *you* and not anyone else who came before or after you?"

Like Bella Goodshine. Where was Bella tonight? Probably at a fancy dinner with white tablecloths. Not in a bad boy's arms watching the sun disappear.

She cleared her throat. "So at least two dozen then?" she teased.

"You'd be surprised at how many girls don't want to get eaten alive by mosquitos," he said. "But seriously, Thorn. It doesn't have to be about hitting the club every night or building schools in third-world countries or doing yoga with a DJ or wearing a secondhand engagement ring and getting spray tans."

"What is it about then?" she asked.

Maybe it was the sunset. Maybe it was the three martinis. Or maybe it was just the really hot guy whose big competent hands were now skimming up and down her arms. It didn't feel fake.

"Being available."

Well, she was definitely single.

"Available for what?"

"Adventure. In whatever form it comes your way." His hands were on her shoulders now, fingers gently kneading the muscles that never seemed to relax.

"That's very rebel Zen of you," she pointed out, trying not to purr at his touch.

His laugh moved her hair.

His thumb hit a knot, and she made an embarrassing moaning noise.

"How do you stay 'available' and still be a responsible adult?" she asked, hoping he wouldn't stop working his magic on her muscles. If his fingers were this good at massage, she could only imagine all the other areas in which they'd excel.

"Responsibility is overrated," he quipped.

"Funny."

"I'm serious. Tying yourself down, committing to something over here means you're going to miss out on all the other things over there. You're making a trade. Like working an eight-to-five job. Sure, you get a paycheck, but those hours are no longer yours."

"Or like monogamy."

"Exactly." His teeth flashed white in the dusk that settled around them like a warm blanket. "Come on, Thorn. Don't you get tired of doing what you're supposed to do all the time? Of being the good girl?"

She bristled. "Maybe I like being good."

"How do you know for sure if you don't give being bad a try?" His hands brushed her hair back from her face before cupping her jaw.

Uh-oh. Mayday. DEFCON Whatever Is the Dangerous One. Warning bells clanged to life in her head.

There was another kind of awakening happening between her thighs. But that was more of a "Hell yes" than an "Oh no."

"You make an interesting point," she admitted.

"I think I want to kiss you right now, Thorn. Have a problem with that?"

"Maybe. I'm not sure. I'm thinking."

"You think too much."

"No one's here for the show," she pointed out. She'd give him that out. If there was no audience, there was no reason for the pretense.

"Maybe this one's just for us."

Oh boy.

"I'll take that under adv—"

The rest of her sentence was cut off by him conquering her mouth. There were a million ways to kiss someone, and she had a feeling Nick Santiago had mastered them all. It started out playful. Teasing. But she wasn't fooled. There was nothing gentle about this man.

His fingers flexed into her hair as if they wanted to be doing something else. Meanwhile, she let hers roam, digging into his T-shirt, his hard chest, his broad shoulders.

The kiss deepened and reincarnated as something else. Something hard and possessive and all-consuming. The heat building between them made her wonder if the sun had somehow come back up. Some primal noise between a groan and a growl worked its way up his throat, and then he was stepping back. He took his heat and her balance with him.

She gripped the rail behind her as her knees went wobbly. "You make me dizzy," she breathed.

He let out a definite growl this time as he paced in front of her. "Riley, honey, you can't tell a guy something like that and expect him not to want to hear it again," he warned.

"But you're immune to me, remember? I'm the committed monogamous type."

He stopped in front of her, but it was too dark to read his face.

"Baby, the way you kiss, there's a bad girl inside you dying to get out and have some fun."

For once in her life, Riley thought there might be some distinct advantages to being bad.

26

Nick managed—barely—to not maul Riley on the bridge before driving them back to her place. This was how guys like him got caught by girls like her. A couple of off-the-charts kisses, a pair of big brown eyes looking up at him like he was a goddamn hero, and he was ready to sign up for a long stint at monogamy.

Hell, he didn't blame guys for happily giving up their bachelor status. It was probably nice pairing off, partnering up. But he was different. He didn't need someone depending on him. Relying on him. Needing him…at least not outside the bedroom.

Riley Thorn would have no problems finding a guy who wanted to be her hero for the rest of his life. Like Gabe.

Man, he hated that guy.

Riley let them in the mansion's back door and held a finger to her mouth signaling for quiet before they tackled the stairs.

Nick didn't mind the journey. It gave him a chance to scope out the situation on the first two floors. Plus, it put Riley's very nice ass in front of him. The house was quieter now, but there were still signs of life. A toilet flush on the first floor and a faint chocolatey smell. A TV and microwave popcorn on the second.

There was a plate on the floor and a note on Riley's door when they got to the third. He peeled it off and read it.

Dear Riley,

I am looking forward to spending time with you tomorrow. Please enjoy this snack.

Love,
Gabe

Great. See? Nick didn't have to worry about Riley falling for *him*. She already had a guy leaving heart-shaped brownies at her door. Freaking great. Just perfect.

Wide-eyed with excitement, she picked up the plate and took a bite of brownie. "Ohmygod. The man's a genius in the kitchen," she moaned. "Want one?"

"No. Gabe has a Gabe-sized crush on you," he complained while she unlocked and opened the door.

"Be nice. He's the first person to ever be impressed with me. I'm not letting you be mean to him."

"Thorn, he is definitely not the first, and he won't be the last."

"Did all your report cards say, 'Does not play well with others'?" she teased.

A few of them had. Also, "Does not take directions."

"I play well with others *now*," he argued.

"Name two people you hang out with on a regular basis who aren't related to you and don't have vaginas," she said.

"Bob and…Biff," he shot back.

"Two *real* people."

Dammit. "I forgot you had the whole psychic thing going for you."

"Yeah, well, watch out. Because that burly brownie baker insists that he's going to teach me how to harness this weirdness," she said. She reached for the hem of her tank and started to lift it.

"Uh, Thorn?"

"Whoops. Sorry. I'm used to coming home alone."

"And getting naked?"

"Changing into pajamas. And yes, I realize how pathetic that makes my life sound."

"Pathetic? You just trespassed to make out with a pretty hot guy—if I do say so myself—on a bridge while the sun went down. Your life is awesome," he argued.

"Great. Now I have a spiritual guide and a life coach," she said dryly. "I'm changing."

She grabbed some clothes out of the scarred dresser and headed for the bathroom.

He hoped she slept in a flannel nightgown and not some cute tank top thing.

He'd already walked off one hard-on from the bridge and then talked himself out of the second one that popped up on the drive home while thinking about the first one.

She was making him regress in hormonal maturity.

It got worse when she came back. Not only was it a cute tank top with one of those completely useless built-in bras, but she was also wearing a slouchy pair of black shorts that could be easily breached from the top or bottom. He tortured himself with a debate on which way he'd go if given the shot.

She bent to put something away in one of the dresser drawers, and he had to turn away.

She had to be messing with him on purpose. The woman was psychic, for Christ's sake. She knew exactly what she was doing to his blood flow.

Two could play at that game, he decided.

"Guess I'll change too." He ducked into the hall bathroom, an outdated museum to bathrooms of the 1960s, and returned.

Riley looked up guiltily from the plate of brownies, which was looking considerably lighter. "You sure you don't want any...uh..."

He felt like he got a piece of his self-esteem back when Riley lost her train of thought and dropped a brownie on the floor.

"Where's your shirt?" she finally mumbled.

"Clean one's in my bag," he said, making a show of flexing his pecs while casually digging through his bag. He took his time pulling a gray T-shirt over his head. "I got these for you," he told her, gesturing at his pants.

"For me?"

"Yeah, I don't sleep in pants."

"What do you…? Oh."

———

They watched three episodes of Riley's favorite survival show and waited. By the time they both knew how to evade a charging bull, his kissable roommate was yawning, and the rest of the house was relatively quiet. Nick had assumed, perhaps unfairly, that the elderly were early-to-bed, early-to-rise folks. It proved to be an incorrect assumption.

It appeared that someone was always awake in the mansion.

After a final listen at Riley's door, he decided it was time to get cracking. Or picking.

"I'm heading over," he said. He dug through his bag, retrieving his gun, gloves, and lockpick set. "You ever have a fiancé who can pick locks?"

She stepped into her kitchen, where she reached into a cookie jar. "You ever have a fiancée who has a key to a crime scene?"

"Smart-ass." He took the key and clipped the holstered gun to his waistband.

She followed him across the hall.

"Where do you think you're going?" he asked.

"I'm going in there with you," she announced.

"Riley, it's a crime scene. I guarantee no one has cleaned anything up."

"I saw his body. Twice. I don't think week-old bloodstains are going to be any worse than that."

"I'm the professional here," he said.

"And I'm the sort-of psychic. Nick, dead people talk to me. Who's more specially skilled than that?"

190

"Point taken. Go put on a pair of gloves." Even if the ghost of Dead Dickie chatted it up with her and told her who put two slugs in his head, they'd still have to find good old-fashioned evidence that the cops couldn't ignore.

He choked back a laugh when she returned wearing elbow-length yellow kitchen gloves. She was fucking adorable. "You're a hell of a girl, Thorn."

"Yeah. Yeah. Let's get this over with."

It smelled like death, sweat socks, and old garbage.

He debated for a minute, then flipped on the lights. Dickie Frick was not a priority on the Harrisburg Police Department's caseload. No one was showing up tonight to comb through the scene of the crime.

"Gross," she said.

But she wasn't looking at the bloodstain on the wooden floorboards. She was eyeing the mess. There was a pile of old takeout containers that spilled from the kitchen counter into a disgusting sink. A haystack of—presumably dirty—underwear occupied the space behind the door. There was a stack of porn, the DVD and magazine variety, next to a sinus-infection-green recliner. There was a sixty-inch flat-screen mounted to the wall and an ancient DVD/VCR combo on the floor.

The bed was a futon. There was a collection of shot glasses displayed on shelves mounted to the wall next to a *Baywatch* poster.

"Living the bachelor dream," Riley quipped.

Nick felt defensive. "My place doesn't look like this." He hadn't bought a DVD in a decade, and he'd given his shot glasses away to the twenty-three-year-olds who lived next door.

"Looks like the cops took any electronics he had here," he said. No laptop or cell phone. No smart home devices or webcams lying around. "There's not much here."

The place was smaller and much more disgusting than Riley's. The dingy windows overlooked the parking lot and alley.

"Look what *is* here." She held up a calendar of the township's summer rec league that had been tucked into a stack of old phone books. Events were circled in red.

"Good eye, Thorn." Nick put the calendar down on the TV tray serving as a dining table and tissue and lotion holder. He was going to get a real table, he decided. And maybe some plants. He could take care of plants. "You said Dickie wasn't around much, right?" he asked, flipping through the calendar and taking pictures of each page with his phone.

"Right. Mostly just to sleep…and watch porn." She peered over his shoulder. "Are coed recreational volleyball and Soccer Shorties leagues really worth getting murdered over?"

"People have gotten themselves killed over stupider shit," he said. "I need to get access to that bar."

"Didn't you already pay them a visit?" she asked.

Nick tucked the calendar back into place and paged through the phone books. "Almost got my face punched in by the bartender. Then one of the servers scammed me out of twenty dollars in return for zero info."

"Dickie sure wasn't living like a business owner and successful bookie," she observed.

She was right. There was nothing in this apartment that hinted at anything but low income. But there were a lot of ways to burn through cash.

"How was he with technology?" he asked.

"Fred had to show him how to change the batteries in his TV remote," she said. "A couple of months ago, he paid Mrs. Penny's great-nephew twenty bucks to hook up his TV to the cable."

"So he might have kept old-school books."

"Like a notebook instead of a database?" she guessed.

"Exactly," he said. Riley wasn't half-bad as a partner, he noted, watching her stand on tiptoe to peek in the cabinets above the sink. He joined her and peered into the fridge.

"Oh my God. What's that smell?" She gagged.

"Two shelves of rotting takeout," he reported, shutting the door.

They did another sweep of the space for a book but came up empty.

"If there was anything here, the cops probably have it," he said. His gaze found its way back to the shiny new flat-screen. Its newness stood out among the refuse.

"Will they tell you if they found his books?" she asked.

"Weber won't. But I have other friendly ears in the department."

"Speaking of friendly," she piped up from her study of the neatly stacked cans of ravioli. "How long did you and Sergeant Jones date?"

"How did—oh. Right. Psychic."

"Not much of one, apparently. Dickie's not sending me any messages from the grave."

"Four dates," he said. "That's how many times Mabel and I went out. A fun little fling between coworkers." Once again, he was telling her more than he intended.

"Four dates?" Riley whistled, then grinned at him.

He caught her gloved hand in his own and stepped her against the wall. "Say the word, Thorn, and we can have our own fun little fling," he reminded her. "If we're that good at kissing each other, imagine how good we'd be at everything else."

"About that—"

They both heard it at the same time. Car tires crunching on gravel.

"Shit," Nick said, cutting the lights in the apartment.

"Who's coming here at two a.m.?" she hissed.

Together they peered through the film of filth on the window to the parking lot below. He made a mental note to see if his cousin Deb was still doing cleaning jobs and if she'd give his own windows a scrubbing.

A dark sedan pulled into the side lot and parked with its engine on and lights off. "Recognize the car?" he asked.

"No."

A figure dressed all in black emerged from the car.

"We need to get out of here," he said.

27

Nick produced a very official-looking gun from the waistband of his pajama pants, and Riley's mouth went dry.

As he dragged her out of Dickie's apartment and into the hall, she thought about how very much she didn't mind the manhandling. She also didn't mind when he pinned her against the wall with his hips, gun trained on the stairs.

She was in the middle of her own romantic suspense movie with the handsome hero when the sound of the front door creaking open three floors below dragged her out of the fantasy and back to the actual real-life danger. Had one of her dingbat neighbors left the front door unlocked again? Had the killer come back? Did they have some unfinished business here in the house? Was there hidden treasure tucked away within these dusty, crumbling walls?

The plot for every Nancy Drew book she'd read as a kid cycled through her head.

Nick clamped a gloved hand over her mouth. "Stay quiet," he whispered in a gravelly, authoritative voice.

When she nodded, he removed his hand but kept his body pressed against hers.

There was most definitely a noise coming from somewhere within the house. A shuffling. Like someone trying to move quietly. It was hard to hear over the racket her own heartbeat was making as it pounded away in her chest. Fear and the weight of Nick's body pressing into hers were doing wild, confusing things to her hormones.

She was acutely aware of her breath—it was loud—and her nipples. They were painfully hard.

Lily never locked her bedroom door. What if the intruder tried that one? What if Mr. Willicott took another middle-of-the-night trip to the bathroom? Was she about to hear one of her poor, sweet neighbors who she'd miss much more than Dickie Frick yelling, "Cabbage casserole"?

There was a noise on the stairs, and Nick stiffened. Riley's heart kicked into overdrive, and her nipples tried to drill their way out of her shirt. *Subtle, nipples. Really subtle.*

Nick's fingers flexed on the gun. It wasn't his only weapon. As best she could tell, the man was also armed with a raging hard-on. Or a large flashlight stuffed in his pajama pants.

She hadn't known bosoms could actually heave, but that was exactly what hers was doing against his chest.

Was it weird that she was terrified and turned on at the same time? Could Nick fight off an intruder if most of his blood was in his pants?

A sound came again, this time on the worn tread of the stairs. It was…familiar. *Shuffle clunk. Shuffle clunk.*

Like someone walking with a—

She heard a wooden scrape followed by the telltale creak, and then a door on the second floor closed.

"Just Mrs. Penny," she whispered. She could feel Nick's breath on her cheek, his heart beating steadily against her own chest. The hand he had at her waist fisted on the hem of her shirt as if he were fighting some conflicting urge.

She felt his hard-on pulse against her and nearly blacked out. Was the danger over, or was it only just beginning?

"Stay here," he ordered.

She had to obey. Her knees had turned to overcooked spaghetti. Walking was not an option.

He left her propped against the wall and silently crossed to the staircase. She felt light-headed, weak-kneed, and really, really ready to get naked. Peeking out of the alcove, she watched him descend to the second floor, the light casting his shadow on the rose and fern wallpaper.

In silhouette, his erection looked like it could take out someone's eye.

She took a moment to calm her breathing and think about anything but Nick's penis. Oops. She was thinking about it again.

"What the hell is an eighty-year-old doing sneaking around at two a.m.?" Nick's harsh whisper startled her. Yelping as her knees buckled, she reached out to catch herself…and caught the waistband of his pajama pants instead.

She—and the pants—went down.

"Thorn?"

"Uh. Yeah." She wanted to look him in the eye, but she couldn't tear her gaze away from another body part that was demanding her attention.

"About the platonic part of this sleepover…"

"Uh-huh?" she breathed. In this exact moment, she would be fine with having sex right here against the wall. She could be quiet. Probably.

"We should really focus on that," he said, interrupting her fantasy.

"Huh?" She looked past his proudly jutting erection to his face.

He reached down and helped her to her feet. Only then did he pull his pants back up.

"We've got a good thing going here," he said, knotting his drawstring. "Maybe we shouldn't complicate things."

"Two questions," she said. "Did you not just offer up a fun little fling three minutes ago? And is that a flashlight shoved down your pants?"

"Uh, yes, I did. And no, it is not."

"So you're saying you've got *that* going on"—she pointed to his heroic hard-on—"and you definitely want to keep things platonic."

He scratched the back of his head. "Yeah."

"You are the worst fake boyfriend I've ever had," she whispered, stomping to her door.

"Come on. Don't be like that, Thorn," he said, following her. "I'm trying to be the good guy here. You're not making it easy."

Thorn women had never been accused of making anything easy. It looked as though she was finally living up to her genetics in more ways than one.

"I'm going down to check that the doors are locked and to make sure that really is Mrs. Penny in her room," Nick said, tucking the gun into the back of his pants.

"You're not knocking on her door like *that*, are you?" Riley asked, eyeing his erection.

He held up three fingers. "Scout's honor. I'm just going to listen creepily at her door."

He won't be the first person to do that in this house, she mused. Defeated, turned on, pissed off, and suddenly exhausted, she went into her apartment and got ready for bed.

While Nick secured the perimeter or interior or whatever the hell he was doing, she poured them both glasses of water and set out a pillow and blankets on the couch for him. There was no way Mr. I Changed My Mind was getting anywhere near her bed tonight. She ducked into the hall bathroom to brush her teeth and nearly shrieked when she ran into his warm, solid torso outside the door. "Crap, Nick. Did you go to ninja school?" she asked, pushing past him.

He gave her a friendly slap on the ass. "Everything's locked up tight, and Mrs. Penny is in her room watching *The Price Is Right*. Your guy Gabe sleeps to a soundtrack of monks chanting."

"Great," she said, too tired to feign interest.

He closed and locked the door behind him, then tucked his gun under the coffee table within arm's reach.

"You could just go home, you know," she said with a yawn.

"I *could*. But how would that look to your roommates at breakfast tomorrow? They might think we had a fight and broke up."

"Or that you were bad in bed and we broke up," she shot back, padding over to her bed and pulling back the covers.

He laughed softly. "Yeah, they'd never buy that."

She shook her head. "Go to sleep," she said grumpily.

He stripped out of his shirt and threw it on her coffee table. She pulled the blanket over her head and refused to be his audience.

"Hey, Thorn?"

"Mmm."

"We're even now."

"Even?"

"I saw you topless. You saw me bottomless."

"I did?" She feigned innocence. "Huh. I forgot all about that."

"Liar." The affection and amusement in his tone hung in the dark between them.

28

*W*hen did spandex come back in style?"

"*...run six miles and still can't get rid of this bra fat.*"

"*Gah! I sucked in a bug...*"

"*Is that the drunk girl from the bar last night?*"

"*Now that guy works out...*"

"Seriously. How do I block this stuff out?" Riley asked Gabe, holding her hands over her ears. For the second time in twenty-four hours, she was strolling City Island with a very attractive man. But instead of whisking her away for a sunset make-out session, Gabe had talked her into going for a run. Something about physical exertion making it easier for the mind to focus. She'd been fueled by enough annoyed sexual frustration to agree.

She'd lasted a whole quarter of a mile before she stopped to almost throw up breakfast. A breakfast that she and Nick had rushed through, awkwardly surrounded by elderly people who assumed they'd had sex last night.

"First, you must decide what you're willing to accept," Gabe said sagely.

If he kept talking like that, she was definitely calling for a ride home.

The couple behind them was bickering about dinner plans. And subconsciously broadcasting their real issues to lucky Riley. He had an online porn addiction, and she had been flirting with a coworker at the mall for two months. This was the downside to finding out she was psychic and not crazy. She was privy to some things that she would have preferred not knowing.

"I mean, can I block stuff out? And if I do, can I open back up? And if I do, can I filter what comes in? And why hasn't Dickie sent me any messages from the beyond? Is his spirit not speaking to me because I didn't do enough to keep him alive? I mean, could I have kept him alive? Should I have tried harder?"

Gabe's smile was blinding.

"What are you so happy about?" she demanded. "I'm basically an accessory to murder."

"I am happy you are taking an interest in your gifts," he said, a little smugly for a spiritual advisor in her opinion. He had her grandmother's fingerprints all over him.

"Are you reporting back to my grandmother?" Riley asked with suspicion.

He shook his head. "Your spiritual journey is a personal one. I report to no one."

Good. She hated to think there was some guild committee poring over notes on her half-assed tiptoeing into clairvoyance.

"I am merely a guide, not an authority here for discipline," he continued.

"Okay. So guide me then," she said, surrendering.

"Let's sit over there. We can stretch and talk," he suggested, pointing at a swath of grass bathed in sunshine.

They sat, and she followed him through a series of stretches that felt kind of okay.

Her burly spiritual guide was taking his fake personal training duties seriously.

A group of moms pushing children of varying ages in strollers slowed to eyeball Gabe's butt as he flowed back and forth from downward dog to plank pose.

One of the women fanned herself with a burp cloth. *"I'd*

take out a second mortgage if that meant I could have him as a personal trainer."

But he was too busy stretching his gigantic muscles and beaming at Riley to notice his fan club.

She studied Gabe as she followed him in the stretches. He was preternaturally attractive. There wasn't a single imperfection about his physical appearance. Plus, he had the personality of Santa Claus. Yet he had zero effect on her hormone levels.

And then there was Nick Santiago, who had winked at her over hash browns and coffee that morning, causing a rain forest in her underwear.

Gabe finished stretching and settled into a meditative posture with a spine so straight it would have brought tears of joy to Wander's eyes.

"Wait. Are we starting?" Riley asked.

"I am ready to begin," he answered.

"Here?"

"Is there something wrong with here?"

"Well, for one thing, we're in public." A group of runners in short shorts and not much else paraded past, illustrating her point.

"Humans always find something wrong with the here and now," Gabe said mysteriously.

"When you say stuff like that, it makes me think you're not a human," she told him.

His laugh drew more eyes. Every woman—and several of the men—in a one-hundred-yard radius stopped what they were doing and looked in their direction.

He didn't seem to notice.

"Can you read my mind?" she asked him.

"Only if you allow me," he said mysteriously.

"I don't know what that means."

"It means that you have much more control over your gifts than you believe. It is not an always on or always off experience. There are ways of refining and filtering what you open yourself to."

"You're saying I could get to a point where I don't get messages just walking down the street? Where I don't get *any* messages *ever*?"

Gabe nodded his perfectly shaped head. "If that is what you wish. Yes."

"Great. Teach me that." She flopped into a cross-legged seat in front of him. She could handle these strangers thinking she was a weirdo if it meant never having to pre-witness another murder.

"In order to learn to close yourself off, you must first learn to open yourself up," her spiritual guide said in a magnanimous Disney-quality baritone.

"Fortune cookie me later, Mufasa."

"You really must explain what this fortune cookie is."

"I'll take you for Chinese," she promised. "Hurry up and teach me stuff."

"Your enthusiasm both pleases me and makes me suspicious."

"As it should."

After another long, suspicion-filled look, he closed his eyes. She followed suit.

"Breathe in the fresh air. Fill your lungs with it," Gabe said, his voice low and soothing.

The guy could make a living recording guided meditations, Riley thought.

"Relax into the present moment. Accept it as it is. Feel the sun on your skin."

She felt an ant strolling up her thigh and brushed it away.

"Smell the river, the scents of this world."

She smelled fish and…dog crap? She opened one eye and spotted a cocker spaniel doing her dirty business a few feet away under a tree.

"Now, listen to the sounds that surround you," Gabe continued, clearly immune to feces fumes.

There were sounds. Her breath. The buzz of a lawn mower on the soccer field above them. A kid shrieking from the playground. There was the hum from a fishing boat out on the river. People. Voices. Laughter.

Thoughts.

She felt it in her stomach. The swoop from normal senses upward to a different place. At least this time it wasn't as vertigo inducing. More of a stomach-tickling lift like a hill on a roller coaster...or kissing Nick. Once again, she found herself surrounded by those puffy pastel clouds.

"If I don't get this job, I'm going to lose the house."

"Candy. Candy. Candy. CANDY!"

"Am I raising a future diabetic? This kid is only happy when he's inhaling sugar."

"Eggs. Chocolate chips. Flour. Don't forget the flour."

"Am I a bad parent?"

"That guy over there has thighs bigger than tree trunks. I want to bite them."

"She seemed really stressed last night. Should I be a good husband and do the laundry today? What if I don't do it the right way? Then she'll end up redoing it."

"Why do my ankles itch when I sweat? Is that some symptom of a rare, fatal disease? Should I tell someone about it? What if I keel over from itchy ankle blood clots and no one ever knows why?"

"How do you feel?" Gabe's disembodied voice floated to her.

"I didn't feel sick or dizzy this time," she told him.

"It is because your mind was calm. Exercise is good for the brain," he explained smugly.

"People sure have busy minds," Riley complained as she dodged another onslaught of internal dialogue from a group of dog walkers.

"Don't poop. Don't poop. I forgot the poop bags again. Don't poop. Ah, crap."

"What now?" Riley asked.

"Use this opportunity to define what you want your guides to share with you." His voice echoed ethereally around her cotton candy clouds.

"Explain it like I'm five, Gabe."

"You may choose to have your guides filter the messages you receive."

"Hang on. You mean like a spam filter on email?" She was excited. Could it possibly be that easy?

"I do not know what spam or email is," Echoey Gabe confessed.

"Of course you don't," she said dryly. "Like a bouncer at a club then? They keep the riffraff out."

"Yes. This simile seems appropriate."

She swooped her hand through a pinky, purply cloud. "So all I have to do is tell them that I don't want any more messages ever?"

"If that is what you wish." Echo Gabe sounded disappointed.

Duh. That was all she'd ever wished.

"As long as you do not want any answers to who murdered your neighbor, that is exactly what you should do," he added.

Damn. The sneaky spiritual guide had her there.

"Don't think I don't see what you're doing," she muttered to him.

Okay. She could do this. Probably.

"Hey, spirit guides. It's me, Riley. I'm new here. You showed me meat loaf before and...well, other stuff. I'm gonna need you to do me a favor and start filtering the crap—I mean, the messages I receive. I don't want to hear the thoughts of strangers anymore. Unless it's, like, essentially earth-shattering or whatever."

This felt like a very awkward conversation. But the clouds pulsed brighter around her, and she took that as a yes.

"Cool. Thanks. We can work on it," she said. "So. Since I have you here. Do you know who killed Dickie?"

No spirit guide took shape in her head. But something else did. The floating orb, the one she'd thought she'd seen through her peephole, bobbed into her mind's eye.

"Great. So he was murdered by a circle. Mystery solved," she muttered dryly.

"Be patient with yourself and the message," Gabe advised from somewhere in the ether.

Is there a spirit guide dictionary? she wondered.

The picture in her mind changed. Now, instead of the murder circle, it was a TV. Wait. No. A computer screen. It was playing a video of her ex-husband.

"What. The. Hell?" Did these spirit guides really think Griffin I-can't-switch-the-laundry-from-washer-to-dryer-because-I-might-damage-my-hands Gentry was capable of shooting a man in the head? Griffin was a lot of things. A self-absorbed pseudo celebrity with a Napoleon complex for one. But he wasn't a murderer. He didn't get his hands dirty.

Something tingled in her periphery. Something that felt important, but she couldn't quite reach it, couldn't blow off the cotton candy swamp fog to examine it.

Then the vision was changing again.

Her spirit guides were probably annoyed with her, she guessed.

"Yeah, well. I'm new at this. Cut me some slack."

When the fluffy clouds cleared, Riley saw herself. She was hefting a pitcher of beer and wearing an indecently short plaid skirt. She had a sash draped across her body decorated with pins that looked like...erect penises.

"Oh shit."

And just like that, her cotton candy bubble popped, and Riley found herself sitting in the grass as a parent explained to little Tyler that no, he couldn't just walk up to other kids and take their candy and snacks. The swift return to her body or the present or whatever the hell it was made her feel a little dizzy.

"Gah." She tipped over backward and lay in the grass, staring up at the sky.

"Excellent work, Riley," Gabe said, like she'd just scored a game-winning three-pointer.

"Mmph."

"Did you learn anything of interest?" he asked.

"*Interest* isn't the word," she groaned. "Tell me again. Am I seeing stuff that's destined to happen, or is it something that might happen?"

"That depends on a number of factors."

She gave a strangled groan. She dragged herself to her feet. "Come on. Let's go."

"Excellent! We can run home." He rubbed his bear-paw-sized palms together, obviously insane to enjoy the thought of more exercise.

She would rather cough up money to Uber back. "Have you ever had ice cream?" she asked.

"I have not."

Definitely not human. She steered him in the direction of City Island's ice cream stand. "It's cold and creamy and sweet. I'll buy you a cone before our next stop." There was no way in hell even Ironman Gabe could run after a bellyful of ice cream.

She bought her spiritual guide a chocolate vanilla twist cone and, while he enjoyed his first licks, called Lily to come pick them up. He polished off his treat in record time, so she ordered him a strawberry milkshake, which he promptly and reverently attacked.

"Sweet goddess of the apocalypse. What is this pain?" he demanded, pressing beefy fingers to his right eye as they headed toward the parking lot. "Am I dying?"

Riley tried not to laugh. "It's called brain freeze." It looked like spiritual guide Gabe was human after all.

He bent at the waist. "I do not like this frozen brain."

She snapped a picture of his contorted face. It was the first time she'd ever seen him look anything less than Buddha-like. "Don't worry. It passes quickly," she promised.

Her phone buzzed in her hand.

Nick: How'd psychic school go? Want to meet for a late lunch?

She hadn't expected to hear from him so soon. Especially after his brush-off last night. But she didn't have the energy to hold a grudge. Sleeping with him would have been a monumental mistake. Fun. But definitely a mistake.

Riley: It was interesting. You're not just asking to lure me away from Gabe, are you?

Nick: That only played a 25 percent factor in the invitation.

Riley: I'm not picking out winning lottery numbers for you.

Nick: Okay. We're down to 50 percent. 25 percent of that is a thank-you for last night.

Riley: What's the other 25 percent?

Nick: Maybe I just want to see you again?

Riley: Ha. You're lucky I'm feeling like Chinese for lunch. I have an errand to run first.

Nick: Come by the office when you're done.

Gabe was upright again and glaring at his milkshake like it had betrayed him.

"You have to take it slower until you build up a tolerance for it," she advised.

Advice that could apply to having Nick Santiago smolder his way into her life.

Hesitantly, he hazarded a small sip. He waited a beat and looked at her when he wasn't struck by a second bout of brain pain. "You are very wise."

"How do you feel about hitting a bar with me before we go to lunch?" she asked.

"I would go anywhere you asked me to," he said proudly.

Lily's station wagon cruised into the lot, windows down and big band music pouring out of tinny speakers. "Yoo-hoo!" She waved out the window.

29

F uck you, line item," Nick snarled at his accounting software. If there was one thing he hated more than paperwork, it was accounting paperwork. Technically, none of this crap was due for another week. However, he was looking for an escape from his exhausting mental gymnastics.

Stage One: Think of Riley. Feel good. Want more.

Stage Two: Remember that the last thing he wanted was to be tied down to anything or anybody.

Stage Three: Think about Riley's body.

Stage Four: Recall the hot AF sunset kiss on the bridge followed by hard-on fest back at the mansion.

Stage Five: Dissect the ball-gripping panic he'd felt last night when he thought someone was breaking in to clean up loose ends named Riley.

Stage Six: Vow to stick to the plan. A life free of complications and responsibilities.

Stage Seven: Remember Riley's breasts. Or her laugh. Or those brown eyes going all molten when he kissed her. It was right about this stage that he'd texted her an invite to lunch.

Stage Eight: Repeat.

"Get out of my head, Thorn," he muttered, dragging his focus back to the menial labor.

Once the last receipt was scanned, one last journal entry made, Nick moved on to less boring things. He fired off an email update to his terrifying ex–gym teacher. He'd swung by the vic's mother's apartment that morning only to get covered in cat hair and choked by secondhand smoke. The woman hadn't spoken to her son in six months. Which was typical for their relationship.

Most of her knowledge of her son came from his childhood and teenage years. She had no idea if adult Dickie had any friends or who—besides anyone who met him—would want him dead.

Nick was just downloading photos of a stakeout to his computer when he heard the front door of the office open.

Riley.

He pushed back from the desk and, annoyed at the swoop he felt in his gut, immediately sat back down.

"Nick?" Riley called from the front office.

First she'd given him the hard-on to end all hard-ons last night. Then there was the fear that someone was trying to hurt her. Now, he was giddy over the fact that he was two seconds away from seeing her face.

Get a grip, Santiago.

He slapped himself in the face, then casually responded with, "Please tell me you're good at QuickBooks, and I'll have your babies." Harmless flirting had always been his go-to defense. No one could take a guy seriously if he was never serious. Only now it didn't feel so "harmless."

"I have no experience with books that are fast, and you do not have a uterus." Gabe's supersized frame filled his doorway, blotting out the light like an annoying eclipse.

"What the hell do *you* want, Human Sequoia?" The high of seeing Riley was smashed into a few hundred pieces by Gabe's stupid face. Nick felt like a four-year-old who'd just been told Santa hadn't shown up.

This was exactly why Nick Santiago didn't get involved with sticky women. He couldn't deal with the stupid roller-coaster ride of emotions.

"Surprise!" Riley called out sunnily from behind the behemoth. "Gabe's joining us for lunch."

She peeked around the giant's elbow, grinning.

"We are going to have fortune cookies," Gabe announced happily.

Great. Now he was pissed off at himself for being disappointed he didn't get to have her to himself. "There aren't enough fortune cookies in the state of Pennsylvania for you," he sniped at his competition.

"If you don't stop picking on Gabe, I won't tell you the good news," Riley said, entering his office, hands suspiciously behind her back.

Gabe preened at her defense.

"What good news?" Nick asked, crossing his arms.

"I got you an insider at Nature Girls," she announced.

"You didn't give that purple-haired server cash, did you?" he asked warily.

"Even better," she promised. With a flourish, she produced a plastic dry-cleaning bag from behind her back.

He eyed the Nature Girl uniform she draped over his desk. "You want me to go undercover as a server?"

"That is amusing," Gabe rumbled appreciatively.

Riley rolled her eyes. "*You're* not going undercover. But *I* am. You're looking at Nature Girls's newest server."

"No."

Her brow furrowed. "No, what?" she asked him.

"No. You're not doing it," Nick snapped. Great. The panic was back. If this was what caring about someone felt like, it was stupid and annoying. "What were you thinking?"

"What I was thinking is that you hired me to help you with this case. You need eyes and ears in that bar."

She looked incredulous, like she couldn't possibly come up with a reason why her working in that shithole wasn't the dumbest, most dangerous bad idea ever. "Yeah. Eyes and ears, not tits and ass," he said.

"I find that remark offensive," Gabe chimed in.

"Stay out of this, Sasquatch."

"Don't call him Sasquatch, shithead," Riley shot back.

Nick closed his eyes and took a breath. "Riley, honey, I get what you were trying to do, and I appreciate it. But you're out of your damn mind if you think I'm going to let you prance around in that third-degree-felony-waiting-to-happen outfit."

"*Let me?*" Her scoff almost bent her in half at the waist. "Last I checked, I'm an independent adult. I don't answer to you."

"Oh, don't play that game with me, Thorn. You'll lose if I have to drag you home with me and lock you in a closet until you come to your senses."

"I would break you out of the closet," Gabe promised her.

"Shut up, Gabe."

"Shut up, Nick," Riley snapped.

"I feel it would be wise for you to reconsider your stance. Perhaps you should take the afternoon to consider it. I will be happy to escort Riley to lunch without you," Gabe offered.

"Gabe, I would very much appreciate it if you'd wait outside so I could discuss this with Riley," Nick said through clenched teeth.

The guy gave an imperious pout followed by a little bow. "Of course." He turned to Riley. "If he tries to lock you in a closet, you know how to reach me."

The second the door closed behind him, Nick and Riley started yelling.

"You're not doing this!" he insisted, rounding the desk to stand in front of her.

"You don't get to tell me what to do!"

"Oh, I'll tell you, Thorn. I'll tell you good."

"Then I won't listen, and I'll do it anyway." She was standing toe-to-toe with him, eyes flashing.

Nick was suddenly faced with one pro of relationships that he'd never before considered. If they were actually dating, maybe he could forbid her from disobeying him on this. Of course, that meant she'd have the power to forbid him from doing stuff. But when it came right down to it, what would he really be giving up? It wasn't like he was still twenty-three and partying five nights a week.

No, he was a man with a business. A grocery list. The sports package on his cable. He went to the gym instead of the strip club and drank protein shakes instead of warm morning beers. Hell, he'd actually mailed his cousin's birthday card on time the other day.

"Why the hell would you even consider working in a shithole like that?"

There would be drunk assholes drooling over her in that short skirt. Dirty hands trying to cop a feel. He was back on that roller coaster again, and there was a double loop coming up.

"Gee, I don't know," she said, her tone dripping with sarcasm. "I thought it would look good on my résumé. Why do you think I'm doing it?"

"First of all, you're not doing it. Second, I don't need you helping me by putting yourself in a situation where I'm going to have to kick in that door and hit some assholes in the face with a table!"

She crossed her arms over her chest. Her jaw was set. "You're fighting with me like a real boyfriend. Besides confusing your let's-keep-this-platonic message, you're ignoring how great of an opportunity this is. No one there knows I have any ties to Dickie. I can ask questions and snoop around without raising suspicion."

The pounding in his head was definitely an early warning sign of an aneurysm. He leaned back against the desk in case this really was it and he was about to crumple to the floor. Life would be so much easier if he could just tell everyone what to do. Hang on. He'd found a loophole.

"You're my employee," he announced triumphantly. "And as your *boss*, I forbid you to work there."

"Show me the employment contract where it says you get to tell me how to do my job," she seethed. The heat from her glare was making his headache worse.

"Fine. I'll have Josie do it," he decided. Josie could at least break faces and pick locks. It would be like sending a shark in to swim with a bunch of eels. Riley, on the other hand, was like punting a golden retriever puppy into a mosh pit.

She took one of those slow deep breaths that women took so they wouldn't go nuclear on someone who usually deserved it. "Look," she said. "Josie's trying to get pregnant, which means timetables and ovulation. They already hired me. Why complicate things? Besides, I…" She trailed off, mumbling something.

He leaned in. "What?"

She bit her bottom lip and rolled her eyes. "I had a vision of myself in a Nature Girl uniform this morning," she admitted.

He didn't know how to argue about the psychic thing yet, especially not when she sounded so self-conscious about it.

He grunted instead.

"If it makes you feel any better, they *also* hired Gabe as a bouncer," she informed him, brightening.

As a matter of fact, that did *not* make him feel better. Now Gabe the Great Wall was going to be protecting her while Nick sweated his ass off in the surveillance van.

"I could also tell you that while one of the waitresses interviewed me, I saw a few stacks of cash exchanging hands. A lot more than a bar tab. The bartender wrote it all down in a book behind the register."

He didn't trust himself to say anything. Instead, he glared at the uniform spread across his desk.

"You were right, Nick," Riley said, changing tactics. "Dickie was running some kind of gambling ring through Nature Girls. It's a lead."

It was the only lead. And this was the best option. And that pissed him off.

Hooking his fingers in the waistband of her running shorts, he pulled her into him.

"What are you doing?" she asked, hands settling on his chest.

"Pretending," he said, nuzzling his face against her hair, down the slim column of her neck.

That weird swoop in his gut was back. Holding Riley in his arms felt...damn good.

"You are really sending some mixed messages, dude," she told him.

"I am aware." He nipped at the spot where her neck met her shoulder. Her skin tasted salty.

He couldn't say why he was torturing himself this way. Or why the edge of her underwear at his fingertips was driving him out of his fucking mind. All he knew was he wanted to be touching her.

She drew in a shuddering breath, fingers digging into his shirt.

"Why did they hire Gabe?" he asked, pushing a curling strand of damp hair off her neck.

The smile she flashed him was guilty and made him want to bite her lower lip.

"He told them he was my boyfriend," she confessed.

The bartender had probably shit his pants just looking at Gabe.

"Are you fake two-timing me, Thorn?" he asked softly. He brushed his thumb against her stomach under the hem of her shirt.

"For as many boyfriends as I have, you'd think I'd be seeing more action," she said airily.

"Mmm." It was the only thing he trusted himself to say.

"You're not really mad, are you?" she asked. "It's a good plan."

It *was* a good plan. One he'd probably have come up with on his own, subbing Josie for Riley, of course.

"I'm not mad," Nick lied. "I'm concerned."

"You don't think I can take care of myself?"

The woman had thrown herself down the stairs chasing a murderer with a hockey stick. "Have you ever taken a self-defense class?"

She nodded. "Of course. In Girl Scouts."

Fuck. "Ever fired a gun?"

She shook her head.

He dropped his forehead to hers. "I don't like the idea of you putting yourself in danger and me not being there to step in," he said.

"Gabe will be there," she said.

"Gabe is a muscly teddy bear. *I* want to be there."

"Careful, Santiago. It almost sounds like you care."

He grunted, then sighed.

"Fine. But you're taking precautions." He could teach her how to use a stun gun, give her a few self-defense lessons.

"I'll carry condoms in my apron," Riley joked.

"Har har. Smart-ass. When's your first shift?"

"Monday night."

She was going to be the death of him.

"I'll get you some pepper spray tomorrow. You can practice using it on the Berlin Wall out there."

"Mean."

30

Riley was killing it in the fake boyfriend department. She had one in a skintight tank top stationed just inside the door of the bar and another probably pacing the floor of his office awaiting an emergency text just in case he needed to ride to the rescue.

Right now, the only rescuing Riley needed was getting Rod the bearded bartender to pour beers faster.

She'd waitressed in college in a dive bar and quickly rediscovered her groove. If one could find a groove on the sticky, uneven floor, dodging hairy-knuckled hands and streams of e-cigarette vapor.

Nature Girls seemed to have its own set of rules. There had been no crash course on the tap list. No employee handbook or HR policies, just an apron to wear over her micro miniskirt. No one asked her about the fading bruises on her arms and legs because no one actually gave a shit.

She started her shift with a minute-long lesson on the greasy register system from Betsy, a bleached-blond, large-breasted girl who seemed a little nervous. Her long, fake, yellow-and-black-checkered fingernails made it nearly impossible to use the touch screen.

"If you two are done playing school, I've got orders to send," snarled the purple-haired server when she came up behind them.

Betsy went wide-eyed and clutched at her heart. "You scared the hell out of me, Liz!"

"Do I look like I give a good goddamn?" Liz sneered, fingers flying over the screen.

"Hi, guys!" A perky brunette with a polka-dot bandanna tied rakishly over her ponytail bounced up to them.

"Hey, Deelia," Betsy said, her gaze on the door. Riley guessed she was probably staring at Gabe. It was hard not to.

"You must be the new girl," Deelia said. She leaned in and gave Riley a surprise hug. "I'm Deelia, and I know we're going to be amazing friends."

"Shut the fuck up, Dee," Liz said, pushing through their little circle to get to the bar.

"Love you, too, Lizard," Deelia sang after her.

Deelia didn't look like she belonged here. She looked like a cheerleader barely out of high school.

"This seems like a lot of servers to have on shift for a Monday night," Riley observed. There were maybe twenty tables in the entire bar.

"Liz is supposed to be training you, which means you're on your own anyway. Plus it's numbers night," Deelia said as if that explained everything.

"Numbers night?" Riley asked.

"Riley, you just holler if you need anything," Betsy said vacantly, still watching the door. "I'll be back in the office."

"Betsy's really good at math. Like freakishly good," Deelia said cheerfully. "You wouldn't know it to talk to her. But—oh! Gotta go. I see some regulars!" The girl sashayed over to a table of menacing-looking men with shaved heads and denim jackets with the sleeves cut off. They greeted her like she was their own personal homecoming queen.

"Move your damn fat ankles and go get that table some refills," Liz snapped as she sailed by with a tray full of empties.

Apparently Riley's training was over.

Nature Girls wasn't exactly a warm, fuzzy environment. But it also didn't seem as life-threatening as Nick had made it out to be. Sure, when the yelling got a little loud, she reassured herself by touching the pepper spray in her apron. But no one had thrown any chairs through any windows yet.

It seemed like a typical dive bar.

Most of the clientele was more than a little rough around the edges. There were a few tables of bikers that appeared to be rivals, a few more of some blue-collar workers drinking off a long day. Besides Deelia, the only person who really looked out of place was a generically good-looking guy in navy slacks and a button-down with the sleeves rolled up. Some guys made that kind of look hot. This guy just looked like he was asking for your vote. He kept a baseball hat pulled low over his face.

Between taking orders, delivering plastic cups of cheap alcohol, and dodging groping hands, Riley paid attention. Everyone seemed unusually engrossed in the local racquetball tournament showing on the two screens behind the bar.

She also noticed that about every half hour or so, Betsy would come out and take what looked like a lot of cash from Rod behind the bar. A lot more than what should have been coming in for two-dollar drafts. She itched to text Nick with an update. Something fishy was definitely happening at Nature Girls.

She wondered if she'd made a mistake in tasking her spirit guides to play bouncer to her psychic visions, if maybe they would have been able to help her connect the dots.

The guy in the hat made a beeline for Betsy the next time she poked her head out of the swinging saloon doors that blocked the hallway to the restrooms and the office. Judging from the girl's face—all dewy and nervous—this was who she'd been waiting for all night.

Riley got a break at 10:30 when the crowd started to thin out. The racquetball tournament was over, and the hardest drinkers had been poured into illegal taxis. There were only a dozen or so patrons left in the clouds of cigarette smoke and cheap alcohol fumes.

There was no actual kitchen here—not that she would have braved a food order from it—just stale mixed nuts that God knew how many unsanitary fingers had been in. So she grabbed a soda and headed for an empty table.

"Bite me, Big Mike," Liz snarled over her shoulder at a customer. "Walk your big ass up to the bar and get it yourself." She flopped down in the chair Riley had been aiming for.

"Oh. Hi," Riley said.

"Don't bother getting comfortable here," Liz said, pulling a pack of cigarettes out of her apron pocket and propping her feet up on the second chair Riley set her sights on. Most of the pins on Liz's sash said some version of Fuck You and Fuck Off.

"Don't mind her," Deelia said with a sorority sister smile. "I think she has polycystic ovary syndrome, and it makes her cranky, like, *all* the time." She pulled up two more chairs and gestured for Riley to take one.

"I told you, Dee," Liz said, lighting a cigarette. "Stop with the Google diagnosing. I was born a raging bitch."

Deelia leaned toward Riley and stage-whispered, "Definitely PCOS."

"PMS, smart-ass," Liz shot back.

"Whatever. I knew your rage was lady-parts related," Deelia said.

"Where's Betsy?" Riley asked.

"She left," Liz snapped through a bad-tempered puff of blue smoke.

Riley did a cursory glance around the bar and noted the well-dressed guy was gone too.

"So who's this dead Dickie guy?" Riley asked, taking what she hoped was a casual sip of her drink. "Some of the customers were talking about him."

Deelia opened her mouth, looking like she was going to be helpful, but Liz shut her down. "Who's asking? You a cop?"

Riley looked down at her belly-baring uniform. "Uh, do I look like a cop?"

"People who come in here asking questions are usually cops," Deelia explained.

"Do you get a lot of trouble here?" Riley asked cautiously.

Deelia shrugged. "Some. Nothing Rod or Dickie—before he got murdered—couldn't handle."

"Dickie was *murdered*?" Riley feigned shock.

Liz snorted, then rotated the stud in her nose. "It happens. Who cares?"

"Did he get murdered *here*?" Riley pretended to look for crime scene tape and bloodstains.

"No, silly!" Deelia said with a wave of her manicured hand. "People mostly just get punched or sometimes stabbed here. And it's hardly ever staff."

Hardly ever. Oh good.

"Guy got double-tapped in the head at his place," Liz said, warming to the topic.

"Wow. Recently, right? I think I heard about it," Riley said.

"Last weekend," Deelia said, drawing a pretty pout on her lips with a lip gloss wand.

"Guy was a douche. He was basically running this place into the ground and playing around with some nickel-and-dime betting racket. Who the fuck cares who wins the Dauphin County Over-Fifty Ping-Pong Tournament?" Liz spouted off, jabbing her cigarette in the direction of the bar.

Bingo!

"So someone murdered him over gambling?" Riley feigned concern.

Liz shrugged. "Nah. Probably just stuck his shriveled dick in the wrong vajayjay."

Riley could tell her line of questioning was wearing thin with Liz. "So if Dickie owned this place, and now he's dead, what's going to happen now that he's gone? Are we all out of jobs?"

"Business as usual until we hear from Dickie's partner," Deelia chirped.

Ding ding ding. Winner winner, chicken dinner.

"*If* we hear from him," Liz corrected.

"I've been here six months now," Deelia calculated. "I've never seen the partner, just his creepy henchman."

"That's because he's a *silent* partner," Liz scoffed.

A silent partner and a creepy henchman? Now *that* was a hot new lead. Riley quelled the urge to dance a celebratory boogie in her chair.

"Well, wouldn't that mean I could *see* him; he just wouldn't *say* anything?" Deelia challenged.

"No wonder you failed out of college."

"I *dropped* out. Not failed out. And that's because I was pregnant. If you don't start being nicer, I'm taking you to the clinic so they can look at your ovaries," Deelia shot back.

"Screw Dickie. And screw my ovaries. What I want to know is who's Tall, Black, and Hot over there by the door?" Liz demanded.

Riley looked up, and Gabe waved to her with a toothy grin that disappeared as soon as he remembered he was supposed to look terrifying. She turned back to the girls. "Oh, him? He's my boyfriend," she said.

Liz looked at her with something besides annoyance and borderline disgust now. "How did *you*"—she gave Riley the once-over—"land *him*?"

Every workplace had a Donna.

"I'm really amazing in bed," Riley announced.

"Good for you! Me too. That's how I ended up knocked up," Deelia said with a little what-are-you-gonna-do shrug. She pulled out a phone in a pink bedazzled case and thumbed through her photos, showing Riley a few shots of a chubby toddler. "This is my little snuggle bug."

"Put the turd maker away," Liz said to Deelia. "What's your story, Hot Guy's Girlfriend?"

"Uh, not much of a story. I divorced a cheating loser who took all my stuff and got me fired."

"Men are fucking assholes," Liz said, stubbing out her cigarette on the tabletop.

"Yo, ladies. Get off your asses," Rod grumbled from behind the bar.

"Case in point," Riley sighed.

Liz snorted in appreciation.

By midnight, they were left with a handful of diehards. Riley was so busy trying not to think about how she had to get up in less than seven hours to go to her actual day job, she failed to dodge the fat hand with the knuckle tattoos that darted out.

Drunk Douche had been aiming for her ass and instead plowed his fingers straight into one of the bruises on her hip.

"Ow! Back off!" Her shouted order brought the rest of the bar to a screeching halt.

Douche thought it was funny and went in for another grab. And that was when all hell broke loose.

Gabe started tossing tables, chairs, and a patron or two out of his way to get to her. The drunk customers took offense to being thrown like Scottish cabers. But Riley was too busy winding up to pay them any attention.

She swung her beer-soaked tray like a major league batter, catching the idiot in his yellow gap-toothed grin. The tray connected with a satisfying *fwap*, and his head snapped back before tilting forward in slow motion.

"No touching," she shouted over the noise as the man's forehead hit the table.

A chair flew past her head, and she ducked. Gabe arrived at her side and hefted the drunk like a sack of dirty, disgusting potatoes. "Perhaps you should take cover," he suggested as a pint-sized man in a cowboy hat gave a "Yeehaw!" and launched himself onto a table of bikers.

The bar was a riot in progress. Patrons threw punches and plastic cups like it was the Wild West. Rod climbed over the bar and started swinging a stool like a club.

Riley crawled around the melee and snuck behind the bar.

"Oh, hi there," Deelia greeted her. She and Liz were sitting cross-legged, drinking straight from a bottle of cheap tequila. "Want a drink?"

"Sure. Why not?" Riley was definitely getting fired for this. Nick was going to be pissed. And he was definitely going to say he told her so. "Does this happen often here?" she asked, scooting closer. She spotted the shotgun wedged under the bar top and wondered what kind of trouble would warrant a gun instead of a stool.

Liz swiped the back of her hand over her mouth and passed Riley the bottle. "Once or twice a month."

She took a drink and congratulated herself on not gagging. She wiggled the bottle at Deelia, but the girl wrinkled her nose. "Hand me the Fireball, will you?" she asked, pointing at a bottle above Riley's head.

There was a loud crash followed by a meaty thud. Riley thought she saw an airborne body fly through the saloon doors into the hallway. There was no sign that the battle was slowing. She hoped Gabe was okay. On the outside, he was a big intimidating guy. But on the inside, he was a teddy bear.

Crouching, she peeked over the bar. She spotted her second fake boyfriend holding one of the bikers at arm's length with one hand on his forehead. The little guy in the cowboy hat dangled six inches off the floor from Gabe's left hand.

Gabe looked like he was enjoying himself. Rod, on the other hand, looked even more pissed off. He held one guy by his scraggly beard while kicking another one in the leg.

Reaching for the bottle, Riley quickly scanned the area for any notebooks labeled DICKIE'S ILLEGAL GAMBLING BOOK. No such luck. Just a stack of mail. She wondered if Betsy had taken it into the back office.

A plastic cup sailed in her direction, and she ducked, dragging the bottle and half the envelopes next to the register down with her.

"Dammit!" An arc of warm beer soaked her hair and shoulders before splattering onto the papers that littered the floor.

"Don't worry. Beer is great for your hair," Deelia said, crawling forward to take the whiskey bottle from Riley.

Liz lit a cigarette and stretched her legs out in front of her. "You're totally fired, by the way," she said.

"Me? Why?" Riley asked innocently. She grabbed one of the less filthy bar towels and mopped at her hair. One of the pieces of mail on the floor caught her eye, and her pulse quickened.

Someone must have hit the jukebox, because "Ring of Fire" cut off midchorus and "Straight to Hell" by Darius Rucker kicked on.

Riley waited until Deelia handed Liz the Fireball before stuffing the envelope into her apron pocket.

"You started the fight," Deelia said with a wince. "Now we won't get tips on all those open tabs."

One of the smaller tables flew over the bar, hit one of the ancient TVs, and landed next to Riley.

"Oops. Sorry," she said.

Riley tried the knob on the mansion's front door and rolled her eyes when she found it unlocked.

"I've never been in an altercation before," Gabe said behind her. "I found it exhilarating."

She looked over her shoulder at him. His black tank top and pants were as spotless as they'd been at the beginning of the night. She, on the other hand, was a beer-bedraggled mess. Her hair hung limply over her forehead. An entire beer could probably be wrung out of her stained blouse. And she'd managed to scratch her leg down one thigh on a broken chair arm, scrambling to get out of the bar.

"How is it that I'm the one who looks like she was in a bar fight?" she asked, stepping into the dark foyer.

"Better question. How is it you're texting me that everything's fine when I'm listening to reports of a fight at Nature Girls on the police scanner?"

Riley gave a little shriek.

The foyer lights flicked on, and she found herself face-to-face with a pissed-off Nick.

"What are you doing here?" she said, hoping her heart would restart at any second.

"What in the hell happened to you?" he demanded, taking her by the shoulders.

"Nothing. I'm fine. Everything's fine," she said.

He sniffed, then leaned in closer. "Are you drunk?" he asked, taking another whiff.

"No. Just doused with beer." She tried shrugging out of his grip, but he wasn't having it.

"You were supposed to keep an eye on her," he growled at Gabe.

"I kept both eyes on Riley," Gabe told him. "I also punched many faces defending her honor."

"I told you this was a stupid fucking idea," Nick complained.

"It was fine until the bar fight," she shot back.

"You got in a bar fight while working undercover?"

"Riley *started* the bar fight," Gabe corrected him. "She hit a man in the face with a tray, and I got to throw him in the gutter."

Nick let her go and pinched his nose between his fingers before starting to count backward from ten. When he got to one, he shook his head and started over again. "This is why I don't work with amateurs," he muttered in the middle of his third countdown.

"Excuse me!" Riley was offended. "This *amateur* confirmed there's illegal gambling happening there and brought you this." She fished the envelope out of her apron and slapped it to Nick's chest.

"What's this?"

"The LLC name of Dickie's *silent partner.* You're welcome. Now, if you gentlemen will excuse me, I'm going to go take a shower and get a few hours of sleep before I have to get up for my real job. So you"—she drilled Nick in the shoulder with her finger—"can go home and thank me tomorrow."

She trudged up the stairs.

"I hope you're proud of yourself, because that was your last shift," Nick called after her.

"Indeed. Riley was fired for starting the altercation," Gabe told him.

Riley brought both hands above her shoulders and extended her middle fingers. "You're welcome," she sang out.

31

Nick leaned against the fender of his SUV and waited for Riley to walk out the door. Sullivan, Hartfield, Aster, Reynolds, and Tuffley's offices were crammed into conjoined row houses. The facades clashed. The floor levels didn't line up. And judging from the looks on every exiting employee's face, the environment was a soul-sucking black hole of time cards, micromanagement, and watercooler drama.

He counted his blessings. Unlike the guy with the mustard stain on his embroidered SHART button-down, Nick had caught an early workout at the gym and then spent the afternoon playing armed security for a lawyer downtown who had pissed off an aggressive interior designer in the same building.

Behind Mustard Stain, the door opened again, and out stepped Riley. She was wearing what Nick considered to be the office uniform—muted, depressing tones that covered every inch of interesting body real estate.

She whipped off her mud-brown cardigan, revealing a sleeveless, high-necked shirt, and lifted her pretty face to the sky like a prisoner enjoying her daily allotment of fresh air. Little did she know, he was here to rescue her.

Riley spotted him and stutter-stepped.

He grinned with just a hint of arrogance. He liked having that effect on her. It made up for the unsettling anticipation he felt every time he knew he was going to see her. It was like moths or manly fire-breathing dragons in his gut. They probably would have gotten bigger and floppier had she smiled at him. But she was giving him a cool glare.

"Hey, beautiful," he said, opening his passenger door for her.

"What are you doing here?" she asked. "Run out of other people to yell at and overreact to?"

Since another group of hamsters freed from the wheel walked out behind her, he decided to press his luck. He reached for her and tugged her in for a quick, hard kiss.

A middle-aged man in a lemon-yellow short-sleeved dress shirt made kissy noises as he passed them.

"Hi," Nick said, drawing back.

This time, Riley's glare came from slightly dazed eyes. Damn. He was losing his touch. Her knees should have been quivering. He was about to give it the ol' college try when she slapped a hand to his chest.

"What do you want, Nick?" she asked, extricating herself from his grip.

"I thought I'd take you for coffee."

"After you apologize for acting like a child, of course."

"Sure. After *you* apologize for taking unnecessary risks."

"I don't feel like coffee."

"What do you feel like?" he asked.

"Punching you in the face."

"Come on, Thorn. Don't be like that."

"Sorry, but once you've hit one guy in the face with a tray, you're filled with bloodlust."

"Let's talk about it over coffee," he suggested, upping the charm and flashing his dimples.

"Nope."

"Come on. I'll buy, *and* I'll pay you for your time."

"You do realize you're being completely transparent, right? You want something from me, and it's not a coffee date."

227

The whole psychic thing made it a lot harder to charm his way around her defenses.

"Fine. I'm meeting Jonesy for coffee in fifteen minutes."

"Ex-girlfriend Sergeant Jones?" Riley asked, at least looking mildly interested now.

"I wouldn't say *girlfriend*," he hedged.

She started to walk away.

"Okay. Fine," he said, stepping in front of her to thwart her exit. "I'm sorry for yelling at you. Jonesy and I never had the relationship talk, so you're welcome to call her an ex-girlfriend even though I wouldn't and she wouldn't. I want you to go with me because people tell you things they wouldn't tell anyone else."

She turned and patted him on the face. Hard. It was one step down from a slap. "There. That wasn't so hard, now was it?"

He grinned. "Is that a yes?"

"What are you trying to get out of her?" she asked.

He shrugged. "I want to know where Weber's investigation stands."

She fished a pair of sunglasses out of her bag and put them on. "And you think she'll tell us."

"I think she'll reassure my fiancée that the cops are doing everything they can to catch the killer."

"Please." She snorted. "I can tell you what the cops are doing. Detective Weber's been following me like I'm a homicidal maniac ready to kill again."

"Following you?" Nick's protective hackles were up. "When? Where?"

"He followed me the first time I went to your office. I saw him again when I went to yoga, and he was outside the hot dog place when I took my lunch break today."

"I'm gonna kick his ass," he muttered.

"Yeah. Pretty sure that's illegal," she pointed out.

"He knows you didn't have anything to do with Dickie's murder," Nick snapped.

"Keep it down, big mouth," she said, looking over her

shoulder to make sure none of her coworkers were within eaves-dropping range. "He knows that I had prior knowledge."

"You're a psychic, not a murderer."

"Will you shut up?" she hissed.

He took out his phone and stabbed at the screen.

"What are you doing?" she asked.

"I'm canceling coffee with Jonesy so I can go kick Weber's ass."

Riley groaned and actually stomped her foot. "No. You're not. Let's go get some stupid coffee."

"You're just saying that so I won't kill Weber."

She sighed. "Well, we can't *both* be murder suspects, now can we?"

———

Nick found a small parking space two blocks from the café and stuffed his SUV into it.

"Wait. Where are we going?" Riley asked, looking stricken in the passenger seat.

"Little Amps," he told her.

"I changed my mind," she said. "You can go beat up Detective Weber."

"What? You have a thing against good coffee?"

"No, smart-ass. I love this place."

"Then what's the problem?" he asked.

"The last time I was here, I gave the barista a warning. From her dead great-grandmother."

He laughed. "Hang on! *You* were the mysterious stranger who told the girl at the register to get her lymph nodes checked?"

She groaned. "You heard about that?"

"The entire city did. It was all over the news. What's the problem? You and the dead grandma were right," he pointed out.

"Yeah. And now, if I go back in there, I'm the weirdo who talks to dead grandmas. It's bad enough dealing with it on my own. I don't need a bunch of people asking me to seek out their dead relatives," she complained.

"So you're not looking to land your own reality TV show?" he teased.

She growled. Riley Thorn was really fucking cute when she was pissed off.

"Relax, I've got this covered."

Two minutes later, they slunk into the café with Riley wearing a Santiago Investigations ball cap low over her eyes with her dark hair fed through the back in a tail.

She relaxed microscopically when she looked behind the register, and Nick guessed the barista she feared wasn't working.

Sergeant Mabel Jones was waiting for them at a too-small table in the back of the shop. She looked fresh and relaxed in hot-pink workout pants and a T-shirt. She might have been out of uniform, but the way she'd put her back to the corner and eyed the room screamed "cop."

"Jonesy," Nick said, greeting her with a hug.

"Hey, Nicky. Riley, good to see you."

"Hi," Riley said, taking a seat.

Nick took the chair between the two women.

"I still can't wrap my head around it. Nick 'the Forehead' Santiago finally settling down. We had bets around the precinct that it was fake," Jones said.

He closed his hand around Riley's knee and gave her a not-too-gentle squeeze. "Real deal here," he insisted.

"Good for you," Jones said, picking up her fancy frothy beverage.

"I'll make the coffee run," Nick told Riley.

"Thanks. I'll take…" She glanced at Jones and smiled. "The usual."

Another reason why he didn't date. Being single carried with it zero requirements to memorize anyone's coffee order or shoe size or birthday. If Riley wanted something specific, she should have told him. Now she'd have to learn her lesson.

Wandering up to the counter, he ordered himself a black coffee and Riley a pink unicorn frappe-something with whipped cream and sprinkles. There was a collection jar next to the register to help with the pink-haired barista's medical expenses. He dropped a ten in the jar.

The women were leaning in now, their voices low. It occurred to him the kind of conversation that could be happening between an ex-sex partner and a perceived current one. Jones burst out laughing and looked his way.

Dammit.

His order came up, and Nick hustled the drinks back to the table. He plopped the unicorn concoction down in front of Riley.

"You're so funny," she said, smiling sweetly as she swapped the drinks. She took a smug sip of *his* black coffee. "Sergeant Jones was just telling me a few stories about when you were a cop."

"Oh great," he said.

"I was telling Riley about the time you tripped over a dog during a foot chase, got pissed off, and tackled the suspect in a kiddie pool," Jones said, clearly enjoying herself. "It popped, and water went *everywhere!*"

"Enough about me," he said. "Jonesy, tell Riley what's going on with the investigation so she can start sleeping again at night."

"I don't have a lot of information," Jones said with guarded sympathy. Just because Nick had once been a cop, it didn't earn him an open line of communication. "I will say this isn't throwing any red flags where we have concerns that the killer would come back. It looks like Dickie was the intended victim."

"Any motives yet?" Nick pushed. He stroked a hand over Riley's back. He didn't know if it was acting or instinct that had her leaning into him, but he kinda liked it.

"Detective Weber hasn't been...forthcoming," Riley added.

"Can't say as I blame him," Jones said, shooting Nick a pointed look.

"Is that why he's treating my fiancée like a suspect?" he shot back. He forgot what he was doing and took a sip of unicorn garbage.

The sugar exploded on his tongue. *Is instant diabetes a thing?*

"Nicky, you know I can't comment on that," Jones said.

"If Detective Douchebag is spending his time following her around, he's not looking for the actual killer," he said.

Riley put her hand on his knee, and he realized he'd been shaking his leg.

"I think what Nick is trying to say," Riley said, giving him a pointed look, "is that I didn't have anything to do with this, and if Detective Weber is only looking at me, the real criminal is out there possibly murdering more uncles."

He could see Jones softening.

"Look, Detective Weber is just doing his due diligence. Honestly, homicide is swamped. I'm not saying that the department isn't concerned that your uncle was killed," she said. "But we've got a heavy caseload right now."

Riley nodded but didn't speak.

Jones pursed her lips. "If it makes you feel any better, we are pursuing other leads."

"Of the illegal gambling kind?" Nick asked, all charm now.

"I heard you got hired. You're not going to turn this into some pissing contest, are you, Santiago?" she asked wearily.

"If I happen to solve the case first, it's not really a contest, is it?"

"So where's the ring?" Jones asked, changing the subject. "Sergeant Fillmore says there's no ring because you're lying, and Hooten in the coroner's office says it's because you're a cheap bastard."

Nick, in the middle of his second foray into diabetes, sputtered whipped cream all over the table.

Riley handed him a napkin. "It's getting sized. He didn't know what my ring size was and got a band that would fit a linebacker," she said.

"That's so on-brand for Nicky," Jones agreed.

"So why do you call him the Forehead?" Riley asked.

"Okay. No more getting to know each other," Nick snapped. "I forbid you from speaking to each other."

The women were still laughing when a new voice observed, "Isn't this cozy?"

Jones's eyes widened when Detective Dickhead pulled up a chair.

Fuck.

"What are you doing, Web? Stalking my fiancée some more?" Nick asked.

"Maybe," Weber said, straightening his stupid suit jacket.

"If she's your main suspect, you are way behind, my friend," Nick scoffed at his ex-partner.

"I'm not your friend, *pal*," Weber snapped. "And my investigation is none of your business."

"If you were half the cop you pretend to be, you'd know she's clean," Nick snapped. "Looks like I took the pretty face *and* the brains when I left the force."

That point landed squarely in a sore spot, he thought with satisfaction as Weber's eyes narrowed.

"Let me remind you again that if you get in my way with this investigation, I'll have no problem throwing a few charges your way."

"I'm not the one in your way, Detective Derp. I'm way ahead of you."

"Careful there, Santiago. Be very careful," Weber warned, his tone steely.

"Hey, who's Beth?" Riley piped up, her nose twitching.

"Oh shit," Jones sang under her breath.

Both Nick and Weber froze. They turned to look at Riley. She was blinking rapidly as if she'd just woken up from a nap. Nick was new to this pretend relationship, but he still recognized the tell. She was getting some message from the beyond. It made his intestines turn to ice.

"Look at the time," Jones said, sparing her bare wrist a glance like she was looking at an invisible watch. "I gotta go very far from here."

"We'll discuss this later, Sergeant," Weber assured Jones.

"Oh, I figured," she said and hauled ass for the door.

"Look, she wasn't gossiping about your half-assed investigation," Nick said. "Jonesy's a good cop."

"What would you know about being a good cop?" Weber sneered.

Nick wanted to throw his unicorn drink in the man's face and then follow it up with a nice right hook.

"I know that following Riley around like she's some kind of criminal is a complete waste of your fucking time. I know that Frick was running a little action on the side out of his bar. And I know he didn't keep the nicest company."

"Yeah? Like Fat Tony. Did you also know that Frick was up to his bloodshot eyeballs in debt to him?" Weber shot back.

"Please. Fat Tony doesn't assassinate debtors," Nick scoffed. "I'd say you're losing your edge, but you never had one."

"Fuck off, loser."

"Make me, shitweasel."

Nick didn't realize they were standing toe-to-toe until Riley shoved her way between them. "Can you both try to remember that you're adults? With an audience. Everyone is staring," she hissed.

The café had gone so quiet that they could hear the folksy guitar music twanging from the speakers. Every pair of eyes was glued to them.

Nick took a mock bow. "Thank you, ladies and gentlemen. If you'd like to see more from our improv troop, come on out to Theater Harrisburg on Tuesdays at noon."

There was confused, scattered applause.

Weber wasn't amused. "Stay out of my way, Nick. And, Ms. Thorn?" He shifted his attention to Riley. "If you step one toe out of line, I will bring you in, and we'll have a nice long chat," he said.

She looked like she was going to barf.

"You made your point, asshole. You've harassed your *witness*. Move the fuck along." Nick stayed on his feet and watched the detective leave. Once he was out the door, he sank back in his chair and took a long hit of pink and green sugar. "I fucking hate that guy."

"Who's Fat Tony? Who's Beth?"

Nick drummed his fingers on the table and stared at a spot over Riley's head. "Fat Tony owns the casino. He's got a history as a biggish bookie. Much bigger fish than Dickie. He's been known to rough up a guy every now and then, but he's a businessman at heart. He wouldn't kill over a debt. He'd find a way to squeeze him dry."

She was waiting for him to answer the second question. But that was a topic not even a psychic could pry out of him.

"Come on. Let's get out of here," he said, suddenly in a hurry to be anywhere but here. He had a new loose thread to pull on. It was time to see what would unravel.

She stood up and gathered her purse. He decided to take his frappe-whatever with him.

They walked out, leaving most of the café staring after them. "Ha. I just realized. Now you can't come back here either," Riley said, grinning at him.

32

The front parlor of the mansion was quiet as Riley worked her way through the yoga studio's social media tasks on the computer. She'd worked at SHART for nine excruciating hours, then squeezed in a meditation with Gabe, during which she accidentally tuned into both Gabe's unconditional worship of her and Lily's obsession with men's butts.

She gave a shudder at the memory and tried to focus on the task at hand. She scheduled two more posts, then updated the spreadsheet on followers and interaction.

Her sister's social media audience was growing by leaps and bounds. Every week, her free live class drew a bigger audience, garnering more followers and shares. Her Instagram account was a carefully curated collection of beautiful pictures and uplifting yogic sentiments.

Wander's star was rising. And Riley's was, well, dim and hard to see.

She was proud of her sister. Not that she understood the desire to step into the spotlight. During their high school careers, Wander had starred in *Annie Get Your Gun*. Riley had been satisfied to make her contributions to the stage crew, hiding out in the wings, rearranging sets only after the spotlights went dark.

Wander had been head cheerleader and homecoming queen. Riley had been second string on the volleyball team and went to Denny's with her flannel-wearing antihero friends instead of the prom.

The pattern continued into adulthood. Now, while Wander experienced steady growth and marched her way toward her goals, the other Thorn sister sometimes felt as stagnant as pond water.

But Riley was proud of Wander's celebrity. Even if it made her life seem a little quiet by comparison. *Okay*, she thought, eyeing the empty room. *Maybe not quiet. More like tomblike.*

A squeaky floorboard and a quiet fart in the hallway ruined her tomb.

"Mrs. Penny?"

Her neighbor poked her head guiltily around the corner. "Oh, hello, dear," she said. It was the same phony grandmother tone she used when she was pretending to be harmless. She was dressed in head-to-toe black. She had a knit cap covering her hair. Even her cane was wrapped in black tape.

"Going somewhere?" Riley asked. She didn't have to be psychic to be immediately suspicious.

"I just have a teensy errand to run," the woman announced.

"Uh-huh. You're not driving, are you?" Mrs. Penny's license had been suspended two years ago after an unfortunate and literal run-in with a city bus.

Mrs. Penny hid her car keys behind her back. "Who, me? Nope. As a matter of fact, I was coming down to ask you if you'd mind giving me a ride."

Lies!

Riley glanced at the horrendous gilt clock on the mantel that ticked noisily. "Are you sure this errand can't wait until tomorrow?"

"Positive. It's just a quickie," her neighbor promised.

Scarred from her accidental reading of Lily, Riley hoped to God it wasn't an *actual* quickie.

"Can I go like this?" she asked, gesturing at her pink

flamingo pajama shorts—a birthday gift from her nieces—and an ancient Hines Ward Pittsburgh Steelers jersey.

"You won't even have to get out of the car," Mrs. Penny promised.

"I'll get my keys," Riley said.

Five minutes later, Mrs. Penny was directing Riley into the heart of the city. The capitol complex was lit up in red, white, and blue in anticipation of the Fourth of July. There would be a 5K, which Riley wouldn't run, and fireworks, which she might see.

Maybe she could talk her parents into going? Or maybe Nick would want to re-create their Walnut Street Bridge kiss?

More likely, Nick would have already solved the murder and vanished from her life.

Or maybe she'd be in jail because being a psychic was a crime.

That was a lot of maybes.

Riley followed the directions and felt her suspicions rise when Mrs. Penny had her turn onto State Street. The dignified glamour of the capitol building faded in the rearview mirror. Here houses got shabbier, churches more run-down. Streetlights cast uneven circles of light on corners.

"What kind of errand is this?" Riley asked when Mrs. Penny had her taking a left on Seventeenth Street.

"Where's that sexy boyfriend of yours? Haven't seen him around lately," Mrs. Penny retorted. "You two fighting? Is he bad in bed?"

Neither one of them felt like answering the questions.

"You can pull over here," the woman said, pointing to an open spot.

Riley pulled up to the curb behind a bumper-less Ford Taurus on blocks. The house next to them desperately needed a new paint job, but there were flowers in planters on the front porch, the exterior light worked, and there was an actual welcome mat at the door.

The little homey touches made Riley feel a little better… until Mrs. Penny opened her mouth again.

"Now, you just wait here with the engine running, and I'll be right back."

"Whoa. Whoa. Whoa. Hang on there. You want me to keep the engine running?"

"Back in a jiffy," Mrs. Penny announced. She yanked the black cap down over her face and peered at Riley through eyeholes.

"Oh shit."

But Mrs. Penny was gone, slipping out of the Jeep and into the night with her cane.

"Shit. Shit. Shit," Riley muttered, wrestling her seat belt off. "My eighty-year-old neighbor just put on a ski mask in the middle of Harrisburg."

She jumped out of the vehicle.

"Mrs. Penny!" she hissed, jogging after the short round figure.

Other shadowy figures were coming into focus on the dark sidewalk at the end of the block. They were converging around her neighbor.

"Oh my God. She's going to get murdered. Detective Weber is never going to believe I didn't have anything to do with *two* murders," Riley muttered, running at full speed now. She elbowed her way into the center of the silent, shadowy mob. "Back off!" she said, putting Mrs. Penny at her back.

"Yo, Stabby McGee. Who is this weirdo?" The voice was nasally and pubescent. It came from a tall, skinny figure in what Riley could only assume was an all-black onesie. He was wearing an Elsa mask.

Mrs. Penny's eyes rolled within the holes of her ski mask. "That's just my getaway driver."

Stabby McGee? Getaway driver? What fresh hell had she stumbled into tonight?

"Uh, Stabby? Can I have a word?" Riley asked, tugging on Mrs. Penny's sleeve.

"Gimme a minute, guys," Mrs. Penny said.

Riley dragged Mrs. Penny away from her army of darkness.

"What in the hell are you doing?" Riley demanded.

"Relax." Mrs. Penny drew out the word like someone who was not worried enough about the consequences of their actions.

"Are you doing something *illegal*?" Riley hissed.

"Look, kid, it's just a quick gig. No big deal."

"A gig? No big deal? Are you in a band?"

"Ha! Yeah. A band. Now, don't you worry your pretty little head. You just sit tight. Keep the engine running. Play some *Tetris*." Mrs. Penny patted Riley on her arm and then pushed her way back into the center of her masked crew. "Everyone understand the plan?" she asked.

Heads nodded. A chorus of assent was echoed in many voices and accents.

Riley frantically scanned the dark sidewalk for band instruments and came up dry.

"Let's get this show on the road," Mrs. Penny, a.k.a. Stabby, ordered.

A man whose beard was poking out from under his Zorro mask snapped together two ends of what looked like a dog leash.

"Maybe we should all go home," Riley began. But the dozen or so weird ninjas ignored her and filed down the ribbon-skinny walkway between two houses.

Please be in a band, Riley chanted in her head. When that didn't allay her fears, she started whispering it out loud as she paced between her vehicle and the mouth of the walkway where Mrs. Penny had disappeared.

The home on the corner had been a nice brick two-story at one point. Now, it had plywood nailed over its windows and piles of trash spilling off its narrow front porch. The door was dented as if by an insistent steel-toed boot. The only house number left was an upside-down seven.

The rest of the neighborhood wasn't bad. A little run-down, a lot in need of some maintenance. But it looked like people lived there. Except for the boarded-up house on the corner that looked like an invading blight.

Riley paced the sidewalk and debated. She should follow

Mrs. Penny. She should go home. She should have pretended not to hear the fart in the hall.

Work—the thing that actually paid her bills—started in just a few hours, and once again, she was out too late for a good night's sleep. She was getting really tired of being really tired.

She heard a sound coming from the back of the house. Breaking glass. Followed by...barking?

A *lot* of barking.

Porch lights flickered on up and down the block.

"Oh, come *on*," she muttered. With one last look at the house that was giving off creepy vibes—and not like hilarious Scooby-Doo-bad-guy mansion vibes—she charged down the walkway.

She was wading through debris in the dark when the shouting started. It was followed immediately by the kind of commotion the human brain can't identify. Through the dim light pouring from the windows of the neighboring house, she could just make out the wooden gate as it swung open toward her.

Something big and black bounded out.

"Ahh!" she shrieked.

The shape raced past her at a dead run. It was too short and quick to be a bear, she decided. Also, it hadn't paused to eat her face. Werewolf? But it wasn't a full moon, and as far as she knew, werewolves weren't actually a thing. Though Gabe hadn't officially answered her question.

Screwing up her courage, she reached for the gate. Two more bulky shadows exploded forth, squeezing their way through the opening. The wood of the gate caught her in the chest and smooshed her against the brick.

As the wind left her lungs, she made a collapsing accordion noise. One of the dark shapes paused, then licked her bare knee before giving a happy bark and rocketing toward the street.

Dogs?

Floodlights went on in the backyard, and Riley had just enough time to jump out of the way of an entire parade of canines racing toward freedom. Tall ones. Fat ones. Fluffy ones. All barking and howling joyfully as they whizzed past.

There was shouting coming from inside the villain house and out on the street.

Riley waited a beat, making sure there wasn't a second canine wave before stepping around the gate.

She should have waited longer.

Massive paws the size of her mother's tea leaf reading saucers hit her in the chest. She was already off-balance when her flip-flopped foot slipped on a crushed beer can.

She went down hard, landing on her ass. The rocket of fur landed on top of her with all million pounds.

"Gah! I need to stop breaking falls," she wheezed. The dog—dear God, please let it be a dog—slurped her face with a long tongue.

She heard the distant wail of sirens.

"Five-oh's coming!" Mrs. Penny burst through the gate, sending it bouncing off Riley's prone body.

"Ouch!"

"Stop fooling around and get your ass up," Mrs. Penny yelled, tottering from using her cane to shove garbage out of the way.

Someone with a headlamp dragged Riley to her feet. The giant lug of a dog stretched leisurely at her side.

She limped her way toward the mouth of the walkway. There was a howling coming from the house, but it sounded… human.

"What's that sound?" she asked.

"It's the sound of vigilante justice," a neighbor in silk boxer shorts and a tank top said as he hung over the railing on his front porch. "Wooooo!" He hoisted a beer in the air.

"Woooo!" repeated the crowd of pajamaed neighbors who had gathered in the street.

"Nobody saw anything," Mrs. Penny shouted to the bystanders.

The growing crowd started applauding.

Riley could see better now that they were under a street-light. The dog glued to her side was long-legged and long-bodied like a lion. He had short reddish fur and a head roughly the size of a wrecking ball. Judging by some dangling anatomy, he was most definitely a he.

"Why are they clapping?" she asked, wondering if she should fashion some kind of leash for the hulking lion dog.

"Because we're friggin' heroes," the androgynous ninja next to her announced.

"Yeah, we just busted up a half-assed puppy mill that some asshole was going to turn into a dogfighting ring!" the nasally teenager in the onesie squeaked.

"We gotta go now," a taller shadow announced in a rumbly church-choir baritone.

"Everybody scatter!" Mrs. Penny ordered before turning and hightailing it toward the crosswalk.

The sirens were rapidly approaching, and Riley could see the flash of lights coming from a few blocks away.

"Wait!" she yelled, flip-flopping after her neighbor, who was jogging in the opposite direction of their getaway vehicle.

Scatter apparently meant clump together suspiciously. Eight vigilantes crowded around them like flies on dog poop, and together they jog-limped across the street.

"You can cut through our backyard and down the alley," said a woman in an oversize Trans-Siberian Orchestra T-shirt, waving from the front stoop of her house.

"We'll keep 'em occupied," another neighbor promised.

"Thanks," Mrs. Penny said, pushing one of the ninjas through the fence gate. "And don't let them run plates on that Jeep down the block!"

Riley and her four-legged friend caught up with Mrs. Penny and four other ninjas in the alley. "We're going the wrong way," she huffed. Why was she more winded than her eighty-year-old charge and the French-kissing dog? She really needed to take Gabe's offer of actual personal training more seriously. "My Jeep is back there."

"Your Jeep is blocked by at least four police cruisers," Mrs. Penny said, throwing herself over a short fence into another yard. The other ninjas followed suit.

The dog looked at Riley. She looked at the dog. Riley shrugged.

They both hopped over into the yard, ducking against the run-down garage with Mrs. Penny when the back porch light came on.

Heads down, they snuck out of one yard and into another. Mrs. Penny waved her arm and pointed. "Let's go down another block before we start breaking car windows."

"No one is breaking any car windows," Riley hissed.

They wove their way through backyards and alleys, vigilantes peeling off and vanishing into the shadows.

"Stay in the car and keep the engine running. How hard is it to follow instructions?" her neighbor grumbled, peering over a forsythia bush.

"I thought you were in trouble," Riley said defensively from her crouched position behind a couch someone left in the alley. She wasn't going to feel guilty. *She* wasn't the one being chased by the cops. Well, technically, she was.

"Yeah, well, now I *am* in trouble, smarty-pants."

"Yeah." Teenage Ninja Elsa poked his head out of a half-dead arborvitae.

Riley gave a little shriek, but it was muffled by a small hand that closed over her mouth.

"Quiet down," Mrs. Penny said. She gave a nod to the figure behind Riley, and the hand disappeared. "Now, how are we getting home without getting arrested?"

33

T he things I do for you, Thorn."
          Nick in sleep pants, a T-shirt, and bare feet—because he'd accidentally grabbed two left sneakers off the floor—navigated his SUV onto the Harvey Taylor Bridge and headed for the West Shore.

Riley was in the passenger seat, looking like someone had yanked her out of bed and dragged her into the night. Her flamingo shorts were pretty damn cute. But her old bruises were covered in fresh new scrapes. She had two muddy paw prints on the boob region of her Hines Ward jersey and was missing a flip-flop.

There were three wannabe ninjas crammed in his back seat, only one he recognized. Despite her ski mask, the giant glasses and peek of purple hair gave her away as Riley's neighbor Mrs. Penny. The other two were still masked. The short, dainty one wore a Richard Nixon mask. The tall guy in the onesie was wearing an Elsa from *Frozen* mask. Then there was the lion-sized dog in the hatch who was slobbering on one of his left Nikes.

Life was weird sometimes. And he was pretty damn glad he'd answered the phone when it rang.

"So," he began. "Who wants to explain why I'm playing Uber for a bunch of kung fu movie extras?"

There was a comical silence as the three back seat passengers looked at each other.

"Who wants to explain why you're supposed to sell life insurance, yet you have a PI license?" Mrs. Penny sniffed.

The quiet ninja snickered.

"You told them I sold life insurance?" Nick asked Riley.

She shrugged. "They put me on the spot. I didn't know what to say."

The police scanner on the dashboard squawked. "Individual found in basement locked inside a dog crate," a monotonous voice stated.

Riley turned in her seat. "You put a *human being* in a dog crate?" Her voice rose high enough at the end of the sentence to have the dog's giant head popping up over the tall, skinny ninja's shoulder, sneaker dangling from his mouth.

"Don't get your panties in a twist," Mrs. Penny snorted.

"Yeah, that dude was a bullet sponge," the skinny ninja in the onesie squeaked.

"You shot him?" Riley screeched.

"No." Mrs. Penny snorted.

"Translation?" Nick asked dryly.

"The guy's a half-assed criminal who the cops have no interest in," Mrs. Penny explained. "He moves in with his girlfriend, who lives with her grandmother. Granddaughter has shit taste in men. He's a real winner. Selling stolen prescription meds out the back door, starting fights with the neighbors. Guy won't leave. Brings a bunch of other half-assed criminals home to party. Girlfriend and grandma move out. The guy's still squatting there, trashing the house, terrorizing the neighborhood, and decides to go into the dog-breeding business."

"Yeah, he starts picking up all the free-to-a-good-home dogs on Craigslist and locking them in cages in the basement," Squeaky added.

"Dumb motherfucker," Mrs. Penny said succinctly.

Nick couldn't help but agree.

The silent ninja nodded too.

"When it turns out half the dogs are already fixed, he decides he'll start a dogfighting ring instead," Squeaky squeaked indignantly.

"A dogfighting ring?" Riley was appalled.

The brute in the hatch blinked at Nick in the rearview mirror.

A pungent aroma with tear gas qualities tickled Nick's nose.

"For the love of God. What is that smell?" he gasped. His throat burned. His nose hairs felt like they'd been seared.

The vigilante ninjas covered their already mask-clad noses.

"Did someone just shit out a skunk?" Mrs. Penny asked.

Nick rolled down the window and stuck his head out into the blast of fresh night air until his eyes stopped stinging.

"No poop. Just dog farts," Squeaky announced cheerfully.

"He smells like my uncle Burt after pork and sauerkraut on New Year's Day," Nick complained.

Riley had her jersey pulled up to her eyeballs. All the windows in the vehicle were down now, and the stench was beginning to dissipate.

"So you just decided to step in and take justice into your own hands?" Riley demanded through her shirt. Nick could hear the good girl horror in her tone.

"Someone had to do something," Squeaky squeaked.

"That someone doesn't have to be *you*," she said, pointing at Mrs. Penny. "Why didn't you just call the police?"

Mrs. Penny's eyeballs rolled violently behind her glasses and ski mask. "You think we didn't try that? The grandma and the girlfriend called. Cops said it was a family dispute, and they should get a lawyer. The neighbors called with noise complaints and reports of criminal activity. Cops said they'd look into it. Never did."

"Did you give them a chance to look into it?" Riley asked, pulling her shirt off her face.

"We gave them two weeks to get their asses in gear and

poke around. Nothing. Nada. Zip," Mrs. Penny said. "What's Alma supposed to do? Just let this asshole destroy her house from the inside out? What are those neighbors supposed to do, let him sell meth on their block? The bacon wasn't gonna do anything."

"So we stepped in," Squeaky said with pride.

Mrs. Penny gave him an approving nod. "Exactly. You think we started out running ops?" she said to Riley. "No! We were feeding the cops information."

"And they weren't doing a darn thing," Squeaky interjected.

The silent ninja nodded vehemently.

"Maybe they were busy investigating other cases," Riley said lamely.

Nick found her faith in a broken system oddly endearing.

"Well, they sure as hell weren't investigating the Meiser Jewelry robbery. That was two dickweeds from Baltimore in a car they stole in York. We sent the cops names, photos, and last known addresses. And what did they do?"

"Nothing," Squeaky said derisively.

"How about the fire on Briggs Street? That was arson. Gang related. We had two eyewitnesses who described the whole thing. And what happened?"

Richard Nixon held up a gloved index finger and thumb in a circle.

"That's right," Mrs. Penny said. "Big fat nada. Kid is still strutting around, vaping like a dumbass and hassling store owners for protection money. And don't even get me started on the hit-and-run by Mount Calvary Cemetery."

Squeaky snorted in a perfect imitation of his elderly leader. "Yeah, don't get her started."

But she was already started.

"We handed that one to them on a silver platter, and they still couldn't get off their asses to investigate. Hell, we sent them footage from one of them there video doorbell things from across the street. Stupid fucking guy gets out of the car to make sure the vic's dead. He's got his name tattooed on his

248

forearm. Plain as day. Cops never even brought him in for questioning."

Nick had a bad feeling about this. A real bad feeling.

"Shit is going down in the Burg, and the cops either don't care or they're getting paid to look the other way," Mrs. Penny announced. Both her compatriots nodded fiercely.

"They showed up tonight," Riley pointed out.

"Yeah, they showed up because a gang of vigilantes seeking justice for the city did their job," Mrs. Penny said.

"Tell them about the tip line," Squeaky prodded.

"What about the tip line?" Riley asked.

"That anonymous tip line for reporting criminal activity? It ain't so anonymous."

Nick met the old lady's gaze in the rearview mirror. "What makes you say that?"

"A couple of the people who called it and left tips on some pretty nasty stuff ended up meeting unfortunate ends," she said.

"Are you saying someone is taking out people who tip off the cops?" Riley asked.

"Do you really think that a fifty-five-year-old woman would park on the railroad tracks and take a nap in the middle of the night two days after reporting her neighbor for running a prostitution ring out of his bagel shop?"

Riley and Nick exchanged a look. Weber had mentioned Riley's call to the tip line.

Now he *really* didn't have a good feeling.

"You can drop me off at the corner up here," Squeaky said, poking his Elsa-masked face between the front seats. "My mom will kill me if she sees me getting out of a car with strangers."

Nick pulled over, and Squeaky and Silent Bob Richard Nixon got out. Squeaky skulked down the block toward a big white house with a yard full of azaleas and statues. Silent Bob gave a little finger wave and jogged off in the opposite direction.

Mrs. Penny poked her head between the seats. "Can we go through a drive-through? Justice always makes me hungry."

Twenty minutes later, they pulled into the mansion's parking lot with two bags of Taco Bell.

"Thanks for the ride, kids," Mrs. Penny announced, taking one of the bags and climbing out of the back seat.

Riley didn't move.

But something did.

"Mother of God!" Nick yelped in manly surprise.

"What?" Riley asked from the other side of the giant dog face that had appeared between them.

"I forgot there was a dog in here."

"Burt is unforgettable," she insisted, moving the bag of tacos away from the sniffing nose.

"How did you end up with him, by the way?" he asked.

"He felt me up, so I thought I should commit."

If he'd committed to every woman he'd felt up...

"Don't worry. It's not contagious," she quipped.

"Did you just read my mind?"

"Oops. Sorry. I'm tired. Sometimes things sneak in that way."

"You know," he said, eyeing the dog. "He could be dangerous."

Burt gave Nick's face a bath with one long, disgusting swipe of his tongue.

"He does seem terrifyingly aggressive, doesn't he?" Smart-ass Riley yawned.

"What are you going to do with a dog this size in an apartment your size?"

She yawned again. "That's Future Riley's problem. Current Riley wants to eat tacos and go to bed."

He turned off the engine. "Let's go, Current Riley."

"You don't have to come up, you know," she said, unclasping her seat belt.

"I want my tacos," he said.

"Then dinner is about to be served," she said, climbing out of the vehicle. Burt the Farting Wonder Dog jumped out after her.

Nick half expected him to lope off into the night in search of an antelope to eat, but the dog merely wandered over to an oak tree at the edge of the lot and lifted his leg.

"It'll be a miracle if that tree survives until morning," he observed.

"It'll match the rest of the property," Riley said, jerking her chin in the direction of the crumbling Tudor-style mansion next door. It looked as if it had been abandoned for a few decades.

He followed her to the back porch, careful to keep back door jokes out of his head since she was in mind-reading mode. "Where exactly did you leave your Jeep?" he asked.

"In the middle of a crime scene."

"You're quite the girl, Thorn."

"So I've heard." The dog followed Riley inside like he'd been shadowing her his entire life.

"I'll check the front door and meet you upstairs," he said.

"I'll try not to feed Burt all your tacos."

Nick double-checked the lock on the door and the windows in all the common rooms on the first floor. Gabe's room was dark, and Nick imagined the man curled up on a futon next to a life-size Riley doll made out of her dirty laundry.

He was the one she called. *He* was the one sharing middle-of-the-night tacos with her. Not her spiritual-advising wall of muscle.

That counted for something.

He took the stairs two at a time. On the second floor, he ran into Mrs. Penny coming out of the bathroom.

"Thanks again for the pickup," she said, throwing him a jaunty salute.

"About those cases you and your skinny friend mentioned," he began.

"Tip of the iceberg, my nosy friend. Be careful there," she warned.

"I'm an insurance salesman. Careful is my middle name," he joked.

"No, it's not. Michael is. Nicholas Michael Santiago, formerly of the Harrisburg PD. Owner of Santiago Investigations."

"You really did run me," he said, impressed.

"Yeah, well, someone's gotta look out for Riley. She's got shit taste in men."

251

"I'm a great catch," Nick argued.

"We'll see if you earn your keep. Maybe it's a good thing they aren't looking too closely at who capped Dickie," she said.

"Why's that?" He already had a pretty good idea.

"They might have some cleanup to do if they find out that our friend upstairs saw more than she's letting on."

Nick didn't like that one bit.

"But if you two do manage to survive this, I wouldn't say no to some investigative gigs. No one ever looks twice at an old lady," she said.

"I'll keep you in mind," he said.

On the third floor, he gave a cursory knock on Riley's door before walking in.

"Holy shit!" He yanked his T-shirt over his nose.

"Nope. Just more farts," Riley said from the other side of the room where she was holding a towel to her face and muscling open a window.

Burt wagged his tail in canine pride from the couch.

"What has he been eating?" Nick wondered. "Dead raccoon and cabbage?" He used the door as a fan and opened and closed it until the cross breeze alleviated the worst of the retina-searing stench.

They ate their tacos at the tiny dining table.

"What do you think of what Mrs. Penny was saying?" Riley asked.

"About dirty cops?"

She nodded.

"Dunno," he hedged. "It happens in a lot of departments. Some get greedy. Some get power hungry."

"Do you think Detective Weber could be a bad cop?" she asked.

"Weber is as by-the-book as they make them. If he's up to something illegal, I'd be shocked."

"He does seem like he's trying awfully hard to point the finger at me," she mused.

"I don't want you worrying about that, Thorn. I'm gonna

find out who did this, and then I'm gonna dance a jig on Weber's desk when I deliver the killer to him."

She laughed, and they ate in silence for a few minutes.

"Well, thanks for the ride," Riley said lamely when they'd finished the last of their food.

Nick stood up and took his shirt off.

Her brown eyes widened. "Uh, what are you doing?"

"Going to bed."

"Bed?" she parroted, staring at the waistband of his pajama pants.

"Burt called dibs on the couch, and someone has to take you to get your car in"—he glanced at his watch—"less than four hours."

"Couch. Four hours," she repeated, now staring at his chest.

The dog sprawled on his back, legs in the air, and let out a happy yawn.

"Come on, Thorn. I'll behave myself," he promised, tugging her to her feet.

"You want to sleep in my bed with me?"

"You're cute when you're really tired," he said, leading her to the neatly made bed. Riley was a woman who appreciated order wherever she could arrange it.

"Fine," she said. "But don't hog the blanket or the pillows."

This was a mistake. He knew it. If he slid between those sheets, things were going to change. Even if it was just sleep. Hell. *Especially* if it was just sleep.

But it was his choice, his mistake to make. He didn't mind mistakes. What he didn't like was not making the decision himself.

He climbed into the bed and pulled the sheet, which smelled like Riley, over him. She waited a beat before turning off the lamp on the nightstand, plunging the room into darkness.

After another moment's hesitation, he felt her weight on the mattress, felt her slide in next to him. They lay there in tense silence on their backs. Nick stared up at the ceiling. Riley held her breath.

A mighty snore broke the silence.

"Was that you?" he teased.

"I think it was Uncle Burt," she whispered back.

Nick laughed quietly.

"Thanks for riding to my rescue tonight," Riley said softly.

"Anytime, Thorn."

34

For a guy who didn't do relationships, Nick was *really* good at snuggling, Riley thought.

His face was buried in her hair, breath tickling the back of her neck. His palm was splayed across her stomach under the thin tank top. Warm, solid, possessive. He held her against him, his thighs cushioning hers. His chest warm against her back. His… Hello!

Her eyes flew open like cartoon window shades. That was some impressive morning wood prodding her in the butt cheek. His breath was hot against her neck, the arm draped over her waist heavy.

Thin flamingo shorts did *not* feel like much of a security measure.

Nick Santiago was just as dangerous asleep as he was awake.

Except he wasn't asleep. His mouth was moving down her neck, across her shoulder, hot brushes of lips and lust. That hand held her tighter from the front as his hard-on greedily introduced itself to her butt. She could feel the pulse of his blood through a layer of clothing.

Her alarm came to life, filling the room with digital monastery chimes and chants.

She flailed and reached for the snooze, but his arm tightened around her.

"Nope," he murmured into her hair. "Staying in bed. All day."

She managed to free one leg from the covers and used her big toe to silence the alarm.

He dragged her back and bit her in the sensitive spot where her neck met her shoulder.

Gah. Shamelessly, she shifted her hips into him.

"Mmm, Riley," he murmured, his lips still moving against her skin.

"Yes?" It was a whisper, a sigh, a plea.

A sleepy groan rumbled deep in his throat. Quite possibly the sexiest sound she'd ever heard in her life.

She promptly forgot about categorizing all the sounds she'd ever heard when his hand shifted just high enough that his fingertips brushed the undersides of her breasts. She was on fire. Never had she gone from asleep to so turned on she might implode this quickly.

She should patent the Nick Santiago wake-up method and sell it as an alarm clock. She'd be a billionaire in a month.

Teeth grazed her shoulder, nipped at the base of her neck. She didn't know how she could be burning up from the inside and yet still have goose bumps peppering every inch of her skin.

Morning breath. Armpits. The weird gunk that collected in the inside corners of her eyes. These were things she should have been concerned with.

But right now, there was only one thing occupying her mind.

One big throbbing, insistent *thing*.

"Where are your pants?" she asked on a laugh and a tremble.

"I'm a night stripper," he said.

"What's a night stripper?" she asked, the words getting stuck in her throat when his mouth settled on the nape of her neck.

"I take my clothes off in my sleep," he explained. "It was really embarrassing in junior high at sleepovers. Now, it's just convenient."

Riley agreed wholeheartedly. She squeezed her thighs together, but it did nothing to relieve that desperate, empty need.

This was a very bad decision. She couldn't wait to make it.

She rolled onto her back, and Nick smoothly slid his unfairly perfect body over hers. She peeked before he settled himself between her open legs. Yep. Unfairly perfect. Every damn inch of him.

The gasp that ripped its way out of her throat when he gave an experimentally masterful thrust of his hips made him grin.

He was so cocky. *Literally. Very literally.*

She arched under him, and he ran his scruffy jaw over her cheek before nipping at her lower lip.

This was the best Thursday morning Riley had ever experienced.

But hang on. She didn't have best Thursdays. She didn't wake up with hot, naked men in her bed.

"Wait, what about the whole contagious monogamy thing?" she asked. It was more of a gasp as he was rocking steadily against her. A promise or a threat of what was to come. She. *She* was about to come.

"I'll risk it," he murmured, lowering his head to take her mouth.

This time, he was the one moaning. Only it was more of a yawning sound than a moan. And then a weird coughing, gagging noise. Followed by a wet sneeze.

Nick pulled back. "Holy shit."

"Oh my God!"

Big brown eyes peered at them inches from their faces.

"I forgot I had a dog," Riley admitted.

"Buddy, I will buy you a year's supply of dog biscuits if you go back to sleep right now," Nick bargained.

But Burt wasn't having it. He put his front paws on the mattress, tail wagging.

"I think he has to go out," she observed.

Burt gave a happy bark, his whiplike tail wagging harder.

Nick dropped his forehead to hers. "I'm trying really hard not to hate him right now," he admitted.

In apology, the dog gave Nick's waist and ribs a slurp.

"Ugh. Gross," he complained.

She couldn't quite smother her laughter.

Nick helped by shoving a pillow over her face. "Come on, jerk dog."

She surfaced from the bed. "I'll take him," she said.

He paused and looked down. "Good call."

The man was totally naked, and his impressive, enthusiastic cock was standing at attention. She lost every train of thought her brain had ever had. Burt barked again, bringing her back to the reality of his doggy bladder.

She felt woozy and fevered. Still staring at the sex god before her, she wrestled on a mismatched pair of flip-flops. She tripped over her own feet and then the dog. Nick smirked at her as she fixed her gaze on him through the gap in the closing door, determined to soak up every second of the view.

Down the stairs she and Burt went, leaving the morning seduction behind. There were signs of life on the second and first floors. Someone was frying bacon in the kitchen. Someone else was watching the morning news at twice the acceptable volume.

Mrs. Penny's door was still closed, and Riley imagined the elderly vigilante was catching up on some much-needed sleep.

Outside, she realized she didn't have a dog leash or a doggy bag. She was entirely ill-equipped to parent a dog. Fortunately, Burt didn't appear to require much parenting. He bounded over to the neighboring lot and did his business. A whole giant mound of it. Followed by a streaming river of it.

Riley made a mental list of dog accessories she needed to buy on her lunch hour. Her lunch hour. Damn it. She had work today. It was a beautiful summer morning. There was a beautiful naked man waiting for her upstairs. But she had to turn her back on both man and dog and go proofread garbage in the windowless offices of SHART.

There was something very wrong with this picture.

Burt bounded back to her, looking proud of himself. A

good dog mom would have offered him a treat. A good dog mom would have *had* treats.

She heard a sharp, shrill whistle and looked up. Nick, still shirtless, was leaning out the third-floor window. "Move that cute ass, Thorn. Gotta pick up the Jeep, and I need coffee."

Burt barked and trotted toward the back door.

Riley sighed.

"How do you feel about dog-sitting?" she called back.

He laughed and shook his head. "Anything for you, Thorn."

She showered and changed in record time. The three of them entered the kitchen, scenting the air.

"Good morning, Riley." Gabe beamed from the stove. "And who is this handsome beast?" he asked, leaning down to pet Burt.

"I'm Nick. We've already met," Nick said.

Riley rolled her eyes and gratefully took the breakfast sandwich Gabe handed her.

"What the hell is that thing?" Mr. Willicott demanded, peering at the dog over his upside-down newspaper.

"This is Burt," Riley said, knowing it was useless to tell her neighbor anyone's name.

"He is a dog," Gabe added helpfully.

Burt trotted over to sniff at Mr. Willicott's empty plate.

"What are you doing here?" Gabe asked Nick with polite disdain.

Nick slung his arm around Riley's shoulders. "Spent the night with my *fiancée* after she called needing some help."

"You were in need of help?" Gabe looked crestfallen. "I am always available, Riley."

Great. She'd snagged less than four hours of sleep, realized her life was a meaningless repeat of terrible days, and managed to hurt her friend's feelings. She threw an elbow into Nick's ribs. He grunted.

"You'll be helping me after work with more training," she promised. "You can even make me go for a run."

Gabe brightened. Nick looked annoyed.

"Good morning," Lily trilled, wandering into the kitchen in a paisley caftan.

"Morning," Riley and Nick said together.

Lily's gasp had the caftan falling off one of her shoulders to reveal that she wasn't wearing anything underneath. "I'm so happy to see you, Nick! Does this mean your sexual performance improved over the first time, and we'll be seeing more of you?"

"Why does everyone think I'm bad in bed?" Nick wondered.

"You seem like a selfish lover," Gabe answered.

Riley choked out a laugh.

"Aren't you going to defend me?" Nick asked her.

Riley noticed that Lily's eyes were riveted on Nick's crotch. The woman looked a little flushed.

"Everyone can keep their noses out of my sex life," Riley said, pushing Lily into a chair and fanning her with Mr. Willicott's newspaper. She couldn't take chances with her neighbors and gravity.

"Oh my goodness! Who is this handsome devil?" Lily asked as the dog shoved his wrecking ball–sized head in her lap.

"This is Burt. I found him last night," Riley told her. "Do you mind if he stays with us for a while until I figure out what to do with him?"

"I've always wanted a time-share dog," Lily said, smushing Burt's face in her hands. The dog was big enough—and probably hungry enough—to eat her in two bites. Instead, his tail swished back and forth on the tile floor.

"What the hell are you going to do with a horse? I hate horses. Refuse to live with 'em," Mr. Willicott said, glaring at the dog.

"Oh dear," Lily sighed. "I suppose we should take a vote. Tonight at dinner."

"I'll keep him with me for the day," Nick promised Lily, flashing her his dimples.

"Well, aren't you a sweetheart, Nick?" Lily was clearly susceptible to dimples.

Riley thought she saw Gabe roll his eyes, a very un-spiritual-advisor-like thing to do.

She hid her smile and poured two coffees into cups and secured the lids.

"We better get going," Nick said, accepting the coffee she handed him.

"See you all later," Riley said. "Thanks for the sandwich, Gabe. That was very thoughtful of you."

"It was my honor," Gabe said.

"Kiss-ass," Nick muttered under his breath.

She thought she heard Gabe whisper, "Disappointing lover," but couldn't be sure.

35

Nick swung into the minuscule back lot of his office and glanced at his passenger. Burt was now bathed, wearing a bright red collar that the dog had picked out himself and holding a stuffed pig in his mouth.

Nick had found a pair of shorts and two matching sneakers in the back of his SUV and sweet-talked his way into a pet supply store before its official opening. He'd enjoyed a brief relationship with the owner back in high school, and she'd been happy to load him up with supplies for his "fiancée's" new dog.

She may have taken advantage of him, he thought, considering the haul he now had to unload. There were two bags of toys in the back seat, another of treats and accessories—who knew dog dental hygiene was a thing?—and a forty-pound bag of organic kibble guaranteed to settle digestive issues.

"Come on, Burt," he said to the dog. "We've got work to do."

Together they climbed the back steps of the building to the second floor.

His apartment was a seven-hundred-square-foot one-bedroom unit. It was in decent shape but a little on the soulless side. A lot of beige on beige. He'd never gotten around to hanging shit on the walls or putting his laundry away. He also hadn't bothered with furnishing the place beyond simple functionality. The bed was king-size. The leather couch had two built-in recliners and faced a flat-screen TV that he still felt he should have gone bigger on. And that was about it. No throw pillows. No books. No art.

But at least he didn't have piles of dirty underwear and porn.

While Nick deposited the pet supplies on the couch, the dog took a sniffing tour of the kitchen, which was minimally stocked with convenience food and takeout menus. If the zombie apocalypse happened, he'd be one of the first to starve to death.

"What? It serves its purpose," he said to the dog when Burt eyeballed him judgmentally.

After he quit the force, Nick had meant to start looking for a house. Get a mortgage. Mow a lawn. Buy a beer fridge for the garage. But the business had sucked up all his time since then. He was growing a reputation, employing people. So what if his home bore an unsettling resemblance to Dickie Frick's? Just because they were both into big TVs and didn't do dishes or blankets or scented candles didn't mean Nick was heading down the same path. A guy could be a bachelor without turning into a lonely old perverted sleazebag. *Right?*

Burt cocked his head at him.

"Don't get comfortable," he told the dog. "We've got shit to do after breakfast."

Nick ripped open the bag of kibble and poured some into a shiny new bowl. Lifestyle judgments forgotten, Burt trotted over and wolfed down the food before moving his massive face to the matching water bowl.

A brisk knock at the door had the hairs on the back of Nick's neck standing up. Burt lifted his head, letting Niagara Falls stream from his mouth to the linoleum floor.

Nobody visited here. Certainly not before nine on a weekday morning.

Tucking the Glock he kept in the utensil drawer into the back of his shorts, Nick eased up to the door.

"Yeah?" he called.

"Santiago?"

The visitor didn't sound like a cop. Nick opened the door.

Two people in cheap suits and sunglasses stared back at him. One was a tall broad-shouldered woman with a slicked-back ponytail. The other was shorter, rounder, and had hairy knuckles. They looked like a knockoff version of the Blues Brothers. Burt stuck his head out the door and gave a deep *boof.*

"Holy shit. 'Zat a lion or a pony?" the short one asked.

"Hey there, boy," the lady said, crouching down and offering Burt her hand. The dog sniffed suspiciously and then plowed into her, giving her face a slobbery kiss.

"Uh, sorry," Nick said, pulling Burt off the woman.

She stood up and brushed the dog hair off her suit. "No problem. I got three just like 'im at home."

"What can I do for you two?" Nick asked, wrestling Burt back inside. The dog shoved his face between Nick's leg and the doorframe.

"Fat Tony wants a word with you," the short one announced.

"He does, does he?" Word certainly traveled fast.

"Yeah. You can leave your pony and that piece you got in your pants here," the guy said.

"I've got work to do," Nick said.

"This'll just take a minute," the dog lover assured him. "He's down in the car." She hooked her thumb in the direction of a shiny black Escalade idling in the alley.

Nick pretended to be annoyed even though they'd just saved him a trip to the casino. He sighed and made a slow-motion show of removing the gun and putting it on the kitchen counter.

He shut the door in Burt's hopeful face. The two stooges sandwiched him on the walk down the flight of stairs.

The tall one knocked on the tinted back window, and the door opened.

The short one gestured for Nick to get inside.

"Nicky, my friend."

Fat Tony was no longer fat. After weight-loss surgery four years ago, he'd lost over a hundred pounds and kept it off by taking up speed walking. The guy did a few laps of his 110,000-square-foot casino every day before work. However, *Skinny Tony* didn't seem to instill the same mixture of fear and respect that *Fat Tony* did. So the original moniker stayed even as the waistband of Tony's shiny sharkskin trousers shrunk.

"Tony. How's the wife?" Nick asked, settling onto the cream-colored leather next to the man.

"Eh. You know neurosurgeons," he said, offering Nick a cup of dark thick espresso. "She's been making me do these sodukey things to keep me 'sharp.'" The man's air quotes were accented with a black onyx pinkie ring and a shiny gold watch. "I keep telling her there ain't nothing dull about Fat Tony."

"Women," Nick said in male camaraderie. He took the coffee.

It was true. The man was shrewd enough that no criminal charges had ever stuck to him. They'd all rolled off him like oil on sharkskin pants. Even as a cop, it had been hard to take offense. The guy was just plain likable.

"Speaking of. I hear you got yourself one finally," Fat Tony said.

This being big news was getting to become old news to Nick. "I do. She's making an honest man out of me."

"Good for you. I always say a guy ain't got nothing if he don't got a woman forcing him to do good shit."

The man was a sage. And his wife, Dr. Mrs. Fat Tony, was the driving force behind the casino boss's generous support of nonprofits. There was a reason the pediatric wing of the hospital was named the Anthony and Elizabeth Martucci Pavilion.

"Thanks. She's a great girl."

"I'll be expecting a wedding invite," Tony told him, taking a dainty sip of espresso.

Nick congratulated himself on not breaking out in hives. "You can count on it," he fibbed. "So what can I do for you?"

"I've kept my eye on you since you left the force, Nicky."

Well, that wasn't a comforting thought.

"You and me, we always got along even when you were trying to bust me for stupid shit, didn't we?" Tony continued.

Nick nodded. "We did." After all the murders, rapes, and assaults, a guy making some coin on the side and evading taxes wasn't exactly a high priority to Nick. Not when there was so much other ugliness out there.

"I'm legit now," Tony said proudly. "Well, mostly. But your old pal Weber seems to think I'm still dabbling."

"That sounds like him," Nick said.

"He's looking at me for Frick's murder."

"I might have heard that rumor."

Fat Tony put down his cup and saucer with a snap. "It wasn't me, Nicky. Yeah, the shithead owed me twenty Gs on the horses. But he paid it off. We both moved on."

"When did he pay it off?" Nick asked.

"Two weeks ago," Fat Tony said. "And before you ask, I don't know where he got the money."

"Okay."

"I didn't have nothing to do with that idiot getting shot." He sliced a ringed hand through the air.

"Why tell me? I'm not a cop anymore."

"I'm hiring you, Nicky."

"Hiring me to do what?"

"Prove I didn't whack Frick the Dipstick. I don't trust that smug Weber shit to figure it out on his own. There's something fishy going on with the cops in this town."

"Heard that rumor too," Nick said, rubbing the back of his neck. A payout from Fat Tony would be nice in the company coffers. But he had a hunch it might not be exactly ethical to take on two clients for the same case. Especially if it turned out that Fat Tony had pulled the trigger.

Damn that Riley Thorn. Her morals were rubbing off on him. "Only problem is, I'm already working the case. Frick's family hired me to find out who pulled the trigger."

"I'm a businessman, Nicky. I got no beef with you double-dipping if it keeps my ass out of an interrogation room."

"You have an alibi for the night Dickie was killed?"

Fat Tony snorted. "I got an alibi for every night of my life."

Nick raised an eyebrow.

"Sorry. Reflex. The wife and I were at the casino for my ma's birthday party."

Fat Tony's mother was a semi-famous singer from the '60s. She wore feather boas to the grocery store and got a Christmas card from Tony Bennett every year.

"Got surveillance footage—undoctored this time—of us there until two a.m. Hell, even got the mayor as an eyewitness."

"What about the Blues Brothers out there?" Nick asked, nodding to where Tall and Short leaned against the brick of the building, hands in their pockets.

"I wouldn't send those two to do any dirty work. He faints at the sight of blood, and she gets winded after a flight of stairs. I can get you the whereabouts of my crew, but it's a waste of my time and yours. I had nothing to do with this."

"One more question. Are you Frick's silent partner in the bar?"

"Do I look like the kind of man who would put his name on that shithole?"

"I don't know. Do you?"

"I'm a classy guy, Nicky. Ain't no way I'd partner with Frick on a dump like Nature Girls."

"Do you know who the partner is?"

"I didn't know there was a partner," Fat Tony insisted. "Who the hell would be stupid enough to go into business with that moron?"

This time, Nick couldn't tell if it was the truth. "You sure?" he pushed.

"Look, Nicky. I got a lot of businesses to oversee. A lot of balls in the air. Dickie Frick was a gnat. An ant. A little, bitty, baby bacterium. I just need you to prove that I didn't whack him." Fat Tony reached into his jacket pocket, and Nick blinked at the wad of cash he produced. "A retainer for your services," Tony said.

Nick's door opened, and Tall gestured for him to get out.

"I'll be in touch, Nicky. Make this right, and you can expect a very generous wedding gift."

Nick watched the Escalade drive off, then glanced down at the pile of cash in his hand and wondered if he'd just fucked up and how badly. He heard a thud and looked up to see Burt's dog face smushed against the window of his apartment.

Never a dull moment.

36

Riley's working life felt like one never-ending dull moment. She was suffocating within the gray walls of SHART.

"Let's circle back to that when we can get our arms around what's really in our wheelhouse," the mid-level manager was saying to the project coordinator. Seven team members were gathered around the conference table in the coffin room with the express purpose of throwing corporate jargon in one another's faces.

"I'd like to take this opportunity to remind everyone that we've made the switch to the new time sheets," a second mid-level manager said, holding up one of the new paper time sheets. "Employees will now be required to bill their time in five-minute increments. We expect everyone to be billing a minimum of seven hours and forty-five minutes a day."

Riley experienced something like an out-of-body experience when she raised her hand. "What about bathroom breaks?"

Pre-Nick Riley would never have spoken up in a meeting, let alone done so passive-aggressively.

The manager gave her a tight smile. "We're anticipating that our employees will be more mindful of the amount of time they spend not working on essential client tasks."

"Look." Leon Tuffley Jr. rose and made a grab for the time sheet with one hand and his crotch with the other. "We ain't asking you for much, for Chrissakes. Just a full day of billable hours every damn day. So stay off the internet and the shitter, and you won't have any problems."

Riley felt itchy and irritated. Like she was allergic to just sitting here in this room. She thought about running from the law with Mrs. Penny last night and about how she could have had sex with a really hot naked guy this morning and then taken Burt for a swim in the river. But instead she'd shown up here for a measly paycheck and crappy health insurance.

"The next item on the agenda is on-time arrivals. Donna is asking that everyone arrive five minutes early so she can lock the side door promptly at eight a.m. rather than waiting until 8:05. And before anyone asks"—the manager gave Riley a steely look—"no, you won't be paid for the extra five minutes."

It took all her willpower not to run screaming out the conference room door.

The rest of the meeting was survived by planning out which mini bottles of liquor she'd start squirreling away in her desk. Vodka for mornings. Whiskey for lunch hours. Tequila for afternoons.

She returned to her desk. Bud the designer was asleep in his chair. Only seven more hours before she could leave. If she didn't work on the first floor and she weren't a new dog mom, she'd think seriously about jumping out a window.

Time for some nonbillable fun. She logged on to Channel 50's social media and cued up the morning newscast. She smirked when Griffin gave a report on last night's vigilante activity.

"Several dogs were recovered from the neighborhood and remanded to the Harrisburg Humane Society," Griffin told the camera in his modulated anchorman voice. "Meanwhile, police are asking anyone with information on the situation to contact them. Over to the beautiful Bella Goodshine for the weather."

Riley rolled her eyes.

The camera cut to the future Mrs. Gentry, who was poured into a baby-pink dress with a deep scoop neck. She was holding a fluffy white dog that looked as though it were about to drown in the woman's abundant cleavage. There was something vaguely familiar about the dog, and Riley realized it was one of the ones that had sprinted past her in the alley last night.

"Thank you, sweetie pie," she chirped. "If anyone is ready to open their homes to a rescue dog, the Humane Society needs your help. Isn't that right, baby?" she crooned to the dog.

Riley could hear the midstate audience swooning at the adorableness and tried not to barf in her desk drawer.

"Help me! Help me!" Bella squeaked, waving the dog's front paw. "Pwease adopt me, Gwiffin!"

Riley choked on her lukewarm coffee. If there was one thing Griffin Gentry hated more than running out of his favorite bronzer, it was dogs. All dogs. He hated dog hair and dog poop. He couldn't stand barking or the smell of puppy breath. The man had once screamed at an entire litter of golden retriever puppies, "Quit whining!" when the sound woman kept picking them up on the audio playback.

They'd all had to pretend it was a joke to smooth things over with the rescue.

"Does Gwiffin want to bwing me home?" Bella baby-talked, waving puppy paws in the man's direction.

He laughed nervously when the camera swung back in his direction. Riley noted the sheen of sweat popping up on his forehead, making his foundation run. "Ha ha! We'll have to discuss that later," he said with a forced smile.

"Oh, but don't you want to be my daddy?" Bella approached, holding the dog out at arm's length. At this point, Riley wasn't sure if Bella was asking that question as the dog or as herself.

"Looks like the Channel 50 family is getting bigger, folks," Griffin's co-anchor announced.

Griffin looked like he was going to vomit when Bella held the dog up to his face. He scooted his chair back from the desk.

The video ended abruptly, and Riley imagined it was because he'd toppled over backward.

She was feeling pretty damn entertained. Until she looked at the stack of job jackets on her desk. *God, this job sucks.*

Maybe it was the moonlighting or playing fake fiancée or her latest stint as a getaway driver, but SHART had gone from sufferable to soul destroying.

The clock on the wall behind her ticked interminably toward noon. Her cubicle mate was awake now and snorting at the YouTube video of bikinied blonds on trampolines. Two supervisors walked by discussing the afternoon staff meeting.

The intercom system clicked on. "Whoever thinks it's acceptable to turn your time sheet in with illegible handwriting will not be paid for hours that can't be read," Jan from accounting announced. Jan was the kind of person you invited to a party if you wanted it to break up early.

Once again, the intercom system beeped. "If someone has a problem with their reading comprehension, perhaps they should personally seek out the employee and ask the question rather than publicly shaming them." It was the fresh-out-of-college vegetarian social justice warrior in project management. Jan was probably going to dock his pay now, Riley thought.

She was surrounded by miserable, bored people. And it was sucking the life out of her.

She still had over an hour before lunch, and she felt like there was a good chance she might die if she waited that long. Especially if she dug into the stack of work that included such exciting projects as a bank's annual report and seven ads for a sleazebag used car dealer whose wife just demanded bigger breast implants.

Hmm. Maybe she could take a few minutes and practice some of her psychic stuff?

She glanced around, making sure no one was paying attention to her before stuffing earbuds in her ears. She cued up one of Wander's soothing meditation mixes and closed her eyes.

It took her a few tries before she swooped into the cotton candy cloud place. But she made it, and all by herself too.

It was nice here. Warm and happy. She felt a nudge on her consciousness. Not exactly a something, but also not a nothing.

"So hey. It's me, Riley. Just practicing here."

She felt the nudge again and wondered if that was their way of saying, "What the hell do you want?"

What did she want? She wanted to find out who killed Dickie and stay out of jail, but so far, those questions weren't resulting in clear answers. Debating for a moment, it popped into her mind almost unbidden. *Beth.* The name had surfaced during Nick and Detective Weber's last bro fight, and neither one had answered the question.

It wasn't like she was prying into Nick's mind. Asking her spirit guides was just an exercise.

"Okay, guides. Who's Beth?"

The clouds thickened, then darkened before they began to thin again.

Detective Weber and Nick appeared through the mists in happier, younger times. There was a young woman with long dark hair and bright pink lips. Short, curvy. Bright and happy. Her arms were wrapped around Nick, grinning up at him. "I thought I told you to keep your hands off her," Vision Weber said to Vision Nick.

Suddenly, Vision Beth disappeared. Poof. Like she'd never been there.

Riley recoiled from the vision so fast she felt like she was having one of those falling dreams. The mists and clouds vanished, and when she reached out to steady herself, she knocked over her water bottle.

Her heart was pounding, and she was sweating. She collapsed back against her chair and tried to catch her breath.

What the hell had she just seen?

37

After Fat Tony left, Nick returned to his apartment. The lingering odor told him that Burt was probably going to need a few more meals of organic kibble before his gut biome regulated itself.

He opened the windows, changed into his work uniform of jeans and a clean T-shirt, and put the dog on his new leash. Together they headed down the back stairs.

Nick wasn't buying the Fat Tony angle of the investigation. He also didn't like the feel of the gambling theory either. Dickie and his rec league gambling was penny-ante shit, and he'd paid his debt to Fat Tony.

He wondered where Frick got the money to pay Fat Tony.

"Yo, coz. Whoa," Brian said when Nick walked in with Burt. "You get a dog?"

Nick shook his head and unhooked the leash. "Not exactly. Long story." Burt trotted in to sniff at Brian's wheelchair, his hand, and his breakfast sandwich before wandering into Nick's office.

"Does it involve why an unmarked cruiser drove by nice and slow twice this morning already?"

Fucking Weber.

"It factors." Nick poured himself a cup of coffee from Brian's fancy machine. His third of the day already.

"Well, table the story. Because I've got updates." His cousin's fingers flew over the keyboard in nerd fluency. Brian turned the screen toward him. "That LLC name that Riley got us at Nature Girls?"

"Shell company?" Nick guessed.

"Yep," Brian said, tapping a pencil on the desk. "Still digging through the layers. But I should be able to find a name eventually. In the meantime, I did find something interesting."

"Interesting like poodles doing parkour or case related?" Nick had fallen for Brian's YouTube rabbit holes before.

"This time case related. But that poodle was fucking awesome."

"Agreed."

Burt seemed to know they were discussing dogs and wandered back out to them. He rested his head on the arm of Brian's wheelchair and stared at the monitor.

"Nature Girls is a shithole, right?" Brian said, giving the dog's head a scratch.

"The shittiest."

"Then isn't it interesting that despite the plethora of one-star reviews on Yelp, it's never once been cited by the health department?"

"I saw a cockroach the size of a toaster walk across the bar while I was there," Nick mused.

"I smell something fishy in Harrisburg."

"There's no way that hellhole would pass a health inspection," Nick agreed. "Can you get me the name of—"

"The inspector? Way ahead of you." Brian held up a sticky note between his fingers.

"Nice work, keyboard warrior," Nick commented, pocketing the name and address. It was his turn to pay someone a visit. "You mind watching the dog for me for an hour?"

———

Walter F. Henry was a sweater. Despite the frigid air circulating in the drab downtown office building, the pit stains continued to grow on his jaundice-yellow short-sleeved button-down. He had a bristly red mustache that twitched under a bulbous nose. Red patches appeared and spread on both cheeks under his wire-rimmed spectacles. He looked fifteen years older than his forty-eight.

"You look nervous, Walt," Nick observed. The guy looked like he was going to piss his pants.

"Nervous? Ha! Who? Me?" To emphasize how not terrified he was, Walt tried to kick back in his chair and in the process knocked over his WORLD'S OKAYEST BOSS mug, spilling cold coffee over his desktop.

"I say Nature Girls and you go into hunted chipmunk mode," Nick said as the man jumped to his feet.

"Ha. Chipmunk." Walt choked out the laugh nervously. "Let me just run out and grab some paper towels."

He hustled out the door. Nick sat and watched the coffee form a brown waterfall over the edge of the laminate.

It was a small cramped office with about as much personality as its occupant. Files were stacked on top of ancient filing cabinets. A red rubber FAIL stamp had a place of honor on the desktop. Where family photos should have been, Nick saw a framed shot of good ol' Walt in front of a shiny red two-seater sports car. Pretty fancy car for a civil servant.

Behind the desk, Nick spotted a roll of paper towels.

Shit.

"Why do they always have to run?" He sighed. He pulled out his badge and jogged out of the office. "Excuse me," he said, dodging a guy pushing a cart full of files and sprinting past two aisles of cubicles.

There was a birthday celebration happening in one of the departments.

"Happy birthday, dear Maaaaaarshaaaaaa," the clump of staffers sang, and Nick sprinted through their midst.

"Sorry. Excuse me. Happy birthday, Marsha," he called as

he cleared the clump. The stairwell door on the other wall was just clicking shut.

"Thank you," a cute redhead holding a piece of cake with a 50 candle in it chirped. "Want some cake?"

"Maybe later!" He shoved the door open and paused to listen. His quarry was heading down. Nick hit the stairs, which smelled like decades of old smoke had baked into the walls and industrial green stair treads.

Good ol' Walt had a head start on him, but Nick was faster…and less asthmatic. Plus, he lived for this shit.

The health inspector had just cleared the exterior door when Nick broke out his old high-school defensive-tackle moves.

They both went down into a hedgerow, landing on a cushion of mulch and low-growing, spiny greenery.

"Please don't arrest me," Walt blubbered, his face still in the mulch.

They'd crash-landed outside a large window cut into the ugly gray stone facade. On the other side of the glass was a conference room. A full conference room. The suited spectators gaped at them. It was probably the most excitement they'd seen all month, Nick guessed.

God, he loved his job. He could have easily been one of those gray-suited hamsters shuffling from meeting to meeting in their little hamster balls, complaining about parking and supervisors. Adhering to the rigid schedules of overlords who didn't trust them to do their jobs without being micromanaged into submission.

In comparison, he just got to chase someone out of a building and tackle them.

He held up his badge to the glass in case any of them felt like doing their civic duty and called the cops.

"I'm not arresting you, dumbass. I told you. I'm a PI. Not a cop."

"I panicked. I'm sorry," Walt wailed.

Hauling Walt to his feet, he took inventory. Nick had a rip in the knee of his favorite jeans. His arm was scraped and bleeding from the stupid bush, and his T-shirt was smeared with dirt and berries from the shrub they'd smashed through. His jaw stung a bit from the health inspector's pointy elbow. Walt was worse. He'd landed facedown in a puddle left from the sprinkler system. It looked like he'd shit himself from the front. The berry stains stood out on his urine-yellow shirt, making it look like he'd been slashed open by an angry bear claw.

"Come on, man," Nick said, slapping him on the back. "I need a beer."

———

Once Walt understood Nick wasn't going to arrest him and didn't give a rat's ass about a health inspector on the take, he stopped sweating.

They hit up a bar on Union Deposit Road. The bartender eyed them nervously when they grabbed neighboring stools. They made quite the picture, Nick imagined. Especially Walt with his sweaty pits and berry-blood front. The missing buttons on his shirt showed off his undershirt and midlife paunch. There was mulch in his comb-over.

Despite his appearance, Walt gave the guy an imperious look. "How's that exhaust fan over the grill?" he asked ominously.

"All fixed," the bartender said, bobbing his head and swallowing hard. While Walt studied the cocktail menu, the guy hurled his filthy bar towel to the floor and grabbed a clean one.

"I'll take the Tröegs DreamWeaver Wheat," Nick said, pointing at a local beer.

"And I'll have a mai tai with extra cherry syrup," Walt decided.

A server cracking gum and playing with a head of wild curly hair wandered up and leaned against the bar. "Yo, what's the special today?" she asked the bartender.

He looked up from where he was scrubbing the register screen and must have given her the death glare while nodding not so subtly in their direction.

Her eyes widened. "Never mind. Just remembered it's my turn to sanitize the fountain heads. Bye!" She scurried back into the kitchen.

Clearly Walt had street cred here.

Nick picked up the food menu. But Walt shook his head. "I wouldn't do that if I were you. They got rat turds the size of thumbs back there."

Nick closed the menu and slid it to the edge of the bar.

Their drinks were served in glasses so clean Nick could taste the dish soap.

"So how's the kickback game these days?" he asked.

Walt choked, and an ounce or two of mai tai shot out his nose.

A wide-eyed manager popped up as if she'd been crouching behind the bar, a neatly labeled bottle of sanitizer in one hand and a fresh towel in the other. She swiped up the mess and disappeared again.

"I don't know what you're talking about," Walt squeaked.

"Sure you do. Look," Nick said, "I don't care if you're blackmailing the governor's husband. All I care about is Dickie Frick."

"Dickie?" Walt swiped a hand over his mustache, probably checking for snot and cherry juice droplets. "You sure you're not a cop?"

Nick sighed and handed over his badge. "Private investigator. A client hired me to look into Frick's murder."

The health inspector telegraphed his move before he made it. Nick clamped a hand down on his shoulder.

"Do you really want me to kick your ass in front of your loyal subjects here?" He recognized the need to be respected and had no problem putting his boot on it.

"No," Walt pouted.

"Then talk."

"I didn't kill him," he whined.

"No shit. Tell me why Nature Girls, an establishment that looks like it's been hosed down in bodily fluids, has never once been cited for health violations."

Walt took a drink and dribbled mai tai down his chin.

"Come on, man." Nick sighed. "I've got other people to tackle today."

"Okay. All right. Fine. So maybe in exchange for a friendly gesture, I might possibly loosen the criteria—"

"They give you cash. You rubber-stamp their inspections. Great. Who approached who?"

Looking left and then right, Walt swallowed hard. "Within forty seconds of me walking in, Dickie handed me a fistful of cash." He said it almost fondly as if Dickie Frick and his dirty money had been a turning point in his life.

"How long's that arrangement been going on?"

Walt shrugged. "Dunno," he said cagily.

"Walt, buddy, I think you do know. And *I* know a lot of things," Nick lied. "Like I said, I'm not here to play judge and jury. I'm not running to the cops to tattle. You could single-handedly help solve a murder here."

Walt sighed. "Six years next month."

"Did Dickie ever mention a silent partner?" Nick asked.

Walt pursed his lips until they disappeared under the bristle of mustache. "No. But one time Dickie wasn't there, and a bald guy met me instead. He wasn't as friendly."

"Name?"

"Something weird. Drew? Down? Durf?"

Only an amateur would have no problem accepting money from a complete stranger without doing any due diligence. "Besides being bald, what did this Durf guy look like?"

"Uh, I dunno. Not real tall, but not, like, super short. Bald," he repeated half to himself.

"White? Black? Latino? Asian?" Nick prompted.

"Maybe white?" Walt guessed.

The health inspector was not the sharpest crayon in the box.

"How about other illegal activity? You ever notice anything else going on at Nature Girls?"

"Not really. I mean, not besides the betting. I won fifty

280

dollars on the U-18 baseball league. But it wasn't like they were cooking meth in the kitchen and selling it."

"Can you think of anyone who'd want Dickie dead?"

"Really anyone who met him. He was a disgusting pig," Walt said fondly.

Nick drained his beer and fished in his pocket for a business card.

"If you think of anything else, give me a call," he said, dropping the business card in front of Walt. He pushed back from the bar and stood. He'd let Mr. Not Very Helpful pick up the tab. "Thanks for the beer."

"Wait!" The health inspector was flustered. "I can't go back to work like this. They're all gonna think I got arrested. Or beat up. Or both. What am I supposed to tell them?"

Reputations, Nick thought. It must be exhausting worrying about one.

"Geez, man, I don't know. Tell them it was a fraternity prank."

Walt brightened. "That's a good idea! I bet it would have been a secret fraternity. Not one of the ones where anyone could get in."

Nick walked out into the July sunshine, leaving Walt to figure out what cool nickname his fictional fraternity brothers would have bestowed on him.

38

W hat?" Nick asked the dog when Burt rested his big face and jowls on Nick's desk. "Are you bored? Don't you have any hobbies?"

He couldn't blame the dog. He'd taken Burt down the block for lunch and to meet Perry of the unstable housing situation. Burt's whiplike tail had wagged the entire walk. He greeted everyone like they were his long-lost best friend. It had been the last fun either of them had. As interesting as Nick's morning had been, what with the wad of cash from Fat Tony and the tackling of the health inspector, the afternoon had consisted of two downtown office serves and reports out the ass.

Nick checked his watch. If he headed over to the mansion now, he could be there when a certain sexy psychic got off work. Maybe he could talk her into dinner and then into revisiting how they'd started the day…before Burt the Beast had cockblocked them.

Pleased with the plan, he backed up his work, shut down his computer, and declined to dissect why he was looking forward to seeing her again.

His gut told him Riley Thorn was nothing but trouble. But that was more of a turn-on than a deterrent.

He walked out into the front room, Burt trotting on his heels.

"Think I'm cutting out," he informed his cousin. "Gonna take this guy home and see if Riley wants to grab dinner."

Brian dragged off his headphones and cocked an eyebrow.

"What?" Nick asked.

"You're into her," Brian observed.

"Of course I am." It wasn't exactly breaking news for Nick Santiago to be into a woman.

"No. You're *into* her," Brian repeated.

"Say it as many times as you want with a different emphasis, and it still doesn't change the meaning, man."

"Ah, but it does. You answered the phone when she called you in the middle of the night. You spent the night with her. You're dog-sitting her pet lion." Burt liked that and gave Brian a slurp with his Gene Simmons tongue. "Good boy. Good lion. And now you're taking her to dinner."

"I've taken women to dinner before," Nick scoffed.

"Not with that stupid look on your face."

He frowned. "What stupid look?"

"The one that rearranges your face every time you know you're going to see her. It's like antici…"

"Pation?" Nick filled in.

"Riley's your Christmas morning."

"Did Josie cut off your oxygen for too long last night?" Nick asked, taking Burt's leash off the coatrack. The dog went from dignified to dancing queen in half a second.

"See that look on Burt's face?" Brian asked. Burt looked crazed and way too enthusiastic. His tongue peeked out the corner of his mouth, ears perked up, brow wrinkled. "That's how you look."

"Your uncle Brian is full of shit," Nick said to the dog. His cell rang, saving him from having to defend himself further. "Hmm," he said, flashing the screen at his cousin.

"Well, that can't be good," Brian said.

Burt continued his tap dance while Nick answered.

"Santiago," he said.

"Nick, it's Katie Shapiro. Have time to meet me for a beer?"

The Sturges Speakeasy was an easy three-block walk from the office and dog-friendly, so Nick brought Burt along.

He found Detective Katie Shapiro on the rooftop terrace at a table with two beers. She was a long-legged, no-nonsense kind of woman. Her hair, a dark blond, was pulled back in a sleek tail. Unlike Weber, she dressed like a normal human being, jeans and blazers mostly. She'd ditched the blazer and kept the tank top, which showed off the arms that had bested more than a few academy-fresh uniforms in push-up contests.

Police work was in her blood. She'd climbed the ranks of the Harrisburg PD behind her father, the now-retired chief of police. She was cool and smart and could wrestle a guy twice her size to the ground without breaking a sweat. She also took everything seriously. Which was why he hadn't taken her up on her offer to get naked after a department ugly Christmas sweater party a few years back.

"A fiancée and a dog," she said, arching an eyebrow over her aviators when he took the seat she pushed toward him with her boot. "What's next, Nick? A 401(k)?"

Actually it was a SEP IRA, but his bad-boy rep had already taken enough hits.

"How's it going, Katie?" he asked, helping himself to the beer she'd ordered for him.

"Another beautiful summer in the city," she said wryly. The hot dogs and fireworks that July brought meant more people were spending more time getting drunk and committing crimes. More assaults, more muggings, and more homicides.

People just couldn't be trusted with good weather.

"I hear homicide is swamped," he ventured, wondering when she'd get around to telling him why she was here.

"You heard right," she said. Her lips were a pale pink that never quite stretched beyond an amused smirk. "And it's about to get hairier now that we're down a man."

This was news. For Harrisburg's fifty thousand residents, there were 175 officers. It wasn't hard to know just about everyone in the department. "Who'd you lose?" he asked, stroking a hand over Burt's furrowed brow.

"Weber. This afternoon. On suspension pending investigation."

He knew she was watching him for a reaction. Rather than climbing on the table and crowing like a rooster like he wanted, Nick took off his sunglasses. "Weber got suspended? For what? The guy was born with the book shoved up his ass."

She lifted a shoulder. "Can't really say. There was some questionable behavior. Some tips getting ignored. Cases not getting closed. Couple of complaints from witnesses."

"You saying he was dirty?" he asked.

"I'm not saying anything," she told him, lifting her beer. "He was looking pretty hard at your girl in the Frick case, wasn't he?"

Nick tapped out a beat on his leg. "She had nothing to do with it. He should have known that."

"She knew something was going down," Katie pointed out. "Enough to report the crime to the cops before it was committed. Twice."

He shook his head. "Just one of those coincidences. She had a feeling."

"Hmm," she said. "She see anything that's not in the report from that night?"

He leaned back and stroked a hand over the dog's broad head. "Nah. She didn't see a damn thing. The shots woke her up. By the time she hit the stairs, the guy was long gone. And I was parked at the wrong angle to catch anyone coming down the fire escape on the dashcam. You catch the case?" he asked.

"Yeah. In addition to the three I'm already working. So I'd appreciate you throwing me anything you come across in your digging. Professional courtesy."

"Same goes."

"I'm not too proud to take help when it's offered. I caught wind of a few rumors about Dickie and some mysterious married woman. No one's coughed up any names yet. But you know how those things shake out. Jealous husband. Bang. Bang."

"So you're leaning away from the gambling angle?" Nick asked.

Her lips curved in that thin almost smile.

"Professional courtesy only goes so far," she reminded him.

"Don't play me like that, Detective. Come on. We go back."

She took off her sunglasses and kicked back in her chair. "Fine. No. The gambling doesn't ring for me. I'm liking the jealous husband."

"May the best man win," he said, lifting his glass to her.

"Oh, she will," she said. "What's wrong with your dog?"

Burt had effusively greeted every person on the deck as he'd pranced to the table. Now, he was staring at Katie, head cocked, tongue poking out of the corner of his mouth. Like he was trying to puzzle her out.

"I'm not sure. I've never seen him make that face before." He couldn't tell if the dog was impressed with the detective or unsure of her.

"Speaking of dogs, you hear about the vigilante shit last night?" she asked.

"I didn't get the details," Nick lied easily. "Something about a break-in and some dogs?"

"A bunch of those weirdos broke into a house on Seventeenth Street and busted a dozen dogs out of the basement."

"Summer in the city," he said.

Her smile was wry. "Tell me you don't miss it."

He grinned. "All those late nights? The rules and regulations? Having to toe the line? No thanks, Detective. I like my gig now."

"Geez. Maybe I should give the civilian life a shot."

39

"Hold this in your hands," Gabe instructed, handing Riley a heavy metal object that had a carved frowning face. She recognized it as a bookend from one of the dusty bookcases in the front parlor. They were seated cross-legged on the floor in her apartment.

Burt was behind them on the couch, happily burying his new favorite toys under the pillows. Nick was off on some non-murder-related surveillance job. He'd pouted when she'd told him she already had plans for the evening with Gabe.

"Shouldn't we be doing this with something of Dickie's?" she asked Gabe. The whole reason she was opening herself up to this crap was so she could help solve a murder. It seemed counterintuitive to be reading a dumb bookend that had nothing to do with anything.

"This is your first time reading an object's energy on purpose. I felt it would be best to begin with something not tainted by homicide," he explained. "So as not to emotionally scar you."

"Ah. Good call," she agreed. She turned the bookend over in her hands. It was the bust of an ugly, scowling man with crazy hair.

"Let us close our eyes and empty our minds," Gabe said, the cadence of his deep baritone soothing like a cozy blanket.

She yawned. "Okay. Emptying."

She needed to schedule a vet appointment for Burt. Eggs. She was out of eggs. Ugh. Next week started the six-week catalog proofing project that she was absolutely not looking forward to. Proofreading SKU numbers and dimensions. Her job was the most boring job in the world. Were stability and normalcy a good enough trade for the hours of her life that ticked away within the industrial gray walls of SHART? She needed the paycheck. With her legal debt to her ex-husband, she didn't really have a choice.

"And bringing your mind back to its focus since it has wandered," Gabe said.

Oh shit. What are we doing again?

Riley yanked her attention back to the ugly object in her hands.

"Good," Gabe breathed. "Now, tell your spirit guides that you are ready to receive messages associated with this item."

She cracked open one eye. "Is there some kind of spirit guide etiquette? Like should I ask them how their day was or something?"

"It is always good to be polite," he said without opening his eyes. He was so calm. He looked like an athletic Black Buddha enjoying enlightenment.

She cleared her throat. "Uh, okay. Spirit guides, I hope you had a good day. I am ready to receive messages about this ugly bookend thing. Please," she added hastily.

"Now, empty your mind again," he instructed.

She took a breath and imagined a blank screen. She was both appalled and delighted when something she hadn't put there popped onto it.

Gabe was still speaking, but he sounded like he was very far away.

She focused on the screen and hung on to the bust while those cotton candy clouds whizzed around her head.

"What are you seeing?" Gabe asked. He sounded like he was in her closet with the door closed.

"Um. A bunch of colorful clouds. Oh wait. They're parting. I see a table with a bunch of crap on it." She uselessly tried to push the clouds away to see more clearly. "Wait. No. It's a yard sale. There's a woman. She's grumpy. She's cheap. Not frugal, but one square of toilet paper cheap. I see a quarter." The picture fuzzed and disappeared behind the clouds. "I don't see anything now," she reported. "Just feel anticipation. Excitement. Young and bubbly. Oh! It's a birthday party. There's a cake and a girl. A teenager."

The grumpy woman popped into the image and handed the girl the unwrapped bust.

The birthday girl would have rather had a new sweater—Riley couldn't blame her there—but she accepted the gift politely. "Thank you, Aunt Gert."

Riley saw a clockface with the hands moving and then Aunt Gert—"Holy shit. Aunt Gert got hit by a tractor? She's dead. Now the ugly bust is important. Valued." Riley opened her eyes, blinked. "Did I do it? Did I get it?"

Gabe was frowning. "I do not understand."

Her shoulders slumped. "Did I get it wrong?"

"This was a gift from Lily's Aunt Gertrude on her eighteenth birthday. It was given to the family by Charles Lindbergh. Aunt Gertrude gifted it to Lily the day before she was tragically killed in a car accident."

She winced. "I think Aunt Gert lied. She bought it at a yard sale and was annoyed by having to get her 'frivolous' niece a gift. And that car accident? She was hit by a tractor when she was trying to steal sweet corn out of a neighbor's field. She thought their farm stand prices were too high."

Gabe was aghast. "Why would Aunt Gert lie to Lily?"

"People lie," she said, feeling like she was telling a kid there was no Santa Claus. "People defraud. People do bad things to advance their own agendas, and they take advantage of other people."

"That is very sad. Lily will be devastated when you tell her this terrible truth."

She blinked. "Hang on. I don't think we really need to tell Lily," she said.

"But she should know that her aunt disliked her and gave her another person's refuse rather than a treasured family heirloom."

"Should she?" Riley asked. "If the truth is just going to hurt someone, what's the point in telling it?"

He frowned again. "I must think about this."

He closed his eyes, and she waited a beat. She waved her hand in front of his face, wondering if he'd fallen asleep sitting up. *Nope. Just meditating.*

She heard a creak from outside her door. Burt popped his head out of the cushion and stared at the door. "Relax. It's probably…" She didn't know who it would be. But her spirit guide people seemed to know something because the hair on her arms stood straight up.

Uh-oh.

"Stay," she said firmly to the dog.

Burt ignored the command and followed her to the door.

Holding her breath, she sidled up to the peephole. Burt shadowed her movements and put his front paws on the door. He gave the wood a lick. She spotted a man in the hallway standing in front of the police tape over Dickie's door.

It definitely wasn't one of her neighbors. He was youngish and well-dressed in khakis and what looked like one of those sweat-wicking golf shirts. Nerves. She could feel them shimmering off him. He stalked to the left, then back to the door. His movements were jerky, tense. He reached out, testing the doorknob.

"Fuck." Riley wasn't sure if he'd said it or thought it.

He paced again and came back to the door. With a squaring of his shoulders, he took a step back and landed a kick to the door above the knob.

"Oh shit," she breathed, turning away from the door. "Shit. Shit. Shit. Where's my phone?"

"*Watch.*"

Riley looked over her shoulder, expecting Gabe to be

standing there. But the whispered command hadn't come from him. He was still meditating over truth and lies.

She grabbed her phone on the coffee table and raced on tiptoe back to the door.

Riley: Everyone go to your rooms and lock the doors now! We have an intruder!

Lily: Where? Is it a he? Do you think he's single?

Mr. Willicott: Who are you people? How did you get my number? How did I get a phone?

Fred: Relax, everyone. If this were a real drill, Riley would have used the code word.

Mrs. Penny: You mean I loaded my Beretta for a drill? Thanks a lot, Riley. I could have shot Willicott.

Fred: Maybe we should have a code word for drill emergencies.

Riley: This is not a drill! Someone just broke into Dickie's apartment!

Lily: She's really dedicated to this practice run.

Riley: Not a practice run!

Fred: THEN USE THE CODE WORD!

Riley smothered a growl.

Riley: Cabbage casserole. Intruder on the third floor.

Lily: You don't mean the census taker I let in, do you?

Mrs. Penny: Christ. I just unloaded the Beretta. You are terrible at this!

Burt gave a low *boof* and stared at the door.

Riley tried to pull up the camera on her phone, but Lily and Mrs. Penny were arguing about the merits of calling the cops with their cabbage casserole situation. Mr. Willicott was asking where his falafel leftovers were.

She pushed her face up against the peephole again. The man was coming out of Dickie's apartment. He was empty-handed and looked even more frustrated. He dragged the hat off his head and swiped a hand over his face.

"Oh crap." She'd seen that face before. *Where?*

The screen in her head coughed up an image from Nature Girls. He was the cute, nervous guy who'd cornered the busty server. Betty? Bitsy? Betsy!

He was still cute, still nervous. But now there was a stink of desperation. She didn't know what he'd been looking for, but she was sure he hadn't found it.

He glanced toward the main staircase, then changed his mind and headed to the back stairs. Riley held her breath and counted to ten before launching herself out her own door and running down the front stairs.

"Come near this door, and I'll fill your face with lead," Mrs. Penny shouted from the second floor.

"Yoo-hoo! Intruder, is that you?" Lily called coyly from behind her first-floor door.

Riley made it down to the first floor without hurling her body into gravity's forces. As quietly as possible, she slipped out the front door and onto the stretch of lawn.

There was a car. A late-model Mercedes in a glossy gray paint job pulling out of the lot onto Front Street. She ducked behind a tree to avoid being spotted.

She pulled out her phone and texted Nick.

Riley: Guy medium height, medium build, looked like a golfer just kicked in the door to Dickie's apartment. Left empty-handed. Drives a new gray Mercedes. Saw him at Nature Girls trying to chat up a waitress. Tried to get video of him, but my neighbors are pains in my ass.

Her phone rang seconds later. Riley sat down on the bottom step of the porch. "Hi, dear, how's your night?" she asked Nick.

"Har har. I'm on my way. Be there in ten," he said. She could hear the RPMs of his engine and knew he was speeding to get to her. "Are you okay?"

"Slow down, Cannonball Run. We're fine. He didn't seem murdery."

"A guy breaks into the apartment where a murder took place a week ago across the hall from my girl? I'm comin' in hot. Where are you?" His voice was casual, but she could sense the urgency from him.

"On the front porch."

"Damn it, Thorn. Get inside and lock the door." All casualness was gone.

"Look, I keep locking the door, and my neighbors keep letting criminals inside."

"I'll yell at them," he promised.

She snorted. "Good luck with that."

She opened the front door and stepped inside.

A shot rang out, and Lily's bedroom door exploded.

"What the fuck was that?" Nick yelled in her ear.

"Mrs. Penny, what the hell?" Riley shouted.

The woman poked her head out into the hall, followed by Lily. "Whoops. And that's why you always cancel the code," she said, waving a handgun.

"Did your neighbor just try to shoot you?" Nick demanded. Riley heard him lay on his horn. "Move your goddamn horse trailer off the goddamn road!"

She covered her phone. "You're in so much trouble," she told Mrs. Penny.

The woman shrugged.

"Riley?" Nick bellowed.

"Everything's fine," she assured him. "Door's locked. Overzealous amateur security contained."

"I'll be there in four," he snapped.

"Should I call the cops?" she asked.

"No," he told her. "I'd like to avoid it if possible. Give them a chance to forget about you for at least a few days."

"I doubt Detective Weber is going to give up tailing his primary suspect," she said dryly.

"Weber's off the case," he said. "He got suspended."

"Over what?"

"Dunno exactly. Sounded like dirty cop insinuations to me. Burt and I met the new detective for a drink today."

A picture of a pretty blond with a badge surfaced in Riley's mind. "You took my dog on a date with another woman?"

"How did you—never mind. It wasn't a date."

"Could Weber be the reason behind all those cases that were being ignored? What about the tip line 'accidents'?" she asked. Her phone vibrated, signaling another call. "Crap. My mom's calling. I better take it."

"Don't you dare hang up—"

She switched over to her mother. "Hey, Mom," she said.

"What's wrong? What happened?" her mom demanded. "My spidey senses are tingling. You're upset. Or in danger. Or your bowels are flaring up."

"Mom, I'm fine. Everything is fine," Riley said, ducking into the front parlor to wait for Nick...and avoid getting shot at by the nearsighted Mrs. Penny.

"Oh! Good. Well, since I have you on the phone..."

Her mother never gave up that easily on an interrogation. Riley was immediately suspicious. "What do you want?" she sighed.

"I want you to bring Nick to dinner tomorrow night," Blossom announced.

Riley could hear the typical domestic background noise on her mother's end. The monk chant album she always played when she and Roger did the dishes together. There was the customary pop of a wine bottle cork, and Riley could envision her dad pouring two glasses to the rim.

"Mom, we're not actually dating."

"You're also not actually engaged," Blossom pointed out. "But if I have to hear from Lily one more time about how charming and polite and 'smoldering with sexuality' my daughter's fiancé, who we've never met, is, I'm going to blow a spiritual gasket. Cheers," she said.

Riley heard the clink of glasses.

"I don't think it's a great idea. It might give everyone the wrong idea," she told her mother.

Blossom scoffed. "Riley, sweetheart, you know I can't lie. And the next time Lily mentions to me how tight your fiancé's butt is, I won't be able to control myself, and I'll just blurt the whole thing out."

"Are you blackmailing me, Mom?"

"I'm not proud of it, but yes. I want to meet him. Even if you're not getting married, he's important to you. Your father and I—"

"I don't give a rat's ass about some fake boyfriend," Roger shouted for Riley's benefit. "This is all your mother."

"You do too care, Roger," Blossom shot back.

"She's just doing this so someone can help me move the couch again," Roger yelled.

Blossom was infamous for inviting guests to dinner with ulterior motives. She'd once invited their gastroenterologist neighbor over for cocktails and proceeded to grill the woman about acid reflux.

Her parents bickered back and forth, and Riley rolled her eyes to the night sky. "Okay. Fine! I'll ask him if he wants to come to dinner. But we're *not* together, and I don't want you getting any ideas."

"Great!" Blossom said cheerily. "Oh, and bring Gabe too. I need to get the Fourth of July decorations out of that cabinet no one can reach."

"Mom, stop putting stuff up there. Half the reason Wander married Raphael was because you needed someone to reach the canning supplies."

But Blossom was already too busy starting her to-do list for her dinner guests, and Nick was flying into the parking lot, sending gravel in all directions.

"I gotta go, Mom," Riley said as Nick slammed his door and stalked up the front porch steps. She hung up and opened the door for him.

He didn't slow down, just picked her up, kicked the door closed behind him, and kissed the hell out of her.

40

"D o you like chicken?" Riley asked her passengers.

"Are there people who don't?" Nick asked.

"I am very fond of chicken. And ice cream," Gabe piped up from where he was crammed into the back seat of her Jeep with Burt.

"*Ask these guys if they know the difference between a spinner-bait and a buzzbait,*" Uncle Jimmy demanded from deep in the recesses of her mind.

"*Not now, Uncle Jimmy.*"

She put on her turn signal and sent up a silent prayer to her spirit guides, asking them to kindly shut up all psychic messages.

She felt something like a garage door closing in her head and waited. No lure trivia. No monologue about river currents and mosquito hatchings. No Uncle Jimmy.

A tickle of guilt formed in her belly, but she brushed it aside. She was about to be smothered in family. The deceased ones could give her a break while she dealt with the living.

It had been another late night with Nick lecturing her neighbors on stranger danger and gun safety. She'd given him a description of the guy and the car, but without a name or a license plate, there wasn't much to go on. Lily had added her own description, which hadn't helped at all unless there was going to be a lineup to identify butts.

Nick had insisted on spending the night in the downstairs parlor to make sure no one else broke in or was admitted. Lily, the earliest riser, had the pleasure of finding him naked on the couch, pants tossed over a wingback armchair, underwear thrown over a stained-glass lampshade.

Riley had left for work while Nick installed security cameras on the front and back doors and Lily described his penis to Mrs. Penny in great detail.

She hung a left into the fast-food restaurant's parking lot.

"Aren't we going to dinner at your parents?" Nick asked.

"Yep," she said, rolling down her window at the speaker. "What do you guys want?"

She placed their order and pulled forward. Nick and Gabe wrestled for the honor of paying. Gabe won, enthusiastically shoving a credit card out the window at the cashier.

A minute later, with a bag full of chicken plus one hot fudge sundae, Riley pulled into a parking spot and distributed the food.

"Why are we pre-eating?" Nick asked her.

"Cabbage casserole," she said.

"Huh?"

"Just trust me. Mom is an…adventurous, vindictive cook. It's better to go on a full stomach."

She popped a nugget into her mouth and handed one to Burt.

"Go easy on the people food," Nick warned her. "We're just starting to get his farts under control."

They ate quickly, and Riley disposed of the evidence in the trash can before driving to her parents' house.

"My family is a little…eccentric," she warned Nick.

"I can handle eccentric," he told her. "But how are we going to fake a relationship around a bunch of psychics?"

"They know we're not together," she said.

"Then why am I invited to dinner?"

"Yes. I too would like to know why he is invited to dinner," Gabe chimed in, a vanilla ice cream mustache coating his upper lip.

She handed him a napkin.

"Why are *you* invited to dinner?" Nick shot back.

"I am a delightful dinner guest," Gabe insisted.

———

"Ain't she a beaut?" Roger Thorn asked, giving Daisy the Spite Cow an affectionate slap on the rump. She was black and white with dead cow eyes and a wet cow nose. "Did you know they hold auctions where you can show up and buy a farm animal?"

"Yeah, Dad. They're for *farmers*," Riley said.

"And recreational livestock raisers," her dad said triumphantly.

Daisy the cow and Burt the dog sniffed noses.

Roger beamed. "Look at her makin' friends."

"Speaking of. Dad, this is Nick. Nick, this is my dad, Roger."

"Hiya," Roger said, offering his hand.

"Really nice cow," Nick said as they shook.

"She is, isn't she?" Roger said with paternal pride.

"The best cow," Gabe cut in, not wanting to be outdone.

"I might be biased, but I agree," Roger said. "Good to see you again, Gabe."

"Excuse me!" The shrill voice had Riley cringing and Burt's hackles rising.

"Who the hell is that?" Nick asked out of the side of his mouth as a rail-thin woman in white capris and six inches of blond bouffant minced down the sidewalk in gold stilettos.

"Chelsea Strump. Next-door neighbor and my father's archnemesis. You met her evil aunt at my office. The eaves-dropping receptionist."

The dog let out a warning *boof*.

"Does anyone else smell sulfur and brimstone?" Roger asked loudly.

"Behave, Dad," Riley hissed.

"Hello," Chelsea said, brandishing a glossy pink clipboard and matching pink pen. "I'm distributing a petition to make housing livestock of any kind illegal in this neighborhood."

"Ha! Good luck with that, Strump. I've already got the Yangs, the Smiths, and the Kapoors on my side."

"Well, I've already got signatures from the Klomps and the Rotterdinks," she said triumphantly.

"The Klomps don't even live here anymore," Roger bellowed. "They moved to Alabama three years ago."

"Mrs. Klomp is prepared to testify that they moved because you threatened them with your livestock ownership plans."

"We should probably go inside before we witness a crime," Riley suggested.

Nick, Gabe, and Burt followed her up onto the porch and into the house.

"We're here," she called.

"Back in the kitchen."

They found Blossom on tiptoe atop a stepladder, pretending to stretch fruitlessly for the out-of-reach cabinet.

Wander was peacefully chopping vegetables at the island. Her indulgent Zen smile wavered for a moment when Gabe walked in. "Hi." Her voice was a high-pitched squeak instead of her usual throaty tone.

"Wander, you know Gabe," Riley said.

Her sister nodded, eyes big, pupils shooting tiny cartoon hearts in the man's direction. "Hi," she squeaked again.

"Hello again," he said.

"And this is Nick," Riley said before her sister could line up husband number three.

With great effort, Wander dragged her doe eyes away from Gabe. "Hello," she said. "I hope you don't mind tofu and children."

"Two of my favorite things," Nick lied, all panty-melting charm.

"Welcome to family dinner, boys. We'll get it started just as soon as I manage to get these gosh darn boxes down," Blossom said from her perch.

"Allow me, Mrs. Thorn," Gabe insisted.

"I can do it," Nick offered. "His muscle mass could shatter that ladder."

"Relax." Riley patted him on the arm. "You're the couch guy."

"Huh?"

She angled her head toward the sliding doors that overlooked the back deck. "Come meet the nieces."

She opened the door, and Burt bounded outside.

"When did you get a dog?" Wander asked, her eyes glued to Gabe's toned butt as he ascended the ladder vacated by Blossom.

"Wednesday," Riley said, stepping outside to supervise.

"Look! A lion!" six-year-old Rain crowed from her upside-down position on the monkey bars. Burt loped over, and she wrapped her arms around his neck in an inverted hug.

"Hello, giant doggy," Janet said, skipping over. "You have big feet!"

Burt's entire body trembled with glee.

"Girls, come in and wash up so you can help with supper," Wander called, regaining some of her ethereal, earth-motherly vibe.

Whines changed to excitement when the girls spotted Riley on the deck. Excitement changed to coy interest when they noticed Nick behind her.

"Aunt Riley, is this your dog?" Janet asked, jogging along-side Burt.

"He is. And this is Nick," she said.

Janet shyly buried her face in Burt's fur.

"Hi, Nick," Rain piped up. "You're cute. Hi, Aunt Riley."

After hugs, they all trooped inside, and the girls shuffled off to wash their hands.

"So this is Burty Boy. Hello, you handsome, handsome boy," Blossom crooned, kneeling down to lavish the dog with love.

Both Nick and Gabe—who was clutching a box of Fourth of July–themed crap—looked as if they wished the compliment was directed at them.

The front door banged open and shut, and Roger appeared, trailed by eight-year-old River.

"You didn't kill that terrible woman, did you?" Blossom asked.

"Nah. I just had River turn the hose on her and made it look like an accident. Now, who wants to help me move a couch?"

———

After a flurry of chopping, steaming, seasoning, and couch moving, they sat down to a meal of what amounted to a mound of steamed vegetables.

"This is why chicken," Riley whispered to Nick as he grudgingly spooned leeks onto his plate.

"You're so wise," he said.

Burt wasn't even trying to beg for scraps. He'd taken one look at the table and wandered into the TV room to curl up on the couch.

"So, Nick," Blossom began.

"Oh boy. Here we go," Riley muttered.

"Tell me all about yourself," Riley's mom said. "What sign are you? Are you an introvert or an extrovert? Do you take any supplements?"

"Mom, we're not actually dating, remember?" Riley said.

"I can be interested in my dinner guests without them dating my daughters," Blossom said with feigned innocence.

Sure. She *could* be. But that was not what was happening here.

"I feel like your intentions—"

"Are you reading my energy right now?" Blossom perked up. "Oh, this is so exciting! I've been waiting years for this."

"Mom, you're dimming Riley's aura," Wander warned.

"That's just a reflex," Blossom said confidently. "She's nervous about finally opening herself up to her gifts. How do you feel about psychic gifts, Nick?"

He choked on a balsamic glazed carrot. His gaze slid to Riley and then back. "I feel...great?"

"So it doesn't bother you that Riley could be reading your energy or receiving messages from a deceased loved one right now?"

"I find it most impressive," Gabe cut in.

Wander looked like she was going to melt out of her chair and into a puddle on the floor.

"You know, not only does Wander see auras, she's clairscent, *and* she's very flexible," Riley said to Gabe.

"I think it's amazing and fascinating," Nick cut in. "The psychic thing, I mean."

Riley looked down at the lump of sautéed kale on her plate and felt a lovely little glow in her chest.

"Hey, who won the 1989 Super Bowl?" Roger asked from the head of the table.

River screwed up her face. "Um, the 49ers?"

"That's my girl," Roger said. "Just for that, I'm gonna teach you how to run the power washer tomorrow."

"Yes!" River pumped her arm in victory.

The doorbell gonged, rousing Burt from the couch.

"Come in," everyone shouted.

There were noises of dog and human greetings, and then Wander's biological dad, a broad-shouldered Black man with a graying frohawk, ducked his head into the kitchen. "Hi, guys," he said.

"Hi, Winston," they chorused back.

The girls pushed away from the table to give more hugs. "Pappy W!" Janet said, making grabby hands at the man.

"Company tonight?" Winston asked.

"Riley brought her men," Blossom said proudly. "Nick, Gabe, meet my ex-lover and Wander's father, Winston."

Wander blew Winston a kiss.

"Uh," Nick said. "Hi."

"Hello. It is a delight to meet you," Gabe said.

"Doing okay?" Riley asked, patting Nick's knee.

"I have a lot of questions," he confessed with a grin.

"Don't you dare ask them because you'll get answers none of us are prepared for," she warned.

"Me and Winston gotta go," Roger announced, pushing away from his barely touched vegetables.

"Trivia night waits for no man," Winston said, rubbing his palms together.

"Have fun, you two," Blossom called, getting up from her chair to kiss Roger.

Wander caught Riley's eye and tilted her head questioningly in Nick's direction. Riley nodded toward Gabe and wiggled her eyebrows. Her sister tugged her braids over her shoulder and hid behind them coyly. It wasn't psychic communication. It was a sister language.

Once the rest of them had spent enough time pushing vegetables around on their plates, Blossom called dinner over. Since Roger had left and taken his cholesterol problems with him, she doled out juicy helpings of homemade strawberry shortcake that made up for the soggy kale.

Nick impressed Blossom with his request for seconds. Gabe volunteered to do the dishes. The kids trooped off to the living room to watch their allotted hour of TV with Burt on their heels.

"Nick," Blossom said as Wander took her plate to the sink. "Have you ever had a tarot reading?"

"Oh no," Riley groaned.

"I haven't. You'd be my first," he said, dimples on full display.

Reluctantly, Riley followed Nick and Blossom into the sunroom with a full glass of wine. She didn't feel good about leaving him alone to be spiritually analyzed. The room had once been a stately study, but her mother had put her stamp on it, adding dozens of plants and crystals and colorful rugs and tapestries. The shelves were now stocked with alternative spiritual tomes and gardening books as well as an extensive collection of gory murder mysteries.

Against the row of windows was a small table covered with a midnight-blue patterned cloth. It was there that Blossom directed Nick to sit.

Riley slouched on the red suede love seat that matched nothing else in the room and picked up a volume on herbs from the bench that served as a coffee table.

Blossom lit fat white candles that lined the windowsill, then produced a deck of cards from a worn vegan leather pouch.

"Since you're a virgin," she said cheerfully, "we're going to do a simple past, present, future reading."

Riley did her best to tune them out, instead focusing on strategies for growing lavender indoors. But her attention continually returned to the low voices at the table.

"This card in your past represents a turning point stemming from a loss. A tragedy occurred. And a decision was made," Blossom instructed, her tarot voice quiet and soothing. "Does that make sense?"

Nick cleared his throat. "Uh, yeah."

Curiosity piqued, Riley couldn't help but listen. Once again, the picture of Nick and the girl with long dark hair popped into her head. Just as quickly as she'd appeared, the girl disappeared.

"The cards say this decision took you on a new path to your present," Blossom continued.

While her mother worked her way through his present and his paths and decisions, Riley again wondered about the mysterious Beth. Who had she been to Nick and Detective Weber? Why was she such a touchy subject for both men?

"*That* doesn't look good," Nick said good-naturedly as Blossom began to flip over the last row of cards. His future.

Blossom laughed. "The Death card very rarely means actual physical death. As long as you don't flip over a Ten of Swords. That's when we'd start to wor—"

"Huh," he said.

"Well, shit," Blossom said.

The sudden wave of "uh-oh" coming from the table caught Riley's attention. She abandoned the herb book and sidled up behind Nick.

She wasn't into divination, but growing up with Blossom Basil-Thorn meant she'd absorbed enough. The Death card sat in the middle of the last row of three cards. To its right, the end of Nick's future, was a card depicting a man lying facedown with ten swords stuck in his back.

"Well, we've all gotta go sometime," he joked.

"Mom!" Riley hissed.

But Blossom's brow was furrowed as she studied the last row of cards. She muttered to herself for a good two minutes before shaking her head. "I'm sorry, dear, but this looks like death to me. And sooner rather than later. Do you have a will? A power of attorney?"

"Aunt Riley?" River appeared in the doorway. Her eyes were glazed, tone flat. "You need to see the TV."

Riley recognized the look immediately. River had been showing signs of her female clairvoyant heritage since she was five.

"Go," Blossom ordered, meeting Riley's eyes.

"We'll talk about this later," Riley promised Nick. To his credit, he didn't look concerned that his fake fiancée's mother had just predicted his untimely demise or that her niece could have been an extra in *The Shining*.

Riley followed her niece into the living room where River pointed at the TV. The evening news was on. "State legislator Rob Bowers was killed in a one-car accident late last night on the Market Street Bridge."

Video footage of the aftermath showed a mangled gray Mercedes with its passenger door ripped open. There was a tarp covering the interior. The white of the bridge was bathed red and blue by emergency vehicle lights.

A distinguished headshot of the victim appeared in the upper left of the screen. "Representative Bowers served the residents of Dauphin County for three years."

"Nick," Riley yelled.

He stepped into the room and put his hands on her shoulders.

She pointed at the screen. "That's him. That's the guy who broke into Dickie's apartment."

41

Riley appeared in the sunroom's darkened doorway when he disconnected the call. "My sister volunteered to drop Gabe and Burt home. I'm coming with you," she announced.

Nick crossed to her and took the keys out of her hand. "Ever been to a junkyard before?"

"You sure know how to show a girl a good time," she joked. But he could feel her nerves.

There was another body now, and every instinct was screaming that the deaths were connected.

After a lightning round of goodbyes, they headed out. It was dark now, and a rainstorm had moved in, saturating the ground and making the road gleam under the streetlights.

"Maybe it's a coincidence," she suggested when he turned off her parents' street and headed toward Route 15.

He shot her a look. "Does it feel like a coincidence?" he asked.

"Not even a little bit."

He navigated around the town of Mechanicsburg on the highway, his mind turning the pieces of information over. It helped to have something else to think about besides the whole he-was-going-to-die-soon thing.

"About that tarot reading," she began. "Those things are really subjective."

He grunted. "Has your mom ever predicted anyone else's death before?" he asked, expecting a negative.

"Well…"

Ah, shit.

"Just a few times," she hedged.

"And? Did they die?"

"Everybody dies eventually, Nick," she said cautiously.

This discussion wasn't helping keep his mind off his impending demise.

He got off the highway and took a meandering road a half mile before the headlights slashed across the sign: EARL'S SALVAGE.

He pulled up close to the chain-link fence, rolled down his window, and stabbed the intercom button.

"Nicky Santiago, how the hell are ya?" crackled a voice through the speaker.

"Not bad, Beefcake. You staying clean?"

Beefcake cackled. "Ish," he said. "Come on in. You got gear, or do you need to borrow?"

"Borrow if you've got it," Nick said. He shot a glance at Riley. "Enough for two."

The gate in front of them whirred and clanked open, and he pulled through. It was a typical junkyard. Refuse was stacked high behind chain-link fences and lit by the occasional stingy pole light. Heavy equipment was parked under the cover of a pair of open-walled car ports.

He followed the dirt path away from the weigh station to a trailer that sat a good eight inches lower on its foundation on the right than it did on the left.

"Come on in," he invited Riley, shutting off the engine.

Together they made the soggy dash for the trailer's cinder block steps. He gave a cursory knock and yanked open the door, shoving her inside.

Earl "Beefcake" Nickelbee was a skinny rooster of a guy

who'd had a few brushes with the law in his younger, dumber days. The only thing that seemed to have changed about the man was that he now sported a skinny mustache and a wedding band.

"Nicky," he said, greeting him with an enthusiastic hug.

"Good to see you, Beefcake. Thanks for opening up for us. This is Riley. Riley, this is my buddy Beefcake."

"Hi," she said.

"You got yourself a looker. New partner? You back on the force?" Beefcake asked.

Nick slid a look at her. "Nah, man. I'm still a PI. Riley's my fiancée."

"No fucking shit? For reals?" Beefcake grinned. "Never thought I'd see the day. No offense, ma'am."

"None taken," Riley said. "I was pretty surprised myself."

"When you know, you know," Beefcake said, holding up his left hand to show off his gold band. "I met the missus two years ago at all-you-can-eat crab legs, and it hit me like a claw cracker to the heart."

"Good for you," Nick said.

"Anyway, help yourselves to some gear." Beefcake waved at the boxes of latex gloves and zippered freezer bags, a stack of cheap plastic-wrapped ponchos, and a collection of banged-up flashlights on the desk.

"How long have you two known each other?" Riley asked when Nick plucked a couple pairs of gloves from the box.

"Feels like centuries sometimes," Beefcake said. "We first met…when was that, Nicky?"

"It was 2005. I busted you for possession and shoplifting from the adult store."

Beefcake snapped his fingers. "That's right. I was mixing it up with the time you got me for writing bad checks. Them were the days. Nicky here was okay for a cop. He wasn't an ass about arresting guys like me. Just doin' his job."

Nick handed Riley a pair of gloves, a poncho, and a headlamp. "Let's get a beer and catch up soon, Beefy."

"I'll bring the missus. We can make it a double," Beefcake said, winking at Riley.

"Sounds great," she said with a smile.

They shrugged into the plastic ponchos, strapped on their headlamps, and headed back out into the rain. Following Beefcake's directions, Nick led the way up the slow rise to the east of the trailer. Wrecks were stacked on top of each other like Tupperware.

"That's a lot of rust," Riley observed as her light cut a swath through the wet night, playing over the sea of cars that began at the crest of the hill and stretched on into the dark.

"Lucky for us, they haven't stashed the Mercedes yet," he said. He pointed to the wreck in front of them.

The hood was crunched back to the dashboard, windshield folded into jagged shards. The driver's side was gouged down the entire length of the car. The passenger door was lashed to the roof, offering a view of that tattered blue tarp that meant death.

She winced. "Looks even worse than it did on the news."

He pulled out his phone and cued up the camera.

"I'm gonna take some pictures of the exterior. If you're comfortable, you can put on the gloves and see if you can find anything interesting in the glove compartment."

"Interesting like what?" she asked.

He shrugged. "Anything that says 'murder'?"

She trudged determinedly to the passenger compartment. He went around to the front of the car, crouching down to look at the damage up close. Then he did the same to the driver's side.

He took pictures of every inch of what had been the hood and engine compartment. Now, it was nothing more than a messy tangle of metal. He played it through in his head, rewinding and starting over.

It had been a while since he'd last landed a crash investigation, but there were a few things that stuck with him. Like the fact that the white gouges and scrapes on the side of the car were consistent with hitting a bridge parapet. However, it was the damage to the front that bothered him. No matter how he played it, the car wouldn't have jumped the sidewalk and slammed head-on into the bridge rail at speed before sliding around to scrape down the side.

But if something had hit the car head-on… It seemed clear to him, a guy several years removed from traffic investigation training. Which meant that someone had intentionally misclassified the wreck.

He really didn't like the idea of dirty cops. And if Shapiro thought they'd cleaned house by suspending Weber, there was obviously still at least one rat on the inside.

"Nick, I found something," Riley called, interrupting his train of thought.

He found her upside down, head under the dash in the passenger seat, and felt his claustrophobia kick in.

"Are you stuck?" he asked, already reaching for her.

But she kicked her legs neatly out the door and popped back up. "This was wedged in a seam under the dash."

He leaned in, his light playing over the object she held between her index finger and thumb. "What the hell is that?"

"A fake fingernail," she said, excitement in her tone. She tugged a baggie out of her pocket and dropped it inside. "I think Rob had a passenger. And I think they made it out of the wreck."

He took the bag and studied the nail. It was yellow with a black crosshatch.

"On the news, I noticed that the passenger side door was open. Which could have been how they got his body out, *but* both airbags deployed," she said, tapping the deflated nylon on the dash.

"Nice work, Thorn," he said proudly. "Maybe we should be partners."

"Hang on to that admiration, because I know exactly who the passenger was."

Nick remained impressed with her for the next thirty seconds. Until she pissed him off by explaining what she thought needed to happen.

"No," he said, still determined to argue the point on the rainy drive home.

"Why not? Think about it. Dickie owns Nature Girls. I happen to see Betty/Bessy/Betsy/What's Her Name, the server with crazy fake nails, all cozy with Representative Rob. Representative Rob shows up at Dead Dickie's apartment looking for something. Then *he* turns up dead hours later, and we find her fingernail under the deployed passenger airbag."

"You're not going back to Nature Girls," he said stubbornly. "You almost got yourself assaulted last time you were there."

"Please," Riley scoffed. "It was a bar fight, not a shoot-out."

"I don't want you anywhere near that shithole," he insisted.

"That's what she said," she shot back.

"Not funny."

"Come on, Nick. It's the only way. This all ties back to Nature Girls. Maybe I'll get lucky, and Betsy will be working."

"And if she isn't, you'll what? Start another bar fight?" he demanded.

"No. I'll find out her last name or where she lives. I had to fill out an application. There's got to be paperwork in that office."

"Riley," Nick said through gritted teeth. "Two people connected to your house and Nature Girls have turned up suspiciously dead. Use your damn head."

"That doesn't make me a target. That makes me the perfect person to figure out the connection," she said.

"No," he said stonily.

"Fine," she shrugged. "Then you come up with a plan."

42

For an early afternoon, Nature Girls was packed. Even the seedier side of society wanted to celebrate their patriotism on the Fourth of July, Riley noted as she picked her way through the crowd toward the bar.

"Play this safe. Get in. Get out. Anyone looks at you funny, I want you out of there," a pissed-off Nick grumbled in her ear.

"Yeah. Yeah. I hear you," she murmured.

She'd won the argument thanks to Josie and Brian voting on her side. It made sense to have her go back in. She had the best chance of fabricating a reason to get into the office.

Nick had played the grumpy sore loser. He'd put a wire on her and parked the surveillance van—with Church of Scientology graphics on the doors—down the block, ready to burst through the front door at the first sign of trouble. Brian told her they'd originally had fake plumber's graphics on the van, but they had too many people knocking on the windows with plumbing emergencies. No one bothered a van full of Scientologists.

She spotted Rod behind the bar and snarky Liz yelling at a table of guys who'd already had too much to drink.

Painting on a smile, she pranced up to a stool and plopped down.

"What the hell are you doing here?" Rod demanded, pouring two beers into plastic cups and hurling some cheap tequila in the direction of a row of shot cups. His long white beard was festively tied with three red rubber bands. "Come back to burn the place down?"

"I left my favorite sweatshirt here on my shift," Riley said, batting her eyes in what she hoped was a look of total innocence. "I think it's in the office. Do you mind if I go on back and grab it?"

"Where the fuck are my Jack and Cokes, you slow-ass bastard?" Liz demanded, hurling her wet tray down on the service bar.

"You'll get 'em when you get 'em, asshole." Rod poured two more drafts and plopped them down in front of two inebriated patrons at the bar.

"Don't be a dick to me. You take this shit out on Betsy. *She's* the one who didn't show."

Riley held her breath. Betsy was a no-show? Was it by choice, or had something very, very bad happened to her after the wreck?

"Christ. Ten seconds in the door, and she's already got them talking about Betsy," Nick grumbled in her ear.

Suck it, Nick.

"You want your drinks, you pour 'em yourself," the bartender snarled.

"I fucking will." Liz ducked under the service bar and popped up on the other side. Yanking a bottle of Jack Daniel's off the shelf, she whirled around to reach for the soda gun and spotted Riley. "What are you sitting your ass down for? Get to fucking work."

"I'm fired, remember?" Riley pointed out.

"She's just here to pick up a sweatshirt," Rod said, grabbing a bottle of Sambuca from under the bar.

"What? You think Baldy is gonna walk his no-neck ass out here and volunteer to do actual work?" Liz snapped at the bartender. She turned her attention back to Riley. "You want

313

your sweatshirt? You're gonna work for it. Take these to those stupid assholes in the cowboy hats, then get the herpes twins' order." She slammed three Jack and Cokes down in front of Riley.

"Stick with the plan, Thorn," Nick warned.

"I thought you said I was a troublemaking moron who didn't know her ass from her apron," Riley said, pointedly staring at the drinks.

"You want an apology? 'Cause it comes with a boot to the vagina. You want some tips and your stupid sweatshirt? Then you work."

"I'll take the tips," Riley said cheerfully and grabbed the cups.

"I am going to kill you, Thorn." Nick's snarl tickled her ear.

"Relax," she said under her breath. "This gives me a bigger window to either get in the office or get some gossip."

"Nope. Definitely killing you," Nick's voice snapped.

She worked, taking orders, delivering drinks, trying to scrape years of sticky filth off vacated tables. By three, things had started to slow, with the first wave of celebrants either heading off to picnics and parties or to sleep off their cheap drinks. By four, she found herself sitting at a table with Liz, feet propped up on a chair, counting her tips.

Yay, surprise money.

"So where's Deelia and Betsy?" Riley asked, pocketing her wad of cash.

Liz snorted, her attention on fishing balled-up cash out of her apron. "Deelia's hanging with her grandma for a bullshit picnic lunch. She's in tonight. Betsy's fucking dead to me. She was on the schedule for today and then no-showed. Rod called me in early, so I'm working a double."

"Does Betsy do that often?" Riley pressed, trying not to sound like she was hanging on Liz's every word.

"Subtle, Thorn." Nick's sarcasm echoed in her ear. She tuned it out. His snark was no different from the usual psychic chatter she'd grown used to hearing.

Liz worked her way through the bills, ordering them from highest denomination to lowest without regard to front, back, or right side up. "Who the frick cares? She's dead to me."

Treading lightly, Riley tried a different tactic. "I worked at Applebee's for a year and always worried that something had happened to the no-shows. Like they were in an accident or got abducted."

"Never that lucky," Liz said, tapping her wonky stash of cash on the table three times before folding it and returning it to her apron. "No-shows are too busy being selfish jackoffs to tell anyone they're not coming in. She's probably shacked up with that on-again, off-again suit she bangs on the weekends."

"I love a guy in a suit," Riley improvised.

"Do they make suits big enough for your guy?" Liz asked.

Riley realized she was talking about Gabe. "Gabe's more of a gym clothes kind of man. How did Betsy land a suit? She seems…" She trailed off, hoping Liz would feel compelled to fill in the blank.

"Dumber than a bucket of hair? Yeah. She never had much going for her up top. Except for the math thing. She always lived with roommates, and then I guess the suit started coughing up cash for an allowance or BJs or whatever. Got her own place over in Camp Hill and almost got kicked out because she didn't realize rent was due every month."

"Why didn't she just move in with the guy?"

"How the fuck should I know?" Liz said irritably. She fished out a pack of cigarettes from her apron. "She was like this even in high school."

Annnnnnd jackpot.

"You went to high school with her? I thought you were a lot younger than Betsy," Riley covered quickly.

"Nope. Just didn't hit the tanning beds quite as much as Little Miss Harrisburg High School Homecoming Queen."

"Nicely done, Thorn," Nick said grudgingly.

Riley felt triumphant.

Liz rose. "Takin' five," she called to Rod, who was eating

a turkey sandwich with one hand and chucking plastic cups in the garbage can with the other.

"Whatever," he said.

"You didn't totally suck today," Liz said to Riley.

"Uh, thanks." With Liz heading out to fill her lungs with poison and Rod shoving food in his face, she could head out or… She glanced toward the dingy hall that led back to the office.

"Get your ass out of there, Thorn. You've done enough today," Nick said.

She felt a pull on her subconscious. A tug toward the hallway.

"I can get in the office," Riley said quietly. "We still don't have a last name or an address." Or whatever lay behind that door.

"No." Nick's tone was stony.

She ignored it and got up from the table. Rod was still eating, but his attention was on the baseball highlights on the TV. Quietly, she moved past the bar and into the hall.

"I swear to God, Thorn, if you don't walk out that front door in five seconds, I'm going to make you very sorry," Nick snarled.

The restrooms were on her left. Years of hands and boots had left their marks on the wood, wearing through the wood stain. The office was just ahead on her right, its door a mismatched green to the metal exit door at the end of the hall.

Her heart was pounding loud enough to drown out Nick's swearing. There were answers on the other side. She could *feel* it.

The knob turned, and before she could react, the door flew open.

She stopped in her tracks and stared in horror as a man stepped out. He was short with the broad shoulders and bulging biceps of a gym rat. He had no neck or hair to speak of.

His shaved head was shiny under the flickering fluorescent bulbs overhead.

Riley's vision tunneled, and for just a second, she found herself peering through her peephole at Dickie's door. The floating orb hadn't been an orb after all. It had been a shaved head.

Shit. Shit. Shit. Okay, maybe it wasn't this shaved head. Maybe it was someone else's bald noggin?

"Can I help you?" No Neck asked gruffly. He had a duffel bag in one hand and file folders tucked under his arm.

Just do it. Just look.

Riley glanced down at his shoes.

Quadruple shit.

Black sneakers with red lightning stripes.

"What the fuck, Thorn? Who is that?" Nick demanded. He was probably punching things in the van.

No Neck's eyes narrowed, and Riley realized she hadn't responded yet.

"Sorry," she said quickly, trying to return her bug eyes to normal size. "Bathroom?" she croaked. She was so super chill under pressure.

"Behind you," he said, jiggling the knob of the door he'd just exited. Testing to see if it was locked.

"Right. Ha," Riley said, trying to shake the vision of Shooty McBalderson taking out her neighbor.

Blindly, she turned around and pushed open the first door she found.

He cleared his throat. "That's the men's room," Baldy said at the same time as she noted the urinals.

"Right," she said again, backing out of the room. "Blood sugar must be low."

She hurled herself through the ladies' room door as if shitty particleboard could protect her from a murderer.

Pressing her ear against the door, she tried to listen.

"Report, Thorn," Nick said.

Riley yanked the earpiece out and stuffed it into her pocket.

"What's with the girl? She wasted?" she heard No Neck the Murderer ask.

Rod's answer was too muffled for her to catch.

"Damn it. Damn it. Damn it," she breathed. Not trusting

her shaking hands to shove the earpiece back in place, she pulled the neck of her T-shirt out. "I just found our murderer. Watch the door for a short, stocky bald guy."

She heard footsteps and froze.

Quickly, she reached into the stall and flushed the toilet.

Then she moved to the sink and ran the water. How long was too long to pretend to wash her hands? Was it suspicious that she was washing her hands in a place like this? Would that tip him off that she was a plant?

She wanted to stay locked in here. She also wanted to run out and break a chair over that murdering bad guy's face.

She made a racket with the paper towel holder and then shoved through the door.

No one was waiting to murder her in the hall. Cautiously, she eased through the saloon doors. No Neck was standing at the end of the bar, facing her.

She tried to walk normally, then realized she had no idea how to do that. Her legs felt too loose in the joints. It went against every self-preserving biological urge to force herself to walk toward a guy who had put two bullets in her neighbor's head.

Did he have a gun? Was that what was in the bag?

"Riley," he said when she pushed through the saloon doors.

How did he know her name? Was he psychic too?

Holy shit. She was psychic. There had to be something in her psychic tool kit that applied to this situation.

Help. Help. HELP! She sent up the plea to her spirit guides, to a god or a goddess—or maybe there was a psychic 911, and she'd just called it.

She felt a wave of calm that definitely wasn't her own wash over her.

Taking a deep breath, she smiled at No Neck the Murderer. "That's me."

"Interesting name," he said finally.

She watched in detached amazement as she extended her hand toward him. "And you are?"

No Neck eyed her hand for what felt like an eternity before

taking it. Cold. It rushed through her like jumping into the deep, dark waters of a lake. There was no rage here. No fit of passion waiting to erupt like a volcano. No nothing. Just cold.

"Dun," he said, dropping her hand.

"Dun?" she repeated. "Are you the owner?" *Shut up, Riley. Shut the hell up.* She wasn't sure if it was her self-preservation sending the message or a higher power or Nick shouting in her ear.

"No." A man of few words and many bullets. "You're new here," he stated.

"Yeah. Well, sort of. I just helped out today because Betsy didn't show up for her shift." She watched his face for a flicker of anything at the mention of Betsy. But there was nothing there. Dead shark eyes. Goose bumps cropped up on her arms.

"Well, look who decided to show up and lend a hand an hour too late." Liz banged her way through the front door and strutted up to the bar, glaring at the cold-blooded killer.

Dun the Neckless turned his dead eyes on the purple-haired woman too abrasive to know she was insulting a killer.

Riley stepped in front of Liz just in case there was a gun in that duffel bag.

Dun ignored Liz's dig and looked at Rod. "Later, man," he said.

"Later," Rod shot back, attention already back on the TV.

Dun the Murderer ignored the front door and headed back down the hall toward the emergency exit. *Dammit.*

She was just weighing her chances of running out the back and getting a picture of the guy when the front door flew open, bouncing off the wall.

"Who the hell are you?" Liz asked, eyebrow raised in what kind of looked like admiration.

Josie, Nick's muscle, strolled in wearing tight motorcycle leggings, a black tank, and a somehow sexy-looking fanny pack. She had a chain choker around her neck, and her steel-toed boots sounded ominous on the sticky floor.

Her gaze was cool as she scanned the room.

"I'm her girlfriend," Josie said, nodding at Riley. "Time to go, cupcake."

43

4:15 p.m. Saturday, July 4

"Give me one good reason why I shouldn't murder you right now," Nick growled, yanking his headset off and hurling it on the console when Riley climbed in the van bubbling with excitement.

"It was him! Definitely him. Big, giant, glowing head that would look like an orb through a dirty peephole in the middle of the night. Same shoes as what I saw in the vision. He went out the back," Riley said with entirely too much excitement for his liking. "Must have come in that way too, because I didn't notice him when—"

Nick grabbed her by the shoulders and shoved her down in the chair he'd just vacated. Her eyes went wide like she couldn't understand why he'd be anything less than thrilled with her. Well, he was going to tell her exactly why. He held up a finger and opened his mouth to let her have it. But those wide brown eyes had him shutting it and stepping away.

His gut had yet to unclench from when she had announced she was just going to pop into the office and search it. For a rule-following good girl, she didn't listen worth shit.

"Uh-oh," Brian said. "Nicky's gonna blow."

Josie climbed in and slid the van door closed. "Relax,"

she ordered. "Everyone's alive and well—minus our two dead bodies. Now we've got more info on our missing passenger and a face to go with the trigger finger. So unclench your sphincter, and let's debrief."

"You're next on the murder list," Nick snapped at her.

Josie stuck her tongue out at him and then slipped it into her husband's mouth.

Maybe Blossom's prediction was about to come true because he sure felt an aneurysm coming on. He was surrounded by idiots who didn't seem to understand or care that Riley had ended up face-to-face with a murderer.

"You were supposed to get in and out. That was *the plan*," he said, trying his best to wrestle his rage into submission.

Riley rolled her brown eyes at him. "I was *supposed* to find out who Betsy is. And now we've got enough to do a little creative internet stalking."

"Elizabeth 'Betsy' Quackenbush. Class of 2012. Voted 'most likely to have peaked in high school.' One year of college on record. Her credit is garbage. Social media is private except for Instagram," Brian read off his screen.

"Looks like she and those boobs like to party," Josie said, leaning over her husband's shoulder.

"Last known address is 513 Oakleaf, Unit 12, Camp Hill," Brian said.

His team was oblivious to the fact that Nick was having some kind of stress-induced brain bleed.

"Well? What are we waiting for?" Riley asked. "Let's go talk to her."

"You're not talking to anyone," Nick snapped.

"She did good, Nicky. Chill out," Josie said, unpacking the pepper spray and blade from her fanny pack to get at a stick of gum.

"She got lucky," he retorted.

Riley scowled up at him. "No need to be a dick, Nick," she said.

"You're not trained for this. You shouldn't be having conversations with trigger-happy murderers or working in places where you're just as likely to get shot, stabbed, mugged, or abducted."

"You're overreacting," she shot back.

"Overreacting? *Me?*" Nick scoffed. His cousin and Josie made it a point to not make eye contact with him, which meant he was embarrassing himself. But he couldn't seem to stop.

Why the hell couldn't she see that she mattered?

"He wasn't going to kill me," Riley argued.

"Why? Because you got so scared you walked into the men's room?"

Her nostrils flared adorably, and Nick immediately squashed the affectionate feelings.

"No. Because he's not a raging lunatic who gets pissed off and pulls triggers. He's cold. Calculated."

He threw his arms in the air. "What the fuck does that even mean?"

"I don't know. I just know," she said, frustrated, "No Neck killed Dickie. But he didn't do it because he was pissed off or evening a score. It was like crossing off a task on a to-do list."

"Like a hired hit?" Josie suggested.

"Maybe," Riley said.

"You could have gotten yourself killed," Nick said, ignoring everything but his own helpless rage.

"You maybe wanna keep it down? We don't want someone calling the five-oh on a van full of screaming Scientologists," Brian mentioned.

"You're officially off the team, Thorn," Nick announced.

Riley gasped, coming out of the chair and into his face. Her anger hit him like he'd just shoved his finger into a socket. "*You* sent me in there, you gigantic moron. Don't take the fact that you're developing real feelings for your fake fiancée out on me."

"Feelings? Ha!" He scoffed as derisively as the lump in his throat would allow.

"Yeah. Feelings," she said again, eyes narrowed. "You're pissed off at yourself. And worried that you won't be able to protect everyone. But you're the one who needs protecting!"

"Get out of my head, Thorn! I didn't invite you in," he yelled.

"I'll do you one better and get out of your van," she said. She wrenched open the door and jumped out onto the sidewalk.

Silence descended on the remaining inhabitants of the van.

"Want me to go after her?" Josie offered.

Nick pinched the bridge of his nose between finger and thumb. "No."

"You know, boss," Josie began. "I get that you've got issues around women who don't want to be protected."

Nick swung around and glared at her. They didn't talk about it. It was their one rule.

Josie held up her hands. "For good reason. I'm just saying Riley's not Beth."

Brian inched closer in his wheelchair. "Regardless of the situation that we are never bringing up again, you just gave a woman you care about the boot in the middle of Harrisburg on a drunken holiday. What my wife is trying to say is you're being a dumbass."

"Fuck," Nick hissed under his breath and climbed behind the wheel of the van.

"What did she mean, 'You're the one who needs protecting'?" Brian asked, reaching for his seat belt.

"Nothing," Nick said sullenly as he started the engine.

"She's a psychic, right? Shouldn't you maybe take her predictions seriously?" Josie said.

"It wasn't her prediction," he said, still watching Riley.

"Good, 'cause I'd miss you at family reunions," Brian quipped.

"It was her mom's," Nick said.

———

He didn't go after her. But he did drive behind her as she stalked down the sidewalk with her phone to her face.

"What? You never saw a van of Scientologists stalking a chick before?" Josie yelled out her window at some suspicious pedestrians.

When Riley came to a stop at a corner and stayed put, Nick swooped into a parking space. They sat in silence and waited.

"I could text her," Brian offered.

"No," he boomed. It was better this way. A clean break. She'd done enough. Just shy of putting herself in the line of fire.

"Okaaaaay then," Brian said, unruffled. "I'll just sit here and brainstorm how to ID a guy named Dun that none of us saw."

"Good. Do that," Nick snapped without taking his eyes off Riley. Anger and hurt radiated off her. Minutes later, a minivan pulled up, and Riley climbed in. Nick verified through binoculars that it was Gabe the Gargantuan driving. Riley stuck her arm out the window and flipped Nick the bird. His lips quirked.

Was it any wonder he was developing feelings—or whatever—for her?

In fact, when all this was over, when he'd bagged the killer and collected his fees, he was going to take Riley out on a date. A real one. He'd just have to figure out how to convince her.

"All right, team. Let's hit the office and brainstorm how to find a guy without a picture or a name," he said, marginally more cheerful now.

"Gee. That sounds way better than the sex we were planning to have," Josie groaned.

44

"I can't believe I basically handed him a murderer on a platter, and he can't even say thank you," Riley fumed in the passenger seat of Mrs. Penny's minivan.

"Nicholas is a very stupid man," Gabe said agreeably.

"I helped, *repeatedly*. And he acts like I was just skipping around, putting everyone in mortal danger," she continued.

"We should throw bathroom tissue at his place of residence," Gabe suggested.

"Huh?" Riley asked.

"Wander and her daughters invited Burt and me to watch a movie with them last night after dinner. The main characters decorated a house with bathroom tissue. It looked like fun, and I promised your very small niece, Janet, that we could do it."

As mad as she was, Gabe crushing on Wander and her house of estrogen was a tiny bit adorable.

"I hope you are not mad at me for dividing my attention," he said gravely.

"Dividing your attention?"

"I am here to serve as your spiritual teacher," he said. "Not to learn to sing songs with children. I feel as though I have let you down."

"Gabe, you're allowed to have a life outside teaching me how to psychically solve murders and stuff."

"You are my priority. I did not mean to frivolously pursue fun when I should have been providing you with spiritual support."

"Uh, I think you're confusing me with my grandmother," Riley guessed. Elanora Basil was a terrifying woman whose superpower, besides being a world-renowned medium, was how skillfully she wielded her disappointment. "You can teach me *and* still live a life."

"I am honored that you would forgive me," he said, relieved.

"Yeah, um, okay."

"So how shall we exact our revenge on Nicholas?"

"Let's beat him to the punch," Riley mused.

"You would like me to punch him? It would be my greatest honor," Gabe said happily.

"No. Well, yes. But no. How about you help me identify a murderer instead?" she suggested.

"Oh. All right," he said, sounding just a little disappointed.

Because a crew of crime scene cleaners was busy erasing all biological traces of murder across the hall from her place, Riley and Gabe got to work in his room on the first floor. The only personal effects the man seemed to possess were a set of large weights, a yoga mat, and a meditation cushion. His bed was a sofa, immaculately made up with sheets and pillows. It looked like it was about two feet short of accommodating his frame.

The rest of the room was crammed with bric-a-brac that spilled over from the front parlor. A broken telescope was tucked in a corner behind a prehistoric-looking palm that had grown at least a foot since the last time she'd seen it.

Shelves were stuffed with books and a collection of…well, everything. There were two old typewriters, a St. Francis of Assisi statue that was missing one arm, and four dozen old film canisters. The furniture was a mismatched collection of yard sale chic and curbside pickup.

"Welcome to my home," Gabe said proudly.

"Thanks," Riley said. "So if I want to figure out who a living person is, how do I do that?"

The idea that she could beat Stupid Jerk-Face Nick in identifying No-Neck Dun gave her a heightened sense of urgency.

"Please, sit," Gabe said, gesturing toward the meditation cushion.

She sat eagerly and closed her eyes without being told.

"First we'll spend half an hour calming your mind—"

"Half an hour?" She opened one eye. "Can't we speed it up? This is kind of an emergency."

"When you rush answers to your questions, you will leave with more questions." He said it as if he were narrating a guided meditation.

She blew out an impatient breath. "Okay. Fine. We'll do it your way. But I want it noted for future lessons that we need to figure out how not to take all damn day."

"So noted," he said.

She let him ramble soothingly about quiet minds and calm focus, waiting for him to get to the point. Somehow, in the middle of it, she let go of the grocery list she'd been composing and the "in your face" victory dance she was definitely going to hit Nick with.

Floating. Her body felt weightless and warm. Giddy with excitement, she realized she was back in the blue ethereal space. This was good. She was totally starting to get not terrible at this.

"You may ask your spirit guides to help lead you to the answers you seek." Gabe's voice sounded very far away.

"Okay, spirit guides. It's me again, your friendly psychic Riley. I'm looking for a man."

The first image that popped into her inner mind was that of Nick Santiago.

"No. Not that one. I'm looking for this guy." She tried to project her memory of No Neck into the ether, but it was like trying to operate Netflix without a remote. "Shit, hang on," she muttered.

"Do not force anything. Move peacefully within the flow," Gabe advised distantly.

She took a frustrated breath, let it out. Bringing her mind back to the bar, she let herself see and hear and smell it. Wobbly tables, sticky floors, the smell of old smoke and spilled liquor. The thud of her heart as she walked toward the office, knowing that a monster was behind the door. Knowing she had to be the one to open the door.

Her breathing seemed louder to her ears. Surely he could hear her. Was he just waiting to lure her closer?

The knob was turning now. It was happening! But before Dun made his appearance, Riley was ripped out of the memory and was instead presented with Griffin Gentry in a red power tie, his mouth working with soundless self-importance. She couldn't hear him, but she could feel the smugness that radiated from his pores.

His face kept blurring, the background sharpening. The stupid red tie expanded until it filled her vision. Red with black and gold stripes.

Shaking her head, she tried to dislodge her spotlight whore of an ex from her brain.

"Ugh! Damn it," she swore, tipping off the cushion and staring up at the ceiling.

"Are you all right?" Gabe asked, looming over her with concern. "You look very shiny and pale."

She was sweating and felt like she either wanted to throw up or eat a breakfast sandwich.

Maybe both.

"I couldn't get any answers," she complained. "They just kept showing me my ex-husband. And Griffin's a cheating, dirty-playing jackass, but he didn't kill Dickie."

"Perhaps this donkey man is involved," he suggested. "The spirits don't lie. But they do encode their messages."

"What would a morning news anchor obsessed with spray

tans and manicures have to do with a dirty old man who runs a gross bar?"

Gabe shrugged his massive shoulders. "That is for you to divine," he said.

"Great," she groaned, climbing to her feet. Her pits were uncomfortably sweaty, and she wondered if she'd remembered to put on deodorant that morning. "Thanks for the lesson and the ride," she said. "I think I'm going to find Burt and take him for a walk. Maybe clear my head."

"I believe Fred took him to the park to see if Burt would help him 'score with the ladies.' Do you know which game Fred is playing?"

"I can guess," Riley said, distracted. Just great. She had a head full of nonsense, no dog to walk, and no answers to rub in Nick's face.

Dejected, she opened Gabe's door. And ran smack into Nick's chest.

"What are you doing here?" she asked his pecs.

"Why are you all sweaty?" he shot back.

Clearly, they were ecstatic to see each other.

Gabe appeared behind her. "I was engaging Riley in some exercise," he said. For a man who probably didn't know what a euphemism was, he'd just pissed off his rival with a good one.

Nick's eyes narrowed. There was no hint of dimples. Nick looked like he wanted to say several things.

"Move it, Santiago," Riley said, stepping around him. "I have nothing to say to you." She *would* have if her damn spirit guides had delivered a name and address instead of stupid Griffin Gentry.

He stepped in front of her. "I *need* to talk to you." He made it sound like he really didn't want to talk to her, and she got the teensiest psychic glimpse of Josie's and Brian's disapproving faces.

"They made you come here to apologize, didn't they?" she asked, feeling a little smug.

He looked like he wanted to put his fist through plaster. That cheered her considerably.

"It was brought to my attention that without your abilities, we don't have much of a chance of tracking this guy down." It sounded like every word pained him.

"But you don't agree?" she pressed.

"Oh, I agree," he said through clenched teeth. "But I still don't want you anywhere near this case."

"Too. Late," she said haughtily.

He ran his tongue over his teeth. "Will you please come to the office with me so we can talk?"

"Sure," she said with feigned sweetness. "On one condition."

"Oh, for fuck's sake," he muttered. "What?"

"Tell me you need my help. Say the words, Nick. Say, 'I need your help, Riley.'"

His jaw clenched. Twice. Then he rubbed at the spot between his eyebrows. "You're being ridiculous."

"You're being an ass."

"You are indeed being a donkey-man," Gabe agreed helpfully.

"Go back to your protein shakes, Big and Tall," Nick snarled.

"Say it, Nick," she prompted.

He was silent for almost a full minute, and she knew his mind was running through all the possible ways he could figure this out without her.

"Fine. I need your help, Thorn."

"Now, say you're sorry for being mean to me when, if it had been anyone else on your team, you would have exploded with pride."

"You're not on my team," he argued. "You haven't been trained. You don't carry a weapon. You don't know how to defend yourself. This isn't just fun and games to entertain you in the middle of your boring, safe life. And you don't get to waltz into the danger zone."

"Do you wish for me to punch him in the face now?" Gabe offered hopefully.

"This isn't even about me, is it?" Riley asked, searching Nick's face. "This is about you and Beth."

"It's about *you* taking stupid and unnecessary risks," he challenged.

"Nice apology, assface." Riley started for the stairs. Nick Santiago could take a long walk off of the Walnut Street Bridge as far as she was concerned.

He grabbed her arm and held her in place. She could feel the frustration in his grip. "Fine!" he said. "I'm sorry for being a dick."

She quit trying to pull away. There was something just beneath the surface. Something like panic and fear.

"Okay. Let's go. But I'm driving separately so I don't have to call for another ride when you piss me off again."

"I am happy to give you all the rides you wish," Gabe called.

"Thanks, Gabe. I appreciate you," Riley said.

"And I am humbled by your appreciation. You are a wonderful human being."

"Oh, bite me, hairless Sasquatch," Nick growled.

45

Nick's mood stayed shitty on the drive back to the office. He tailed Riley's Jeep, never letting her out of his sight. He couldn't shake the bad feeling in his gut. Something was about to go down, and he was man enough to be scared shitless that it was going to go down around her.

His brain helpfully ran through all the possibilities. What if this Dun guy recognized Riley somehow from the mansion? What if he'd been casing the place before the murder? He'd have seen her coming and going.

And she'd just walked right up to him and started a conversation.

Did she have any idea how much damage someone could inflict in the minute it would have taken him to get to her? Brian had grabbed him as he'd tried to get out of the van to drag her ass out of there. Then Josie had wrestled him back into his chair.

Nick really needed to start lifting heavier weights.

They'd made him sit and listen. *They'd* trusted her to handle herself. But his reaction hadn't been about trust. It was experience. If the bad guy was bad enough, nothing would stop him. Nick knew this.

But Riley wasn't Beth. She was tougher. Smarter. Older. But she still needed protection. And he was fucking terrified that he couldn't give it to her.

Her Jeep swung into a spot across the street from his office. He parked behind her, not willing to let her out of his sight for the amount of time it would take him to park around back.

She ignored him as he jogged to catch up to her. She pushed through the office door two steps ahead of him.

"Let's get this party started," Josie said. She had her feet propped up on the empty desk and was filing her nails.

"Thanks for forgiving my thickheaded cousin," Brian said cheerfully from his workstation.

"I didn't," Riley said, shooting Nick a look. "But I'm here to help if I can."

"While you were doing your apology tour," Brian said to Nick, "Jos swung by Betsy's place."

"She hasn't been seen since yesterday morning. She just got back two days ago from a spa day courtesy of her—" Josie whipped out a notebook, consulted it. "Snookums. Guy meeting the description of Dead Rob has been seen around the complex. I may have accidentally picked the lock and had a look around. Place was messy, but it wasn't tossed. No phone. No purse. Her toothbrush was missing. There was some bloody gauze and bandage wrappers in the bathroom trash. Looks like she might have figured out she was in trouble, patched herself up, and went into hiding."

"So we've got no Betsy. And a guy with no picture, no name besides Dun, who our friendly neighborhood psychic fingered for the kill," Nick summarized. "Have any other visions since then?"

"Don't be a smart-ass," Riley said, looking a little guilty.

He turned away from her and flopped down in one of the vinyl armchairs. It was uncomfortable and ugly, and he had the urge to pick it up and throw it through the window. His temper had been legendary in his teens and early twenties. Being a cop had evened him out. Then not being a cop and being his own boss had smoothed out the remaining rough edges. But every once in a while, things flared to the surface.

"Let's start from the top," Brian suggested. "Riley, can you give us a description of the guy?"

She took the second chair and pointedly turned away from Nick.

"Okay. So he's not very tall. He's bald. Shiny, shaved head. Big shoulders. No neck whatsoever. Kind of looks like a brawler."

Nick noticed Josie's gaze fix thoughtfully on Riley's face.

"He definitely works out. And pretty hard-core too."

"Sounds like the guy you saw coming out of the back office when you were there," Brian mused to Nick.

He'd forgotten. Rage had clouded his mind and his instincts. Calling it up from the memory banks, he played it through. "Yeah." He nodded. "Big short guy. Crazy eyebrows."

Josie's feet hit the floor. "Looks constipated? Wears fancy sneakers?"

Now Riley was leaning forward. "Yeah! With a red lightning stripe on them."

"I think I know our guy," Josie announced smugly.

"You've got to be shitting me," Nick said, anticipation rising and pushing away the dredges of anger, fear.

"Nope. Gym rat at a place I used to go until we moved over here. Duncan something."

"Now, we're talking," Brian said, turning back to his monitors, fingers flying over the keys. "Was he a selfie guy? Sounds like a selfie guy. He could have tagged himself or checked in at the gym."

Josie got up to look over her husband's shoulders. "I remember him preening in the mirror, but I don't remember any 'welcome to the gun show' selfies or 'watch me lift' footage."

"Footage." Riley said it quietly, but Nick still heard her. She had a funny look on her face. Her nose twitched twice as she pulled her phone out of her bag.

He had too much energy to sit, so he paced and thought while his team worked.

Why would a no-necked gym rat take out a skinny, crappy bar owner who he obviously knew? Was it a woman? Gambling? Drugs? Money?

He turned it over again, returning to what Riley had said in the van. Cold. Like an item on a to-do list. Like a...job.

"Duncan Gulliver," Riley said quietly. Her face was pale. Those heavily lidded eyes were open wide. She held out her phone to Nick, and he took it.

"Holy shit!" Brian said gleefully as he keyed in the last name. "Did you just psychically come up with that? Because that's fucking cool."

Josie ruffled his hair affectionately. "Don't make it weird, babe."

It was a video on the screen from the Channel 50 News Facebook page. An interview between asswipe Griffin Gentry and Harrisburg mayor Nolan Flemming. Griffin Gentry was fiddling with his too-fancy red power tie.

"Look at the thirty-second mark," Riley told him.

Nick fast-forwarded. "Well, fuck me."

"Oh shit," Josie said.

At the same time, Brian announced, "We've got a problem, Nicky."

Nick looked up at Riley, who managed to look both scared and excited. In the B-roll of the interview, Flemming was doing a ribbon cutting for a new restaurant on Second Street. To his right was Mr. No Neck himself, shoved in a suit and looking constipated.

"Duncan Gulliver, communications director for Mayor Flemming," Brian read from the screen.

"What the hell does a communications director do?" Josie asked.

"Apparently they pull triggers," Nick speculated.

"Are you saying it's possible that Duncan of Clan No Neck is a hired gun for the mayor of Harrisburg?" Brian asked.

"Get me everything you can on Gulliver and Flemming," Nick said.

"You know none of this is admissible," Riley reminded him. "You can't just go to the cops with nothing but a psychic's word. I've already burned my credibility to the ground with them by warning them and then telling them I didn't see anything."

"You would have burned it even worse by telling them you saw a shiny orb go into your neighbor's apartment," Nick argued.

"She's got a point, Nicky," Josie agreed.

But he was already shaking his head. "We just have to work backward. We've got our hired gun and a potential bloodthirsty bastard who did the hiring. Now we work our way back and find a connection that'll stand up in court." He stopped his travels across the carpet. "Bet you twenty bucks Flemming is the silent partner. That's our connection." He felt it in his gut. Now, all he needed to do was prove it.

"Let me see if I can get my hands on the liquor license paperwork," Brian said.

"We need Betsy," Riley said to Nick.

He nodded, in agreement for once.

"By all accounts, she's not the sharpest crayon in the box. She wouldn't have gone far. Maybe she's hiding out at a friend's place?" she suggested.

"Our murderous mayor's making an appearance at some swank shindig at the casino tonight," Josie said, reading over Brian's shoulder.

"Hold that thought," Nick said, handing Riley's phone back.

It was time to step on some toes.

Nick pulled out his own phone and brought up the contact.

"Nicky. I can only assume you're calling because you've cleared my name."

"I'm working on it, Fat Tony. I need a favor."

46

H a! Look at the boss," Josie said, angling her phone to show Riley.

Nick was dressed in a suit, looking dapper as hell and maybe just a little pissed off about it. He looked *really* good.

"Mmm." Riley remained noncommittal. She was still mad at him. But at least he hadn't stupidly tried to forbid her from taking part in the search. They'd split up, guys to the casino to scope out the mayor and the girls—plus Gabe—to track down Nature Girl Betsy.

"I still can't believe he gets to go to a party while we play hide-and-seek all over the East and West Shores for Boobs McGee," Josie complained.

There was a knock on her window, and Josie opened the door before slipping into the back. Gabe hefted his muscly bulk into the passenger seat and triumphantly held up a bag. "I have returned with sustenance."

"Stakeout snacks," Josie said, making grabby hands for the bag.

"Good job, Gabe," Riley said. "If we get lucky and find Betsy, I'll take you for ice cream tomorrow."

"That would be most wonderful," he said happily.

They divvied up the burgers and fries. Riley produced the list of addresses Brian had compiled of all Betsy's known associates. "Okay, where do we start? Whose door do we knock on first?" she asked.

"We gotta be careful about who we talk to," Josie said, her mouth full of fries. "Someone might tip her off that we're looking for her."

Gabe ate his cheeseburger in three bites. Riley wondered how much trouble she was going to get in with her grandmother for introducing Gabe "the Bod" to junk food.

"Let's start with a drive-by of her parents' house," Riley suggested. "Maybe we'll get lucky."

———

An hour and a half later, they still hadn't gotten lucky, and everyone—except Gabe—was cranky.

They'd scoped out the parents' neat and tidy ranch house in Shiremanstown, but given the neighborhood, it was impossible for a Jeep full of people to remain inconspicuous on the street. After a few passes, they'd moved on to the sister's apartment in Mechanicsburg. There was a parking lot for them to stake out. But Josie was already bored and buzzed the apartment from the intercom.

"No answer," she reported, climbing into the back seat again. "This is lame."

A boring stakeout was still ten times more exciting than what Riley did for a living. And there was something humming in the back of her head. An anticipation of something yet to come.

"Let's start on the friends' places," she suggested. If Riley were in trouble, she'd go to Jasmine before she went to her parents.

They made a pit stop at a gas station for pee breaks and snacks, and then worked their way through the short list of Betsy's girlfriends. It was getting too late to ring doorbells, so they settled for drive-bys, looking for big blond hair and boobs.

"Bingo," Josie said, pointing at the next house on their

list. 423 Springs Road was a crappy little ranch house on a big weedy lot. Judging from the thump of music and the dozens of cars lining the street, the occupants were having a party. A loud one.

"Let's go mingle," Josie announced. "Cover story. We're Betsy's BFFs, and we got worried when she didn't show up for work today."

"Good enough for me," Riley said.

Together, they headed up the walk to the front door. When no one answered the bell, they let themselves in. The living room had a dark green linoleum floor that peeled up at the corners. The furniture screamed "broke college student." The couch was covered in a dirty slipcover. There were two chairs. One was a papasan with a stained beige cushion, the other a pink inflatable armchair.

The paneled walls—more green—were covered in movie posters hung with thumbtacks.

A shirtless guy wearing a necktie around his forehead and blue paint on his bare chest jogged through the living room whooping. He was followed by a very short, very drunk girl whose shirt was on backward. She was wearing one shoe.

"Gimme back my Red Bull and vodka, Jared," she whined.

"Oh, to be young and dumb again," Riley sighed.

"Let's go scare the shit out of these kids," Josie said.

"Let's not. Blend in, stick to the story," Riley advised.

"Party pooper." Josie pouted.

They walked into the kitchen and out the back door to where the action seemed to be. The lawn had a wicked slant to it, but that hadn't stopped the partiers from setting up beer pong tables and wading pools with water levels that listed dangerously downhill. The fence had seen better days but still served its purpose by corralling fifty young drunk people.

"Let's get in and out before they burn down the house with fireworks," Riley suggested.

They split up, dividing and conquering. Riley grabbed the first smiley drunk girl she passed and asked if Betsy was there.

"Who's Bessie?" the girl slurred under the pirate hat that sat askew on her head.

"Betsy Quackenbush."

"Dunno. Want a Jell-O shot?"

"No thanks. Whose party is this?" Riley asked.

Smiley Drunk spun around, sloshing beer out of her cup in a wide arc. "Um, see that girl with the hair?"

She was pointing at a volleyball court with a sagging net. No one was on it.

"Which girl with what hair?" Riley tried again.

The drunk closed one eye and adjusted her point. "That one. With the brownish hair and the polar bear."

There indeed was a brunette clutching a polar bear pool float.

"Great. Thanks. What's her name?"

"Whose name?" the girl asked, turning back and dousing Riley with beer.

"Never mind."

Riley picked her way through the revelers and up to the polar bear girl.

"Hi," she said. "Is Betsy here?"

The brunette screwed up her nose. She cocked her head so far to the right, Riley had to grab her before she tipped over.

"Gravity sucks," she sang.

"Yeah. Sucks. Do you know Betsy?"

"Sure! We're practically besties!"

"Do you know where she is?"

"Nope! She was supposed to be here. But she was all like, 'I'm a lame loser and can't come to your awesome party tonight.'"

"You talked to her today?" Riley pressed, her pulse ratcheting up a notch.

"No talk. Text." Snagging her cup in her teeth, the girl dug through the pockets of her obscenely short cutoffs before producing a phone. It took her three tries to get the code right. "See?"

She shoved the phone in Riley's face, narrowly missing her retinas.

Riley took the phone.

Betsy: I can't come tonight. Something bad happened. I have to go away for a while.
Sharlene: You suck. Hate you.
Betsy: I'm serious, Shar. Shit went down, and I think I'm in trouble.
Sharlene: You're dead to me. Unless you show up tonight. Bring ice.

Sharlene's concern for her friend was underwhelming.

"Do you know where she would have gone?" Riley asked Sharlene.

"Nooooooope," she sang, then burped. "Don't care." She twirled off and added a pool noodle to her collection of floaties, leaving Riley holding her phone.

With nothing to lose, Riley hit the call button.

It rang a few times before going to a generic voicemail. Well, at least they had Betsy's number now. Riley plugged it into her own phone before putting Sharlene's down on top of a can of warm beer and going in search of her friends.

Gabe was fending off the advances of three girls who looked barely legal. Josie looked like she was threatening the life of the blue-chested boy.

Riley rescued her team, and they regrouped at the Jeep.

"I learned that blue chest guy deals prescription ADD meds on the side," Josie announced.

"I learned that young, intoxicated women are a danger to themselves," Gabe said, climbing into the back seat.

"I got Betsy's phone number and a text she sent her friend saying shit went down and she has to disappear for a while."

Josie gave a low whistle. "Nice work, newbie."

"It would be nicer if we knew where she disappeared to. She didn't pick up when I called her from her friend's phone."

Josie tried from her own phone and got the same voice-mail. "I'll text the hubs and see if there's any way to get a fix on her phone."

While Josie texted, Riley drummed her fingers on the wheel in frustration. "How do we find a girl who doesn't want to be found?" she asked.

"Perhaps you should try searching for her in a different way," Gabe said obliquely.

She chewed on her lip. She'd thought that her mystical spirit guides had turned up bubkes on No Neck when in fact they'd been trying to push her toward the video of Griffin's interview. She just hadn't listened closely enough.

Maybe she could get a read on where Betsy was hiding. She grabbed her bag and rifled through it, triumphantly producing the baggie. "Aha!"

"You want to do manis right now?" Josie asked, eyeing the fake fingernail.

"Nope. I'm asking my spirit guides where she is."

"That was my next guess," Josie said.

"I am very proud in this moment," Gabe announced.

"Everyone be quiet," Riley insisted. She closed her eyes and focused on her breath while holding the nail between her finger and thumb. She didn't know if it was the urgency of the situation or the fact that she *really* wanted to prove herself useful to Nick. Whatever the reason, she dropped into the blue state fast enough that it made her dizzy.

"What's she doing?" she heard Josie hiss.

Gabe shushed her.

"Okay, spiritual people. Me again. I need to find Betsy Quackenbush," Riley informed her guides.

"Are they going to, like, give her an address?" Josie wanted to know.

"I do not know how they will reveal their truths," Gabe said.

Riley blocked out her audience and focused on the nothing-ness that surrounded her.

Something was coming out of the fog, solidifying into a blurry picture. She reached out, slapping blindly at Josie.

"Yo, watch the boob grabbing," Josie complained.

"Paper. Pen," Riley told her, snapping her fingers without opening her eyes.

The vision was coming in clearer now.

"Ah, shit. Okay, hang on." After a few seconds of what sounded like wild pawing through the glove compartment, Josie pressed a pen and fast food napkin into Riley's hand.

"I'm seeing a house," Riley said slowly. "I think. Front porch. A circle? What the hell is that? A pizza?" She moved the pen over the napkin, hoping she was sketching her vision and not writing all over her leg. "Shit. It's fading."

"Did you get any house numbers on the pizza?" Josie asked when Riley blinked her eyes open.

Riley looked at the scrap paper. The sketch kinda sorta resembled a box with a circle divided into fours. There were no numbers.

"No. Damn it. Just a weird pizza."

"Perhaps this beautiful drawing will link to one of the other addresses on the list," Gabe suggested, peering over her shoulder.

"Not a bad idea, big guy," Josie said, slapping his gigantic bicep with enthusiasm. "We'll just pull up Google Maps, drop into Street View, and see if any of these buildings make pizza." She secured her tongue between her teeth and went to work on the remaining addresses.

"Why can't they just give me an exact location?" Riley complained.

"Because they do not speak the same language as you," Gabe said patiently.

"Well, things would be a hell of a lot easier if they spoke my language or if they gave me a translator."

"You are your own translator," he explained. "They use symbols that will mean something to you."

Hence Griffin's douchey tie, Riley realized.

"Those spirit guides are some sneaky-ass geniuses," Josie said gleefully. She held up the phone so they could see the screen.

It was a stately Victorian painted midnight blue with purple trim. The porch wrapped around the side. On the second floor just above the porch roofline was a circular window divided into four.

"Holy crap," Riley breathed. "It worked!" For the first time in her life, this whole psychic thing didn't seem so annoying.

"Let's go catch us a witness," Josie said.

———

Josie stabbed the doorbell of 604 Market Street. Behind her on the porch, Riley shifted her weight from side to side. Behind *her*, Gabe studied a hanging basket that was at his eye level.

The door opened, and a woman who coasted in just under five feet tall glared at the strangers on her porch.

"Is this one of those distract-me-at-the-front-door-so-one-of-your-slimeball-friends-can-break-in-the-back-door-and-steal-my-prescription-medicines schemes?" Betsy's great-aunt Fanny demanded. She was wearing a bathrobe and curlers in her hair.

"Can I keep her?" Josie whispered in delight.

"We have no interest in violating your back door, venerable elder," Gabe promised.

Riley elbowed Josie out of the way. "We're sorry to bother you so late, ma'am. We're looking for your niece Betsy."

"Betsy? Ha! That girl is probably off handing out BJs at some sex party." The curlers trembled on top of her head.

"So she's not here?" Riley pressed.

"I haven't seen that girl since last Thanksgiving. She brought a bottle of Diet 7UP and half a bag of stale Twizzlers as her contribution, if that tells you anything about her. What do you want with her anyway? She owe you money?"

A thump sounded from the second floor directly above the door.

"Do you live here alone?" Riley asked. She wasn't picking

up on any untruth to Great-Aunt Fanny's statement. But it was a huge house. It was possible that Great-Aunt Fanny didn't know she had a roommate.

"Achoo!" The sneeze echoed down to them through an air vent in the foyer ceiling.

"Bless you," they all said to each other.

"Oh, don't mind that," Fanny said with a dismissive wave of her gnarled hand. "This place is old. Haunted. Ghosts come and go. Leave sandwich fixin's and dirty dishes in the kitchen. Make a guest room bed look like someone's been sleeping in it. Couple of years ago, I'd swear there was a ghost party going on in the attic almost every weekend. I called an exorcist, but nothing worked. Then one day, poof! All the ghosts were gone. Matter of fact, last night was the first time I've heard any ghostly activity in a long time."

"Perhaps you could offer to connect with the spirits," Gabe suggested eagerly to Riley.

"A door-to-door exorcist?" Fanny asked. "Well, ain't this my lucky day?"

"I don't think we're going to need an exorcist or a medium," Riley guessed.

Josie held up her phone and dialed.

A familiar tune echoed tinnily down to them from upstairs, followed by a frantic "Oh! Shit!"

"Ghosts don't usually have cell phones with Nicki Minaj ringtones, ma'am," Josie pointed out.

"Betsy, come on down. It's Riley from the bar," Riley called over the elderly woman's head. "We just want to talk to you."

"Betsy Quackenbush, is that you?" Great-Aunt Fanny screeched. "You get your scrawny ass down here right this instant."

Riley breathed a sigh of relief when a barefoot, bandaged Betsy slunk down the staircase.

"What in the devil happened to you?" Fanny demanded, turning to face her niece. "You didn't get beat up by that MMA fighter's girlfriend again, did you?"

"No, ma'am," Betsy said miserably. She had a bandage on her forehead and one on her right arm just above the wrist.

She also had only nine long yellow-and-black-checkered fingernails.

"Betsy, we know about Rod, and we know you were in the car with him," Riley said gently.

Her blue eyes widened. "I don't know *anything* about anything. I didn't have anything to do with the blackmail or the wreck."

Riley and Josie exchanged a look.

"Who said anything about blackmail?" Josie asked.

"We need to talk," Riley said.

47

This was exactly the kind of shindig Nick avoided whenever possible. The Hills Casino and Racetrack squatted on fifty acres of what had been farmland just northeast of Harrisburg. Downstairs, chain-smoking old ladies in cat sweaters worked the slots. Upstairs, men and women in slick clothes mingled and made small talk, trying to out-wealth everyone else.

Nick would rather be at a backyard BBQ in shorts with a beer in his hand than duded up in a suit, trying not to burp out loud. His feet already hurt, and he was sweating through the damn shirt under his jacket.

Floor-to-ceiling windows looked out over the well-lit horse track. Servers in white shirts and black ties circulated with trays of drinks and useless finger foods that a guy would have to eat four trays of just to take the edge off his hunger.

The dignified music came from a bored-looking DJ in the corner.

"Can you hear me?" Nick muttered under his breath as he brought his beer to his mouth.

"Crackly and not very clear, but yeah," his cousin said in the earpiece. "Cell service is shit in there. Is that, like, the third Tony Bennett song since you've been there?"

"This place is like a giant tomb," Nick agreed. He flashed a reflexive grin at the woman who wandered by and gave him the eyes.

He was wired. A conversation recorded without consent or a warrant would never hold up in a Pennsylvania court. But that was for the DA to worry about later. All Nick had to do was connect the dots for the cops, get the bad guy off the street, and collect his fees. If he got the mayor to say anything, it would be a starting point for the cops to work backward from.

"So what's the story? You just gonna walk up to Mayor McMurder and ask if he's had anybody whacked recently?"

Nick had had eyes on the mayor and the mayor's muscle-bound henchman a couple of times so far. The relief he felt knowing that Riley was miles away from the bad guys and that they'd have to get through him to get to her was intense.

"I'm an investigator. His name came up in connection with a case I'm working on. I just have a few questions seeing as how his name is on the Nature Girls' liquor license right next to Dickie's," Nick said.

"Don't get yourself killed," Brian sighed.

Nick's thoughts returned to Blossom's tarot cards. But he shrugged it off. Tonight didn't feel like the night he was going to die.

He spotted a woman making her way toward him through the crowd.

"Hang on. Incoming," he said quietly.

"Nick Santiago," she said, holding out her hand. "We haven't met yet. I'm Jasmine Patel."

"Riley's best friend. Sure," he said. "I recognize you from Riley's Facebook picture."

"And I recognize you from the intensive online stalking I did when my BFF mentioned you the first time," Jasmine said crisply. She wore a sleeveless red dress that stopped several inches above her knees. It looked way more comfortable than his stupid suit. "It's nice to finally meet you. Is Riley with you?" she asked.

"Riley's running some errands for me tonight," he said evasively.

Her dark eyes sharpened. "You're either here with someone else and cheating on my very best friend in the world, or you're working. And for both our sakes, you better hope that you're working."

Nick swallowed hard. "Definitely working."

Her smile was deadly. "Good."

"You do know that Riley and I aren't actually together though, right?" he said.

"Hmm. I know that's what you both *say*," she said, liberating a glass of champagne from a server's tray.

"Ha! Busted!" Brian crowed in his ear. "You like a girl!"

"I'm not much of a relationship guy," Nick told Jasmine.

"Well, you better turn into one before you let her get away. Riley Thorn is one of a kind," she warned him.

He thought about her facing down a hired hitman alone. "Yeah. She's definitely that."

"Let me give you a few Riley hacks," she said. "In case you come to your senses and decide to lock her down."

"I'm all ears."

"She needs the kind of man who will support her. Not like sugar-daddy support her. But someone who will help her spread her wings. A guy who will break her out of the boring safety cocoon she's crocheted herself into. She needs the kind of man who will help her be herself, not expect her to play fan club president while he runs off and has a good time."

Nick cringed inwardly.

"So what she's saying is, you shouldn't have doubted her abilities, shamed her, and kicked her off your team," Brian mused in his ear.

"I'm not here having a good time," Nick told Jasmine. "I'm here to get answers to questions."

"And what's Riley doing tonight? Buying you groceries? Scanning your receipts?"

She was doing something she couldn't possibly get hurt doing.

"Look, I'm dying to break her out of that good-girl bubble, but not at the expense of her safety. And just because I don't want to see her get hurt doesn't mean I don't respect her," Nick snapped.

She cocked her head and studied him coolly, then grinned. "Okay. You passed the best friend test."

His shoulders dropped away from his ears. "You're terrifying," he confided.

"And don't you forget it," she said brightly. "Now, who are we spying on?"

"Nicky, I've got a window." Fat Tony barreled into their conversation.

"Hi, Fat Tony," Jasmine said with affection. "Window for what?"

"Hi, sweetheart. How the hell are you? Thanks again for helping with my mother-in-law's estate," Fat Tony said, giving her a noisy kiss on the cheek.

"Fat Tony's introducing me to the mayor," Nick explained.

"Ooh! Can I come? He's super cute," Jasmine said.

"No. He's not," Nick argued. Were all women happy to hurl themselves headfirst into danger? It was fucking exhausting.

"Nicky, didn't anyone ever tell you not to argue with a beautiful woman?" Fat Tony chided, linking arms with Jasmine.

"Listen to Fat Tony, Santiago," she said.

"This is a clusterfuck," Nick muttered as he followed them across the room to the windows overlooking the track where three men were deep in conversation. Two of those men were most definitely criminals.

"Nolan," Fat Tony said to the man in the impeccable blue suit. "I want you to meet my friend, Nick Santiago. Nicky, this is Mayor Flemming."

Nolan Flemming was an okay-looking guy, if Nick was pinned down for an opinion. He had wavy blond hair and a tan that made him look a little bit like a displaced surfer. His nose was perfectly straight, his teeth perfectly white, and his face was a canvas for the perfect political smile. Interested but distant.

"Great to meet you, Nick," he said.

"Likewise," Nick said, shaking the man's cool, smooth hand.

Fat Tony introduced Jasmine, and as expected, Flemming's demeanor warmed for the beautiful constituent.

No one introduced Duncan Gulliver.

The conversation restarted, and Nick observed. On the surface, Flemming said and did all the right things. But there was that buzz just beneath the surface. Nick had interviewed his fair share of murderers and bad guys. Most of them got caught up in circumstances or bad environments. But it was the vacant, charming ones you had to watch for.

And he was watching very closely, which meant he noticed the quick flare of temper when someone accidentally knocked into Flemming from behind. The cool, flat look that met the woman's apology.

Nick's warning system came online and alerted him to a low-level threat.

Jasmine didn't seem to notice. She was laughing and tossing her hair and doing all the little things women do when they're sizing up a potential mate. Riley was right. Her best friend had terrible taste in men.

Duncan had the personality of a robot. He stayed on the outskirts of the circle and made no attempt to join in the conversation. He looked like Nick felt, as if he'd rather be anywhere but here.

Nick leaned in to Fat Tony. "I'm going to need you to get her out of here before the mayor takes too much of a liking to her," he said, tilting his head toward Jasmine.

Fat Tony gave a subtle nod. A few minutes later, the man whisked Jasmine away to his wife so they could "girl talk" about estate planning an endowment for a clinic in the city.

Nick was weighing his options for how to proceed when a familiar and unwelcome face joined the conversation.

"Mayor Flemming. Great to see you again," Griffin Gentry bubbled enthusiastically.

His handshake was like the rest of him. Too eager.

Gentry's fiancée, Riley's replacement, glittered on his arm in a white sequined dress that was doing its best to contain her ripe upper half. Her silver-blond hair was done in thick ropelike waves, and she'd either played tonsil hockey with a vacuum nozzle or gotten a few syringes of filler in her pink shiny lips.

Nick shuddered. That was not the kind of woman who would pull on a ball cap after a long night of sweaty, acrobatic sex and say yes to greasy diner food. Bella Goodshine was the kind who would spend two and a half hours getting ready to be seen at the gym and then take selfies the entire time.

"Griffin." Flemming's tone was indulgent. "Do you know Nick Santiago?"

"I don't think I—" Gentry's eyes widened, and he took a step back, bumping into Bella.

"Hey!" she squeaked.

"Oh, I think you remember," Nick said, flashing him a hard grin.

Gentry giggled nervously, a high-pitched sound incongruous with his for-the-cameras voice.

"You've met?" Flemming asked.

"It's a small world," Nick said, hoping he'd leave it at that. Gentry was a moron, but he knew enough about Riley to be dangerous in this situation.

"He's dating my ex-wife," Gentry announced in a voice much higher than usual.

Shut. The. Fuck. Up. Man.

Bella was bored with the conversation and stood raking her fingers through her curls.

"I'm sure your fiancée doesn't want to hear stories about your ex-wife," Nick said with feigned courtesy.

But Gentry was one of those nervous morons who tended to babble.

"We met when I generously offered to interview her to get her side of the story when she was the prime suspect in her next-door neighbor's murder."

Yep. Nick was going to have to maim the guy. Maybe beat him with a chair or smother him with his soon-to-be wife's thirty pounds of hair extensions.

"You keep interesting company, Griffin," Flemming said, sounding bored.

"I mean, Riley was the only witness to the guy getting shot in the head. Naturally she's going to be a suspect."

"Riley?" It was the first and only word Duncan "Trigger Happy" Gulliver had uttered. Now Nick had two guys to beat with chairs. "What an interesting name."

Nick hoped to God his cousin was hearing this and sending out an SOS to the girls. Griffin Gentry had just connected the fucking dots for a trigger-happy henchman.

Flemming was eyeing Duncan with interest. "So your ex-wife actually witnessed the crime?" Flemming asked, turning back to the buffoon in the suit.

"She didn't see anything," Nick said icily. He held Flemming's gaze.

Gentry noticed that no one was paying attention to him again and did what he did best: performed for the spotlight. "Anyway, good luck with the ol' ex, and don't fall for any of her family's psychic mumbo jumbo. I never bought into it."

Nick reached out and snagged Gentry by the lapels. "You look thirsty. Are you thirsty?" He hauled the man away. "You are the dumbest sack of shit I've ever had the misfortune of meeting."

"Hey! This is a custom Thaddeus, and I just got it back from the dry cleaners. You're sweating all over it," Gentry complained.

"You're fucking lucky I'm not making you bleed all over it. Now get the hell out of here, and don't ever mention Riley's name to anyone again."

Bella appeared out of the crowd. "Baby, I'm thiiiiirsty. Will you get me some champaaaaaagne?" Her whine was accompanied by a pronounced pout as she tugged on his jacket sleeve.

"Uh, sure, babe. Yeah," Gentry said, mustering his haughtiest look before sashaying away from Nick.

"Yo, coz. You there?" Brian's voice crackled in his ear.

"Tell me you just heard what went down," Nick growled in the direction of the mic.

"Missed it. Jos just called. The signal was all broken up, but they got the Quackenbush girl. The waitress doesn't know anything about Mayor McMurder, but she did know something about a blackmail scheme."

Nick swore under his breath.

"Listen, the shit just hit the fan here, so I'm gonna give it a quick stir before I leave. Start the van and keep it running. We might have some trouble."

"Copy that," his cousin said.

Another woman walked by, shooting him a quizzical look, and he realized how he looked whispering at his crotch. "Just giving him a pep talk," he told her.

Her eyebrows winged up.

Nick made his way back to the mayor, who was now in conversation with a couple of smarmy suits who looked like they probably had a few sexual harassment lawsuits between them. Duncan was nowhere to be seen.

"Mayor Flemming, do you have a few minutes to answer some questions?" Nick asked, using his cop voice.

Flemming picked up on the change in tone.

"Anything for a voter," he said.

They walked a few feet away and enjoyed a view of the racetrack, where horses were being corralled at the starting gate.

"I'm here because your name came up in conjunction with an investigation."

"You're a cop?" Flemming asked, showing only mild interest.

"Not anymore. I'm a PI. I was hired to look into a murder."

"Ah, your fiancée's neighbor," he guessed.

Nick decided to throw some shit and see what stuck. "Actually, Representative Rob Bowers," he said. "You knew him?"

Flemming's brow furrowed. "No. I knew of him, but we didn't know each other personally. I'd heard that was ruled an accident. A tragic one, of course."

"You heard wrong. It was a homicide. Another driver hit him head-on on the bridge, then drove off. Their mistake."

"Mistake?" Flemming repeated.

"If they had stuck around, they would have seen his passenger get out and walk away."

It was subtle. Nick wouldn't have spotted it if he hadn't been studying the man's face. But something dark flickered in those creepy plastic doll eyes.

"Interesting. Who hired you?" Flemming asked.

"I'm afraid I can't say. But I would like to ask you about your whereabouts on the night in question," Nick said, his smile full of sharp teeth. "Your muscle's too. He looks like he could kill a couple of people without breaking a sweat."

"If you'd like that information, then you're going to have to speak to my attorney," Flemming said. Nick finally got a peek at the hellfire beneath the politically correct facade.

Maybe Duncan pulled the trigger coldly, but Flemming ordered the kill with a raging hatred.

"Maybe I'll do that," Nick said. "Well, I've got work to do. I've got a witness to interview. Should be interesting. She said she has information about a blackmail plot, which coincidentally ties to Dickie Frick, your partner at Nature Girls. I'm sure I'll be seeing you again."

"Oh, I'm positive our paths will cross again," Flemming said in a hiss.

Nick gave him a two-fingered salute and headed toward the door. He waited until he was in the hallway before breaking into a run.

"Coming out, Bri. Might have a tail, so get ready to drive fancy. We need a rendezvous point with the girls. Tell them to bring the waitress and not to go to Nature Girls under any circumstances."

Duncan already had a head start, and he already knew where Riley worked and lived.

"About that," Brian said. "We've got a problem."

48

I still feel like this could be kidnapping," Betsy said again from the back seat of Riley's Jeep, where she was crammed against Josie. They were heading out of Mechanicsburg without a firm destination in mind.

"More like abduction," Josie corrected her.

"It's *neither*," Riley lied. She'd just abducted a human being. She couldn't possibly get much further from rule-abiding good girl if she tried. "If we found you, they can find you too. We're going to get you someplace safe where they'll never look."

"Who's they?" Betsy asked.

"The people who killed your boyfriend, Rob," Riley said grimly.

At his name, Betsy started to cry. A loud, heaving wail. Gabe dug through the glove compartment and handed her a fistful of fast-food napkins.

"Walk us through the blackmail again," Josie demanded over the sobbing.

The busty blond dabbed daintily at her eyes. "There's really not much to tell," she said. "The bald creepy Duncan guy with no neck would show up at the bar once every couple of weeks with evidence and instructions. Dickie would make contact, apply the pressure, and collect the cash or favor or whatever."

Riley's eyes met Josie's in the rearview mirror. Betsy's crayon was sharper than it looked.

"You sure noticed a lot," Josie said. "We were led to believe that you were an idiot."

"Josie!" Riley chastised.

"What?" Josie shrugged.

"Oh, I get that a lot," Betsy said, giving her hair a fluff. "Pretty, dumb girls get more attention than pretty, smart girls. If you're smart, everyone assumes you can take care of yourself, so you're stuck paying your own mortgage, mowing your own lawn, and buying your own jewelry. But if you're dumb, someone always steps in to take care of you."

"So you're not dumb, just lazy?" Josie guessed.

Betsy rolled her baby blues. "Why should I do all the work when it makes someone else happy to do it for me? Really, I'm doing them a favor. At least I was. Now Rob's dead." The wailing began again.

Gabe dug through the stakeout snacks and handed the crying woman a pack of cupcakes.

"Oh! My favorite," Betsy said.

"What did Dickie have on Rob?" Riley said the man's name carefully and hoped the sobbing would be temporarily stemmed by processed sugar.

"Besides me?" Betsy asked.

"Yeah, I guess."

"Something about campaign finance fraud. I mean really, that was probably his campaign manager's fault, or it could have been blamed on him. But Robby was married *and* seeing me. So he couldn't really take his pick on the blackmail charges."

"Did Dickie know you knew about the blackmail stuff he was doing?" Riley asked.

Betsy shrugged. "I doubt it. To him, I was just another big-boobed bimbo. But I knew there was going to be trouble the day Dickie died. He and Dun had an argument that afternoon in his office. They got pretty loud."

"What were they arguing about?" Josie asked.

"Something about Dickie skimming off the blackmail scheme. And 'the boss,' whoever that was, wasn't happy."

"How was he skimming?" Riley asked, driving aimlessly now.

"Dun said something about how the boss was saving Rob for later and Dickie squeezing twenty-five K out of him now was a stupid move." Betsy said all this through a mouthful of cupcake. "Even stupider, Dickie didn't have most of the twenty-five K anymore."

So Dickie had broken into the blackmail stockpile and helped himself to a piece of the pie. That was enough of an oopsie to get him dead.

"Did the cops get the blackmail evidence when they searched the office?" Riley asked.

Betsy shrugged in the mirror. "Dunno. Doubt it. He had some kind of hiding spot. Somewhere behind the desk. I walked in on him one time when he was all hunched over behind it. He yelled at me to get the fuck out, which was totally rude and uncalled for. I looked for it after he left but couldn't find anything. I don't think Dun knew where he hid the evidence either. He asked Dickie for it that day, and Dickie said, 'Fuck off, cocksucker.'"

The underestimated waitress was a fount of information.

"You think what he had on Bowers is still there?" Riley asked Josie.

"Could be," she mused. "If we found it, it could tell us exactly what Flemming was planning."

"Ooh! Are you talking about Mayor Flemming? He's sooooo cute," Betsy purred.

"Trust us," Josie said. "You can do better for a sugar daddy."

"I can forgive a lot for good looks and a big wallet," Betsy countered.

Riley shook her head.

"I am concerned for your well-being," Gabe told the girl.

"Well, aren't you sweet?" Betsy said, fluttering her lashes. "What's your financial portfolio look like?"

"No!" Riley said sharply.

"You know," Josie mused. "Brian said that Dun and Flemming are both at that party."

Riley chewed on that for a moment. "Maybe it couldn't hurt to swing by the bar and take a look when we know they're both occupied miles away. Although I think Trigger-Happy Dun keeps the office locked now."

"Oh, Rod's got a key behind the bar by the ice machine," Betsy said confidently.

"Problem solved," Josie said. "Of course, Nick wouldn't be happy about it…"

It was the right button to push at the right time.

"Let's go have a drink," Riley said, exiting the highway and heading toward Nature Girls.

They couldn't decide who should go in and who should stay behind. So they all went inside together. Gabe, Josie, and Betsy were supposed to stay at the bar and create a distraction while Riley snuck into the office and did some snooping.

The distraction proved easier than originally thought, because as soon as the bandaged Betsy walked in the door, Liz got in her face. "Look, everyone, it's Boobs McNo-Show."

Their loud argument and Betsy's third round of tears for the evening soon had the attention of everyone in the place.

Josie sidled up to the bar, leaned over the counter, and plucked the key out of the cup while bartender Rod poured a round of shots and ignored the shouting women. Smoothly, she held out the key behind her back, and Riley palmed it before ducking into the hallway and hurrying to the office door.

With Rod occupied and Duncan miles away, she didn't have a thing to worry about. But nerves still made her hands shake. Her whole body was vibrating as if there was a message trying to get through. But she shoved it aside. She didn't have time for a dead grandpa trying to tell her where the keys to the Buick were.

Unlocking the door, Riley took another peek over her shoulder. Seeing no one, she snuck inside and locked the door behind her.

The office was just as disgusting as the rest of the bar. But it had the distinction of housing a stale, farty odor. The ghost of Dickie, she supposed. Making her way behind the desk, she pulled out the creaky-wheeled chair and sat. She wisely decided not to think about the fact that the last two people who sat in this chair were a murder victim and his murderer.

She peered at the floor. It was concrete under vinyl tile in here just like the rest of the bar, only slightly less sticky. There were some peeling tiles, but nothing that looked like a hidey-hole.

"Where is it?" she whispered to herself.

If she were a gross old guy doing dastardly things, where would she hide the dirt?

Her nose twitched when she looked at the vinyl baseboard. Odd that it only existed on one wall. Another twitch. With only a little bit of disgust, she knelt to get a closer look. There was a foot-long section that poked out from behind the shelving unit that seemed like it fit just a little more flush to the wall than the rest of it.

She ran her fingers over the top of the baseboard where it met the wall, then did the same along the floor. She found a paper clip on the desk and wedged it into the seam.

"Well, would you look at that," she murmured as the piece of trim slid up to reveal a dark hole. Her heart was pounding, but this time, it wasn't from fear or Nick pheromones. It was the thrill of discovery. Finding typos at work never felt like this.

She whipped out her phone and fumbled with it until she turned on the flashlight function. It was indeed a small compartment built into the block wall. Inside, she found two food storage bags with photographs and two flash drives. The top photo in the first bag was a shot of Representative Rob with his tongue down Betsy's throat.

"Jackpot."

Mission accomplished, she grabbed the stash, stuffed it into her purse, and replaced the trim.

Her heart was thundering in her chest with adrenaline. Finally, solid evidence that even the cops couldn't refute. Nick was going to be pissed and would definitely have to apologize. That made her even happier.

Elated, she slung her bag over her shoulder and opened the door.

Her elation turned to an iceberg of dread when the emergency exit door was yanked open.

A pissed-off-looking Duncan seemed just as stunned to see her as she was to see him.

"We meet again, Riley." Her name coming from the mouth of a cold-blooded killer was unnerving, to say the least. The door clicked shut behind him.

"I forgot my—" Excuses ceased to matter when she noticed the gun he had in his hand. She sent up a sarcastic "Thanks a lot, guys" to her so-called spirit guides for not alerting her to her own death. Then, because there was nothing else she could do, she hurled the office key at Duncan's face, and when he made a move to catch it, she took off running toward the bar.

It was hard to run in a zigzag in a hallway like *Made It Out Alive* suggested, but Riley did her best, also throwing in some ducking in case he was ready to shoot up a bar to get what he wanted.

She charged through the swinging doors back into the bar area, where it appeared hell had also broken loose. Betsy and Liz's argument had escalated into a physical fight. Gabe was trying to hold Liz back, but she was fighting dirty with fingernails. Betsy was screaming insults while hurling plastic cups of beer at Liz. Deelia, with a festive sparkler headband, was begging both of them to calm down and address their issues outside. Patrons were getting in on the action, either by laying odds on the women or by starting their own fistfights. Josie was at the bar, watching the action with a beer of her own.

"GUN!" Riley shouted at the top of her lungs and dove to

the floor just as Duncan squeezed off a shot. The bullet meant for her put a hole in a very large, very bearded man's beer.

Duncan barreled out into the bar, and everything came to a screeching halt...including the girl fight. The eyes of every patron locked on the guy with the gun. For a second, the only sound was the twangy musical stylings of Garth Brooks singing about his pals in low places.

A knife sliced through the air and embedded itself in the wall two inches from Dun's face.

"Dang it. I pulled it a little too much to the left," Josie complained.

All hell proceeded to break loose again.

Guns were produced from God knew where. More knives were thrown, some at Dun, some just in abandon. Rod popped out from behind the bar with the shotgun. He fired it at the ceiling, but as far as warning shots went, it only encouraged everyone else to open fire. Guns and cheap beer were not a great pairing, Riley decided as a hail of bullets took out the glass windows and peppered the block walls.

"Let's roll," Josie shouted to Riley, producing a small handgun from an ankle holster.

Riley crawled after her toward the door.

Gabe threw a gentleman in a Confederate flag tee into two drunk guys dueling with chairs. Then he pushed Betsy to the floor. She joined the hands-and-knees parade.

Josie kicked the door open and stood brace-legged in the opening. She fired off a couple of shots as Riley and company crawled through her spread legs. Gabe was too tall though and ended up taking Josie with him on his back like a pony. The platonic reverse cowgirl would have been funny had they not been escaping a gunfight at the Not So OK Corral.

The second the door slammed shut on the chaos inside, they bolted, hunched over, for the Jeep.

"Son of a bitch!" Riley stopped short and looked in horror at the bullet-ridden, smoking hood of her vehicle.

The door sprang open again, and everyone braced for

a hail of bullets. "You assholes aren't leaving us behind!" Liz yelled as she and Deelia sprinted toward them. Deelia's sparkler headband bobbed comically.

"We need wheels," Josie said.

"You think?" Riley shot back. "Sorry. Uncalled for. I'm stressed."

"Forgiven," Josie said. "How about that one?" She pointed to a tinted-windowed Escalade.

They crouched and ran, and just as they got to the SUV, some joker shot the shit out of the windshield and set off the car alarm.

"Plan B," Riley yelled.

"Oh, for fuck's sake! This one," Liz said, pointing at a big, rusty pickup. "It's Luther's. He hides his keys in it so we can't take them from him."

Luther's pickup was indeed unlocked, and they unceremoniously piled in.

"Yes!" Riley hissed when the keys fell from the sun visor.

"Oh my God. Get your lard ass off me," Liz screeched from the back seat.

They could hear sirens in the distance. Riley didn't want to get caught at this particular crime scene. Not with hot evidence to deliver. And not with potential dirty cops answering the call.

"Everyone, buckle up and shut up," she said, shoving the keys into the ignition. The engine gave a lazy wheeze and then roared to life. So did Ram Jam's "Black Betty" at full volume from the CD player.

Josie twisted the volume knob to no avail.

"Turn it off," Liz yelled, covering her ears and elbowing Deelia in the process.

"Ouch! My boob!"

"Volume's stuck," Josie shouted. She looked down at the knob in her hand. "And the off button doesn't work."

"Uh-oh. Here comes Dun, and he looks pissed," Betsy observed from the back.

"Get down!" Riley yelled as she threw the truck into reverse and stomped on the accelerator.

"How many damn bullets does that guy have?" Josie complained as Dun opened fire.

Keeping her head low, Riley peeked over the dash, shifted into first, and floored it again…straight at Duncan. He squeezed off a shot that splintered a lovely little hole in the windshield right where Riley's face should have been. There was a fleshy thud, and Riley cut the wheel to the left.

"You hit him!" Josie said, impressed.

"Is he dead?" Riley asked.

A shot rang out and broke the back window, causing the occupants, including Gabe, to shriek.

"Nope. Just limping. Now he's *really* pissed," Josie observed.

Riley edged around the building. "What kind of car does he drive?"

"Uh. Some shiny red sports car," Betsy shouted over the music.

Riley spotted it parked outside the back door of Nature Girls. It was a spiffy little two-seater. She gunned the engine.

"What the fuck are you doing?" Liz screeched.

"Disabling his car." The pickup truck smashed into the back end of the car, embedding it in the block wall.

"Uh, guys? He looks even madder now," Deelia said as Dun limped around the side of the building.

Riley aimed for the alley and floored it again as a hail of bullets tore through the truck's metal body.

"Wooooooo!" Betsy hooted.

"You guys, sometimes I get super carsick," Deelia said from where she was crammed partially under Gabe's bulk.

"Do not fucking puke on me," Liz growled.

"Perhaps we could stop for some ginger ale," Gabe offered.

"Nobody is puking, and we are definitely not stopping," Riley said, gripping the wheel with her left hand and dialing her phone with her right. She couldn't hear over the music and couldn't tell if the call had connected or not.

"Nick, if you can hear me, we're in big trouble!" she yelled.

49

S he took the turn onto the street a little too fast and nailed a trash can.

"You hit something else," Josie reported.

"I noticed," Riley shouted over the music. She stuffed her phone in her bra and prayed Nick was listening on the other end of the call.

"At least it wasn't another person," Josie yelled.

Riley made two more turns, took an on-ramp way too fast, and then popped out on the interstate. A dark sedan appeared behind her. "Heading south on 83 toward the bridge. We've got company," she reported, gritting her teeth.

"Oh my God. She's lost it. She's talking to her tits," Liz groaned.

"I talk to mine all the time. Don't you?" Betsy said.

"I do not know if I speak to any body part," Gabe mused. "Perhaps I should try it."

"You people are *not* normal," Deelia told them.

Josie rolled down her window and slammed fresh magazines in both guns.

"It looks like the cops," Riley said. Red and blue lights flashed in her rearview mirror. "You can't shoot at cops!"

Unless they were dirty. And there was only one way to find that out.

She jammed her foot down on the accelerator. The stolen pickup truck lumbered up to speed. There was a loud bang, and Betsy shrieked. "They're shooting at us! Bad cops!"

Just then, the night sky lit up.

"They're not shooting at us," Riley insisted. Fireworks exploded to their right as City Island's pyrotechnics crew went balls to the Fourth of July wall. There was a baseball stadium full of families enjoying both the nation's favorite pastime and birthday.

She desperately wished she could have been one of them. Innocent. Normal. Her only concern the overpriced beer. But no. One stupid mistake, one seemingly innocent decision, and now she was going to end up in the Susquehanna River in a stolen car full of weirdos without ever having sex with Nick.

The car behind her veered into the left lane, and the vision of the driver's plan hit her so hard her nose spasmed. *Definitely bad cops.*

"Everybody get down!" Riley shouted and slammed on the brakes.

All five of her passengers hit the deck just as a hail of bullets took out the windows on the driver's side.

"Pretty sure they're shooting at us now," Smart-ass Liz pointed out.

"You think?" Riley said.

Glass rained down, and the smell of burning rubber assailed her nostrils.

"We're taking fire," she yelled in the vicinity of her breasts.

If Nick was there and saying anything, she couldn't hear him. Not over the fireworks or the screaming or the song wailing at full blast on the radio she couldn't control.

She peered over the wheel. Black tire tracks snaked their way up to the stopped car sitting sideways across the bridge's southbound lanes. Two men got out and slowly began to advance on the truck, guns drawn. There was only one way to get past gun-toting bad guys barricading the road to freedom.

"Everybody hang on," Riley said.

"What's the plan?" Josie asked calmly, racking the slides of her guns.

"I'm gonna ram them," Riley said grimly. A shower of golden sparkles rained down from the sky above, drifting toward the inky black of the river.

Step one. Accelerate to thirty miles per hour.

"I blame you, Nick Santiago," Riley yelled to her breasts again and mashed the gas pedal to the floor. Two men stood, legs braced and guns blazing, in front of the sedan.

"Ohhhhhhmmmmmmmm," Gabe hummed from the back seat, partially buried under a pile of waitresses.

"What the hell is Studly doing?" Liz demanded.

"How should I know? Maybe we should hum with him?" Deelia suggested.

Riley couldn't tell which pops and booms were gunfire and which were fireworks. It was hard to distinguish sounds over the music and the humming from the back seat.

Step two. Aim for the center of the front wheel.

Her passengers abandoned the communal *ohm* and started screaming. Moments from each of their lives flashed before Riley's eyes.

"I should have stayed in school!"

"I never should have given that guy a BJ!"

"I should have had that second hot fudge sundae!"

Pop. Pop. Pop. The shooters peppered the truck with bullets.

Riley never should have answered the knock on her door two weeks ago.

Boom.

The impact was more satisfying than she thought it would be. She'd calculated just right, hitting the car on its front quarter panel and sending it in a slow spin that both shooters had to dodge by jumping over the barrier and into the northbound lanes. The car's front end smacked into the concrete barrier. Josie climbed out her window and stylishly shot out the two passenger side tires.

"Suck on that, assholes," she shouted before sliding back into the pickup.

"Everyone okay?" Riley asked as they cruised toward freedom at eighty miles per hour.

One by one, the back seat occupants popped their heads up.

"No! Deelia blinded me with her dumb fucking headband," Liz complained.

"Oh, shoot! I broke two more nails," Betsy whined.

The song ended, and they could hear Josie's phone ringing.

"Babe!" she shouted as the next track began. "You are not going to believe how many people I got to shoot at tonight!"

Riley's brain was scrambling. They needed to rendezvous with Nick and Brian. They needed to change cars—because this one was stolen and she'd left hers at yet another crime scene—and they needed a safe place to go to regroup.

"What's that? We're *burned*? *All* of us? Now what the fuck did Nick do?"

Riley took the exit. "I have a plan," she shouted.

"You guys. I don't feel so good," Deelia groaned loudly.

Gabe rolled down his window just in time. Deelia leaned over him to barf out the window as the fireworks finale began behind them. Another explosion, a little more fireball than firework, lit up the sky.

"Ha! I knew I hit the gas tank," Josie said victoriously.

50

Nick took the left off Front Street into the mansion's driveway a little too fast and ended up jumping the curb. He left his SUV running in the front yard, not bothering to close the door.

Every light in the mansion was on.

He bounded up the porch steps and burst through the permanently unlocked front door.

"You do not need to pack your vinyl collection," he heard Riley yell from the second floor. "Only essentials, people!"

"Riley!" he barked.

"Nick?" She leaned over the handrail. Burt the dog couldn't fit his head through the balusters, so he jumped up, resting his front paws on the railing like a person.

She was fine. He told himself that as he took the stairs two at a time. She met him halfway and jumped into his arms. He hugged her hard. It was only relief that had him kissing her like his life depended on it. At least that was what he told himself.

He didn't stop until her knees went out, and she sagged into him.

"I started a gunfight in a bar and then hit a cop car while they shot at us," she said in a rush. "They were definitely bad cops."

"You are in so much fucking trouble," he said.

"I think we all are," she said. She gave him another hard kiss on the mouth before pulling back. "Let's go, people! We need to be gone in two minutes!"

"I wish you'd give us more notice," Fred complained as he slipped past Riley on the stairs carrying two yoga mats, a backpack, and a humidifier.

"I'll keep that in mind for next time a crazy murderer is after us," she said.

If there was a next time, Nick was afraid he wouldn't survive it.

"I need some help lashing my mattress to the roof," Mrs. Penny yelled up from the first floor.

"Mrs. Penny, you are not taking your mattress. I don't care how bad your back is," Riley shouted. "There are beds where we're going. Beds and no record players."

Mr. Willicott, arms full of vintage vinyl, huffed and stomped back into his room.

"You need to get your things," Nick said, pushing Riley up the stairs.

"On it. Oh, and someone pack a bag for Gabe," she shouted over her shoulder.

"I'll do it," Lily volunteered with enthusiasm. "I can't wait to see that man's underwear."

They jogged to the third floor as her neighbors creakily made their way out of the house with their most treasured possessions. "So, dear. How was your night?" Riley asked.

"I pissed off the mayor—who is definitely a bad guy, by the way—threatened the life of your ex-husband, and met your best friend," he reported.

"You met Jasmine? Isn't she the best? Wait, was she at the party? With the mayor?"

"Fat Tony promised to keep her away from him," he said. "But you can call her from the road to make sure."

"Okay. Mrs. Penny's going to drive her minivan. It can fit all of them and their stuff. I'll ride with you. Josie was taking

Gabe and the three waitresses to my parents' house, where Brian is meeting them. They're going to ditch the stolen truck, load everyone else up, and meet us at the rendezvous point."

Nick blinked.

"What?" she asked, unlocking her door.

"You're pretty fucking hot when you're all logistical," he said.

She rolled her eyes and left him in the hall.

Since he was there, he checked the little Wi-Fi camera he'd hidden on the curio built into the wall near Riley's door. The batteries would be good for another twenty-four hours. He hoped it would be enough time.

"What are you doing?"

Riley was standing in her doorway, holding a black duffel bag and eyeing him suspiciously.

"Just checking the camera," he said.

"Checking the *camera*? You put a camera outside my apartment and didn't tell me about it?"

"Relax," he said. "It's not like I put it in the toilet."

"First of all, ew. Second—"

"Should I take the frozen lasagnas with us?" Lily wanted to know from the first floor. Burt galloped down to investigate.

"No, you should not!" Riley shouted back.

"What?" Lily said.

"No!" Riley said again.

"I can't hear her. I'm just going to take three," Lily bellowed.

"If we get out of here alive, it'll be a miracle," Riley muttered under her breath.

"Did you pack that fast?" Nick asked, looking at the bag in her hand.

"No. I keep a go bag. And back to this camera thing. How long has it been there? Sometimes I walk to the bathroom in my underwear, you know."

"Oh, I *know*," he said.

She punched him in the chest.

"Ow! I'm just kidding. I put it there the night Dead Rob tried to break in."

"You could have told me you put a camera—" She stopped midsentence, eyes going wide. "Oh my God, Nick!" She hit him in the chest two more times.

"What?" He looked behind him in case Mayor Flemming or Duncan the No-Neck Henchman had come up the back stairs.

"Dickie had a camera," she said, hitting him again.

"What are you talking about?"

"Before he died, I didn't hear him in his apartment and got worried," she said, crossing the hall to Dickie's door. The crime scene tape was gone, but the latch had yet to be fixed. "I put my ear against the door to listen, and he scared the crap out of me when he flung it open. He said something about what was I doing with my big ear pressed up against his door."

"I think you have very normal-sized ears," Nick said.

"Thank you. I thought so too, but then I wondered if one was bigger than the other and it was this secret people were afraid to bring up to me. Anyway, I think he had a camera out in the hall."

"I thought you said he was technologically stupid?" he asked.

"He was," she said, her gaze scouring the walls. "But how else would he know that I had my regular-sized ear up against his door?"

"It would have to be well hidden for the cops not to find it," he mused, eyeing the ceiling. And Dickie would need to be able to view the footage easily. Nick left her scouring the corner curio cabinet in the hall and opened Dickie's door and flipped on the lights. The crime scene cleanup team had done good work erasing the biological matter, but the place still screamed miserable bachelor.

His gaze tracked to the flat-screen on the wall.

Playing the odds, he found the remote and pressed Power. "Well, holy shit."

"Did you find something?" Riley poked her head in the door. In the two seconds he'd left her alone, she'd gotten cobwebs in her hair and dirt all over her face.

372

He hooked his thumb toward the screen and stepped out into the hall.

"I knew it!" she said, dancing triumphantly in front of the screen showing a live video feed of the hallway and Dickie's door. "I'm so smart! I'm so smart!" Burt returned from his sniffing reconnaissance and barked happily.

"Riley, I packed Gabe some thongs and tanning oil," Lily hollered from the first floor, interrupting her victory song and dance.

"Pack him some clothing too," she yelled back. "And deodorant! Mrs. Penny, is that a gaming system you're lugging?"

She abandoned Nick to herd the neighbors.

Meanwhile, he took another look at the screen and started to calculate the angle and position of the feed. It took him less than two minutes to find the fingertip-sized hole in the ceiling tile. He grabbed one of the kitchen chairs from Riley's apartment and dragged it over.

He heard feet on the stairs, and Riley jogged into his line of sight. "I got them all in the van. I think we need to go now," she breathed, sagging against the railing.

"Just one second," he said, carefully freeing the lens from the hole. It was a snazzy little flexible fiber-optic camera. "Got it."

He replaced the tile, shoved the chair back into Riley's apartment, and jogged across the hall to turn Dickie's TV off. "Let's get the hell out of here."

By the time they made it downstairs and out the door, they could hear the faint wail of sirens. Burt loped to the SUV and jumped neatly into the passenger seat.

"In the back, buddy," Nick said, giving him a nudge into the back seat.

"I never thought I'd be the kind of person to hear police sirens and have to run," Riley admitted as she climbed in and secured her seat belt.

He gunned the engine and drove through the yard into the parking lot.

Mrs. Penny and company were—miraculously—buckled

in and ready to go. He flashed his headlights at the minivan, which responded with a rev of the engine. Together, both cars peeled out into the alley and fled north.

"So where are we going?" Nick asked.

Riley grimaced. "The commune."

"Say what now?"

———

Twenty miles down the road, Nick disconnected a call and tossed his phone into a cupholder. "That was Brian," he said. "They just got to the, uh, commune with your parents, your sister, and her kids, and your dad's cow."

"The cow? How? Never mind. I don't want to know." Riley sighed. "Mrs. Penny brought her Xbox, so why wouldn't my father bring his spite cow? And why should my best friend answer any texts about staying away from Mayor McMurder?"

A snore sounded from the back seat. Nick adjusted the mirror to look at Burt sleeping soundly with his paws in the air.

Her phone screen lit up, and she rolled her eyes. "Mrs. Penny and the gang are going through a drive-thru. They want to know if we want anything."

He frowned. "I wouldn't say no to a burger."

"Amateurs," she muttered under her breath.

Despite everything, he found himself grinning.

"You know, Thorn, there's no one else I'd rather be running from the law with."

She shot him the side-eye. "You're just saying that."

"I'm really not."

She thumped her head against the seat. "Nick, how are we going to get out of this? I stole a car, hit a human being with it, and then smashed into a cop car."

"Doesn't count if they're crooked," he said. "Wait. What human being did you hit?"

"Just Duncan. And I'm serious."

He sighed. "I know. Look, I let Flemming know that I knew about his blackmail scheme. So you're not alone on the BOLO."

"BOLO?"

"*Be on the lookout.*"

"Oh God. I'm a BOLO," she moaned.

"Where's your Jeep?"

"Shot to hell at yet another crime scene."

"Classic Riley. Since we've got a few more miles to go, let's talk," Nick suggested.

She looked at him suspiciously. "I thought that was what we were doing."

"There are some things you should know about me," he began.

She perked up.

"Like what?"

"Like when I was a cop, I headbutted my partner and broke his nose."

She frowned. "Why did you headbutt him?"

"He accused me of not doing my job. A witness I was watching disappeared. He blamed me."

"No. I meant why not punch him?" she clarified.

Man, he was so into her.

"I was handcuffed at the time," Nick told her.

"I'm going to need you to back up and explain."

He sighed. "Weber and I were partners. We were tight. Our families were tight. His little sister, Beth, witnessed a crime. It was drug-related. Weber wanted her to 'do the right thing' and testify. I thought she'd be safer not saying anything. Figured we could close the case without her testimony. We disagreed. Loudly."

He saw Riley's nose twitch in the dim light of the dashboard.

"Beth disappeared. Weber accused me of hiding her and fucking up the case. Tried to have me arrested. By the time we both got our heads out of our asses and realized she was missing, the trail was cold."

"I'm so sorry," Riley said, squeezing his hand. "Were you and Beth...involved?"

He shook his head. "No. We flirted, but that was just to annoy Weber." Nick lapsed into silence for a long beat. "It's not that I don't respect the law," he said finally. "I just don't trust it to protect the law-abiding citizens all the time. It can be abused and distorted. Or in this case, completely fubared."

"Did you ever find out what happened to her?" she asked.

His hand tightened on the wheel. "No. She's a cold case now."

"I'm so sorry," she said again.

He felt the weight of her gaze on him and took her hand.

It was Riley's turn to sigh. "I guess this makes it my turn for a confession. I tried not to be psychic because I accidentally broke up my parents' marriage and sent my mother into the arms of Winston—Wander's biological dad—when I was four years old."

"Uh, what?"

"I kept telling Dad that Mommy was kissing a man."

"Oh. Shit."

"Yeah. They didn't realize I was seeing visions of the future. Dad thought I was telling him something that had already happened. Mom didn't even meet Win until a month after my dad left. They hooked up. She got pregnant. My dad realized he made a mistake, and they got back together. They realized pretty soon after why I'd said what I'd said."

"How'd they figure that out?" Nick asked, taking the left onto a bumpy dirt and gravel road.

"I predicted Great-Uncle Tyrone's death."

Of course she had.

"You're a hell of a girl, Riley Thorn."

"You just hang on to that thought when you meet my extended family," she warned, pointing ahead of them where the trees thinned and shadows of buildings appeared.

"Is that a tepee?" Nick asked.

51

The commune was just as weird as Riley remembered it. It consisted of a ramshackle barn, a dozen acres of half-assed fences that chickens and goats were constantly escaping from, and a random collection of buildings, including a few tepees, yurts, and even a wigwam.

She couldn't see it in the dark, but she knew the patchwork garden was loaded with squash somewhere to the south, and the creek in which she and Wander had spent hours of their childhood meandered through the woods beyond the house.

She directed Nick to pull in front of the pink farmhouse that stretched out in all directions thanks to additions built without aesthetics—or permits.

"Welcome to Happy Acres," Riley said grimly.

Despite the late hour, lights were on everywhere. She spotted Brian's van and her sister's hybrid SUV.

The purple-and-tangerine front door—another new paint job since she had last visited—opened, and a familiar figure stepped out onto the porch.

"You ready for this?" she asked Nick. Exhaustion was beginning to play at the corners of her mind now that the adrenaline had started to fade.

"Baby, I practically spit in a murderer's face tonight. I think I can handle meeting more of your family," he teased.

They got out and unloaded Burt and their bags from the back.

"You brought me a lion!" the woman on the porch said cheerfully. She knelt in her homemade linen caftan to lavish Burt with attention.

"Karen, this is Burt the dog and Nick the guy. Nick, this is my mom's second cousin Karen."

"Nicky Santiago! Long time no see. Look at you wearing clothes for once," Karen said with a saucy wink.

Riley choked on her laugh when Nick turned the shade of a radish skin.

"Oh, hey, Karen. How's it going?" he said weakly.

"Tell me you didn't sleep with my mom's second cousin," Riley whispered out of the corner of her mouth.

"I was eighteen, okay? She taught me a lot."

"Oh, I bet she did," she said, finding the connection perhaps a little funnier than she should.

Another set of headlights panned over the front porch. Nick tensed next to her, then relaxed when Mrs. Penny laid on the minivan's horn.

"We got snacks and shit," she hollered through the window.

"Sounds like we're having ourselves a party tonight," Karen said cheerfully as four senior citizens climbed out of the dusty minivan.

———

They helped lug bags, seniors, and livestock to their respective temporary homes. Daisy the Spite Cow was happily pastured with the commune's goat herd. Burt followed his nose—and the sound of fast-food wrappers—to the yurt Liz, Deelia, and Betsy claimed. Nick and Mrs. Penny had their heads together over her Xbox setup in the farmhouse's turquoise and eggplant living room. Gabe was in the upstairs bunk room reading a bedtime story to Wander's girls while Wander and Lily made huge thermoses of tea and prepped seven breakfast casseroles.

Riley took a moment to step out onto the back porch. The sky was so big and bright out here. It made her feel small, insignificant. Just like her life pre–Nick Santiago.

She let out a long, weary sigh.

"You look like you could use this." Her mother appeared with two mugs of tea. She was in her summer loungewear, a long black skirt that swished around her ankles when she walked and a Van Morrison T-shirt that had seen a few decades of washes and Van Morrison himself three times.

Riley accepted one of the mugs. "Thanks, Mom. I should be bringing you tea. I'm the reason you're in this mess."

"Oh, stop. This is the weekend getaway I've always dreamed of," Blossom said, lying like any good mother.

A loud fart erupted from the tepee closest to them.

"Willicott! You just singed my nose hairs," Fred shouted.

"Okay, not exactly the getaway I've always dreamed of. But my hubby is here, my girls are here. I've got my grandkids and my husband's stupid cow. And we're all safe. That's not so bad."

"Mom, I admire your ability to put a silver lining on a steaming cloud of old-man farts, but seriously. This is a disaster. I never wanted any of this. I just wanted to be normal," Riley lamented.

"Normal?" Blossom scoffed. "What fun is normal?"

"Normal is great," Riley insisted. "It's stable, predictable. Normal people don't witness the murder of next-door neighbors. Normal people don't end up in high-speed chases or get shot at by bad cops. Kudos to you and Dad for believing that, by the way. Normal people don't have to pack up everyone they love and drive them to a commune in the middle of Pennsylvania."

"Oh, puh-lease," Blossom scoffed. "Normal is dry cleaning and paying your taxes and—"

Daisy the cow lowed happily from somewhere in the dark. Burt answered her with a cheerful bark.

"Normal is not having spite cows or stolen dogs," Blossom finished with a demonstrative wave.

"I don't think you're making the point you think you're making. Wait, you and Dad don't pay your taxes?"

"Let's focus on you right now." Blossom didn't seem nearly concerned enough with IRS authority.

Riley was definitely revisiting the tax thing when there wasn't a murderer to catch.

"My point is no one is normal. And the people who strive for normal or perfect or respectable miss out on all the good stuff."

"I never asked for this." Riley sighed.

"The best gifts are the ones you don't ask for. Maybe you should stop trying to return it. Unwrap it. Open it up. Try it on."

"You're really committing to that metaphor, aren't you?"

Blossom nudged Riley with her shoulder. "All I'm saying is maybe it's time to stop being so afraid all the time. Bad things happen. But so do a lot of good things."

"I wouldn't mind seeing a few good things," Riley confessed. "All I get are murders and dead people."

"Drink your tea."

Riley sipped, then gasped. "What the hell is this?"

Blossom snickered. "Warmed up lemon-honey moonshine."

Riley took another more tentative sip. "Where did you get it?"

"You don't think they survive on organic vegetables and macramé alone here, do you? You should see the pot field in the back pasture."

"Mom!"

Riley finished her hot moonshine and, feeling significantly better about everything, went in search of Nick. She found him high-fiving Mrs. Penny as the woman hurled her headphones to the floor and broke into a victory dance.

"Are you two playing games?" she asked.

"Only if doing kick-ass investigative work counts as playing games," Mrs. Penny hooted.

"We got the footage," Nick said with an underwear-melting grin.

"What footage?"

He turned and pointed toward the TV. The state-of-the-art flat-screen that definitely hadn't been here last time she visited.

"Mrs. Penny, did you seriously bring your TV?"

"Worry about that later," she said, her fingers working the game controller. "Check this shizz out."

The blank screen flashed to the mansion's third-floor hall and Dickie's door.

The timestamp in the corner of the screen read 1:32 a.m., June 21.

"You didn't," she whispered.

"Oh, we did," Nick said gleefully. "Turns out Mrs. Penny's great-nephew Terrence did a little IT work for Dickie that went beyond just connecting his cable."

"How?" Riley asked, impressed.

"Kid's an online gamer," Mrs. Penny explained. "Cost us some Bitcoin and I had to promise to stop calling him Turd Face at family reunions, and he gave us the login to the cloud storage."

Nick gave Mrs. Penny's shoulders a squeeze. "You can work for me anytime, Penny."

"I might take you up on that," the woman mused.

They watched as a figure came up the darkened stairs and approached Dickie's door. The bald head glowed on-screen. Riley chewed on her lower lip.

"You can see the gun, but you can't see his face," she worried.

"Just wait," Nick said, slipping an arm around her waist.

True to his word, No-Neck Duncan shifted to the left, gazing toward the back staircase before raising his fist to knock.

Riley pressed her face to Nick's chest. She didn't need to watch the rest. She'd lived it enough times already.

"Oh! This is my favorite part," Mrs. Penny snickered.

Riley peeked at the screen in time to see herself running down the stairs with a hockey stick clutched in her hands. Thankfully, the angle mostly blocked the view of her spectacular fall.

"You know what this is, Thorn?" Nick asked, giving her another comforting squeeze.

"What?"

"Irrefutable evidence that Duncan Gulliver killed Dickie Frick. Combine that with the blackmail evidence you stole, which Brian has already scanned into some secret nerd vault, and we're gonna win this, Thorn."

She saw the evidence baggies of photos and papers she'd liberated from the hole in the wall on a doily-laden sideboard.

Nick's confidence was comforting, except for that creepy, icy tingle working its way around her chest cavity.

"By this time tomorrow," he said, "we'll be free and clear, and those two sons of bitches will be behind bars."

"Then maybe you can help me and the rest of the vigilantes look into police corruption," Mrs. Penny suggested with a gleam in her magnified eyes.

"One case at a time," Riley said, fighting off a yawn.

"You two want to see your room?" Karen asked from the doorway.

"Please." Riley wanted very much to see a bed right now. She wanted to lie down, pull a pillow over her head, and not think about anything.

They said their good-nights to Mrs. Penny, who looked as though she were settling in for a long night of gaming.

"We've got one room left, so you two will have to bunk up," Karen explained, leading the way back down the hall on the first floor.

"Not a problem," Nick answered for both of them.

Karen delivered them to their door, told them breakfast was at six, and left them.

Nick gestured for Riley to wait in the hall before opening the door to do a habitual sweep of the room. Not that there was anything remotely threatening at Happy Acres. But still, she found comfort in the protective gesture.

When her big bad bodyguard gave her the all clear, she stepped into the room. And her world came to a screeching halt.

382

The walls were paneled in faux wood grain. The pea-soup-green carpet was worn through in spots and ripped up in others. A lava lamp burped orange bubbles on a rickety nightstand. The only other piece of furniture in the tiny room was a full-size bed. It was covered with a hideous orange-and-green floral bedspread.

The hideous orange-and-green floral bedspread that had haunted her visions for the last two weeks.

Riley looked from the bedspread to Nick and back again.

Here. They were always meant to come here.

He shrugged and dropped his bag on the floor. "I've stayed in worse places." He never saw it coming.

Riley launched herself at him.

Recovering quickly, he caught her. Boosting her up, he wrapped her legs around his hips. And then that dimpled sex god drove his tongue into the mouth she planted against his.

52

H*e should definitely stop kissing her,* Nick's inner good guy whispered from the recesses of his mind. This was clearly an adrenaline thing. She might regret it in the morning. But there wasn't enough blood left in his head to really focus on the pitfalls.

Not when Riley Thorn was plastered against him, kissing the hell out of him. That situation demanded every iota of his attention.

He'd been waiting for this. Hoping for this. Ready for this. *Well, almost. Shit.*

He pulled back from her very eager, very talented mouth.

"I don't have a condom, Riley," he groaned.

Mrs. Zimmerman would be disappointed in him.

She sank her teeth into his lower lip. "I have six in my go bag."

"Oh God. You are the sexiest, most prepared woman I've ever met in my entire life," he said between devouring her mouth and shoving a hand under her T-shirt.

"Yeah, I'm awesome," she said, her breath catching as his hand found her breast.

The sexy little whimper that made it out of her throat had

him tossing her on the ugliest bedspread he'd ever seen and ripping open her bag.

He found the condoms as well as a pocketknife and a fire starter in the exterior pocket. The woman was a marvel. There was no way he was going to just walk away from her. Not after tonight. And not even after the bad guys were behind bars.

He grabbed a condom, looked at her sprawled across the bed, and grabbed a second one.

"Shirt," he commanded.

Eagerly, she dragged her shirt over her head and threw it at him. Her bra was red, white, and blue with silver sparkles representing what he could only assume were fireworks.

He responded in kind, yanking his own T-shirt off over his head before diving for her.

It felt so right to settle his weight over her, to kiss her again as his cock throbbed behind the zipper of his jeans. The friction of skin against skin was exactly what he'd been missing.

"Are you sure about this?" he asked, hoping, praying she was.

"Don't you dare wuss out on me now, Santiago. I can handle the love 'em and leave 'em," she promised.

He stared into her brown eyes under those gorgeous heavy lids. Like molten chocolate. And suddenly he wasn't so sure *he* could handle it.

Maybe he could do the relationship thing. Hell, if different-girl-every-weekend-in-college Brian could eventually transition into faithful husband, Nick could sure as hell do the boyfriend thing.

"Talk later," he decided. There were more urgent, pressing matters at hand. Like removing pants and kissing every inch of her body.

"Good idea," she said.

He dragged his lips away from her mouth and trailed them over her neck, pausing to sink his teeth into the sensitive flesh at the base of her neck.

She shuddered and bucked her hips against his.

He groaned at the exquisite torture of being separated by mere layers of clothing.

If he got any fucking harder, he was going to have to have his zipper surgically removed from his dick.

Eyes on hers, he moved lower, to the edge of her very festive bra. She arched against him as his tongue danced just under the edge of the barrier.

She let out a moan that had his blood pulsing harder.

"Pants," she breathed. "Take off your pants."

He wrestled his way out of his jeans, kicking them into a crumpled heap on the floor.

"Nice thighs," she whispered, running her hands over his legs to his dark-green boxer briefs.

"Thanks. I work out," he said humbly.

Her head hit the pillow, and she laughed. The lava lamp cast a warm glow over her skin. He dove for her again. They were a tangle of teeth and tongues, of whispers and soft laughter. He dipped his head to lick and taste a trail down her body, pausing to pay special attention to her breasts, her stomach, the insides of her thighs.

By the time he was done tasting and teasing, she was trembling. She reached for him, her fingers dipping into the waistband of his underwear. But he stopped her. "Not this first time, Thorn."

"The second time?" she asked, looking disappointed.

He shoved his underwear down, freeing himself to roll the condom down his shaft. "Maybe the third time." He grinned.

"God, I love your stupid dimples," she said with a laugh.

"Anything else about me that you love?" he asked as he settled himself between her thighs.

"I'd really like to find out right now," she said, looking down at where their bodies were almost joined.

He gave a small testing thrust, and her head fell back onto the pillow. The second she opened for him, he forgot all about going slow and sweet. He forgot about murder and danger and dogs and old ladies. He drove into her with one swift stroke.

"Nick!" Riley squirmed beneath him, her nails digging into his shoulders.

How long had he been waiting for this moment? It felt like all his life.

He lost himself to the rhythm. To the feel of her surrounding him. To the sound of her breath in his ear as she gasped and moaned. *This* was what he'd been missing. This was what he didn't know he wanted.

The headboard hit the wall hard and rattled. Once. Twice. He adjusted them, dragging her body crossways on the mattress. The next thrust was quieter if he didn't count her sharp intake of breath.

This was what he was never letting go of.

Rolling, he landed on his back and anchored her above him. "Ride, Thorn."

His grip on her hips was harder than he intended. But he needed to hang on for dear life as she moved above him, over him, around him.

Their gazes locked, their breath synced, and their bodies began to move as one.

"Thorn?" It came out through gritted teeth.

"Yeah?" she breathed.

"Are you with me?" He squeezed her hips harder.

"I'm with you."

"Good. Then hang on." He rolled them again, pinning her to the mattress and letting her body guide his rhythm.

"Nick. Nick. Nick," Riley chanted.

It was music to his fucking ears. She was getting wetter and tighter. Her nails were digging deeper.

"Now," he muttered. "Now."

And for once, she didn't argue. They came together in a synchronized release that had his eyes rolling back in his head and his muscles going rigid then limp like a marathoner's legs just before the finish line.

He rode it out, carried her with him, and when it was over, he collapsed with a heroic groan.

For a moment, there was nothing but the sound of their breath coming in short gasps.

"Good for you, kids," Blossom called through the wall.

"*Mom!*" Riley called back, embarrassed. "Stop listening!"

"Don't worry! Your father has his headphones in. He's listening to a sleep story," Blossom bellowed.

"What the hell's all the racket?" Roger yelled. "Is Daisy okay?"

"Daisy is fine! Everyone is fine. Go to sleep!" Riley shouted back. She buried her flaming face in the crook of Nick's neck. "I'm too satisfied to be humiliated," she confessed.

"That oughta put an end to all the Nick's-bad-in-bed rumors," Nick said with satisfaction.

53

Yep. He was still there.

And he was still naked.

Nick Santiago was spooning her sans clothing. The much-hyped comforter was in a crumpled pile on the floor. Finally, a vision worth having.

She stifled a yawn and wiggled closer to the man who'd just rocked her world so hard and long that she'd gone psychically blind and deaf and lost the ability to form coherent words.

If sex with Nick was listed on Yelp, her review would include glowing words like *orgasmic, expert level, very large penis,* and *totally satisfied.*

No matter what happened in the morning, this had been the best bad decision she'd ever made.

One second, she was curled up in the protective cocoon of his arms, and the next she was standing in broad daylight.

She dropped into the vision just like she was dropping into a dream. But this was no dream.

Nick was standing in front of her, looking pissed off as hell.

"Drop the gun!" he said, pointing his own shiny pistol at someone. His eyes were steely.

Her Nick. Always the hero.

But time was moving slow. Or speeding up. And the sound of water was muffling everything. She felt cold and hot at the same time.

There was the sound of a gunshot, and Riley watched in horror as a bullet tore its way through the air, closing in on Nick.

"Noooo!" Vision Riley shouted.

But the bullet was sinking into his flesh. And he was falling backward into the water. His eyes closed in slow motion, and the water turned red around him.

She launched herself out of bed, hands clutching her chest. This wasn't a nightmare. This was a vision. A vision of the future.

She felt sick. Her mother's cautionary tarot reading came back to her.

"No. No. No," she whispered.

She needed to fix this. To stop this. Nick was not going to die if she had anything to say about it. Whatever plan he'd concocted was going to get him killed. Today.

Her phone vibrated on the nightstand. It was Jasmine. She snatched up her phone and sat on the bed. Her momentarily relief shifted to anxiety. Middle-of-the-night calls were never good news.

"Jas? Are you okay? What's wrong?"

Nick stirred beside her.

"Riley Thorn, you're a hard woman to find." The man's voice was smooth, amused, and laced with poison.

"Who is this?"

"Just your friendly city mayor calling to see if I can count on your vote in the next election."

Mayor Nolan Flemming was calling her from her best friend's phone.

"What have you done with Jasmine, Flemming?"

Nick's hand clamped on her thigh. She switched the phone to speaker with shaking hands.

The mayor's laugh was a cruel chuckle. "Nothing. Yet."

The *yet* hung in the air.

"Where is she?" she demanded.

Nick sat all the way up and turned on the bedside lamp.

"I'm afraid your friend didn't get your text warnings soon enough," he said smugly. "Jasmine and I are enjoying a little private time together. We'd love it if you could join us."

How anyone in their right mind could find this sleazebag handsome was beyond her.

"What do you want?" Riley asked.

"You have something I want. I have something—or someone—you want. I'd like to orchestrate a trade."

She looked at Nick. He nodded.

"You want me to trade you the blackmail evidence I found at Nature Girls for Jasmine?"

"Such a smart girl," he crooned.

"I want to talk to her," she said.

"Of course you do. Jasmine, darling, say hello to our friend."

"Riley, don't fall for this piece of shit's games!" Jasmine shouted in the background. "He's not actually handsome up close. He's a kidnapper! And he smells like piña coladas!"

Definitely a turnoff.

"I told you it was the spray tan," Nolan yelled back.

Good God, just how many unhinged, spray-tanned weirdos were lurking out there?

"Jas, are you okay?" Riley asked, tears filling her eyes.

"Besides the fact this asshole won't let me take off my eye makeup, I'm fine."

"Where are you?" she demanded.

Nolan tut-tutted into the phone, and Jasmine went eerily silent. "I don't think that's of consequence right now."

"What do you want me to do?" Riley asked, pulling her knees up against her chest.

Nick's big warm hand settled on her back. But instead of comforting her, it reminded her that in mere hours, that hand would be cold and lifeless. She was going to barf.

"I'd like you to meet me at the back entrance to the State Museum at three p.m. today."

"Three p.m.? Oh, come on!" Jasmine shouted in the background. "You honestly can't expect me to wear day-old fake lashes and eyeliner that long."

Nick's fingers squeezed Riley's shoulder.

"Three p.m. at the State Museum?" she repeated.

"Come alone and bring what you stole from me."

"What guarantee do I have that you'll let us go?" she whispered.

"If you want a guarantee, buy an air fryer." The demented mayor laughed at his own joke.

"Dude, that wasn't even close to being funny," Jasmine called.

"Shut up," Nolan told her. "I'm a businessman at heart, Ms. Thorn. If you prove your usefulness to me, your loyalty to me, I think we can reach an amicable agreement."

Yeah, right.

"I don't think we need to share this information with your investigator boyfriend, and I know for a fact the police are much more interested in bringing you in for blowing up a department vehicle and endangering officers' lives. I'm personal friends with a few of Harrisburg's finest. So let's keep it just you and me and Jasmine."

"What about Duncan?" she asked.

"He might stop by to say hi, but I'll keep him on his leash."

Riley doubted that very much.

"Three p.m.," he said. "Come alone and bring what's mine."

He disconnected, leaving Riley with a racing heart and staring at the phone in her hand.

"Nick," she whispered.

"I know, baby. But I've got this. Jasmine is going to be fine," he promised. "Everything is going to be fine."

He got out of bed.

"Where are you going?" she demanded.

"Riley, I've got this," he said with that dimpled grin that made her vagina do a cartwheel. "I promise you, I've got this under control. I'll go wake up Bri and Josie. We're going to get

Jasmine back, and I'm going to get to kick this idiot in the nuts before he heads downtown in cuffs."

"Do you have an actual plan?"

"My plans have plans," he said, all cocky hero. "Trust me."

She did trust him. But he didn't know all the information.

"About that tarot reading my mom did…" she began.

"You have nothing to worry about, Thorn," he assured her with confidence she felt was not entirely called for.

She knew it then. Even if she told him that he was going to get shot and die in the next twelve hours, he'd *still* show up. He'd *still* try to save the day. He'd *still* die.

Yep. She was definitely going to barf.

"Let me wake up Bri and Jos and make a few calls. I swear to you on my life that I will fix this, Thorn."

She didn't trust herself to speak. So she settled for nodding.

He pulled on his jeans, leaving them unbuttoned, and grabbed a shirt off the floor, not realizing it was hers until he couldn't get it over his nipples. "Fuck it," he said, taking it off. "Stay put. I'll be back."

She nodded again.

He leaned in and pressed a hard kiss to her mouth. "I know you're worried, but I swear to you this all ends in just a few hours."

That was exactly what she was worried about.

He kissed her one more time and ran a hand through her tangled hair. "I'll be back soon."

He was already dialing his phone when he opened the bedroom door.

"We've got a problem, and this time it's not your fancy shoes and your stupid face," he said into the phone.

The guy sure knew how to ask for a favor.

Scrambling out of bed after he closed the door, she found his T-shirt halfway under the bed. It was the one from her vision. She grabbed a sports bra and dragged Nick's shirt on over it. She nodded at the mirror.

He couldn't get shot in this shirt if she was the one wearing it, she reasoned.

And he couldn't get shot if she rescued Jasmine first.

She found her shorts, then unpacked her running shoes and socks from the bag. Tucking the mini can of pepper spray into her waistband, she stuffed a twenty-dollar bill into her sock and grabbed her spare phone charger.

Riley looked back at the rumpled bed and remembered with aching clarity what had transpired there only hours before.

Nick was going to be so pissed. But at least he'd be alive, and Jasmine would be safe. She hoped he'd forgive her eventually.

Riley dug through the nightstand until she found a tablet of recycled paper, then quickly scrawled a note that was probably just going to piss him off even more.

She knew what she had to do.

Hitting dial on her phone, she held her breath.

"There's been a change of plans," she said.

54

City Island on a Sunday morning was eerily quiet. She ignored the almost empty lot and cruised up over the steep hill toward the stadium. Great. It looked like sleepy early morning volunteers were setting up for a 5K. The finish line arch was halfway inflated. Well, at least there would be witnesses to her spectacular and untimely death.

Hmm. Witnesses. That gave her an idea. A really desperate one.

There was another smaller parking lot on the west side of the baseball and soccer fields, and she nipped into a space.

"Okay, spirit guides. I know we don't know each other that well, and we're probably going to be meeting pretty soon. But I could really use your help getting Jasmine out of here today," she said, fiddling with her phone. Opening Facebook, she went to the yoga studio's page. A few clicks later, and she stuffed the phone into her bra strap. "It's go time," she whispered and climbed out of the SUV. She left the keys on the seat and the door unlocked so Nick wouldn't have to swing by the morgue before picking up his car. *Gulp.*

Her heart was hammering in her chest. Adrenaline made her sweaty and breathless. A bit like last night in bed with Nick. Only not nearly as good. Her poor adrenaline system. After so many years of not being used, it had been in overdrive for twelve hours straight.

She followed the pavement to a skinny thruway between the stadiums.

With every step, she felt her senses sharpen. She was a doe approaching an open meadow during hunting season. The pulse of blood in her head was loud, and she wondered if her carotid artery was up to the task. One thing was certain—there was no way she was making it out of this day alive.

"Mom, Dad, I'm really sorry it came to this," she said under her breath as her feet moved of their own volition toward the meeting point. "And, Nick, I had to do this. I hope you understand. Also, last night was beyond amazing. No regrets. Please take care of Burt and Gabe for me. And I'm going to shut up now."

The morning air was thick and humid. She was sweating profusely and shivering at the same time. Maybe she had the flu.

To her right, the tall metal supports of the baseball stadium's first baseline bleachers gleamed in the sunlight. She heard something up ahead, just on the other side of a small squat building. This was it.

"Don't throw up. Don't throw up," she chanted.

A figure stepped onto the asphalt a few paces in front of her. Half blinded by sweat, Riley swiped a hand over her eyes. Mayor Nolan Flemming flashed her his trademark political smile. The hairs on her arms stood straight up. The man may have been dressed in shorts, running shoes, and a T-shirt that proclaimed his love of recycling, but she knew without a doubt that she was in the presence of evil.

"Well, well, well," he purred, a sleek cat eyeing a dish of tuna juice. "It's nice to finally meet you, Riley Thorn."

"Where's Jasmine?" she demanded, not willing to waste banter on a murdery villain.

Mayor McEvil gave a signal.

A second figure holding a gun with a silencer stepped out from behind the building. The muscly henchman, Duncan Gulliver, was a protein-powder-fueled beast. His shaved head seemed to attach directly to his shoulders. Both he and the mayor had several small round bruises on their faces and arms. They must have made the mistake of coming at Jasmine while she still had her stilettos on.

Duncan reached behind the building and produced her very angry, barefoot best friend. Jasmine's hands were secured behind her back. She was still in last night's slinky cocktail dress, and her makeup was smeared, those bastards. But her beautiful, silky hair hung in its perpetual reality-rejecting curtain of perfection. Above the duct tape on her mouth, her eyes flashed a nuclear warning. Riley knew if Jasmine saw an opening, the henchman was going to lose his balls.

"Duncan, I swear to my spirit guides, if you laid one hand on her—" Riley growled.

"Nothing personal," he said. His sneer was cold, careless. A flicker of something caught at her mind. *Duncan. A pole. A woman. Wild, not-found-in-nature hair. Whispers.*

"Oh, it's *very* personal," she promised.

"Excuse me," Nolan announced grandly as if he didn't like his audience's attention off him for too long.

"So how does this work?" she asked, hoping to buy a little time. She needed a diversion. *Come on, spirit guides. Send in the big guns or little guns,* she telegraphed. She wasn't picky. She was desperate.

"Tell me, Jasmine," Mayor McDouche said, strolling over to cup her by the chin. "Just how stupid is your friend?"

Riley could feel the moment rising like a physical, palpable thing.

It was hard to tell through duct tape, but it sounded like Jasmine enunciated, "Fuck you." If humans could murder with their eyes alone, Nolan Flemming would be nothing more than pink mist.

He grinned in Riley's direction, and she could see something, feel something she'd never noticed in interviews. A black oozy murk. A dirty film on his soul that made her feel light-headed.

Keep him talking. At this point, she didn't know who the voice in her head belonged to, and it didn't matter.

"I'm here to make a trade. So let's trade," she said stubbornly. "The blackmail evidence you had on Representative Bowers for Jasmine."

Flemming produced a small handgun from behind his back and scratched his temple with the barrel. "You know, Ms. Thorn. I think I've changed my mind. I'm going to take you, your friend, *and* the evidence."

"That wasn't the deal," Riley said.

"Why on earth would you think that I'm a man of my word?" He looked genuinely perplexed.

Duncan still had Jasmine in a death grip, but his gun was pointed at Riley.

Okay. Two bad guys with guns against two exhausted, pissed-off ladies. Not great odds. But it could have been worse.

"I can't let your pretty friend here just run off and tell everyone that the mayor of Harrisburg kidnapped her," Nolan said. "And I'm certainly not going to let you wander off in the direction of the closest cop. Now, turn over the photos and whatever else you found."

Riley kept her hands in the air, her weight in the balls of her feet. If she had to move suddenly, she wanted to be ready. "Like you said, the cops aren't going to believe a word I say after you had them try to kill me and a pickup truck full of innocent people last night. Why *are* you doing this? Why did you have Dickie Frick and Rob Bowers killed? What could they possibly have done to you?"

"Please," the mayor scoffed. "This isn't the movies where the bad guy confesses his motives."

"It's not like I really care anyway." She sniffed. "I'm sure it all stems from you having a micro penis."

Jasmine snickered and mumbled something that sounded like "Haa! Good one."

Nolan's eyes went frigid, and Riley hoped she hadn't gone too far too fast.

"My penis doesn't need defending," he announced haughtily.

She cocked her head and peered at his crotch. "I'm not really seeing any evidence. How about you, Jas?"

Jasmine made a point of squinting, then shrugged and shook her head.

Duncan's face remained impassive and murder-happy, but Riley could feel a vague kind of amusement from him.

"Ladies!" Nolan snapped. His voice carried and echoed off the bleachers behind him. "Need I remind you that you're both about to meet an untimely end. Now, hand over the photos, and I'll turn you over to my associate so I can go to brunch."

She could hear voices from the soccer field. The grounds crew was out. People meant witnesses.

"Need I remind you that City Island is not a deserted island. What are you going to do? Shoot us and leave us for the soccer players to find?" Riley asked.

He rolled his eyes. "Ms. Thorn, you and your friend are not my first murder. We are by no means rookies at this."

"And who would ever look at the mayor and his communications director for motive?" she said. "Do you even have a motive, or is this just the way you two spend your Sunday mornings?"

"Your neighbor Dickie was an example for people who don't do as they're told," he said smugly.

"What was that weasel even capable of doing to you?" she scoffed.

"Frick took advantage of my generosity," he said coldly. "He tried to cut me out of one of my own enterprises."

"You don't mean Nature Girls," Riley prompted.

"I have a nice side hustle that involves collecting information and using that information as leverage."

"Blackmail," she said helpfully.

"You call it blackmail. I call it data storage."

"I went through the 'data.' You had evidence of campaign finance fraud on Bowers," Riley said.

"I wouldn't have asked for much," Nolan said with an

exaggerated wave of his gun-wielding hand. Everything this guy did was for an audience. Just like Griffin. "Just his seat in the legislature, but my stupid partner got greedy and squeezed him for cash on another matter. Shortsighted moron."

She blinked. "You did all this to move up the food chain? Why didn't you just, oh, I don't know, *run against him*?"

He laughed like she was an adorable, stupid toddler. "Rules are for sheep like you. I bet you've always been the good girl, haven't you? Always played by the rules. Always done the right thing. And where has that gotten you?"

Her blood was starting a slow, roiling simmer. "At least I haven't killed anyone."

"And you won't get your chance to either. Because your time is up," Flemming said with a sneer.

"Too bad I didn't bring the files with me," she said quickly.

"I beg your pardon?" He looked appalled.

"The photos and the files I found at Nature Girls. I didn't bring them here," Riley said.

Flemming brought the barrel of the gun to the spot between his eyebrows and closed his eyes. "I'm afraid I don't understand. That was *the deal*. You were going to bring the blackmail material to swap for your best friend, and I was going to kill you both," he said, walking through it step-by-step.

"Well, I had a feeling that was your plan, so I stashed everything before I came here. It's safe. I'll tell you where it is if you let Jasmine go."

"No," he said.

"Fine. Then, in just a few hours, someone is going to find the envelope I left with your blackmail material and my note explaining it all, and you'll be arrested. I can wait," she said, feigning patience.

"No, no, no. You'll tell me where you squirreled away my property, or I'll shoot your best friend in the head."

Dear God, she hoped this bluff would pay off.

"If you shoot my beautiful friend in her beautiful head, I'm not going to tell you where I hid the stuff."

"Then I'll shoot you," he decided, pointing his gun at Riley.

She rolled her eyes. "Think, man! If *you* shoot *me*, and I'm the only person who knows where the only evidence tying you to the murders of Dickie Frick and Rob Bowers is, how are you going to find it and destroy it?"

"Well, this is a pickle," Flemming said, pacing back and forth between Riley and Jasmine and her captor. Jasmine tried to lash out with a long leg to kick him but missed. "I've decided," he said, stopping in his tracks. "I'll risk it. If someone tries to come forward with the information, I'll just have one of *my* cops pay them a visit."

"Aren't you running out of friendly cops? The two from last night are probably in the hospital after that mess. And Weber got himself suspended."

Flemming frowned at her thoughtfully as if considering her point. Then he shook his head. "No. Nope. I'm bored with this. Kill them both, and I'll take my chances with the evidence."

Duncan leveled the gun at Riley again. "Say goodbye, ladies," he said.

Nolan swiveled around to face his henchman. "Dun, what have I told you before?"

The henchman winced. "You get the cool last line," he said as if by rote. "Sorry, boss."

Flemming gave him a stiff nod. "Ladies, I'm afraid your time as loose ends has come to an end." He gave Duncan a "carry on" gesture.

Riley's heart was pounding in her head now. "Stepping into your spotlight, isn't he, Nolan? Here and there. Trying it on for size. Speaking of loose ends, you're probably going to have to have a talk with Duncan's girl. He told her all about the leverage he's got on his greedy boss."

Nolan scoffed. But Riley caught the whiff of doubt.

"Nice try. But me and the boss are always bros before hoes," Duncan snarled.

"That's not what you told—" *Debbie.* The name floated to her on the ether. "Debbie."

A direct hit. Duncan turtled his neckless head back, recoiling from her words.

"You told your *stripper girlfriend* about this?" Nolan's voice was shrill.

"She only dances part-time," Duncan argued.

"She also works part-time in a craft store," Riley added helpfully. "She's really into scrapbooking. And glitter."

"What the fuck, Duncan?" Nolan demanded. "Where is your head at?"

"I'm actually wondering where his neck is," Riley said.

Duncan stretched his gun hand toward her, ready to do the deed. "Don't listen to her, boss. She's lying."

Jasmine shook her head violently. "Naaa ee naw!"

"What?" Nolan asked.

"Naa. Ee. Naw!"

"She said, 'No, she's not,'" Riley translated.

"Fy kig!" Jasmine enunciated. "Fy kig!"

Impatient, Nolan stormed over and ripped the tape off of Jasmine's mouth.

"Ouch! You motherfucker!" Jasmine snarled.

"What were you saying?" Nolan demanded.

"She's psychic," Jasmine said. "And you're really going to regret waxing my face, dumbass."

"Psychic? Ha," Duncan snorted. But that curl of worry was wrapping its way around his body.

"Her entire family is," Jasmine insisted. "Her grandmother's a famous medium. But Riley here is seriously powerful. She knows everything."

Nolan turned to study Riley. "Is that true?"

She took a breath, then nodded. "Yeah. It's true."

"What number am I thinking of?"

Oh, for fuck's sake. Seriously? Every time. Except Nick.

"Your first thought was sixty-nine but you dismissed that as too easy, so you changed it to thirty-three point three."

"That's exactly right," Nolan said, eyeing her with a nauseating combination of surprise and interest.

"Lucky guess," Duncan said, nerves in his voice.

Riley blew out a breath and dropped her shields, inviting everything in. It hollowed her out and then refilled her. The rush of power, of knowledge was heady and disorienting. She felt drunk.

"You named your teddy bear Steven, but you couldn't pronounce Ts, so you called him 'Seeven' until you ripped his head off during a temper tantrum when you were six. Your aunt Phinola is not happy with how you swiped the mantel clock from the den during her funeral. It was supposed to go to your mother, who, by the way, is secretly afraid she raised a monster. She sees a therapist in Mechanicsburg about you. Oh, and it's definitely not normal to piss the bed every time you drink too much."

"Damn, girl," Jasmine said, nodding with approval. Then she turned back to Flemming. "Ha! Bed pisser with a micro penis!"

"And you," Riley said, pointing at Duncan, who paled noticeably. "Your plan to steal the mayor's cash stash and then kill him by lacing his smoothie with ground-up peanuts is pretty good. Might actually work."

"I'm allergic to peanuts," Flemming shouted in disbelief.

"Uh, yeah. That's kinda the point, dumbass," Jasmine said.

Both men were staring at Riley in shock and horror.

Just then, her spirit guides really went to bat for her.

She locked eyes with Jasmine and blinked three times. Their girl code for "Time to go."

55

Duncan hid his gun behind his back and tried to maintain his grip on Jasmine. Nolan surprised Riley with his speed when he moved to her side and wrapped a hand around her arm in a vicious hold.

"Not. One. Word," he hissed, tucking his own gun into the waistband of his shorts as nine women in oversize fluorescent green T-shirts proclaiming their love of Jesus and the Enola Brethren Church power walked into their midst.

"Drive those elbows back, ladies," the leader of the pack ordered. "Keep those abdominals tight. The bus should be here any minute."

The tension was so palpable Riley wondered how the walkers didn't bounce off it.

"Riley?" the second-in-command squawked, coming to a halt in front of them. It was Donna, the front desk troll. She was glaring judgmental daggers in Riley's direction.

Nolan tightened his grip on her, and Riley had to smother her desire to scream.

"Oh, hi, Donna. You know Mayor Flemming and his communications director, Duncan Gulliver, don't you?" She put a lot of emphasis on her hostage takers' names.

A woman with her pearlescent glasses on a chain made of

tiny crucifixes elbowed her way to the front. "Mayor Flemming, you spoke at our ladies' bazaar last winter and said that my ham and bean soup was the best you ever had."

Mayor McMurder had two choices—either order his henchman to kill a whole pack of church ladies or let Riley go and shake the woman's hand. But she already knew what choice he'd make. Image was everything, after all.

He pasted a phony smile on his gruesomely handsome face. "It's a pleasure to see you again," he said, releasing Riley's arm.

"She has a fiancée *and* a boyfriend, and now the mayor's her workout buddy?" Donna complained none too quietly to her walking partner.

"Now!" Riley shouted. She thumbed the cap of the pepper spray open and gave the mayor a spritz. The church ladies—more accustomed to name-calling over bingo cards—were slow to react as she pushed her way through them toward Duncan. Jasmine bent at the waist, raised her arms off her back in a show of flexibility that would have made Wander proud, and brought them down sharply. The zip tie securing her hands broke just as Riley hit Duncan at half speed in the chest, knocking him off-balance.

His gun hand came up and over, knocking the pepper spray out of her grasp. The church ladies started screaming like a flock of startled chickens.

"You idiot," Nolan howled.

"That's the last time you call me an idiot," Duncan said.

"You're right, it is." The mayor drew his gun and pointed it at his poison-planning pal.

Uh-oh.

"Everybody run!" Riley yelled. She and Jasmine took off at a sprint while the church ladies bounced off one another like panicked pinballs. "This way!" The authority in her voice and a gunshot broke through the panic.

They followed her like ducklings toward Championship Way, an optimistically monikered road that led to the front of the baseball stadium and the parking lot.

"Run in a zigzag, people," she ordered. "It makes it harder for a shooter to hit you!"

Everyone obliged.

"What the fuck is going on?" Jasmine shouted as she zigged barefoot behind Riley.

"Mayor bad," Riley puffed, zagging to the left.

"Yeah. Kinda got that when he abducted me last night. Where the hell is Nick?"

"At the commune. We rounded everyone up after I T-boned a cop car on the bridge last night."

"Girl, he is going to murder your ass."

"Has to catch me before Mayor Nolan Flemming," Riley shouted into her cleavage.

"Why are you yelling at your boobs?" Jasmine asked, hiking up her slinky red dress.

"It's a thing. Okay?"

There was a quieter popping sound, and the metal sign on Riley's left dinged.

"Zag, people!" she screeched.

"There's the bus!" someone shouted behind her. A seventy-year-old turned on the gas and motored past Riley. *Damn.* She really needed to work on her cardio. At least if she lived through this.

In front of them, a short bus in lime green and navy blue crested the hill.

"Everyone get on that bus," Riley gasped.

There was another popping noise, and the 5K's inflatable finish line made a slow farting sound and began to collapse.

Riley stopped at the open bus door and manhandled a woman with a neck brace aboard. "I need you to get these ladies out of here and to the closest police station on the West Shore. Tell them everything that happened. Okay?"

They pushed a woman in pink flamingo pants up the bus stairs.

The driver looked confused.

"I'm not leaving you!" Jasmine announced.

There was another muffled ping, and the side mirror of the bus shattered behind Riley's head.

"Argue later!" She grabbed her best friend and shoved her on the bus. "Get them out of here. I'll lead them away."

"You're an idiot," Jasmine said, dragging the elderly driver out of his seat. "Sorry, Gramps, but I'm gonna need access to the accelerator."

"I love you!" Riley yelled.

"Love you back, you dumbass," Jasmine said, slamming the door in Riley's face. Then she threw the bus into reverse and floored it down the narrow road carved into the hill, laying on the horn the whole way. The woman sure knew how to make an exit.

Riley didn't waste time watching her go. She had her own escape to plot. There was no way she was doubling back for Nick's SUV. It was kind of her thing now, leaving cars at crime scenes. Running wasn't going to get her very far. The pedestrian bridge was in front of her, and so was a bike rack.

"Good enough," she muttered.

She grabbed the first bike on the rack that wasn't locked. It had a basket, a pink banana seat, and matching streamers. She pushed off and started pedaling like a demon. This was where her free-range childhood served her. She'd logged more miles on bikes than she had her own feet.

"Turn around," she shouted at a pair of joggers who were just coming off the bridge. "Gun!"

They made a U-turn without breaking stride.

She hit the open grates of the bridge and yanked the phone from her sweaty cleavage. The screen was fogged. She stabbed at the screen, hoping it was the right spot. Posting had never been more essential than right this second.

"Dang it!" She swiped it across her tank top, and it vibrated in her hand.

"Mrs. Penny, I can't talk right now. I'm kind of in the middle of something," she yelled into the phone.

She heard the ominous rev of an engine behind her and looked over her shoulder.

"You have got to be shitting me," she said, exasperated.

There was a panel van sitting at the entrance to the pedestrian bridge. It revved its engine.

Riley pedaled faster and threw the phone in the basket.

"Where are you?" she heard Mrs. Penny ask distantly. "We woke up, and you were gone. Nick was yelling. And that got the goats all stirred up until he left."

"Nick left? Where is he?" Riley screeched. "Gun!" she warned the next jogger. The woman stopped in her tracks, then did an about-face and sprinted toward the Harrisburg side.

"He went after you, dummy," Mrs. Penny said from the basket. "He borrowed a motorcycle from the commune."

"No. No. No. He can't come here. He can't catch up to me!"

"I heard him yelling at one of his cop friends. They're tracking your phone."

"Shit!" Riley hissed. Her legs were on fire. She should have grabbed a road bike or a ten-speed. She should have done a lot of things differently.

"Do you need our assistance?!" Mrs. Penny shouted.

The van engine revved again, and she heard the squeal of tires as the wheels bit into the gravel and asphalt.

"Damn it." She picked up the pace as Harrisburg loomed in front of her. "Listen, Mrs. Penny. This is a code cabbage casserole. I repeat, code cabbage casserole. You need to make sure Nick doesn't get back to Harrisburg. If he finds me, he's going to die. Do you understand me?"

"Er—copper—ah—breakfast—ee…" The line went dead.

"Have some situational awareness, man. Van!" she screamed at a guy texting while walking two dogs onto the bridge. The dogs understood the warning before the man did and dragged him back to the city side.

The metal grates were vibrating under her now as the van picked up speed.

"Spirit guides, I could really use a hand," she said, sucking in a breath and pedaling for her life. The van was right behind her, but Front Street was so close. Riley nipped off the bridge

408

and took a hard right. The van plowed straight ahead into a concrete bench with a statue.

She couldn't tell if it was the evil villain or henchman driving as she hopped the curb and dodged a Nissan changing lanes. She pedaled onto Strawberry Street, a tight alley with not nearly enough witnesses. Pumping her legs and sweating her ass off, she popped out on Second Street, facing the empty Crowne Plaza Hotel.

"Oh, come on! Where the hell is everyone?" she wheezed, maneuvering up onto the sidewalk. For a street that was bumper to bumper every damn weekday and lined with drunks and pickpockets on a Saturday night, it was abandoned on a Sunday morning. *Damn it.* The one time in her life that she wanted attention, she couldn't find anyone to give it to her.

If she could survive a little longer, if she could surround herself with people, someone would call the cops. The good cops. She just needed to hang in there...

Something hit her from behind. As she went airborne, she realized it was the front bumper of the van, which was now on the freaking sidewalk and, oh good, smashing into a streetlight. Then it was her turn to smash into something. A human something.

"That's why you should always wear a helmet," a helpful homeless guy yelled from across the street.

Riley pulled herself onto her knees and apologized to the twentysomething skateboarder she'd knocked down. Once again, every damn part of her body hurt.

The driver's side door of the van flew open, and evil mayor Nolan Flemming stumbled out. He was bleeding from his left arm. But, *lucky her*, it looked like he was a righty.

"I just can't catch a break," she said through gritted teeth. Her fingers clamped around the skateboard.

"Time to die, bitch," Nolan spat, raising the gun. This one wasn't the little handgun he'd had on City Island. This one was bigger.

The skateboarder crab walked backward, eyes as big as the manhole covers on the street. Riley looked down at her hands and breathed. In her mind, she saw Nolan limping to a stop behind her and raising the gun.

"You've got witnesses," she warned him.

But he was beyond caring. Also clearly beyond sanity.

She felt him shift his aim to the kid whose wallet chain seemed to be stuck on a trash can.

She twisted and rose. In one mostly seamless move, she brought the skateboard up and slammed it with satisfaction into Nolan's face. It crunched gloriously just as the gun went off.

"That's for Dickie and Jasmine and that Rob guy, and for even *thinking* about killing Nick!" She swung again, connecting with the side of his head, and he went down on his knees. "You okay?" she called to the kid.

"That fucker shot me! He shot me in the foot!"

Flemming stirred on the ground.

"Uh, yeah. I'd suck it up and start running if I were you," Riley advised.

They took off in opposite directions. She hadn't even made it half a block when she heard an unholy howl behind her. Apparently Flemming's murderous brain was protected by a really thick skull.

As she chugged up Market Street, a side stitch reared its ugly head, and so did an idea. There was one place that was guaranteed to have an audience *and* cops.

Glancing behind her, she spotted a bloodied Nolan jog-limping after her. She guessed sometimes it took more than a gunshot wound, a van accident, and a skateboard to the face to end evil. *Again, lucky her.*

She whipped down an alley, ignoring the side stitch that was getting steadily worse but finding comfort with the fact that even if Nick was still tracking her phone, he'd find it blocks away from where she was probably going to die.

The green globe on top of the Capitol rose between buildings, and she felt a teeny tiny spark of hope.

Maybe she really could do this. Save the day. Get the guy. Live to have more sex with Nick.

"You're dead, Thorn," Flemming snarled behind her, popping her little bubble of hope. He was gaining. Stupid runner's endurance.

A dozen scrapes and cuts sang as she pumped her arms and legs. The adrenaline was probably exploding blood out of the openings.

Finally, the capitol loomed in front of her. She started for the steps. All 1.7 million of them. "Who built this damn building on a damn hill?" she huffed. Her breath was a thin, pathetic wheeze now, and her side felt like her appendix had decided to rupture. She also may have pulled a butt muscle.

Twenty.

Twenty-one.

Twenty-two.

There were too many goddamn steps.

A woman in uniform appeared in Riley's line of sight near the top of the steps. One of the capitol police.

Riley opened her mouth to yell for help or vomit—she wasn't sure what had a greater likelihood of coming out. But that murderous son of a bitch beat her to it.

"Look out! She's got a gun!" Nolan shrieked behind her.

56

Riley didn't know who was more shocked with the mayor's announcement, her or capitol security. Shaking her head, she held her gunless hands over her head and kept running.

She couldn't afford to stop and defend herself against the accusation. They'd both end up full of holes. So she sprinted for the giant statues of naked people that flanked the main entrance to the capitol.

"Gun!" Nolan yelled again behind the cop who had recovered from the shock and was in pursuit. "She's got a gun!"

The guards at the desk to Riley's right looked up from their fresh coffees. "Say what?" one of them said.

"No gun!" she managed to rasp as she dashed through the metal detector, hands up. "See?" she wheezed over her shoulder when it didn't beep. "Other guy has one! Bad guy!"

The rotunda was a beautiful space full of incredible architecture. She'd come here in the third grade on a field trip and remembered being fascinated and comforted by the *Sesame Street* lamp-style lighting and the huge dome above. Third-Grade Riley had no clue that Future Riley was most likely going to die here.

Nolan was shouting at the guards to give chase. And, *oh*

great, the cop from outside had drawn her weapon and was running after her. Riley jogged through the group of people standing at the foot of the grand staircase. A private capitol tour, she guessed. Parents harnessed their gaping children and hid them behind their backs as the madwoman approached at full gallop.

"Mayor has gun. Not me," she hyperventilated to her audience as her sneakers slapped the rust-colored tile mosaics. "Mayor bad!"

"Stop where you are," the cop ordered in a terrifying bad-dog voice.

Riley *wanted* to obey. She *enjoyed* following rules. But this time, being a good girl would get her killed.

Adrenaline was the only thing that had her legs pumping. Soon, her body was going to turn into one of those marathoners who lose all control of their limbs and bowels. God, she hoped she didn't crap herself before they shot her.

She charged past the grand staircase, dismissing it as an escape since there was no way in hell that she could run up more stairs.

Lady Luck showered her bountiful grace down on Riley and delivered unto her a guy pushing a mail cart full of files just beyond the staircase. "I'm so sorry about this," she wheezed and shoved the mail cart over on her way past.

"Hey!" the guy yelled as folders and papers flew everywhere.

She spared another glance behind her. The cop tripped over a package. The woman's sensible shoe planted on a file folder, which slipped out from under her like a banana peel, and down she went.

"Thank you," Riley breathed to whoever the hell was looking out for her.

She cut to the left down a hallway. Here, the grandeur of the dome and rotunda gave way to normal, oldish office space. She tried a door. Found it locked. Damn Sundays. *Wasn't government a twenty-four seven kind of job?*

The next door was locked too.

Hearing fast footsteps approaching, she picked up the pace. Just as she turned a corner, a door on the left opened. She half tackled the door and its operator, forcing both back into the room.

"What the fuck is your problem?" a nice-smelling woman in a pantsuit screeched from the floor. Lying on the floor sounded so good to Riley right now. *Just a little nap. Maybe some water. Dry heave in a trash can.*

She kicked the door shut and turned the lock. Bending at the waist, she gave the dry-heaving thing serious consideration.

"What the hell is this?" the woman demanded. "Are you one of those PETA freaks? Is this some publicity stunt?"

The nameplate on her desk read Janice Ettinger, Chief Clerk.

Still trying to catch her breath, Riley held up a finger.

"Are you on drugs?"

"Not. Drugs." But stringing words together proved to be too much. She grabbed a large glass vase and dry heaved.

"Don't you *dare* vomit your meth or whatever you're on into a hand-blown Jean-Pierre vase."

"Come out with your hands up," someone authoritatively shouted from the other side of the door.

"Help me! She's vomiting and holding me hostage!" her accidental hostage shrilled.

Another good heave, and Riley felt much better. She swiped at the sweat and blood on her face with the hem of her tank top.

"Oh my God, is that a *hole* in your abdomen?"

"Oh, shit," Riley said, looking down at the dark hole just above her hip bone. "I thought it was a side stitch." She tried to look behind her but couldn't quite manage it. "Did it go through?" She didn't know much about bullet wounds, but according to TV, it was better if it went straight through.

"Uh-huh." Chief Clerk Janice nodded, considerably paler now.

Riley pulled her tank back into place and handed her hostage the vase. "Here. Just in case you need it."

"You need to surrender now, ma'am," shouted the cop on the other side of the door. There was a ruckus coming from the hallway, and Riley imagined a pileup of capitol police plotting the best way to smoke her out.

"I need to get out of here," she wheezed to herself.

There were two ways out. The door. *Hard nope.* Or the old-school horizontal half window.

Her hostage barfed loudly into her prize vase.

"Listen," Riley said, clearing away items that blocked the window. "I know this sounds crazy, but the mayor is trying to kill me. He had my neighbor Dickie Frick murdered. Then he killed Representative Bowers. I think he killed his communications director on City Island this morning, and then he drove a van across the pedestrian bridge and tried to run me down. Also, he apparently shot me," she said, grabbing the water bottle she found on the desk. She sucked it down in three big gulps. Her side was on fire now, and she wondered if the water she'd just swallowed was going to shoot back out of the wound. "He's out there now saying I have a gun. And I'm basically going to die all because I had this vision that Nick—that's my fake fiancé who I for real slept with last night—was going to die today."

"You slept with your fake fiancé?"

"Janice, if I get murdered today, the highlight of my life will be sex with Nick Santiago," she said, dumping an entire stack of file folders onto the floor and climbing onto the ancient radiator. Her wound was really starting to throb now that she knew it existed.

"Nick Santiago is your fiancé? Ha! Now I know you're crazy! Nick would never willingly get engaged."

"Don't make me show you my bullet hole again, Janice." Riley pushed the window out as far as it would go. They weren't very far off the ground, but it was still going to hurt. A lot. She had to go now before capitol security secured the perimeter or whatever the hell they called it.

She *really* could have used another five minutes of rest. But she wasn't sure if she had five more minutes left to live, and she wasn't going to spend her remaining time with Janice.

"Help me! She's delusional," her nauseous hostage shouted.

Rolling her eyes, Riley fell out the window.

"Oof!" She landed ungracefully on top of a spiny, woody bush that immediately crumpled under her weight. "Ouch. Ouch. Ouch." She crawled her way through the landscaping, staying against the building. The landscaping theme on this side of the building appeared to be "thorny."

She could hear sirens and didn't trust that they were coming to her aid. Peeping through the needles of some bitey evergreen, she spied Commonwealth Avenue to the east. It was a busy road, even on the weekends. If she could make it there, she could flag down a car, borrow a phone, at the very least thank Nick for the orgasms before…before.

She had to go now. It was her only chance. Hunching low, she jog-waddled her way along the east wing. The fountain spurted to life just ahead. From above, it looked like half of a perfect boob. But from the ground, it was much more dignified. Today, the waters spewing forth into the air were still a toilet-bowl blue for the Fourth of July weekend.

Behind her, the sounds of angry law enforcement grew louder. It was now or never. One deep breath that *really* made her side hurt, and she was off and running again.

The sidewalk in front of her was empty. It opened onto the fountain's courtyard, which also appeared to be sublimely devoid of gun-toting people ready to shoot her. Fueled by hope, she pounded across the concrete, making a beeline for the road. There were cars cruising by. She felt the spray from the fountain's jets as she neared it. Almost there.

Maybe this would work. Maybe she would live through this after all.

Something hit her from behind. And then she was airborne, sailing into the toilet-blue waters. She went under. Her brain found the unanticipated warmth of the water a little gross. And then she realized she couldn't breathe. Someone pulled her up.

"When I say don't move, I mean don't fucking move, lady." It was the capitol cop, who was super pissed off but not currently pointing a gun at Riley. "Damn it. I just ironed this shirt," the officer complained.

"He's trying to kill me. Mayor Flemming has a gun. He shot me," Riley said after spitting out a pint of fountain water.

The cop slapped a cuff on one of her wrists. But Riley was slippery when wet, and she flailed her other hand free.

"The mayor's trying to kill you. Yep. Uh-huh." The cop reached for Riley's other wrist.

"I'm serious. Look. He shot me." She yanked her bloody tank top up.

"Damn, girl. You got shot right through the muffin top."

"He had Legislator Bowers murdered because he wants his seat," Riley said in a rush. "He shot his henchman, Duncan Gulliver, on City Island. Call. Ask. Please! I'm not lying, Shanna. Just ask. For the love of cheese and crackers, save my life and ask," she begged.

"How do you know my name?"

"I'm a psychic. Your PIN number is 0733, and when you were twelve, you kissed the neighbor boy, but you wished it was his sister." It came out in a frantic rush.

"This is Officer Billings," the cop said into the handset on her shoulder. "We got any police reports coming in from City Island?"

There was a crackle of static as Riley's life hung in the balance.

"Got a report of gunfire and someone kidnapping a bus full of church ladies. Then some asshole drove his van across the pedestrian bridge, trying to mow down a girl on a bike. Just another day in paradise."

"Me! That was me. I'm the girl on the bike," Riley said, nodding so hard her teeth chattered.

Cars continued to whiz past on the road, either not noticing the wrestling match in the fountain or immune to it. Officer Billings had stopped reaching for her other hand.

"If what you're saying is true—"

The sound of a shot echoed in Riley's head, and she watched in horror as a tiny hole appeared in Billings's chest and began to bloom red.

"No. No. No." Riley grabbed the woman's arms and tried to hold her up, but the officer's knees buckled in slow motion. Riley lowered with her, resting Officer Billings against the lip of the fountain.

"Gun," she whispered to Riley before her eyes rolled back in her head.

"You stupid, psychotic son of a *bitch*," Riley seethed as Mayor Flemming limped closer, casually wielding his gun.

"I had a feeling you'd come this way. Maybe I'm psychic too. Best of all, I reported a woman fitting your description trying to break into the State Museum, so it's just you and me, Ms. Thorn," he sneered. His laugh was unhinged, and she knew whatever sanity that had kept him from exposing himself as a monster was officially gone. She'd probably knocked it out of him with the skateboard…along with what looked like one of his canine teeth. *Cool.*

"You didn't see this coming, did you?" Riley said, yanking Billings's gun out of the holster and pointing it at him.

Why, why, why hadn't she taken Nick up on the shooting lessons? Was there a safety? If so, how did she unsafety it? Was there a round in the thing? Was she supposed to pull back a hammer-majiggy?

This was bad. She couldn't outshoot him. The only chance she had was luring him closer and beating the crap out of him.

Eh. Worth a shot? Ha. Little about-to-be-murdered pun there.

Riley dropped the gun to her side and crossed her eyes. "I'm getting a message from the beyond for you," she said in a robotic monotone. She jerked back and forth like she was being electrocuted. She hoped the gravely wounded Officer Billings didn't have a stun gun submerged in the water.

Flemming limped closer, still pointing the gun at her.

"I'm getting a motherly presence. Also the letter *F*," Riley reported. "Mother Ffffffff…"

He was inching closer and closer. "Great-Aunt Frances?" he guessed.

She shook her head. "No. More like motherfu-u-u-u-cker!" Everything seemed to happen in slow motion as she hurled the gun at him. He put his hands up as if to catch it, just like *Made It Out Alive* said he would. Flemming wasn't fast enough though. It hit him in the forehead with a satisfying *thwack*.

She dove sideways just as his finger tightened on the trigger. The shot went wide. At least she assumed it did when she didn't feel any new holes in her body.

She surfaced and tried to jump to her feet, but the jig was up. A howling, bleeding Nolan sloshed his way toward her.

Riley, out of weapons, splashed him as he came closer, gun raised.

"Say good night, bitch," he snarled.

"You're so original with your bad-guy lines," she complained, squeezing her eyes shut and keeping up the waterworks even as he pulled the trigger.

When there was no bang, when she didn't feel the life drip out of her body, she opened one eye. Nolan was staring in horror at his empty magazine. *Click. Click. Click.*

Their eyes met over the barrel of the now-useless weapon.

She opened her mouth and let out an entire adulthood of pent-up rage in a terrifying battle cry. He took a floundering step backward. Riley lunged for him, and they grappled in the blue, blue water. It was a blur of limbs and toilet water. He yanked her hair, and she landed a stunning jab to his already wounded mouth.

He attempted a headlock hold, which she countered with a nasty bite to the bicep. A lucky punch slipped past her defenses and caught her right in the bullet hole. It took the breath out of her, and Nolan pressed his advantage, flopping on her with all his body weight. She went under and, with horror, felt hands tighten on her throat. He had her pinned against the floor of the fountain, a foot of water between her and precious, precious oxygen.

She bucked and punched and slapped. But she was growing weaker. A haze of red filtered through the water in front of her eyes. Just like her vision. Only it was *her* blood. Not Nick's. She'd done it. She'd saved Jasmine and Nick. And if this was the way things had to end, she'd die knowing everyone she loved—or in Nick's case really, really, *really* liked—was safe.

The red and blue were getting darker and darker and darker as the world gently disappeared.

57

"Riley!" Her name ripped its way out of his throat as Nick ran toward her. Toward the madman intent on drowning the woman he wanted to do a lot of things to.

The entire ride back to Harrisburg, he'd planned out exactly how loud and long he was going to yell at her.

Stupid.

Irresponsible.

Selfish.

The plan had been to find her and then spend the next week or so shouting some sense into her.

He wasn't exactly conscious of jumping into the fountain, of diving for the murderous monster, of his gun slipping out of his waistband and sinking. But the second his body collided with Flemming's, instinct took over.

Dragging Riley to the surface with one hand, he held Nolan under with the other, jabbing a knee into the man's balls.

"Breathe, baby," he demanded, giving Riley a little shake. Her lips and skin had a blue tinge to them. Actually, so did her hair.

Her eyes—thank fucking God—fluttered open. She coughed and choked and drew in a breath.

"I am so pissed at you, Thorn," he told her as the world's most evil mayor thrashed against his grip.

She pawed at him, trying to say something, but choked out more water instead.

He leaned in closer. "What?"

"Get out of the fountain!" she rasped. There was panic in her eyes.

"I'm a little busy saving your life," he argued.

"Get out of the damn fountain, Nick!"

"As soon as I'm done kicking this weasel's ass."

He gave her one hard kiss and released her. Riley continued to shout nonsensically at him to get out even as she sloshed over to the unconscious cop.

Nick dragged Flemming back to the surface.

"Nobody fucking drowns my girlfriend," he snarled. He grabbed the man by his stupid hair and landed a right hook that would have made Floyd Mayweather shed a tear of pride. Flemming deflated like a bagpipe.

Reaching down, Nick grabbed the poor excuse for a man by the back of the neck. He was in the middle of trying to decide whether to kick him in the face or step on his trachea when someone else shouted his name.

"Hands the fuck up!"

Detective Weber, in jeans and a T-shirt, stood against the lip of the fountain, gun pointed. A cop car with lights and sirens screeched to a halt on the street behind him.

"Don't justh sthand there, you moronths!" Flemming sputtered through holes where teeth used to be. "Arresth theeth athholeth! They athaulted me!"

"Harrisburg PD! I wanna see some hands!" This command came from Detective Katie Shapiro, who vaulted out of the car, gun trained on them.

Nick saw the shift from terrified to smug as it played out on Nolan's face. He tightened his grip on the man.

"Let the mayor go, Santiago," Shapiro ordered.

"Weber," Nick said. "You remember that thing in Tijuana?"

"Already ahead of you, brother," Weber said, shifting his stance to point his gun at Shapiro.

Riley gasped. "Wait! Weber isn't dirty?"

"That's exactly what you wanted everyone to think, isn't it, Katie?" Nick said.

The detective's face remained an impervious mask. "I don't know what you're talking about," she said.

"Okay, she's definitely lying," Riley said, pointing at Shapiro. "And, Nick, I swear to God, if you don't get out of this water right now—"

But her threat was cut off by the arrival of the capitol police. There were more cars. More guns. More people. And lots more yelling.

Nick had about twenty weapons trained on him and, after a brief internal debate, decided the best course of action was to release the son of a bitch. Momentarily.

"They tried to kill me!" Flemming sputtered while he flailed around in the water, and two officers ran up to the cop slumped at the fountain's edge. "They did that! *They* thot tha offither," Flemming said, pointing while he tried to get to his feet.

"It's true. I saw the girl shoot her," Shapiro called out.

Nick gave Flemming a kick to the chest and sent the man sprawling backward.

"Don't fucking move," five or six cops yelled at the same time.

"You lying sack of weasels," Riley bellowed. She started coughing again, and Nick edged toward her. "The mayor shot Officer Billings. He also abducted my best friend and shot his communications director, which doesn't really matter because he was a bad guy too," she told the crowd between coughs.

"Riley, honey. Maybe you want to shut up for a second and breathe," Nick suggested.

"Oh, *and* he shot me too," she announced.

"*He shot you?*" Just when Nick thought he couldn't possibly get more pissed off.

Flemming frantically tried to backstroke away from him.

"Stop moving, Flemming, or someone is going to put a bullet in you," Weber shouted.

"You don't have a badge, Weber," Shapiro reminded him.

"Then consider this a citizen's arrest," Weber shot back. "You're next."

Nick eased to the left, putting himself between Shapiro's gun and the woman he was probably going to have to marry for real. He was running calculations in his head. If they could get out of this fountain alive, they'd have a chance at getting someone to listen to the truth. But as the seconds ticked by, the odds of that were getting slimmer and slimmer.

"Halt!"

Nick blinked. Once. Twice. Even after a third blink, he was still seeing the same thing. A dozen masked vigilantes converged on the fountain. He recognized Richard Nixon and Elsa from *Frozen* from his late-night pickup service. But he didn't see Mrs. Penny.

"The mayor is lying!" the kid in the Elsa mask squeaked, holding up a phone.

"Back off *now*," Detective Shapiro shouted. "This is official police business."

"What in the fuck is going on? Who are we supposed to shoot?" growled one of the capitol cops.

"Show him," Nick told Elsa the Ninja, pointing with his raised hands at the grumpy cop.

Obligingly, the pubescent vigilante trotted up to the cop.

"What am I looking at?" the officer groused. "I don't have my reading glasses."

"Dude, it's a Facebook Live. This mayor guy tried to kill the hot chick in the fountain on City Island and again on Second Street."

"Hot chick? Aww, thanks, Elsa," Riley croaked.

Nick rolled his eyes. And then realized he'd made his mistake. He'd let Flemming out of his sight.

"*Nick!*" Riley shrieked. He spun around in time to see

the sopping wet mayor level a gun at him from the lip of the fountain.

"Ah, shit."

He wasn't going to have the chance to yell at Riley. He wasn't going to find a house and figure out what settling down meant. He wasn't going to get to give his cousin and Josie the raises he'd planned. He wasn't going to wake up to another morning with Riley naked in his arms.

"Put the gun down, Mayor," someone yelled. But it was too late.

Flemming pulled the trigger just as something wet and hard hit Nick from the side. He went under the water and stayed there, wondering when it would start to hurt. Maybe it was a kill shot, and he was already dead? That thought pissed him off. Maybe he was just super manly and pain didn't affect him? He liked that better.

Then hands were grabbing at his shirt, his shoulders.

He wondered if this was heaven or hell. Most likely hell, he guessed. He'd been a real pisser as a teenager and a twenty-something. He broke the surface of the water and dragged in a breath.

Huh. Hell looked a whole lot like Harrisburg in the middle of a gunfight.

The capitol cops were hunkered down behind vehicles and stone balustrades, taking fire from one pissed-off Detective Shapiro and the city's soggy-ass, blue-tinged mayor who had Nick's fucking gun. The vigilantes had scattered to take cover behind trash cans and stone benches.

"You okay, man?" Weber asked, dragging him backward behind the fountain's concrete center.

"When did you get in here?" Nick asked, feeling a little dazed.

Weber dropped him unceremoniously next to Riley.

She grabbed him and held on tight. "You're not dead!"

"Are you okay?" he asked, returning the embrace.

"Ow," she said. "Except for my side."

"She pushed you out of the way," Weber said grimly.

"I can't believe that guy shot you," Nick croaked, staring in horror at the wound in her side.

"I know," she groused. "He got me in the love handle when I was running...or maybe it was when I was on the bike. I thought it was appendicitis."

"We're sitting in a lot of blood for one bullet hole," Weber observed.

She swiveled her head back to Nick. He started to feel a strange stinging beneath him. "Oh, come on," he said.

Weber grinned and pushed Nick onto his side. "Congratulations, brother. You've got yourself an extra hole in your ass."

"For Pete's sake! All my freaking heroics, and you *still* get shot?" Riley yelled over the sounds of gunfire.

"I got shot in the ass? That's not sexy," he complained.

A bullet pinged into the concrete above their heads. Weber positioned himself to return fire. "We might want to save the arguments for when we're not taking fire," he suggested.

"Nick?" Riley's pretty brown eyes were watery.

"Yeah, Thorn?"

"If we don't get out of here, I just want you to know that I had a really good time last night. Like *really* good," she yelled.

His male pride puffed up automatically. "You're damn right, you did," he shouted. "And we're getting out of here. So don't try to say some dramatic goodbye."

"How are we getting out of this?" she asked as bullets flew over their heads.

"It'll take a miracle, but you're pretty damn lucky. I'll take my chances with y—"

The sound of squealing wheels and a revving engine cut him off. They poked their heads up and watched in sick fascination as a dusty gray minivan jumped the curb and hurtled toward the fountain.

"Is that...?"

"Cabbage casserole," Riley breathed.

Detective Shapiro and Mayor Dirtbag Flemming were too busy in their murderous rampage to pay attention to the minivan as it accelerated toward them. It hit Flemming first, sending his body bouncing over the hood and into the windshield before the man rag-dolled onto the sidewalk. It didn't slow when it struck Shapiro, tossing her a good ten feet. She hit the fountain's concrete centerpiece with a sickening thud, followed by a belly flop into the water. The minivan came to a crunching halt when it slammed into the concrete bollards that ringed the front of the fountain.

"Cabbage casserole that, motherfuckers," Mrs. Penny shouted with satisfaction as she emerged from behind the wheel, hands on her head as a dozen stunned officers trained their weapons on her.

There was a long beat of silence, and then the world started spinning again.

Burt the dog loped out of the minivan and jumped into the fountain to deliver face licks to Riley, Nick, and Weber. Satisfied that his people were alive, he shifted his attention to trying to bite the jets of water that arched into the center.

"We're coming out," Weber yelled, holstering his gun and gesturing for Nick and Riley to follow him.

Hands up, they limped and sloshed their way as a three-some to the lip of the fountain.

Cops and EMTs moved in barking orders, searching for wounds and weapons.

The vigilantes high-fived and took a selfie…with the unmasked Josie.

"No fucking way," Nick said, pointing to his employee. "Richard Nixon."

"Oh, you didn't know?" Riley asked innocently.

"You did? She didn't say a word in the car."

"I'm a psychic, remember?" She grimaced and looked over her shoulder to make sure no one had heard her confession.

He shook his head and grinned. He slipped an arm around her waist, being mindful of her gunshot wound. In return, she wrapped an arm around his hips.

"Which one of us is holding the other up?" she asked as they limped toward the paramedics.

"We're holding each other up. That's what partners do," he told her. "By the way, where's my car?"

She grimaced. "Left it in the middle of a shoot-out on City Island."

"Nice."

A feral howl came from behind them. They turned to see a sweaty, bloody Duncan Gulliver swaying on the sidewalk ten feet away. The hand that held the gun was shaking.

"Oh, for fuck's sake," Nick said, jostling Riley behind him. He tried to take a run at the gunman, but the bullet in his ass and the girl jumping on his back impeded him.

"Another gun!" someone yelled.

"Christ! How many more fucking bad guys are there?" one of the cops yelled, unholstering her weapon.

Before anyone, including Duncan, could react, ninety-two pounds of pissed-off dog flew into the air.

"Burt!" Riley yelled.

The dog's trajectory had him plowing into the henchman's arm and knocking the gun free before he slammed into the man's chest.

Duncan crumpled to the cement like tissue paper.

Burt pinned him to the sidewalk with two beefy paws on his shoulders and barked once in his face.

"Whose lion is this?" bellowed a capitol cop with pants wet to the knees and gun drawn.

"Mine," Riley said, sliding off Nick's back.

"Ours," Nick corrected her.

"Aww." She grinned at him.

Nick whistled Burt off the blubbering bad guy. The dog bounded over, tail wagging.

"Buddy, you are getting the biggest rib eye I can find tonight," he told the heroic canine.

Burt danced around in a circle, oblivious to the carnage and confusion around them.

"You two wanna get those souvenirs looked at?" Weber asked, gesturing at their matching wounds.

While Nick flopped facedown on a gurney to give the lady paramedic a peek at his ass, he watched Riley sit on the curb to pet the very, very good boy and let an EMT fuss over her wounds.

His heart did a stuttery thing in his chest. Yeah. Marriage might be in the cards, and he wasn't even mad about it. Sometimes it was just better to surrender.

"Okay there, lover boy?" the paramedic asked.

"Better than I've ever been," he said.

"Uh-huh. Well. Your hands and feet and ass are blue. You've got yourself a slug lodged in your ass, and your girlfriend looks like she went a few rounds with a hangry reality TV housewife. You're both going to the hospital," the lady paramedic told Nick briskly.

He swore ripely, and when her back was turned, Nick climbed out of the ambulance and limped his way toward his girl.

"Whiner," Riley teased from her seat on the curb.

"Yo, Weber," Nick called.

The detective looked up from the heated conference he was in with the officer in charge of the scene.

"We under arrest?" Nick asked.

Weber gave a rueful headshake. "Not as of this moment."

"Good. You can drive us to the hospital."

Nick's phone rang, and he paused to fish it out of his pants pocket. He swiped the water droplets off the screen. It was Perry, his semi-homeless wise man. "Hey, Perr. What's up?" he said.

Riley swiveled her head to look up at him, and Nick saw her nose twitch.

"I don't know if you've heard but you're gonna need a new office space and apartment," Perry told him.

Nick pinched the bridge of his nose. "And why is that?"

"Burnt to a crisp. Arson, of course. I mighta got a peek at the firebugs before they fled the scene."

"Shit," Nick said. "Fuck. Anyone hurt?"

"Not as far as I could tell."

Nick gritted out a sigh. "Okay, man. Thanks. I'll buy you lunch this week."

"What burnt down?" Riley asked, eyes wide when he hung up.

"Damn," Weber said, ambling over. "Someone beat me to it."

"Beat you to what?" she demanded, her hands stilling on Burt's red fur.

"Nick's apartment and office burned to the ground early this morning," Weber announced. "Guessing it was Shapiro's dirty work. Probably the two cops who tried to take out your Nature Girls gang last night on the 83 bridge."

"Maybe you shouldn't have knocked on my door," Riley said to Nick. She was wearing his T-shirt, and he thought that was fucking adorable.

"Are you kidding, Thorn? This is the most fun I've had in a long time," he said, reaching down to help her up.

"I'm sorry about your place," she said, brushing her blue hands on her damp shorts.

Nick shrugged it off. It wasn't much more than a few tons of paperwork and takeout menus. "Son of a bitch. Now, I'm going to have to buy all new dog stuff," he complained.

"Hey, man. It also means you get to buy a new flat-screen," Weber pointed out.

Nick considered that a win. "I'm going eighty-inch with this one."

Riley winced. "Getting shot sucks almost as much as running."

"But think of the big screen we'll get to recover in front of," he told her cheerfully.

"Where are you going to hang a big screen if your apartment and office are in ashes?" she asked.

"I'll figure something out," he promised.

Weber led the way to his car. They followed behind at a leisurely pace conducive to limping.

"When were you guys in Tijuana together?" Riley asked.

"Never," Nick said with a grin. "We just thought it made us sound cool when we were rookies."

"That's adorable," she said.

He held on to her a little tighter with his blue hand. "I don't know if anyone's ever told you this before, but you're a real pain in the ass, Thorn," he quipped.

"Ha. I'm sorry. I didn't hear you because I was too busy wondering if it was too soon to use 'Get the lead out.'"

"Very punny," he said, dropping a kiss on top of her Smurf-tinged hair. "I'm still pissed at you though. We're definitely having a fight about this."

"I'll pencil you in," she promised.

"Riley! Hey, Riley!"

"You have got to be kidding me," she muttered.

Griffin Gentry was running toward them with a camera crew on his heels. "Is it true you shot several police officers and tried to drown your lover in the capitol fountain?" he yelled into the microphone in his hand.

"Oh, honey, I got this," Nick promised. He handed Riley over to Weber, walked up to Gentry, and punched the guy right in the face. Gentry crumpled to the concrete. Nick stepped over him and inhaled a lungful of summer morning air and nodded. "Yeah, this is a good day."

58

They parted ways in the emergency department. Nick was wheeled off to meet with what Riley could only assume was a butt surgeon. Weber stayed with her while the nurses fussed over her wounds. The detective had changed out of his waterlogged clothes into blue scrubs that matched his feet in the plastic flip-flops someone had found for him.

"I gotta ask," he said after the flurry of gauze and tape and antibiotics fed through a very sharp needle. "What were you thinking meeting Flemming alone like that?"

"I knew Nick was going to get shot if he showed up today," she said. "I thought I could change the future."

"By sacrificing yourself," Weber said.

She shrugged. "Seemed like a good idea at the time."

He sighed. "It was a very brave, very stupid thing to do."

"Yeah, but Nick and Jasmine are alive, aren't they? And Flemming isn't getting anyone's seat in the legislature anytime soon."

"You could have been killed," he said sternly.

"But I wasn't. Wait. Jasmine is okay, isn't she? She didn't die in some kind of church bus shoot-out did she?" Riley asked, sitting up.

Weber held up his hands. "She's fine. The walking club is a little shaken and maybe confused about what constitutes kidnapping. But Jasmine is fine."

She relaxed back on the bed. "Now it's my turn to ask a question."

"Shoot," he said, then winced. "Sorry."

"How did Nick know he could trust you?"

He gave her a grin. "Because I'm always the good guy."

Riley rolled her eyes. She was starting to collect arrogant men the way her aunt Sage collected erotic snow globes.

"Did you both know Detective Shapiro was dirty?" she asked.

"I had my suspicions," Weber said.

"Which were confirmed when she had you suspended and took over the case."

He nodded. "That one pissed me off. Nicky eventually figured it out too. He's a lot slower than I am." Weber glanced at his watch.

"Have to go?" she asked.

"Yeah. My lieutenant and the chief scheduled a contest to see who can yell the longest at me for running an off-the-books op while on suspension."

He didn't look too worried about it.

"They want to have a conversation with Nicky too, so I called your dad to come pick you up," he explained.

She felt a jab of disappointment. Oh, wait. Maybe that was just the hole in her love handle. She'd had a cute fantasy of limping out of the hospital arm in arm with Nick and going home to have some less acrobatic, more gentle sex than last night's round. And then food. A lot of food.

That was the thing about fantasies. Unlike psychic visions, they didn't come true. Considering the fact that there was no reason for them to pretend to be engaged anymore, she'd be lucky if she ever saw him again.

She moped until she was discharged, handed her bloody T-shirt—well, Nick's bloody T-shirt—in a biohazard bag, and wheeled to the hospital's entrance.

"What the—"

Her dad was waving from behind the wheel of Nick's Scientology van.

"You sure you want to get a ride home in that?" the orderly asked.

She laughed. "Yeah. I guess so."

The orderly helped her out of the chair, and Riley, suddenly bone-weary, lugged her body into the passenger seat.

A large wet nose snuffled at her hair.

"Dad. Why are you in Nick's van? And why is your cow sniffing my head?"

Roger beamed at the heifer. "Had to get my girls back home, didn't I?"

Daisy mooed in agreement, right in Riley's ear. Man, cows were loud.

Her father and his spite cow were picking her up at the hospital after she'd been shot.

She'd never had a chance at turning out normal.

"Where's Burt? Where's Mom?" she asked, wincing as she secured her seat belt.

"Gabe picked up Burt and drove him and the rest of your neighbors home since Mrs. Penny's minivan is now evidence. Your mom, sister, and the girls are staying up at the commune for the day. And your waitress friends said something about helping in the back pasture," he said, easing the van onto Second Street, where just hours ago, his daughter had pedaled for her life with a madman on her tail.

"How mad is Mom?"

Roger shrugged. "Eh. About as to be expected with her daughter getting herself shot over some guy."

Nick Santiago was not merely "some guy." But until she found out where things were going now that the fake engagement was for real over, she'd keep her opinions to herself.

"How mad are you?" she asked.

"I've been madder," her dad mused. "Besides, I've done

some dumb shit in my day. Like thinking I was gonna dump your mom for crushing on some guy she hadn't even met yet."

"Dad, I'm really sorry about that," she began.

"Sorry? You were four. What the hell do you have to be sorry about?"

"I broke you guys up."

Roger shook his head. "That's bullshit. I broke us up."

"Yeah, but you wouldn't have if I hadn't told you Mom was kissing another guy."

"Those three months and nine days without having you and your mom around were the longest of my life. One week into it, I knew it was the biggest mistake I'd ever made. But without it, I wouldn't have known how much I really loved your mom and how ready I was to be a husband and a dad."

Daisy shoved her giant face between the seats and mooed.

Roger chuckled and gave the cow a little scratch between the ears. "Yeah, I love you too, Daisy girl."

"You honestly aren't mad about it?" Riley pressed.

"Mad? We got your sister out of the deal. I got a trivia night partner. And I've got three little cuties who call me Pop-Pop and build birdhouses with me."

"That's very Blossom Basil-Thorn of you," she observed.

"What can I say? You Thorn women rub off on a guy." He grinned.

She couldn't help but smile back. "But seriously. You left your wife, and she got pregnant by another man because I opened my big fat mouth."

"Ah, Rye Bread. You always were too hard on yourself." Roger sighed. "Lemme ask you this. This Nick fellow. You did what you did because you had a vision or something that he was gonna get shot in a fountain, right?"

"Yes."

"Did he or did he not still get shot in a fountain today?"

"He did," she said slowly.

Nick *had* gotten shot in a fountain.

Dickie *had* gotten himself murdered.

Her parents *had* broken up over a man her mom hadn't even met.

"Wait," Riley said, straightening in her seat and then wincing at the full-body soreness. "What are you saying?"

"I'm saying I don't know how this woo-woo stuff works. But maybe you saw those things happening because they were gonna happen no matter what."

She thought of the ugly comforter at the commune. Of Nick ranging his gloriously naked body over hers. Then she remembered she was in a vehicle with her dad and his pet cow.

"Are you saying you think all that stuff was fate?"

"I'm not really sure what I'm saying," Roger said. "But it's something to think about, isn't it? It's a possibility you were seeing things that were gonna happen no matter what you did. Maybe you should ask your grandmother about it."

They both shivered.

"Maybe I'll have Mom ask her," Riley said.

"Good call." Roger yawned. Daisy mooed. "Let's get some tacos and then get you home."

———

Her dad left her in front of the mansion with a greasy bag of tacos and one of queso and chips before driving off with his cow.

The heavy interior door was open behind the screen, and Riley could hear the sounds of the house and its residents. Mrs. Penny was yelling for Bloody Mary ingredients from the front parlor while Lily and Fred argued over who was Great-Aunt Esther's favorite growing up. Riley could smell fresh laundry in the dryer.

Just across the road, the river gleamed under the summer sun. Birds sang. Neighbors mowed their lawns.

Things were blissfully, comfortingly normal.

She sat down in the rocking chair and took a breath. Things were going to change. Several of them. But it didn't seem quite as scary now that she'd faced down bad guys with guns. She'd survived getting shot and almost drowned. She'd survived spending the night with Nick in her bed. She could survive being less normal.

She heard a scrabble of nails from inside. Burt gave a happy bark and bounded through the screen door. He trotted up to her and shoved his face into her lap, looking up at her with love-struck brown eyes.

"Hey, buddy. Who's the best boy in the world?" she asked, leaning down to hug him.

His tail slashed through the air, back and forth in dangerous happiness.

The screen door creaked open again, and Gabe appeared. He was dressed in his usual skintight workout wear and holding a bowl of ice cream in one hand and a gym bag in the other.

"Riley! You are back!" In his rush to hug her, he threw the bowl over his shoulder. The dog dove for it.

Riley returned his hug one-armed.

"Thank you for telling Nick where to find me," she said.

He looked surprised. "How did you know?"

She tapped her temple. "Psychic, remember? Also, how else would Nick have figured out where I was? I had his car with the police scanner."

"I was honored to use our spiritual connection to aid you today," he said humbly. "It has been an honor to serve you, Riley Thorn."

The man looked like he was about to cry. She eyed the gym bag he'd dropped.

"You're not going somewhere, are you?" she asked.

His eyes were more puppy-doggy than Burt's, and his lips were pressed in a firm line.

"I assumed my work here was complete," he said, toeing a seam between porch planks. "Since you have embraced your powers."

The parlor phone rang. "Yeah, what do you want? I'm in the middle of a bucket of Bloody Marys," they heard Mrs. Penny answer.

There was a beat of silence.

"Look, I'll tell you what I told your seventeen other journalist buddies. Ms. Thorn isn't giving interviews or psychic readings. At least not without a five-figure booking fee."

"Mrs. Penny!" Riley yelled.

"Whoopsie. Never mind," the woman said into the phone. "You've got the wrong number. Bye!"

"Journalists are calling?" Riley asked.

Gabe nodded. "It would seem that your live video on social media became contagious."

She leaned against the back of the chair and closed her eyes. She'd claimed and then shown off her psychic abilities to an invisible audience. "Well, shit," she sighed.

"Sorry, kiddo," Mrs. Penny said, poking her head out of the front door. "We've been getting calls all day long. You're famous!"

Riley groaned. Her new internal rejection of normal for the sake of normal was going to be unfairly and publicly reinforced.

"You coming out is perfect timing," Mrs. Penny said cheerfully. "I'm looking for a new gig now that the vigilantes have to disband under penalty-of-the-law bullshit. Did those cops even say thank you to us for running justice for them? Maybe a little, but it's not like they coughed up any cash reward or anything. Anyway, I'll be your manager. Come on inside and have a Bloody Mary. We'll talk appearance fees."

Riley could only deal with one crisis at a time.

"I'll be in in a minute. I need to talk to Gabe first."

"Okey dokey! I'll start your Facebook page as soon as you show me how to use Facebook. Your video got way more views than Wander's downward dog ever did," she said chipperly.

Burt, hearing "downward dog," lay down in the ice cream he was still lapping up.

"Gabe," Riley began when Mrs. Penny banged back into the house. "What would you say if I told you I thought we had more work to do?"

He perked up. "I would agree wholeheartedly."

"I can't afford to pay you," she said quickly.

"My work is not linked to a paycheck," he said magnanimously.

"Yeah, but how do you afford stuff?"

"The universe provides," he said, opening his palms and looking up. Fat stacks of cash did not fall from the porch rafters.

"Uh-huh. We'll come back to that. Money aside, if you're still up for teaching me how to get better at this stuff, I'd like to learn," she told him.

He bowed his perfectly shaped head. "It would be my greatest honor."

"Good," she said.

"Excellent."

"Okay then," Riley said.

"If you will excuse me, I will replace my sadness ice cream with happiness ice cream," Gabe said, beaming.

"Have at it, man."

"Yoo-hoo! Riley?" Lily called from somewhere in the house. "Do you have any pictures of Nick's butt? I want to show it to my friends at pottery class!"

Fred poked his head out of the parlor when she stepped inside.

"Jasmine called. She wants to come over for drinks tonight. Lots of drinks, she said."

"That sounds good," Riley said wearily. The steps looked insurmountable. So she flopped down in the lift chair and pushed the button.

She sighed. It was a new normal.

59

"M rs. Zimmerman. I was just getting ready to call you," Nick said into his phone as he eyed the smoldering wreckage of his office and apartment.

According to the fire marshal, it was a total loss. But it didn't really feel like one to him. It felt like the right excuse for a new beginning.

"I can't say I'm not disappointed," his client said stonily. "Imagine discovering that the PI I hired solved my nephew's murder without telling me."

Nick ran a hand over his bandaged ass. "Yeah, I can see how disappointing having your nephew's murder solved would be."

"Ah, there's that sarcasm I'm not at all fond of," she said. "I suppose, since you did deliver on your promise, I should pay up."

One of the last remaining shingles on what was left of the roof cracked off and landed at his feet. "I'd sure appreciate that," he told her.

She sighed. "And I suppose I could include a small bonus for you socking that Gentry moron in the mouth. I've been waiting years for someone to do that," she grumbled.

"Happy to oblige," he told her.

There was a beat of silence. "You did an acceptable job, Nicholas," she said grudgingly.

It was the gold star of compliments from the gym teacher who had looked the brand-new school record holder for the fastest mile in the eye and said, "Well, if that's the best you can do."

"Thank you, Mrs. Zimmerman," Nick said, fearing that he was about to get misty-eyed.

"I'll mail the check to your office," she told him.

A piece of glass the size of a football fell from a broken upstairs window and landed shard-point down in a still-smoking piece of wood. "Uh, maybe mail it to my cousin instead?" he suggested.

"What's next, boss?" Josie asked when he disconnected the call.

"I've got a couple of stops to make. You up for riding along?" he asked.

"Sure."

"On the way, you can tell me all about how you forgot to mention to me you were doling out vigilante justice all over the city."

She shrugged. "Work was slow. I was bored."

———

Between stops, they listened to the radio, and Josie debriefed him.

The damage count for Mayorgeddon—as one of the stupid media outlets dubbed it—was impressive.

Mayor Nolan Flemming suffered a broken nose, eye socket, and right pinkie finger, along with two superficial gunshot wounds, and was in the hospital under police custody.

Detective Shapiro didn't fare any better. She took four bullets to the vest, one to the neck, and earned two broken legs from Mrs. Penny's minivan. Since the news of her arrest broke, witnesses had come out of the woodwork to share their Crooked Katie stories.

Duncan Gulliver spilled his guts in the hospital on both Flemming and Shapiro.

Officer Billings and the skateboarder Flemming shot were both expected to make full recoveries.

Josie was annoyed that she had arrived too late to the action to try out her new knife.

Riley's Facebook Live of the shoot-out on City Island already had seventy-five thousand views.

As for Nick, he'd earned himself a heart-shaped suture job from the joker of a surgeon who'd dug out the bullet and stitched his ass back up.

And it was only lunchtime.

He pulled up to the curb and studied the house. It was a modern Greek monstrosity with columns and plaster and urns everywhere. No matter how hard he tried, he couldn't imagine Riley living here. "Ready for this?" he asked Josie.

She cracked her neck to the left, then the right. "Oh yeah."

The front door was painted gold. Metallic flake gold. Nick ignored the lion-head door knocker and used his fist to announce their arrival.

The door swung open, and they were met by a swollen-nosed, even shorter than usual Griffin Gentry. He was barefoot.

"No! Back! Go away!" the man squeaked as he tried to wrestle the door closed.

But Nick wasn't waiting for an invitation to come inside. He shoved the door, knocking it into Gentry's forehead, and strode across the threshold. "Thanks, we'd love to come in," he said.

The foyer, with its beige textured walls and gold tile floor, seemed soulless and tasteless, just like its owner.

"You need to leave, or I'm calling my lawyer," Gentry whined.

"Yeah, about that," Nick said, pulling the papers out of his back pocket and slapping them against the man's chest. "Sign these."

Gentry sputtered and snorted, taking the papers and giving them a quick scan. "You want me to release Riley from her financial obligation to me? Ha! That's not happening. Not now, not ever," he said, braver now that he'd backed out of Nick's reach.

"I'm so glad he said that," Nick said, grinning at Josie. She smiled wickedly and advanced on Gentry.

He backed up a step and then another one.

"If you don't sign these papers," Nick explained, "I'm going to call Claudia at Channel 49 News. You remember her, don't you? She's the anchor your dear old dad fired so he could give you her job right out of college."

"Big deal," Gentry snorted, still backing away from the advancing Josie until they were in a room with a piano and very ugly furniture.

"A very big deal," Nick agreed. "You see, Gentry, I'm a private investigator. I investigate things. I follow people. I catch people doing things they wouldn't want their mistresses-turned-fiancées finding out about."

On cue, Josie pulled an envelope out of the back of her jeans and tossed it at Gentry. He bobbled it, and when it landed on the cold tile, a series of black-and-white photos fell out. His eyes went wide, and he scrambled to pick them up, but Josie pushed him back with a boot to the chest, forcing him down onto an overstuffed pink ottoman.

He stared in horror at the photos that showed him entering and leaving motels with two different scantily clad women, neither of whom were Bella Goodshine. And neither of whom had any problems with very public, very illegal displays of affection.

"You know, I think your viewers would love to know how you use your expense account to pay for motel rooms and prostitutes," Nick mused.

Gentry sputtered but didn't manage to form any actual words.

"You can make it all go away, just by signing those papers," Nick told him.

"And if you don't," Josie said, leaning into the man's space, "we'll tell everyone you wear lifts in your shoes."

His tangerine complexion faded to an ashy orange. "They're arch supports!"

"Oh no, they're not, Mr. Size Six and a Half," she hissed. "That's right. We got your shoe guy."

"Not Lionel!" Gentry gasped. The man was more upset about the lifts than the prostitutes.

"Sign the papers, Gentry, and no one needs to know anything," Nick insisted.

Josie produced a pen, somehow managing to make the gesture threatening. "Sign."

"Griffy, do we have company?" a breathy voice called from the grand staircase.

Gentry grabbed the pen, signed like his life depended on it, and then swept the photos under the ottoman with one tiny bare foot.

"There you are!" Bella pranced—because there was no better word for describing the way she moved—into the room wearing a pink silk robe with furry lapels and five-inch stilettos with matching furry puffs on the toes. She was carrying a small scruffy dog in a bedazzled collar. "Look, LaLa," she baby-talked to the dog. "We have guests!"

"They were just leaving," Gentry said, his face satisfyingly terror-stricken.

Nick took the crumpled papers that Josie handed him and scrawled his signature at the bottom. "We just stopped by for autographs," he said.

Josie whipped out her notary stamp the way someone would produce a knife, causing Gentry to fall back down on the ottoman.

"Y-y-yeah. Autographs," he stuttered.

"Pleasure doing business with you," Nick said with a lazy salute.

Josie leaned into Gentry's space once more. "I hope we'll meet again," she told him with a wicked gleam in her eyes.

"Daddy's so famous, LaLa," Bella crooned to the dog, oblivious that her fiancé was two seconds away from pissing his pants.

They said polite goodbyes, and Nick and Josie showed

themselves out. "Your friend is so tall and handsome," Bella said to Dirtbag Gentry just before Nick closed the door.

He stretched his arms overhead and squinted up at the blue sky. "Another satisfying job."

"Are you seriously not going to tell Bella Cartoon-Birds-Sing-in-My-Head Goodshine about that dick?" Josie asked as Nick limped toward his SUV.

He grinned and slid behind the wheel. "Check the glove box," he said.

Josie found another, similar envelope. Inside it was a series of similar pictures. Only instead of Gentry with prostitutes, it was Bella making out with—and sometimes doing more with—a handful of men who were all much, much taller than her fiancé.

"Oh shit. Is this…?"

"Yep. That's Gentry's old pal, Mayor Nolan Flemming. Seems he and Mrs. Gentry to Be had a quickie behind a dumpster at a fundraiser a few nights after he had Frick murdered," Nick said, driving down the long leg of the circular driveway.

"A match made in the sulfurous fumes of hell," Josie mused.

He stopped at the bottom of the drive, signaled, then floored it. His front fender took out the mailbox and sent it flying.

Josie didn't so much as blink. "So you've been tailing them since he showed up at the hospital and shoved a microphone—which totally represents the penis size he wishes he had, bee tee dubs—in Riley's face?"

"Yep," Nick said, heading in the direction of the city.

"Man, you've had it bad for Thorn from the beginning," she mused.

"Yep," he said again. "So what are you going to do now that your vigilante days are over courtesy of Detective Do-Right?"

Josie stretched all catlike. "I dunno. Guess get preggo and bake shit. Also, I really want to learn hatchet throwing. What are *you* going to do now that the fake engagement is over?"

"I'll tell you what I'm gonna do, Jos," Nick said, gripping

the wheel tighter. "I'm going to drop you off at your house so you and my cousin can make babies or throw hatchets at each other or whatever the hell you do behind closed doors. Then I'm going to drive over to Riley's and yell at her for a few hours about being careless and irresponsible. Then I'm gonna tell her that if she wants the honor of being my girl, she needs to get her head out of her ass."

Josie nodded smugly at his stupid, stupid plan. "Sounds like a Nick Santiago plan."

60

3:07 p.m. Sunday, July 5

Riley didn't know what day it was, let alone what time it was, when the knock at the door woke her. Judging from the ache in her side, it was still Sunday, and she still had a bullet hole in her muffin top. Burt hurled himself off the couch and galloped to the door, where he sat and growled until Riley wrenched it open.

"Did you even look who it was?" Nick demanded and limped past her with an armload of bags.

"Nice to see you too. I'm fine, thanks." She yawned.

"Why does it smell like mushroom fertilizer and dead groundhogs in here?" he asked, dumping his haul on the couch.

She yawned again. "Burt ate an entire bowl of ice cream."

The dog in question nudged Nick in his wounded butt cheek, then grinned like it was a game when he yelped.

"Burt, don't be a dick," Riley said. She stretched, then winced. Her entire body felt like it had…well, done all the things it had actually done.

The dog scented something besides stale canine farts wafting in the air and jogged happily out into the hall and down the steps.

Nick kicked the door shut behind him.

"What are you doing here?"

"What am I doing *here*? What am *I* doing here?" he demanded, pacing unevenly in front of her. "I'll tell you what I'm doing here." He reached into his pocket and pulled out a piece of paper and read the words out loud.

Dear Nick,

Please forgive me. I had to do this. You were going to get shot and killed. I saw it right before Flemming called. I couldn't let that happen. Thanks for last night. For every-thing really. Please take care of Burt for me.

Love,
Riley

"Uh-huh," she said, shuffling over to the coffee maker on the counter and stabbing buttons. She needed caffeine if there was going to be yelling.

"Stop making coffee, and come back here so I can yell at you, Riley Whatever the Hell Your Middle Name Is Thorn."

She ignored him, so he followed her into the tiny kitchen space and started unpacking the bags in jerky, angry motions. Riley took inventory. New bowls for Burt. Another bag of dog food. More leashes and toys. Two rib eyes, one for Burt and one for his people. The remaining shopping bag held a few new articles of clothing and toiletries. Remembering his home and office had been torched, she allowed herself to feel the teensiest bit sorry for him.

As the appliance gurgled to life, Riley dug into her tiny fridge and produced the small bag she'd stashed there.

"Here's what's going to happen," Nick continued. "I'm going to yell at you until you see the error of your ways."

"Uh-huh," she said.

"Then I'm going to tell you that I'm moving in."

"Moving in? Together?" she repeated.

"Technically across the hall, but yeah. It's gotta be here because my place is charcoal."

"Should I apologize for that too?" she asked with a yawn.

"No. That one's on me. I pushed Flemming's buttons too hard at the party last night," he admitted. "But I've got plenty of other stuff you need to apologize for."

The coffee maker spat a stream of caffeinated goodness into a mug. The second the stream stopped, Riley yanked the mug out and breathed deeply. "Okay. You're moving into Dickie's old place."

He shook his head. "You're not hearing me, Thorn. We aren't going to *just* be roommates. We're going to be—"

She held up a finger and drank deeply. This time when her eyes opened, they were clear, focused. She felt more coherent.

Nick was waving a pair of salad tongs in her face.

"What are you doing with my dirty Dickie underwear tongs?" she asked.

"I'm retiring them. You don't live with a dirty old man anymore. You're living with me now. And we're not roommates. We're dating. You're my girlfriend. I'll remember your damn birthday and take you out for dinner and buy you shoes or whatever as soon as you apologize for being a headstrong idiot."

"Here. I saved you a taco," she said, handing him the bag.

He looked down at it and opened his mouth. Then closed it. Hugging the bag to his chest, he looked back up at her. "You could have died, Riley."

"You too," she shot back.

"That's beside the point!" And he was back to yelling.

"Yeah? Well, then your point is *also* beside the point," she shouted.

He was looking at her with that patented Nick Santiago hunger, and she felt something tingle to life in her nether regions.

There was a knock on her door. "Riley! That Leon Tuffley guy is on the phone for you. He says something about Human Resources investigating you for kidnapping a receptionist and making terroristic threats?" Fred called. "They want you to come in early tomorrow."

Nick was back to staring at the taco.

"Hang on one second," Riley said to him. She limped the five steps to the door and opened it. "Tell that crotch-scratching, bottom line–licking dumbass that I quit."

"Crotch-scratching, bottom line–licking dumbass. Crotch-scratching, bottom line–licking dumbass. Got it," Fred said cheerily and then uncovered the cordless phone.

She shut the door and turned to face Nick, feeling a combination of giddiness and terror and determination.

"You just quit your job," he said, looking a little bewildered.

"You need a place to stay? I need a job," she said, advancing on him unsteadily.

"You want to work for me?"

"We can play it by ear," she said, sliding her arms around his neck. She thought about boosting herself up but didn't trust her current vertical leap or Nick's ability to catch her with that extra hole in his tush throwing off his center of gravity.

He, however, had no such qualms. He grabbed her by the butt cheeks and picked her up off the ground. When he pressed her against the wall, she realized it would take a lot more than a gunshot wound to the ass to dampen Nick Santiago's libido.

"I didn't get to yell at you enough yet," he complained when she nipped at his bottom lip. "I also didn't get to impress you with what I did to your ex-husband."

"Impress me after sex," she breathed.

"Hey," he growled.

"Sorry. That came out wrong." Riley laughed.

He kissed her and stumbled in the direction of the bed. It felt like falling, she realized. That dip in her gut during free fall. The thrill of it. The adventure. But they were in it together.

He pitched them forward, and together they fell onto her bed.

"Ouch," they muttered between kisses.

Epilogue

A few weeks later

The Susquehanna River flowed over Riley's feet and ankles, making the summer swelter seem a little more manageable. Cicadas buzzed in the trees. Sunshine sparkled and danced on the surface of the water, baking vitamin D into her skin. She soaked it all in, luxuriated in it.

Music of the Jimmy Buffett variety wafted to them from the speakers in the bullet-ridden Jeep onshore.

"This was a really good idea, Thorn," Nick murmured next to her.

She tipped her head to the side and peered at him. He was kicked back in a partially submerged lawn chair next to her. His ball cap was pulled down over his eyes. There was a cold beer in his hand, half a sub in his lap, and a smug smile on his face.

"Actually, it was my Uncle Jimmy's," she said with a grin.

"Remind me to thank him when I meet him," he said lazily.

She bit her tongue and waited.

"He's dead, isn't he?" Nick said finally.

"Yep. He haunts the Jeep," she told him.

"Of course he does."

"Anytime you get sick of the weirdness, you're free to start sleeping across the hall," Riley teased. Their relationship was still fresh, still intoxicating. They'd bonded over murder and wound care and now found themselves settling into a quieter normal with no murders to solve, no innocence to prove.

They were only a few weeks into this new normal. But it was good. *Really* good.

Nick had moved in across the hall into Dickie's old space, but they spent every night together in her bed. Riley was dipping a toe into the private investigating waters by studying up on criminal justice and investigative techniques while working part-time as an office manager for Santiago Investigations. Her financial burden had lightened considerably thanks to Nick forcing Griffin to declare Riley's legal debt to him settled.

She also had a slot reserved in an upcoming firearms safety course.

Thanks to the media attention from the Mayor McMurder case, Nick was juggling a heavy caseload and shopping for a new office space. Preferably one with a sprinkler system.

Best of all, they both were still sleep deprived because every time they got near a bed or a flat surface, sex happened.

Really great sex.

A massive splash snagged their attention. Burt motored toward them with a small tree clutched in his mouth. Nick put the beer in his cupholder and made a grab for the tree. "Buddy, I told you. Smaller branches. Not entire trunks." He broke off a branch and hurled it into the water. Burt bounded toward it, sending river water everywhere.

"How was Perry today?" Riley asked before biting into her half of the sub.

"He's good. I took him chicken salad and some new socks. Said the cops talked to him about the arson, and he IDed the perps from mug shots. Same two who tried to take you out on the bridge. Weber thinks they're going to roll on Shapiro if the deal's right."

"Good," she said with a satisfied sigh.

"No one associated with that mess is going to see the outside of a cage for a very long time," he said.

"Have you noticed Mrs. Penny's been acting weird lately?" Riley changed the subject.

"Define weird. She's always weird."

"She swears she's not doing the vigilante thing anymore, but she's been sneaking around. Some days it looks like she's in disguise."

"Yeah," he said. "About that. I've been meaning to tell you—"

But Burt bounded back, looking very proud of himself with five feet of rotting log.

Nick repeated the process, tossing a foot-long piece of bark into the river.

"Hey, Thorn?" he said.

"Mmm?"

"What time is it?" he asked.

She peeked at her phone. "11:17 a.m."

His dimples appeared. "What day is it?"

"Wednesday."

"What are we doing right now?"

Her grin nearly split her face. No more hours wasted behind industrial gray walls. No more snide receptionists or accounting for every minute of her day. "Whatever the hell we want."

"Cheers," he said, tapping his beer to hers. "Oh, shit. What time did you say it was?"

"11:18 now," she told him.

"We gotta go," he said, standing and folding his lawn chair.

"Why? Where?"

"It's a surprise."

"You can't surprise a psychic," Riley warned him as a dozen messages tried to ping onto her internal screen.

"No cheating," he said, pulling her out of the chair.

"It doesn't work like that," she said dryly.

"Tell your spirit guides that you don't want to know," Nick said.

"Hear that, spirit guides?" she said wryly. "I don't want to know any surprises for the rest of the day."

He whistled for Burt, and the muddy, wet dog romped toward them.

———

Back at the mansion, Nick parked next to a large delivery truck idling in the parking lot. "What are my parents doing here?" Riley asked, noticing their car was parked where Mrs. Penny's minivan used to sit.

"Let's find out," Nick said, putting his hands on her shoulders and pushing her toward the house. While he closed the dog gate on the porch, Riley pretended to ignore the hand-painted No Trespassing and No Psychic Readings signs on the front of the house. She hoped fervently that in a few weeks, they could come down once everyone in the city forgot about the whole psychic thing. But for now, the phone rang off the hook, and letters from people asking for help or calling her a fraud continued to arrive.

They left Burt outside to dry off and went inside, finding the usual amount of chaos.

There seemed to be a lot of extra people in residence. Two uniformed delivery men were trooping down the steps. Riley's dad was talking gin with Mrs. Penny in the front parlor.

Fred and Lily were having a spirited discussion in the kitchen about seasoning and the second season of *Gossip Girl*.

Nick peeled off two twenties from his wallet and handed them to the delivery guys. "Any trouble?" he asked.

"Thanks, man. Had to maneuver around the lift chair, but nothing we ain't done before," the first guy said.

Nick dragged her up the stairs past Mr. Willicott, who had moved a bench from his room into the hallway and was reading a newspaper from the 1990s.

On the third floor, they found Riley's mom and Gabe and a cloud of pungent smoke.

Riley coughed. "Mom, what are you smudging?"

Blossom swirled around, making the long orange skirt float out around her. "It's your housewarming, sweetie!"

"I've lived here for a whole year," she pointed out.

"Not like this," Blossom said with a very unsubtle wink at Nick. "Ta-da!" She threw open the door to Nick's room.

Riley poked her head in. "What the"

Nick gave her a nudge inside.

What had been a mostly empty room with a few half-emptied bags of new personal effects now housed a very large king-size bed, matching nightstands, a tall dresser, and a huge dog bed.

"Uh. This is nice, but where are you going to watch TV?" Riley asked, hopping on the bed and lusting after the comfy mattress.

"The question is, where are *we* going to watch TV?" he said, pulling her to her feet.

"I'm so excited I could just die," Blossom squealed.

Back in the hall, Gabe bowed low and opened Riley's door with a flourish.

"Holy shit."

Her bed and god-awful couch were gone. A new, deep sofa with fat pillows sat in front of an obscenely large flat-screen TV. There was another dog bed next to it, this one shaped like a couch. Her rickety card table had been replaced with an actual dining table with four chairs.

In the dormer, a pair of cushions rested on the floor next to a low bench that held a collection of candles and a few books that she recognized from her mother's personal library.

Exploring Your Psychic Abilities
Guiding Your Spirit Guides
Great Psychics of the Seventeenth Century

"That's for your future training with Mount Everest over there," Nick said, nodding toward Gabe.

Gabe beamed his benevolence at Riley, and something behind him on the wall caught her eye. It was a framed photo, a still from the *Cumberland Sentinel* of Nick and Riley, arms around each other, bloody and battered, as they limped away from the capitol fountain. They were both grinning.

She crossed to it and ran her fingers over the plain black frame.

"It's, uh, our first picture together," Nick said, sounding a little embarrassed. He scratched nervously at the back of his head. "Thought it looked pretty cool."

And just like that, Riley's heart threw itself down the stairs of her chest. Tumbling madly into real-life, honest-to-goodness love. Not that she was going to tell him right this second. They'd moved way too fast to get to this point. She could give him a few months to settle into monogamy.

"You did all this?" she asked, turning to him.

Unable to contain her excitement, Blossom danced around Gabe. "It's a living room! You have a bedroom and a living room now! Isn't this exciting?"

It was the little things for Blossom Basil-Thorn.

Nick flashed her his dimples, and Riley felt a little light-headed. "My renter's insurance check landed. Figured I might as well do something with the money."

Nick Santiago had moved them in together. Without asking. It was a very Nick-like thing to do.

"You realize what you've done, right?" she asked.

"What?" he asked.

"You moved us in together. Like officially. Like no safety net of you having your own space."

He reached for her, settling his hands on her hips. "I am aware, Thorn."

"And you're okay with this?" she asked.

"Uh-huh," he said, pulling her closer.

She slipped her arms around his neck. "You're really sure about this? You're ready to say goodbye to your bachelor glory days?"

"Oh yeah," he said, his mouth zeroing in on hers.

Riley's lips were already parting. Her body was already responding to his touch.

456

"Ahem!" Blossom cleared her throat loudly. "We'll give you some privacy to break in the new furniture in a few minutes. But first, I think it's time for another tarot reading," she said, producing a deck of cards from the folds of her skirt.

Instinctively, Riley stepped between her mother and Nick. "Mom, do you think that's a good idea? Remember what happened last time?"

"Oh, pfft. That was weeks ago. I have a very good feeling about your future."

Riley sighed. "Fine. But we're doing this with alcohol."

They trooped downstairs, and Blossom bustled ahead of them into the parlor where she confiscated an ornate marble side table.

"Mrs. Penny, a round of whatever you feel like making," Nick said.

"Straight bourbon it is!" Mrs. Penny announced, whipping out a bottle.

"I think I will get some celebratory ice cream," Gabe mused and headed off to the kitchen.

Riley and Nick sat down on the velvet settee. Blossom dragged one of the heavy wingback chairs up to the table while Roger noodled out a tune on the organ in the corner.

"Mom, I really don't think this is necessary," Riley began.

"Nonsense. We'll just make it a quickie. Not a sexual quickie, of course." Blossom giggled.

Riley laid her hand on Nick's knee and squeezed. Hard.

"We'll just do a linear spread," Blossom insisted. "Now, you both handle the deck."

"I beg your pardon?" Nick said.

"*Deck*. She said *deck*," Riley said.

"Bourbon's up," Mrs. Penny said, shuffling over with three glasses with very generous pours in her grip.

Riley gave the cards a half-hearted shuffle and then handed them over to Nick. He did the same, only with more enthusiasm. Another reason why she liked him. He was nicer to her family than she was.

"Okey dokey," Blossom said, taking the deck back and dealing out three cards. "We'll just do a little past, present, future." She flipped over the first card. "I think we can all agree that this is an accurate read of your recent past."

"The Knight of Wands," Riley said to Nick.

"Mmm. Uh-huh," he said, slinging an arm around her shoulder.

"It means action and adventure and lots of fearlessness," Blossom supplied. "Now, let's take a peek at your present. Oooh. The Six of Cups. That's very nice."

"Happiness, healing, and familiarity," Riley explained.

His thumb was distracting her nicely with its little circles on her shoulder. She couldn't wait to go back upstairs and try out that new bed.

"Now for the future," Blossom said.

"If she draws the dead guy stabbed full of swords, I'm out," he joked in a whisper.

"Don't be silly, Nick. I see nothing but happiness and adventure in your fut—fuck."

"Mom!"

But Blossom was staring down at the card she'd just flipped. "It's the Tower. The major arcana card known as chaos."

"Eh, better than the dead guy, right?" Nick said, peering at the card.

It was a card of upheaval and destruction, as illustrated by the stone tower collapsing in a shower of fire and sparks into a dark river.

Riley did not have a good feeling about this.

Roger hit a two-handed cacophony of sharps and flats on the organ, and not one second later, the doorbell rang.

"Uh-oh." Riley and Blossom stared wide-eyed at each other.

"Oh no. She wouldn't have come without calling first," Blossom said, shaking her head back and forth.

"She can't be here," Riley hissed.

"Didn't you sense her coming?" Blossom asked.

"Nick made me shut up my spirit guides so he could surprise me!"

"Well, that was a stupid thing to do," her mother complained.

"What? Who?" Roger asked.

"What's going on?" Nick asked, standing up to face the unknown threat.

The front door swung open on its own, and a tall woman with ramrod posture and a pinched frown swirled into the foyer. She was dressed in head-to-toe black in flowing layers. Her lipstick was a dark purple on a tight mouth bookended with deep lines. She had bird feathers tucked into her short silver hair.

Everyone in the room came to their feet.

"One would think that one's family would have prepared a proper greeting," she announced coolly.

Blossom picked up her tumbler and knocked back four fingers of bourbon in one gulp.

"Who the hell is that?" Nick whispered out of the side of his mouth.

"Trouble," Riley whispered back.

"Mom!" Blossom said, gasping out bourbon fumes. "I'm so happy to see you."

"No, you're not," Riley's grandmother snapped.

Riley heard a gasp. "Elanora!" Gabe dropped his bowl of ice cream at the woman's feet. Burt galloped over and started hoovering up the dairy.

"Great. He'll be farting for days," Nick groaned.

"I see you've managed to corrupt my star student, Riley," Elanora announced with derision.

"Hi, Grandma," Riley said, giving the woman a little wave and feeling like she was eight years old all over again.

"What are you doing here, Mom?" Blossom asked.

"I'm here on behalf of the guild to fix the recent unfortunate publicity surrounding Riley's..." She trailed off, gaze skimming over Nick. "Gifts."

"Oh boy," Riley breathed.

"Not good?" Nick asked.

"Very not good."

"You staying at a hotel, Elanora?" Roger asked hopefully from the organ stool.

Apparently that was a preposterous suggestion. "I am not," she scoffed. "I will be staying with my daughter."

"Oh. Good," Roger said with zero enthusiasm.

"Yay," Blossom said weakly.

"Gabriel, now that I am here, I will expect you to resume your commitment to your holistic studies," Elanora announced.

"Yes, of course, Elanora," Gabe said with his head bowed. "I would be honored."

"I think that Tower card just made its play," Nick whispered to Riley.

"Yeah, I guess things couldn't get much worse."

It was such a stupid thing to say.

The universe must have agreed, because the doorbell rang again.

No one moved.

"This is the last time I ever give my spirit guides the day off," Riley muttered.

"I'll never surprise you again," Nick promised.

"I'll get it," Fred sang. He danced down the hallway, avoiding spilled ice cream and lapping dog and disapproving grandmother.

He opened the door with a flourish that had his toupee billowing up off his scalp before settling back down.

"Uh-oh," Riley said.

Detective Kellen Weber walked into the parlor. "I hope this isn't a bad time," he said, eyes locking on Riley.

"Define *bad*," Nick said.

Riley elbowed him in the gut. "What can we do for you, Detective?"

"I need your help on a case."

Want to know what happens next?

Read on for an excerpt from
The Corpse in the Closet,
book 2 in the Riley Thorn series

1

This was not how she was going to die, Riley decided. Not sitting on a concrete floor in a musty TV studio surrounded by idiots.

The helmet-headed blond on her right was muttering under her breath about lawsuits. On her left, Riley's ex-husband, Griffin Gentry, rocked in place and whimpered about the dry-cleaning fees for his mohair suit.

Neither of them was smart enough to realize just how much trouble they were all in.

But Riley knew that, barring a miracle, none of them would be walking out of Channel 50 alive.

"How long are we going to have to stay like this?" the blond demanded. "This lighting is giving me a headache, and I need to make four dozen cupcakes for the marching band bake sale tomorrow."

"That's my chair," Griffin complained when the gunman sat down behind the anchor desk.

"Let the man with the gun sit in your chair," Riley advised.

"Just great," Griffin whined when the gunman lowered the seat. "It's going to take me forever to get it back to the right height."

"Oh, please," Valerie hissed from her position between cameras one and two. "You put it as high as it goes, and we all pretend you're a normal-size human."

"Let's focus on the real problem here," Riley said. "That guy has killed several people so far, and he has more on his list."

"No one wants to kill me! Everyone loves me," Griffin insisted.

"Have you continued to devolve, or was I really that stupid when I married you?" she wondered.

"Personally, I think it was a combination of both," the camera one operator at her feet chimed in.

"Hey, Don," she whispered. "Long time, no see."

"How's it going?" the hefty mustachioed man asked.

"So what's he going to do after he's done messing up my chair?" Griffin hissed, tugging at his collar. "You don't think he'll do something terrible like—"

"Kill you? Anything could happen at this point," Riley said.

"*Kill me?*" he croaked. "I was going to say *make me look silly on the air*."

Her ex-husband had gone from indignantly inconvenienced to anxious. Beads of sweat appeared on his spackled forehead.

Griffin was a nervous sweater. And he was very, very nervous. He looked as if he'd been hosed down.

"Look. He's one guy with a gun. There's sixteen of us in here. If we attack him in order of least important person to most important person, most of us will survive," the blond said.

"Obviously, I'm the most important," Griffin said, latching on to her idea.

"You read things from a teleprompter and wear makeup," the woman scoffed. "I'm a *mother*. I'm raising the future of our country."

"Your kids are in college," Riley pointed out.

"And they still need their mother! I'm last. Griffin can be next to last," the woman conceded.

"Bella should be next to next to last," Griffin decided.

On cue, Bella Goodshine, perky weather girl and his new fiancée, popped up next to him and held out a hand to Riley. "Hi! I'm Bella!"

"I know who you are!" Riley yelled.

The gunman spun around in his chair to glare at her.

"Sorry," Riley said. "But she keeps introducing herself to me!"

"Didn't she steal your husband?" the blond asked.

"She sure did," Griffin said. He was still sweating.

"This must be really awkward for you," the blond observed.

"It's not great."

"Don't mind Bella," Griffin said, reaching for Riley's hand. She snatched it away. "She has female face blindness."

"Female face blindness?" Riley repeated.

Griffin nodded. "She only recognizes men. It's a medical condition."

Riley blinked slowly, then shook her head. "I'm not dying here with you people."

"So who should be first in line to attack this guy?" Griffin asked. "I never cared for Armand. I don't like his urinal cake placement."

"Fine. He'll go first," the blond decided. "Then maybe that guy over there by the bagels. I don't like his shirt."

"That's Rose. She didn't sign my birthday card this year. Maybe she should go first?"

"You people can't just decide who lives and who dies," Riley hissed. This was what was wrong with the world. People like Griffin, who had an overinflated sense of importance, wielding power over others.

Nick was going to kill her. That was if she survived her own murder.

2

Abso-fucking-lutely not," snarled Nick Santiago, dimpled private investigator and barely reformed bad boy as he fisted his hands in the cop's shirt and bared his teeth.

Life could go from blissful summer day to bonkers in a very short period of time, Riley realized as she clung to her boyfriend's back. Not ten minutes ago, she—Riley "Middle Name Unacknowledged" Thorn—had officially moved in with him. But before they could christen the new king-size bed, everything had, of course, gone straight to hell.

She blamed her batty mother's tarot prediction for copious amounts of strife and turmoil.

The universe waited all of twenty seconds before delivering said strife and turmoil in the form of a surprise visit from Riley's formidable grandmother. Elanora Basil, president of the North American Psychics Guild, had proceeded to cast a pall of judgmental disdain that could be felt throughout the entire run-down mansion and large portions of Harrisburg, Pennsylvania.

It had gone downhill from there.

Now Nick was assaulting a cop. Not just any cop. His ex-partner and frenemy Detective Kellen Weber.

"Calm the hell down," Riley demanded through gritted teeth as she tried to pry Nick off the detective.

"Do you require my assistance?" The deep baritone came from the large, impossibly muscular Black man in the doorway.

"Stay out of this, Empire State Building," Nick snarled.

"I got it, Gabe," she promised her part-time spiritual guide and full-time friend. "But thanks."

"I am always available for punching Nick in the face if necessary," Gabe promised. After the briefest of hesitations, he gracefully dodged the melee in the kitchen and helped himself to a frozen Snickers, which he devoured in two bites before squaring his massive shoulders and disappearing again.

Elanora had that effect on people.

"Don't make me arrest you, Santiago," Weber rasped from his prone position on the kitchen table.

Nick growled in response. The pony-size dog at their feet mistook the noise for a game and barked joyfully.

"Not now, Burt," Riley told the dog as she landed a series of slaps to Nick's hands.

Finally, he released the detective.

"The last time she got involved with an investigation, she got shot," Nick snarled. "The answer is no. She's not doing your job for you."

Detective Weber stood and straightened his tie. He was an attractive man, always dressed as if he was ready to take a disapproving in-law to the Olive Garden after church. "Assaulting an officer is against the law, dick," he reminded Nick.

"Pretty sure a jury would make an exception for you, assface."

She slid off Nick's back. "Can you two idiots keep it down? If my grandmother hears—"

"This is precisely why I am here."

The mint-green kitchen suddenly seemed very small and very cold as Elanora, terrifying matriarch and nationally known psychic medium, stepped into the room. Her sniff was full of derision.

She was petite with ramrod posture and looked as if she wore a coat hanger under her layers of flowing black. With her pinched frown and sterling hair swept back from her face with bird feathers, she reminded her granddaughter of an old, disappointed Stevie Nicks.

Briefly, Riley wondered if her grandmother had murdered the bird that donated the feathers. Nothing seemed out of the realm of possibility when it came to Elanora.

"Your behavior is positively unseemly. My granddaughter is most certainly not getting involved in another homicide," Elanora announced briskly, glancing at the case file Weber left on the table. "She is dangerously untrained, and I have absolutely no faith in her ability to control even the most basic of powers. Look at the two of you. One minute alone in a room with her, and you're behaving like children."

Riley rolled her eyes. "Thanks, Grandma." Elanora preferred *Grandmother*. Riley preferred to mess with her just a little bit.

Nick pointed in Elanora's direction as he leaned into Riley. "Listen to your scary grandma. You're not doing it."

He was lucky he was hot even when his dimples weren't on full display. He was also lucky that Riley was a patient woman. He was new at this boyfriend thing. So she could ignore the occasional gung-ho alpha blunders and tolerate the adorable macho overprotectiveness. Because deep down, she knew he was still tied up in knots over their recent adventure in taking down the city's mayor, his communications director, and a few bad cops.

Both she and Nick had walked away with a bullet hole apiece as souvenirs. While she'd moved on, he was still stewing about it, and like a good girlfriend, she was giving him the space to stew about it.

Elanora gave Nick an imperious glance followed by a stiff nod. "Perhaps you're not as useless and uneducated as you appear to be, Nicholas."

It was practically a gold star.

"Thanks?" he said.

"While I appreciate you all feeling as if you have the right to make decisions for me, you don't," Riley announced. "None of you do."

"That's right. This is Riley's decision," Weber said smugly.

"Kiss-ass," Nick snapped.

"You two, out." She nudged her grandmother and boyfriend toward the door.

Burt barked and cocked his gigantic head.

"You can stay. You trust my judgment," she told the dog.

Elanora's eyes narrowed. "I did not come here to be ignored while you continue to make a mockery of the guild."

"No, but you did arrive unannounced. You can't expect us to drop everything and entertain you."

"*Entertain* me?" Elanora scoffed. "My daughter and granddaughters are blessed with psychic gifts that should have foretold my arrival."

"Yeah, well, they didn't. So you can't expect me to drop everything right now. Go home with my parents. Drive them nuts. You like doing that. We'll catch up soon."

The disapproving lines on her grandmother's forehead deepened. "I am very disappointed—"

"In me. And everyone else. And life in general. I got it, and I'm not saying you're wrong. We'll deal with it later, Grandmother."

"We most certainly will."

Elanora swept from the room in a huff, and Riley turned to face Nick. "And you," she said.

"Me?" He pointed at himself and produced both dimples. Weapons of mass devastation.

"Yeah, you. You're the one who said you could handle dating a psychic." She didn't exactly choke on the word, but she did cough.

"Thorn, this has nothing to do with you talking to dead people and reading minds. I don't give a shit about your psychic training. You haven't been trained to defend yourself. You barely survived the last time you got tangled up in a case. Hell, you threw a gun at the bad guy. You can't expect me to pat you on the back and tell you to get back out there and bring home a win."

"You really do need to teach her to shoot," Weber cut in.

"I don't if she stays away from murderers."

"Oh, come on. You're being dramatic," she complained. "One measly bullet hole in a love handle didn't put me anywhere near death's doorstep."

"Don't tell me it was one 'measly bullet hole' when you almost let a madman drown you in the goddamn capitol fountain."

Oh, that.

"Nick." She crossed her arms over her chest. He was putting on a front, but underneath it, she could sense the fear that kept him up at night.

Not again. I can't lose her.

She slammed the metaphorical garage door shut in her head. As a psychic girlfriend, she tried very hard to give Nick and his inner monologue privacy.

"Riley." He mirrored her posture, hiding his inner turmoil under a cocky, sexy facade.

"Let me hear Detective Weber out," she said gently. "Looking over a case file isn't going to put me in mortal danger." At least she hoped it wouldn't. "You have to trust me."

His jaw clenched under his sexy stubble, making his dimples pop again. "For the record, I don't like it. And you," he said, turning on Weber. "If she ends up in trouble or gets hurt, I will personally choke you to death with your stupid tie collection."

"Nick." She sighed.

"I'm not leaving," he insisted, pulling out a chair from the table and attacking one of the banana muffins Gabe had baked that morning. The man was an angel in the kitchen. Burt trotted over and put his head in Nick's lap so he could inhale muffin crumbs.

The problem was, Riley didn't really *want* to consult on a case. Especially not another murder. Especially not when, as her grandmother so meanly pointed out, her powers were not exactly under her control at all times. Which technically was her own fault for denying their existence for the past thirty-four years.

However, she'd also spent the last several years doing what she'd been told in both a dead-end job and her deader-end marriage. She was due for a rebellion.

Author's Note

Dear Reader,

This story has been with me since before I wrote *Pretend You're Mine*, so quite the long-ass time. I don't know when I decided to make Riley psychic, but I do remember when I had the idea for the book.

When Mr. Lucy and I first started dating, he was working as an investigator for a PI and took me along to a junkyard to retrieve personal possessions from a wrecked car. He sure knows how to show a lady a good time!

So thanks, Mr. Lucy, for that romantic trip to the junkyard, because without you, Riley Thorn would never have existed. I hope you loved Riley and Nick and Gabe and Mrs. Penny because there is more to come!

In the meantime, feel free to shower me with accolades in a review or tell thirty of your closest reader buddies that you have the book for them! And then tell them that book is this book... in case I was being too subtle. Which usually never happens. Thanks for reading! You look lovely today!

Xoxo,
Lucy

Acknowledgments

- As always to Mr. Lucy for maintaining the proper ratio of tacos, hugs, and "stop whining and go write."
- To Joyce and Tammy for always keeping me on track with work and showering.
- To my Street Team and ARC Team. I don't deserve you and I hope you never figure that out.
- To Kari March Designs for once again delivering a fantastic cover and graphics.
- To the editing dream team of Jessica, Amanda, and Dawn.
- To the rest of #TeamLucy including Audio Dan, Heather, Rachel, and Marketing Guy Rick. You guys are the best!
- To BRAs, you are my happy place.
- To you, dearest reader, for picking this book.
- To the essential workers and frontline medical staff who kept us alive, fed, and in business during the COVID-19 pandemic.
- To rainbows and hot sauce, Peloton rides (@thebigscore) and ice cream sandwiches, to missing out on London and Edinburgh and staying home to write books instead.
- #BlackLivesMatter
- To my author friends for reminding me that all good things are hard.

About the Author

Lucy Score is a #1 *New York Times, USA Today,* and *Wall Street Journal* bestselling author. She grew up in a literary family who insisted that the dinner table was for reading and earned a degree in journalism. She writes full-time from the Pennsylvania home she and Mr. Lucy share with their obnoxious cat, Cleo. When not spending hours crafting heartbreaker heroes and kick-ass heroines, Lucy can be found on the couch, in the kitchen, or at the gym. She hopes to someday write from a sailboat, ocean-front condo, or tropical island with reliable Wi-Fi.

Sign up for her newsletter by scanning the QR code below and stay up on all the latest Lucy book news. You can also follow her here:

Website: lucyscore.net
Facebook: lucyscorewrites
Instagram: scorelucy
TikTok: @lucyferscore
Binge Books: bingebooks.com/author/lucy_score
Readers Group: facebook.com/groups/BingeReaders Anonymous
Newsletter signup: